# STARCROSSED

# STARCROSSED

## JOSEPHINE ANGELINI

An Imprint of HarperCollins*Publishers*

HarperTeen is an imprint of HarperCollins Publishers.

Starcrossed

Library of Congress Cataloging-in-Publication Data
Angelini, Josephine.
Starcrossed / by Josephine Angelini. — 1st ed.
    p.  cm.
Summary: When shy sixteen-year-old Helen Hamilton starts having
vivid dreams about three ancient, hideous women and suddenly tries
to kill a new student at her Nantucket high school, she discovers that
she is playing out some version of an old tale involving Helen of Troy,
the Three Furies, and a mythic battle.
    ISBN 978-0-06-201199-2
    [1. Supernatural—Fiction. 2. Mythology, Greek—Fiction.
3. Nantucket Island (Mass.)—Fiction.] I. Title.
PZ7.A58239St 2011                                    2010040425
[Fic]—dc22

Typography by Erin Fitzsimmons
11  12  13  14  15   LP/RRDB   10 9 8 7 6 5 4 3 2 1
❖
First Edition

*. . . for my beloved husband*

# ONE

"But if you bought me a car now, it would be yours when I go away to school in two years. Still practically new," Helen said optimistically. Unfortunately, her father was no sucker.

"Lennie, just because the state of Massachusetts thinks it's okay for sixteen-year-olds to drive . . ." Jerry began.

"Almost seventeen," Helen reminded.

"Doesn't mean that I have to agree with it." He was winning, but Helen hadn't lost yet.

"You know, the Pig only has another year or two left in her," Helen said, referring to the ancient Jeep Wrangler her father drove, which she suspected might have been parked outside the castle where the Magna Carta was signed. "And think of all the gas money we could save if we got a hybrid, or even went full electric. Wave of the future, Dad."

"Uh-huh" was all he'd say.

*Now* she'd lost.

Helen Hamilton groaned softly to herself and looked out over the railing of the ferry that was bringing her back to Nantucket. She contemplated another year of riding her bike to school in November and, when the snow got too deep, scrounging for rides or, worst of all, taking the bus. She shivered in anticipated agony and tried not to think about it. Some of the Labor Day tourists were staring at her, not unusual, so Helen tried to turn her face away as subtly as she could. When Helen looked in a mirror all she saw were the basics—two eyes, a nose, and a mouth—but strangers from off island tended to stare, which was really annoying.

Luckily for Helen, most of the tourists on the ferry that afternoon were there for the view, not her portrait. They were so determined to cram in a little scenic beauty before the end of summer that they felt obliged to ooh and aah at every marvel of the Atlantic Ocean, though it was all lost on Helen. As far as she was concerned, growing up on a tiny island was nothing but a pain, and she couldn't wait to go to college off island, off Massachusetts, and off the entire eastern seaboard if she could manage it.

It wasn't that Helen hated her home life. In fact, she and her father got along perfectly. Her mom had ditched them both when Helen was a baby, but Jerry had learned early on how to give his daughter just the right amount of attention. He didn't hover, yet he was always there for her when she needed him. Buried under a thin layer of resentment about the current car situation, she knew she could never ask for a better dad.

"Hey, Lennie! How's the rash?" yelled a familiar voice. Coming toward her was Claire, Helen's best friend since birth. She tipped unsteady tourists out of her path with artfully placed pushes.

The sea-goofy day-trippers swerved away from Claire like she was a linebacker and not a tiny elf of a girl perched delicately on platform sandals. She glided easily through the stumbling riot she had created and slid next to Helen by the railing.

"Giggles! I see you got some back-to-school shopping done, too," Jerry said as he gave Claire a one-armed hug around her parcels.

Claire Aoki, aka Giggles, was a badass. Anyone who took a look at her five-foot-two frame and delicate Asian features and failed to recognize her inherent scrappiness ran the risk of suffering horribly at the hands of a grossly underestimated opponent. The nickname "Giggles" was her personal albatross. She'd had it since she was a baby. In her friends' and family's defense it was impossible to resist calling her Giggles. Claire had, hands down, the best laugh in the universe. Never forced or shrill, it was the kind of laugh that could make anyone within earshot smile.

"Fo-sho, sire of my BFF," Claire replied. She hugged Jerry back with genuine affection, ignoring his use of the dreaded nickname. "Might I have a word with your progeny? Sorry to be so rude, but it's top secret, high-clearance stuff. I'd tell you . . ." she began.

"But then you'd have to kill me," Jerry finished sagely. He shuffled obligingly off to the concession stand to buy

3

himself a sugary soda while his daughter, the chief of the food police, wasn't looking.

"Wacha got in the bag, dad?" Claire asked. She grabbed Helen's loot and started rifling through. "Jeans, cardigan, T-shirt, under . . . whoa! You go underwear shopping with your dad? Ew!"

"It's not like I have any choice!" Helen complained as she snatched her bag away. "I needed new bras! Anyway, my dad hides at the bookstore while I try everything on. But trust me, even knowing he's down the street while I shop for underwear is excruciating," she said, a smile on her reddening face.

"It can't be all that painful. It's not like you ever try to buy anything sexy. Jeez, Lennie, do you think you could dress more like my grandma?" Claire held up a pair of white cotton briefs. Helen snatched the granny panties and shoved them to the bottom of the bag while Claire stretched out her magnificent laugh.

"I know, I'm such a big geek it's gone viral," Helen replied, Claire's teasing instantly forgiven, as usual. "Aren't you afraid you'll catch a fatal case of loser from me?"

"Nope. I'm so awesome I'm immune. Anyway, geeks are the best. You're all so deliciously corruptible. And I love the way you blush whenever I talk about underpants."

Claire was forced to adjust her stance as a couple of picture-takers barged in close to them. Working with the momentum of the deck, Claire nudged the tourists out of the way with one of her ninja balance moves. They stumbled aside, laughing about the "choppy water," clueless that Claire had even touched them. Helen fiddled with the heart necklace she always wore and took the opportunity to slouch down against the railing to better meet her friend's small stature.

Unfortunately for achingly shy Helen, she was an eye-grabbing five feet nine inches tall, and still growing. She'd prayed to Jesus, the Buddha, Muhammad, and Vishnu to make it stop, but she still felt the hot splinters in her limbs and the seizing muscles of another growth spurt at night. She promised herself that at least if she topped six feet she'd be tall enough to scale the safety railing and throw herself off the top of the lighthouse in Siasconset.

Salespeople were always telling her how lucky she was, but not even they could find her pants that fit. Helen had resigned herself to the fact that in order to buy affordable jeans that were long enough she had to go a few sizes too big, but if she didn't want them to fall off her hips, she had to put up with a mild breeze flapping around her ankles. Helen was pretty sure that the "wicked jealous" salesgirls didn't walk around with chilly ankles. Or with their butt cracks showing.

"Stand up straight," Claire snapped automatically when she saw Helen slouching, and Helen obeyed. Claire had a thing about good posture, something to do with her super-proper Japanese mother and even more proper, kimono-wearing grandmother.

"Okay! On to the main topic," Claire announced. "You

know that huge kazillion-dollar compound that the New England Patriots guy used to own?"

"The one in 'Sconset? Sure. What about it?" Helen asked, picturing the house's private beach and feeling relieved that her dad didn't make enough money at his store to buy a house any closer to the water.

When Helen was a child she had very nearly drowned, and ever since had secretly believed that the Atlantic Ocean was trying to kill her. She'd always kept that bit of paranoia to herself . . . though she still was a terrible swimmer. To be fair, she could tread water for a few minutes at a time, but she was rotten at it. Eventually, she sank like a rock no matter how saline the ocean was supposed to be and no matter how hard she paddled.

"It finally sold to a big family," Claire said. "Or two families. I'm not sure how it works, but I guess there are two fathers, and they're brothers. They both have kids—so the kids are cousins?" Claire wrinkled her brow. "Whatever. The point is that whoever moved in has a bunch of kids. And they're all about the same age. There are, like, *two boys* that are going to be in our grade."

"And let me guess," Helen said, deadpan. "You did a tarot reading and saw that both of the boys are going to fall madly in love with you and then they'll tragically fight to the death."

Claire kicked Helen in the shin. "No, dummy. There's one for each of us."

Helen rubbed her leg, pretending it hurt. Even if Claire

had kicked Helen with all of her might, she still wouldn't be strong enough to leave a bruise.

"One for each of us? That's uncharacteristically low drama of you," Helen teased. "It's too straightforward. I don't buy it. But how about this? We'll each fall in love with the same boy, or the wrong boy—whichever one doesn't love us back—and then you and I will fight *each other* to the death."

"Whatever are you babbling on about?" Claire asked sweetly as she inspected her nails, feigning incomprehension.

"God, Claire, you're so predictable," Helen said, laughing. "Every year you dust off those cards you bought in Salem that time on the field trip and you always predict that something amazing is going to happen. But every year the only thing that amazes me is that you haven't slipped into a boredom coma by winter break."

"Why do you fight it?" Claire protested. "You know eventually something spectacular is going to happen to us. You and I are way too fabulous to be *ordinary*."

Helen shrugged. "I am perfectly happy with ordinary. In fact, I think I'd be devastated if you actually predicted right for a change."

Claire tilted her head to one side and stared at her. Helen untucked her hair from behind her ears to curtain off her face. She hated to be watched.

"I know you would. I just don't think ordinary's ever going to work out for you," Claire said thoughtfully.

Helen changed the subject. They chatted about their class

schedules, running track, and whether or not they should cut bangs. Helen wanted something new, but Claire was dead set against Helen touching her long blonde hair with scissors. Then they realized that they had wandered too close to what they called the "pervert zone" of the ferry, and had to hastily backtrack.

They both hated that part of the ferry, but Helen was particularly sensitive about it; it reminded her of this creepy guy that had followed her around one summer, until the day he just disappeared off the ferry. Instead of feeling relieved when she realized he wasn't coming back, Helen felt like she had done something wrong. She had never brought it up to Claire, but there had been a bright flash and a horrible smell of burnt hair. Then the guy was just *gone*. It still made her queasy to think about it, but Helen played along, like it was all a big joke. She forced a laugh and let Claire drag her along to another part of the ferry.

Jerry joined them as they pulled into the dock and disembarked. Claire waved good-bye and promised to try to visit Helen at work the next day, though since it was the last day of summer, the outlook was doubtful.

Helen worked a few days a week for her father, who co-owned the island's general store. Apart from a morning paper and fresh cup of coffee, the News Store also sold saltwater taffy, penny candy, caramels and toffee in real crystal jars, and ropes of licorice whips sold by the yard. There were always fresh-cut flowers and handmade greeting cards, gag gifts and magic tricks, seasonal knickknacks for the tourists,

8

and refrigerator essentials like milk and eggs for the locals.

About six years ago the News Store had expanded its horizons and added Kate's Cakes onto the back, and since then business had exploded. Kate Rogers was, quite simply, a genius with baked goods. She could take anything and make it into a pie, cake, popover, cookie, or muffin. Even universally loathed vegetables like brussels sprouts and broccoli succumbed to Kate's wiles and became big hits as croissant fillers.

Still in her early thirties, Kate was creative and intelligent. When she'd partnered up with Jerry she revamped the back of the News Store and turned it into a haven for the island's artists and writers, somehow managing to do it without turning up the snob factor. Kate was careful to make sure that anyone who loved baked goods and real coffee—from suits to poets, working-class townies to corporate raiders— would feel comfortable sitting down at her counter and reading a newspaper. She had a way of making everyone feel welcome. Helen adored her.

When Helen got to work the next day, Kate was trying to stock a delivery of flour and sugar. It was pathetic.

"Lennie! Thank god you're early. Do you think you could help me . . . ?" Kate gestured toward the forty-pound sacks.

"I got it. No, don't tug the corner like that, you'll hurt your back," Helen warned, rushing to stop Kate's ineffectual pulling. "Why didn't Luis do this for you? Wasn't he working this morning?" Helen asked, referring to one of the other workers on the schedule.

"The delivery came after Luis left. I tried to stall until you got here, but a customer nearly tripped and I had to at least pretend I was going to move the blasted thing," Kate said.

"I'll take care of the flour if you fix me a snack," Helen said cajolingly as she stooped to pick up the sack.

"Deal," Kate replied gratefully, and bustled off with a smile. Helen waited until Kate's back was turned, lifted the sack of flour easily on her shoulder, and sauntered toward the workstation, where she opened the sack and poured some flour into the smaller plastic container Kate used in the kitchen. While Helen neatly stacked the rest of the delivery in the storeroom, Kate poured her a bubbly pink lemonade, the kind that Helen loved, from France, one of the many foreign places she was dying to visit.

"It's not that you're so freakishly strong for someone so thin that bothers me. What really pisses me off," Kate said as she sliced some cherries and cheese for Helen to snack on, "is that you never get winded. Not even in *this* heat."

"I get winded," Helen lied.

"You sigh. Big difference."

"I've just got bigger lungs than you."

"But since you're taller, you'd need *more* oxygen, wouldn't you?"

They clinked glasses and sipped their lemonade, calling it even. Kate was a bit shorter and plumper than Helen, but that didn't make her either short or fat. Helen always thought of the word *zaftig* when she saw Kate, which she had a notion meant "sexy curvy." She never used it, though, in case Kate took it the wrong way.

"Is the book club on tonight?" Helen asked.

"Uh-huh. But I doubt anyone will want to talk about Kundera," Kate said with a smirk, jingling the ice cubes in her glass.

"Why? Hot gossip?"

"Smokin' hot. This crazy-big family just moved to the island."

"The place in 'Sconset?" Helen asked. At Kate's nod, she rolled her eyes.

"Oh-ho! Too good to dish with the rest of us?" Kate teased, flicking the condensed water from the side of her glass in Helen's direction.

Helen play-shrieked, and then had to leave Kate for a moment to ring up a few customers. As soon as she finished the transactions, she came back and continued the conversation.

"No. I just don't think it's that strange for a big family to buy a big property. Especially if they're going to live in it year-round. It makes more sense than some old wealthy couple buying a summer home that's so huge they get lost on the way to the mailbox."

"True," Kate conceded. "But I really thought you'd be more interested in the Delos family. You'll be graduating with a few of them."

Helen stood there as *Delos* ran around her head. The name meant nothing to her. How could it? But some echoey part of her brain kept repeating "Delos" over and over.

"Lennie? Where'd you go?" Kate asked. She was interrupted by the first members of the book club coming early, wound up and already in the throes of wild speculation.

Kate's prediction was right. *The Unbearable Lightness of Being* was no match for the arrival of new year-rounders, especially since the rumor mill had revealed that they were moving here from Spain. Apparently, they were Boston natives who had moved to Europe three years ago in order to be closer to their extended family, but now, suddenly, they'd decided to move back. It was the "suddenly" part that everyone spent the most time discussing. The school secretary had hinted to a few of the book club members that the kids had been enrolled so far past the normal date that the parents had practically had to bribe their way in, and all sorts of special agreements had to be made to ship their furniture over in time for their arrival. It seemed like the Delos family had left Spain in a hurry, and the book club agreed that there must have been some kind of falling-out with their cousins.

The one thing Helen could confidently gather from all the chatter was that the Delos family was rather unconventional. There were two fathers who were brothers, their younger sister, one mother (one of the fathers was a widower), and five kids, all living together on the property. The entire family was supposed to be unbelievably smart and beautiful and wealthy. Helen rolled her eyes when she heard the parts of the gossip that elevated the Delos family to mythic proportions. In fact, she could barely stand it.

Helen tried to stay behind the register and ignore the excited whispering, but it was impossible. Every time she heard one of the members of the Delos family mentioned by name, it drew her attention as if it had been shouted, irritating her. She left the register and went over to the magazine rack, straightening the shelves just to give her hands something to do.

As she wiped down the shelves and stocked the candy jars, she mentally ticked the kids off in her head. *Hector is a year older than Jason and Ariadne, who are twins. Lucas and Cassandra are brother and sister, cousins to the other three.*

She changed the water for the flowers and rang up a few customers. *Hector won't be there the first day of school because he's still in Spain with his aunt Pandora, though no one in town knows why.*

Helen pulled on a pair of shoulder-length rubber gloves and a long apron, and dug through the garbage for stray recycling items. *Lucas, Jason, and Ariadne are all going to be in my grade. So I'm surrounded. Cassandra is the youngest. She's a freshman, and only fourteen.*

She went to the kitchen and put a load in the industrial dishwasher. She mopped the floors and started counting the money. *Lucas is such a stupid name. It's all wrong. It sticks out like a sore thumb.*

"Lennie?"

"What! Dad! Can't you see I'm counting?" Helen said, slamming her hands down on the counter so hard she made a stack of quarters jump. Jerry held up his hands in a placating gesture.

"It's the first day of school tomorrow," he reminded her in his most reasonable voice.

"I know," she responded blankly, still unaccountably irritable but trying not to take it out on her father.

"It's almost eleven, honey," he said. Kate came out from the back to check on the noise.

"You're still here? I'm really sorry, Jerry," she said, looking perplexed. "Helen, I told you to lock the front and go home at nine."

They both stared at Helen, who had arranged every bill and every coin in neat stacks.

"I got sidetracked," Helen said lamely.

After sharing a worried glance with Jerry, Kate took over counting the change and sent them home. Still in a daze, Helen gave Kate a kiss good-bye and tried to figure out how she had missed out on the last three hours of her life.

Jerry put Helen's bike on the back of the Pig and started the engine without a word. He glanced over at her a few times as they drove home, but he didn't say anything until they parked in the driveway.

"Did you eat?" he asked softly, raising his eyebrows.

"I don't . . . yes?" Helen had no idea what or when she'd last eaten. She vaguely remembered Kate cutting her some cherries.

"Are you nervous about the first day of school? Junior year's a big one."

"I guess I must be," she said absentmindedly. Jerry glanced

over at her and bit his lower lip. He exhaled before speaking.

"I've been thinking maybe you should talk to Dr. Cunningham about those phobia pills. You know, the kind for people who have a hard time in crowds? Agoraphobia! That's what it's called," he burst out, remembering. "Do you think that could help you?"

Helen smiled and ran the charm of her necklace along its chain. "I don't think so, Dad. I'm not afraid of strangers, I'm just shy."

She knew she was lying. It wasn't *just* that she was shy. Any time she extended herself and attracted attention, even accidentally, her stomach hurt so badly it felt almost like the stomach flu or menstrual cramps—really *bad* menstrual cramps—but she'd sooner light her hair on fire than tell her father that.

"And you're okay with that? I know you'd never ask, but do you want help? Because I think this is holding you back. . . ." Jerry said, starting in on one of their oldest fights.

Helen cut him off at the pass. "I'm fine! Really. I don't want to talk to Dr. Cunningham, I don't want drugs. I just want to go inside and eat," she said in a rush. She got out of the Jeep.

Her father watched her with a small smile as she plucked her heavy, old-fashioned bike off the rack on the back of the Jeep and placed it on the ground. She rang the bell on her handlebar jauntily and gave her dad a grin.

"See, I'm just peachy," she said.

"If you knew how hard what you just did would be for an average girl your age, you'd get what I'm saying. You aren't average, Helen. You try to come off that way, but you're not. You're like *her*," he said, his voice drifting off.

For the thousandth time Helen cursed the mother she didn't remember for breaking her father's sweet heart. How could anyone leave such a good guy without so much as a good-bye? Without so much as a photo to remember her by?

"You win! I'm not average, I'm special—just like everyone else," Helen teased, anxious to cheer him up. She nudged him with her hip as she walked past him, wheeling her bike into the garage. "Now, what is there to eat? I'm starving, and it's your week to be kitchen slave."

# TWO

S till without her own car, Helen had to ride her bike to school the next morning. Normally at a quarter to eight, it would be cool out, even a little chilly with the wind blowing off the water, but as soon as she woke up, Helen could feel the hot, humid air lying on her body like a wet fur coat. She had kicked her sheets off in the middle of the night, wriggled out of her T-shirt, drunk the entire glass of water on her nightstand, and still she had woken up exhausted by the heat. It was very un-island weather, and Helen absolutely did not want to get up and go to school.

She pedaled slowly in an attempt to avoid spending the rest of the day smelling like phys ed. She didn't usually sweat much, but she'd woken up so lethargic that morning she couldn't remember if she had put on deodorant. She flapped her elbows like chicken wings trying to catch a whiff of herself as she rode, and was relieved to smell the fruity-powdery scent of some kind of protection. It was faint, so she must have put it on yesterday, but it only needed to hold on until track practice after school. Which would be a miracle, but oh well.

As she cruised down Surfside Road she could feel the baby hairs around her face pulling loose in the wind and sticking to her cheeks and forehead. It was a short ride from her house to school, but in the humidity, her carefully arranged first-day-of-school hairdo was a big old mess by the time she locked her crummy bike to the rack. She only locked it out of tourist-season habit and not because anyone at school would deign to steal it. Which was good because she also had a crummy lock.

She pulled her ruined hair out of its bonds, ran her fingers through the worst of the tangles, and retied it, this time settling for a boring, low ponytail. With a resigned sigh she swung her book bag over one shoulder and her gym bag over the other. She bent her head and slouched her way toward the front door.

She got there just a second before Gretchen Clifford, and was obliged to hold the door open for her.

"Thanks, freak. Try not to rip it off the hinges, will you?" Gretchen said archly, breezing past Helen.

Helen stood stupidly at the top of the steps, holding the door open for other students, who walked past her like she worked there. Nantucket was a small island, and everyone knew each other painfully well, but sometimes Helen wished Gretchen knew a little bit less about her. They'd been best friends up until fifth grade, when Helen, Gretchen, and Claire were playing hide-and-seek at Gretchen's house, and Helen accidentally knocked the bathroom door off its hinges while Gretchen was using it. Helen had tried to apologize, but the next day Gretchen started looking at her funny and calling her a freak. Ever since then it seemed like she'd gone out of her way to make Helen's life suck. It didn't help matters that Gretchen now ran with the popular crowd, while Helen hid among the braniacs.

She wanted to snap back at Gretchen, say something clever like Claire would, but the words caught in her throat. Instead, she flipped the doorstop down with her toe to leave the door propped open for everyone else. Another year of fading into the background had officially begun.

Helen had Mr. Hergeshimer for homeroom. He was the head of the English department, and had mad style for a guy in his fifties. He wore silk cravats in warm weather, flashy colored cashmere scarves when it was cold, and drove a vintage convertible Alfa Romeo. The guy had buckets of money and didn't need to work, but he taught high school, anyway. He said he did it because he didn't want to be forced to deal with illiterate heathens everywhere he went. That was his story, anyway. Personally, Helen believed he taught because he absolutely loved it. Some of the other students didn't get him and said he was a wannabe British snob, but Helen thought he was one of the best teachers she'd probably ever have.

"Miss Hamilton," he said broadly as Helen stepped

through the door, the bell ringing at exactly the same time. "Punctual as usual. I'm certain you will be taking the seat next to your cohort, but first, a warning. Any exercise of that talent for which one of you earned the sobriquet *Giggles* and I shall separate you."

"Sure thing, *Hergie*," chirped Claire. Helen slid into the desk next to her. Hergie rolled his eyes at Claire's mild disrespect, but he was pleased.

"It is gratifying to know that at least one of my students knows that *sobriquet* is a synonym for *nickname*, no matter how impertinent her delivery. Now, students: another warning. As you are preparing for your SATs this year, I shall expect you all to be ready to give me the definition of a new and exciting word every morning."

The class groaned. Only Mr. Hergeshimer could be sadistic enough to give them homework for homeroom. It was against the natural order.

"Can *impertinent* be the word we learn for tomorrow?" asked Zach Brant anxiously.

Zach was usually anxious about something, and he had been since kindergarten. Sitting next to Zach was Matt Millis, who looked over at Zach and shook his head as if to say, "I wouldn't try that if I were you."

Matt, Zach, and Claire were the AP kids. They were all friends, but as they got older they were starting to realize only one of them could be valedictorian and get into Harvard. Helen stayed out of the competition, especially because she had started liking Zach less and less the past few years. Ever since his father had become the football coach and started pushing Zach to be number one both on the field and in the classroom, Zach had become so competitive that Helen could barely stand to be around him anymore.

A part of her felt bad for him. She would have pitied him more if he wasn't so combative toward her. Zach had to be everything all the time—president of this club, captain of that team, the guy with all the gossip—but he never looked like he was enjoying any of it. Claire insisted that Zach was secretly in love with Helen, but Helen didn't believe it for a second; in fact, sometimes she felt like Zach hated her, and that bothered her. He used to share his animal crackers with her during recess in the first grade, and now he looked for any opportunity to pick a fight with her. When did everything get so complicated, and why couldn't they all just be friends like they were in grade school?

"Mr. Brant," Mr. Hergeshimer enunciated. "You may use *impertinent* as your word if you wish, but from someone of your mental faculties I shall also be expecting something more. Perhaps an essay on an example of impertinence in English literature?" He nodded. "Yes, five pages on Salinger's use of impertinence in his controversial *Catcher in the Rye* by Monday, please."

Helen could practically smell the palms of Zach's hands clam up from two seats away. Hergie's powers for giving extra reading to smart-ass students were legendary, and he seemed determined to make an example out of Zach on the first day. Helen thanked her lucky stars Hergie hadn't picked on her.

She'd rejoiced too soon. After Mr. Hergeshimer handed out the schedules, he called Helen up to his desk. He told the other students to speak freely, and they immediately launched into excited first-day-of-school chatter. Hergie had Helen pull up a chair next to him instead of making her stand and talk across his desk. Apparently, he didn't want any of the other students to hear what he was going to say. That put Helen a little more at ease, but not for long.

"I see you decided not to enroll in any Advanced Placement classes this year," he said, looking at her from over his half-moon reading glasses.

"I didn't think I'd be able to handle the extra workload," she mumbled, tucking her hands under her thighs and sitting on them to keep them still.

"I think you're capable of much more than you are willing to admit," Hergie said, frowning. "I know you aren't lazy, Helen. I also know you are one of the brightest students in your class. So what's keeping you from taking advantage of all that this educational system has to offer you?"

"I have to work," she said with a helpless shrug. "I need to save up if I want to go to college."

"If you take AP classes and do well on your SATs, you will stand a better chance of getting enough money for school through a scholarship than by working for minimum wage at your father's shop."

"My dad needs me. We aren't rich like everyone else on this island, but we are there for each other," she said defensively.

"That's very admirable of you both, Helen," Hergie replied in a serious tone. "But you are reaching the end of your high school years and it's time to start thinking about your own future."

"I know," Helen said, nodding. She could see from the worry puckering his face that he cared, and that he was just trying to help. "I think I should get a pretty good athletic scholarship for track. I got much faster over the summer. Really."

Mr. Hergeshimer stared at her earnest face begging him to let it go, and finally conceded. "All right. But if you feel like you need more of an academic challenge, you are welcome to join my AP English class at any point this semester."

"Thank you, Mr. Hergeshimer. If I feel like I can handle AP, I'll come to you," Helen said, grateful to be let off the hook.

As she went back to her desk, it occurred to her that she had to keep Hergie and her father away from each other at all costs. She didn't want them comparing notes and deciding that she needed to be in special classes and go out for special awards. Even the thought gave her a bellyache. Why couldn't they all just ignore her? Secretly, Helen had always felt she was different, but she thought she had done a pretty good job of hiding it her whole life. Apparently, without realizing it, she'd been sending out hints of that buried freak inside of her. She had to try to keep her head down, but she wondered how she was going to do that when she kept getting taller and taller every damn day.

"What's up?" Claire asked as soon as Helen returned to her seat.

"Just another motivational moment from Hergie. He doesn't think I'm applying myself," Helen said as breezily as she could.

"You don't apply yourself. You never do your work," Zach replied, more offended than he should have been.

"Shut it, Zach," Claire said, crossing her arms belligerently. She turned and faced Helen. "It's true, though, Lennie," she told her apologetically. "You never do your work."

"Yeah, yeah. You can both shut it," Helen said, chuckling. The bell rang and she gathered her things. Matt Millis gave her a smile but hurried away as they left the room. Feeling guilty, Helen realized that she hadn't spoken to him yet. She hadn't meant to ignore him, especially not on the first day of school.

According to Claire, "everyone" knew that Matt and Helen were "supposed" to be together. Matt was intelligent, good looking, and captain of the golf team. He was still sort of a geek, but because Helen was practically a pariah ever since Gretchen had started spreading rumors about her, it was a compliment that everyone thought she was good enough for someone like Matt.

Unfortunately, Helen never felt anything special for him. Zero tingles. The one time they had been shoved into a closet together at a party to make out, it had been disastrous. Helen felt like she was kissing her brother, and Matt felt like he was being rejected. Afterward, he was sweet about it, but no matter how many times he cracked jokes, there was a weird tension between them. She really missed him but she worried that if she told him he would take it the wrong way. *It feels like everything I do lately is being taken the wrong way,* Helen thought.

The rest of the morning Helen wandered on autopilot from class to class. She couldn't concentrate on much of anything, and every time she tried to make herself focus she felt nothing but irritation.

Something about the day was off. Everyone—from her favorite teachers to the few acquaintances she should have been happy to see—was annoying her, and every now and again while she was walking down the hall she would suddenly feel like she was inside an airplane at ten thousand feet. Her inner ears would block up, all the sounds around her would become muffled, and her head would get hot. Then, as suddenly as it had come on, the discomfort would go away. But even still, there was a pressure, a pre-thunderstorm energy all around her, even though the skies were lovely and blue.

It got worse at lunch. She tore into her sandwich thinking that her headache was the result of low blood sugar, but she was wrong. Jerry had packed her favorite sandwich— smoked turkey, green apple, and brie on a baguette—but she couldn't force herself to take more than a bite. She spat it out.

"Your dad make another dud?" Claire asked. When Jerry had first partnered up with Kate he'd started experimenting with creative lunches. The Vegemite and Cucumber Disaster of Freshman Year was legendary at their table.

"No, it's good old number three. I just can't eat it," Helen said, shoving it away. Claire gleefully picked up the remainder and started eating it.

"Mmm, 'is really good," she mumbled around a full mouth. "Us a 'atter?"

"I just don't feel right," Helen said.

Claire stopped chewing and gave her a worried look.

"I'm not sick. You can go ahead and swallow," Helen assured her quickly. She saw Matt approaching and chirped, "Hey!" trying to make up for that morning.

He was deep in conversation with Gretchen and Zach and didn't respond, but still came to his habitual spot at the geek table. Both Gretchen and Zach were so engrossed in what they were saying that they didn't notice that they had wandered into geek territory.

"I heard they were movie stars in Europe," Zach was saying.

"Where did you hear that?" Matt asked, incredulous. "That's ridiculous."

"I heard from at least two other people that Ariadne was a model. She's certainly pretty enough," Zach argued passionately, hating to be wrong about anything, even gossip.

"*Please.* She's nowhere near thin enough to be a model," Gretchen hissed bitterly, before catching herself and adding, "Of course I think she's *pretty*, if you go for that exotic, voluptuous look. But she's nothing compared to her twin,

26

Jason—or her cousin! Lucas is just *unreal*," she gushed.

The boys shared a knowing look but silently agreed that they were outnumbered by girls and should probably let it go.

"Jason is almost *too* pretty," Claire decided solemnly, after giving it a moment's thought. "Lucas, however, is an über-babe. Quite possibly the most beautiful boy I've ever seen. And Ariadne is a stone-cold fox, Gretchen. You're just jealous."

Gretchen gave an exasperated huff and rested a fist on her hip. "Like you're not," was all she had for a comeback.

"Of course I am. I'm almost as jealous of her as I am of Lennie. But not quite." Helen felt Claire turn to her to see her response, but she had her elbows on the table and her head cradled in her hands, rubbing her temples.

"Lennie?" Matt said, sitting down next to her. "Does your head hurt?" He reached out to touch her shoulder. She stood up abruptly, muttering an excuse, and hurried away.

By the time she got to the girls' room she felt better, but she splashed a little cold water on her face for good measure. Then she remembered that she had put mascara on that morning in an attempt to make an effort. She looked at her raccoon eyes in the mirror and burst out laughing. This was the worst first day of school ever.

Somehow she made it through the last three periods, and when the bell finally rang she gratefully made her way to the girls' locker room to change for track practice.

Coach Tar was all fired up. She gave an embarrassingly optimistic speech about their chances to win races that year

and told them how much she believed in them, both as athletes and as young women. Then she turned to Helen.

"Hamilton. You'll be running with the boys this year,"
Coach said bluntly. She told everyone to hit the trail.

Helen sat on the bench for a moment, debating her options
while everyone else filed out the door. She didn't want to
make a fuss, but she was mortified by the thought of having
to cross the gender line. The muscles in her lower abdomen
started to spasm.

"Go talk to her! Don't let her push you around," Claire
said indignantly as she left.

Confused and afraid she was going to get a bellyache,
Helen nodded and stood up.

"Coach Tar? Can't we just do it the way we always do?"
she called out. Coach Tar stopped and turned around to listen, but she didn't look happy about it. "I mean, why can't
I just train with the rest of the girls? Because I am a girl,"
Helen finished lamely.

"We've decided that you need to start pushing yourself
more," Coach Tar responded in a cold voice. Helen had
always gotten the feeling that Coach didn't like her much,
and now she was sure of it.

"But I'm not a boy. It's not fair to make me run cross-
country with them," Helen tried to argue. She jabbed two
fingers into the spot between her belly button and her pubic
bone.

"Cramps?" Coach Tar asked, a touch of sympathy creeping into her voice. Helen nodded and Coach continued.

"Coach Brant and I have noticed something interesting about your times, Helen. No matter who you're running against, no matter how fast or slow your opponents are, you always come in either second or third. How can that be? Do you have an answer?"

"No. I don't know. I just run, okay? I try my best."

"No, you don't," Coach said harshly. "And if you want a scholarship, you're going to have to start *winning* races. I talked to Mr. Hergeshimer. . . ." Helen groaned out loud, but Coach Tar continued, undeterred. "It's a small school, Hamilton, get used to it. Mr. Hergeshimer told me that you were hoping for an athletic scholarship, but if you want one you're going to have to earn it. Maybe forcing you to match the boys will teach you to take your talent seriously."

The thought of displaying her speed for the world to see had a physical effect on Helen. She was so afraid that she was going to get some kind of cramp or bellyache that she started to have a mini panic attack. She began to babble. "I'll do it, I'll win races, just please don't single me out like that," she pleaded, the words tumbling out in a rush as she held her breath to hold back the pain.

Coach Tar was a hard-ass, but she wasn't cruel. "Are you okay?" she asked anxiously, rubbing Helen between her shoulder blades. "Put your head between your legs."

"I'm okay, it's just nerves," Helen explained through gritted teeth. After catching her breath she continued, "If I swear to win more races, will you let me run with the girls?"

Coach Tar studied Helen's desperate face and nodded, a

bit shaken from witnessing such an intense panic attack. She let Helen go to the girl's trailhead but warned her that she still expected wins. And more than just a few.

As she ran the trail, Helen looked at the ground. An academic scholarship would be great but that would mean competing with Claire for grades, and that was out of the question.

"Hey, Giggles," Helen said, easily catching up. Claire was panting and sweating away already.

"What happened? God, it's so hot!" she exclaimed, her breath strained.

"I think the entire faculty is trying to see if they can climb up onto my back at the same time."

"Welcome to my life," Claire wheezed. "Japanese kids grow up . . . with at least two . . . people up there. . . . You get used to it." After a few more labored moments of trying to keep up with Helen, Claire added, "Can we . . . slow down? Not all of us are from . . . planet Krypton."

Helen adjusted her pace, knowing that she could pull ahead in the last half mile. She rarely exerted herself in practice but she knew that even without trying hard she could easily finish first. That fact scared her, so she did what she usually did when the subject of her freaky speed came up in her head. She ignored it and chatted with Claire.

As the two girls ran down Surfside and out across the moors to Miacomet Pond, Claire couldn't stop talking about the Delos boys. She told Helen at least three times that Lucas had held the door for her at the end of class. That act proved he was not only a gentleman but already in love with her as well. Jason, Claire decided, was either gay or a snob because he had only glanced at her once before quickly looking away. She also took offense at how nice a dresser he was, like he was European or something.

"He's been living in Spain for, like, three years, Gig. He kinda is European. Can we please stop talking about them? It's giving me a headache."

"Why are you the only person in school that isn't interested in the Delos family? Aren't you even curious to get a look?"

"No! And I think it's pathetic that this entire town is standing around gawking at them like a bunch of hicks!" Helen shouted.

Claire stopped short and stared at her. It wasn't like Helen to argue, let alone start yelling, but she couldn't seem to stop herself.

"I'm bored to death of the Delos family!" Helen continued, even when she saw Claire's surprise. "I'm sick of this town's fixation with them, and I hope I never have to meet, see, or share breathing space with any of them!"

Helen took off running, leaving Claire standing by herself on the trail. She finished first, just like she'd promised, but she did it a little too quickly; Coach Tar gave her a shocked look when she recorded the run time. Helen blew by her and stormed into the locker room. She grabbed her stuff and bolted out of school, not bothering to change or say goodbye to any of her teammates.

On the way home, Helen started crying. She pedaled past the neat rows of gray shingled-sided houses with their black or white painted storm shutters and tried to calm down. The sky seemed to sit particularly low on the scoured land, as if it was pressing down on the gables of the old whalers and trying to finally flatten them after a few centuries of stubborn defiance. Helen had no idea why she'd gotten so angry, or why she'd abandoned her best friend like that. She needed a little peace and quiet.

There was a car accident on Surfside; some gigantic SUV had tried to turn onto a narrow, sandbanked side street and turned over. The drivers were okay, but their beached whale of a car blocked off traffic from end to end. Annoyed as she was, Helen knew she couldn't even pedal past the boneheaded off islanders without losing her checkers. She decided to take the long way home. She turned around and headed back toward the center of town, passing the movie theater, the ferry, and the library, which, with its Greek temple architecture, stuck out like a sore thumb in a town that otherwise was an ode to four-hundred-year-old Puritan architecture. And maybe that's why Helen loved it. The Atheneum was a gleaming white beacon of strange smack-dab in the middle of forget-me-now drab, and somehow, Helen identified with both of those things. Half of her was no-nonsense Nantucket through and through, and the other half was marble columns and grand stairs that just didn't belong where they had been built. Biking past, Helen looked up at the Atheneum and smiled. It was consoling for her to know that she might stick out, but at least she didn't stick out *that* much.

When she got home, she tried to pull herself together, taking a freezing-cold shower before calling Claire to apologize. Claire didn't pick up. Helen left her a long apology blaming hormones, the heat, stress, anything and everything she could think of, though she knew in her heart that none of those things was the real reason she had flipped out. She'd been so irritable all day.

The air outside was heavy and still. Helen opened all the windows in the two-story Shaker-style house, but no breeze blew through them. What was with the weird weather? Still air was practically unheard of in Nantucket—living so close to the ocean there was always wind. Helen pulled on a thin tank top and a pair of her shortest shorts. Since she was too modest to go anywhere dressed so scantily, she decided to cook dinner. It was still her father's week as kitchen slave and technically he was responsible for all the shopping, meals, and dishes for a few days yet, but she needed something to do with her hands or she'd use them to climb the walls.

Pasta in general was Helen's comfort food, and lasagna was the queen of pasta. If she made the noodles from scratch, she'd be occupied for hours, just like she wanted, so she pulled out the flour and eggs and got to work.

When Jerry came home the second thing he noticed, after the amazing smell, was that the house was swelteringly hot. He found Helen sitting at the kitchen table, flour stuck to her sweaty face and arms, worrying the heart-shaped necklace, which her mother had given her as a baby, between her thumb and forefinger. He looked around with tense shoulders and wide eyes.

"Made dinner," Helen told him in a flat voice.

"Did I do something wrong?" he asked tentatively.

"Of course not. Why would you ask that when I just cooked you dinner?"

"Because usually when a woman spends hours cooking a complicated meal and then just sits at the table with a pissed-off look on her face, that means some guy somewhere did something really stupid," he said, still on edge. "I have had other women in my life besides you, you know."

"Are you hungry or not?" Helen asked with a smile, trying to shake off her ugly mood.

Hunger won out. Jerry shut his mouth and went to wash his hands. Helen hadn't eaten since breakfast and should have been starved. When she tasted the first forkful she realized she wouldn't be able to eat. She listened as best as she could while she pushed bits of her favorite food around her plate and Jerry devoured two pieces. He asked her questions about her day while he tried to sneak a little more salt onto his food. Helen blocked his attempts like she always did, but she didn't have the energy to give him more than monosyllabic answers.

Even though she went to bed at nine, leaving her dad watching the Red Sox on TV, she was still lying awake at midnight when she heard the game finally end and her father come upstairs. She was tired enough to sleep, but every time she started to drift off she would hear whispering.

At first she thought that it had to be real, that someone was outside playing a trick on her. She went up to the widow's walk on the roof above her bedroom and tried to see as far as she could into the dark. Everything was still—not even a puff of air to stir the rosebushes around the house. She sat down for a spell, staring out at the fat, black slick of the ocean beyond the neighbors' lights.

She hadn't been up there in a while, but it still gave her a romantic thrill to think about how women in the olden days would pine away on their widow's walks as they searched for the masts of their husbands' ships. When she was really young, Helen used to pretend that her mother would be on one of those ships, coming back to her after being taken captive by pirates or Captain Ahab or something just as all-powerful. Helen had spent hours on the widow's walk, scanning the horizon for a ship she later realized would never sail into Nantucket Harbor.

Helen shifted uncomfortably on the wooden floor and then remembered that she still had her stash up there. For years, her dad had insisted she was going to fall to her death and had forbidden her from going up to the widow's walk alone, but no matter how many times he punished her, she would eventually sneak back up there to eat granola bars and daydream. After a few months of dealing with Helen's uncharacteristic disobedience, Jerry finally caved and gave her permission, as long as she didn't lean out over the railing. He'd even built her a waterproof chest to store things in.

She opened the chest and dug out the sleeping bag she kept in there, spreading it out along the wood planks of the walk. There were boats far out on the water, boats she shouldn't be able to hear or see from such a distance, but she could. Helen closed her eyes and allowed herself the pleasure of hearing one little skiff as its canvas sails flapped and its teak planks creaked, way out on the gently lapping swells. Alone and unwatched, she could be herself for a moment and truly let go. When her head finally started to nod she went down to bed to give sleep another shot.

*She was standing on rocky, hilly terrain, blasted so hard by the sun that the bone-dry air wriggled and shook in streaks, as if parts of the sky were melting. The rocks were pale yellow and sharp, and here and there were angry little bushes, low to the ground and lousy with thorns. A single twisted tree grew out of the next slope.*

*Helen was alone. And then she wasn't.*

*Under the stunted tree's crippled limbs three figures appeared. They were so slender and small Helen thought at first they must be little girls, but there was something about the way the muscles in their gaunt forearms wove around their bones like rope that made Helen realize that they were also very old. All three of them had their heads bent, and their faces were completely covered by sheets of long, matted, black hair. They wore tattered white slips, and they were covered in gray-white dust down to their lower legs. From the knees down, their skin grew dark with streaks of dirt*

*and blackening blood from feet worn raw with wandering in this*
*barren wilderness.*

*Helen felt clear, bright fear. She backed away from them com-*
*pulsively, cutting her bare feet on the rocks and scratching her*
*legs on the thorns. The three abominations took a step toward*
*her, and their shoulders began to shake with silent sobs. Drops*
*of blood fell from under the skeins of rank hair and ran down the*
*fronts of their dresses. They whispered names while they cried*
*their gory tears.*

Helen woke up to a slap. There was a prickly numbness in
her cheek and the steady note of a dial tone whining in her
left ear. Jerry's face was inches away from hers, wild with
worry, and starting to show signs of guilt. He had never hit
her before. He had to take a few shaky breaths before he
could speak. The bedside clock read 3:16.

"You were screaming. I had to wake you," he stammered.

Helen swallowed painfully, trying to moisten her swollen tongue and closed-off throat. "S'okay. Nightmare," she
whispered as she sat up.

Her cheeks were wet with either sweat or tears, she didn't
know which. Helen wiped the moisture away and smiled at
her dad, trying to calm him down. It didn't work.

"What the hell, Lennie? That was not normal," he said in a
strange, high-pitched voice. "You were saying things. Really
awful things."

"Like what?" she croaked. She was so thirsty.

"Mostly names, lists of names. And then you started

repeating 'blood for blood,' and 'murderers.' What the hell were you dreaming?"

Helen thought about the three women, *three sisters,* she thought, and she knew she couldn't tell her father about them. She shrugged her shoulders and lied. She managed to convince Jerry that murder was a pretty normal thing to have nightmares about, and swore that she would never watch scary movies by herself again. Finally, she got him to go back to bed.

The glass on her nightstand was empty and her mouth was so dry it felt tender and sore. She swung her legs out of bed to get water from the bathroom and gasped when her feet touched the hardwood floor. She switched on her lamp to get a better look, but she already knew what she was going to see.

The soles of her feet were cut deep and peppered with dirt and dust, and her shins were scratched with the hatch-mark pattern of thorns.

# THREE

In the morning when Helen woke up and looked at her feet, the cuts were gone. She almost believed that she had imagined them—until she saw that her sheets were dirty with dried, brown blood and grit.

In order to test her sanity, Helen decided to leave her sheets on the bed, go to school, and see if they were still dirty when she came home. If they were clean when she got home, then the whole thing was an illusion and she was only a little crazy. If they were still dirty when she came home, then she was obviously so crazy that she was walking around at night and getting dirt and blood in her bed without remembering it.

Helen tried to eat a bowl of yogurt and berries for breakfast but that didn't work out very well, so she didn't even bother to take her lunch box. If she got hungry, she could try buying something more tummy friendly like soup and crackers later.

Riding her bike to school, she noticed that it was unbearably hot and humid for a second day in a row. The only wind was the breeze created by her spinning wheels, and when she locked her bike up at the rack she realized that not only was the air still, but it was also lacking the usual insect and bird sounds. All was unnaturally quiet—as though the entire island was nothing but a ship becalmed in the middle of the vast ocean.

Helen arrived earlier than she had the day before, and the halls were crowded. Claire saw her come in. When her face broke into a smile, Helen knew she had been forgiven. Claire fought the flow of traffic to double back and join her on the walk to homeroom.

As they made their way toward each other, Helen suddenly felt like she was trying to trudge through oatmeal. She slowed to a stop. It seemed to her that everyone in the hallway vanished. In the suddenly empty school Helen heard the shuffling of bare feet and the gasping sobs of inconsolable grief.

She spun around in time to see a dusty white figure, her shoulders slumped and quivering, disappearing around a corner. Helen realized that the sobbing woman had passed behind someone—a real person staring back at her. She focused in on the figure, a delicate young girl with olive skin and a long, black braid trailing over one shoulder. Her naturally bright red lips were drawn into an O of surprise.

To Helen she looked like a china doll, so perfect she could not be entirely real.

Then the sound switched back on and the corridor was full of rushing students again. Helen was standing still, blocking traffic, staring at a glossy black braid swinging against a tiny girl's back as it vanished into a classroom.

Helen's whole body shook with an emotion that took her a moment to recognize. It was rage.

"Jesusmaryandjoseph, Len! Are you gonna faint?" Claire asked anxiously.

Helen made her eyes focus on Claire, and she took a wobbly breath. She realized that she was drenched in cold sweat and shivering. She opened her mouth, but nothing came out.

"I'm taking you to the nurse," Claire said. She grabbed Helen's hand and started to tug on it, trying to get her to move. "Matt," she called out over Helen's shoulder. "Can you help me with Lennie? I think she's going to faint."

"I'm not going to faint," Helen snapped, suddenly alert and aware of how strange she was acting.

She smiled bashfully at them both to try to take the sting out of her words. Matt had put his arm around her waist and she patted his hand softly to let him know he could release her. He gave her a doubtful look.

"You're really pale, and you've got circles under your eyes," he said.

"I got a little overheated riding my bike," she started to explain.

"Don't tell me you're fine," Claire warned. Her eyes were flush with frustrated tears, and Matt didn't look much happier. Helen knew she couldn't brush this off. Even if she was going crazy, she didn't have to take it out on her friends.

"No, you're right. I think I might have heatstroke."

Matt nodded, accepting this excuse as the only logical one. "Claire, you take her to the girls' room. I'll tell Hergie what happened so he doesn't mark you late. And you should eat something. You didn't eat any lunch yesterday," he reminded her.

Helen was a little surprised he remembered that, but Matt was good at details. He wanted to be a lawyer, and she knew that someday he would be a great one.

Claire drenched Helen in the girls' room, dumping cold water all the way down her back when she was supposed to just wet her neck. Of course they wound up having a gigantic water fight, which seemed to calm Claire down because it was the first normal response she'd had out of Helen in a few days. Helen herself felt like she had passed an exhaustion barrier and now everything had become funny.

Hergie wrote them hall passes, so the two friends took their time getting to their first classes. Having a hall pass from Mr. Hergeshimer was like getting one of Willy Wonka's golden tickets—a student could go anywhere and do anything for a full period and not one teacher would put up a stink.

In the cafeteria they got oranges for Helen's low blood sugar, and while they were at it they split a chocolate chip muffin. Helen choked it down and miraculously started to feel better. Then they went and stood in front of the six-foot-tall fan in the auditorium to cool down, taking turns singing into the whirling blades and listening to each other's voices get chopped into a hundred pieces until they were both laughing their faces off.

Helen felt so giddy after playing hooky on a Hergie hall pass and eating raw sugar on an empty stomach that she couldn't even remember what class she was supposed to be going to. She and Claire were casually strolling down the wrong hallway at the wrong time when the bell signaling the end of first period rang. They looked at each other and shrugged as if to say, "Oh well, what can you do?" and burst out laughing. Then Helen saw Lucas for the first time.

The sky outside finally exhaled all of the wind that it had been holding for two days. Gusts of stale, hot air pushed through every open window into the sweltering school. It caught loose sheets of paper, skirt hems, unbound hair, stray wrappers, and other odds and ends, and tossed them all toward the ceiling like hats on graduation day. For a moment it seemed to Helen that everything stayed up there, frozen at the top of the arc, as weightless as space.

Lucas was standing in front of his locker about twenty feet away, staring back at Helen while the world waited for gravity to switch back on. He was tall, over six feet at least, and powerfully built, although his muscles were long and lean instead of bulky. He had short, black hair and a dark end-of-summer tan that brought out his white smile and his swimming-pool blue eyes.

Meeting his eyes was an awakening. For the first time in Helen's life she knew what pure, heart-poisoning hatred was.

She was not aware of the fact that she was running toward him, but she could hear the voices of the three sobbing sisters rise into a keening wail, could see them standing behind the tall, dark boy she *knew* was Lucas, and the smaller, brown-haired boy next to him. The sisters were tearing at their hair until it came out of their scalps in bloody hanks. They pointed accusing fingers at the two boys while they screeched a series of names—the names of people murdered long ago. Helen suddenly understood what she had to do.

In the split second it took for her to close the gap between them, Helen saw the other boy lunge at her, but he was stopped by Lucas, who threw out an arm and sent him flying back into the lockers behind them. Then her whole body stopped and strained.

"Cassandra! Stay where you are," Lucas called over Helen's shoulder, his face no more than an inch away from hers. "She's *very* strong."

Helen's arms burned and the little bones in her wrists felt like they were grinding together. Lucas was holding her by the wrists to keep her hands away from his neck, she realized. They were locked in a stalemate, and if she could get her fingers half an inch closer, she could reach his throat.

*And then what?* a little voice in her head asked. *Choke the life out of him!* answered another.

Lucas's achingly blue eyes widened in surprise. Helen was winning. One of her long nails grazed the pulsing skin covering the fat artery she itched to slit. Then, before she could process what was happening, Lucas spun her around and clamped her to his chest, restraining her arms against her breast and standing between her legs. The position he'd forced her into kept her off balance and unable to bring her heel down on his instep. She was immobile.

"Who are you? What is your House?" he breathed into her ear, giving her a rough shake to punctuate his point. She was beyond understanding language.

Outmaneuvered and helpless, she started to scream with rage, then stopped herself. Now that she couldn't see his eyes she was becoming aware of the fact that half the school's faculty was trying to tear her off him. Everyone was staring.

Helen doubled over in agony as her abdomen seized up with cramps. Lucas immediately let her go as if she'd turned into a lit match, his body convulsing spasmodically, and she dropped to the floor.

"Miss Hamilton! Miss . . . Helen. Helen, look at me," said Mr. Hergeshimer. He was kneeling on the floor next to her while she panted, trying to relax her muscles. She looked up at his sweaty face. His hair was messed up and his glasses had been knocked sideways on his face in the fight. She wondered for a moment if she had been the one to hit him, and then she burst into tears.

"What's wrong with me?" she whimpered softly.

"It's all right, now. Calm down," Mr. Hergeshimer said sternly. "All of you had better get to class. Immediately!" he roared to the throngs of kids standing around with their mouths open. Everyone scattered as Mr. Hergeshimer stood up and took charge.

"You boys," he pointed at Lucas and Jason, "are to come with me to the principal's office. Mr. Millis! Miss Aoki! You are to take Miss Hamilton to the nurse's office and then go *directly* to your next classes. Understood?"

Matt immediately stepped forward and put Helen's arm over his shoulder, helping her to stand. Claire took Helen's hand and held it reassuringly. Helen glanced up and saw Lucas looking back over his shoulder at her as he went quietly with Mr. Hergeshimer. Another wave of loathing broke over her, and fresh tears lined up in her eyes. Matt guided her while she cried, awkwardly patting her hair and getting her to walk toward the nurse at the same time. Claire walked on Helen's other side, shaken and silent.

"What did he do to you, Lennie?" Matt asked hotly.

"I've never seen him b-b-before in my l-l-life!" Helen hiccuped and cried even harder.

"Great idea, Matt! Ask her questions! Can you shut the hell up now?" Claire snapped, trying to get hold of herself.

They walked the rest of the way without talking. When they got to the nurse's office, they told Mrs. Crane what had happened and made sure to add that Helen had come to school with heatstroke that morning. Mrs. Crane had Helen lie down with a cool towel over her eyes and went back into her office to call Jerry.

"Your father's on his way, dear. No, no, keep your eyes covered. Darkness will help," Mrs. Crane said as she passed by Helen's cot. Helen heard her rush out to the hall to speak to someone briefly, then come back in and sit behind her desk.

Helen lay under the towel, grateful that she was being left alone and in relative privacy. She couldn't think two coherent thoughts in a row, let alone explain herself to anyone. What scared her the most was that for some reason she knew that what she had tried to do was *right*, or at least that it was expected of her. Deep inside, she knew she would have killed that boy if she could, and she didn't even feel guilty about it. Until she saw her father.

He was a mess. Mrs. Crane told him everything that had happened, explaining that Helen was suffering from a serious case of heatstroke and that it may have caused her strange outburst. He listened patiently and then asked Mrs. Crane for a moment alone with his daughter, which she gave them.

Jerry didn't say anything at first; he just sort of hovered over Helen's cot while she sat up and fidgeted with her necklace. Finally, he sat down next to her.

"You wouldn't lie to me right now, would you?" he asked softly. She shook her head. "Are you sick?"

"I don't know, Dad. I don't feel right—but I don't know what's wrong," she told him earnestly.

"We've got to take you to the doctor, you know."

"I figured," she said, nodding. They smiled at each other, and then suddenly they both turned their heads at the sound of hurried footsteps coming toward the nurse's office.

Jerry stood up and faced the door, putting himself in front of Helen. A tall, impossibly fit man in his early forties burst into the room. Helen jumped off the cot and stood on the other side of it, glancing around instinctively for another exit. There wasn't one. Helen had the feeling that she was going to die.

In the corner of the tiny office, one of the sobbing sisters appeared. She was hunkered down on her knees, her face covered by her filthy hair, moaning names and saying "blood for blood" as she hit her forehead repeatedly against the wall.

Helen put her hands over her ears. She pulled her eyes away from the horror in the corner and mustered enough courage to look back at the large man. A spark of recognition passed between them. She had never seen him before, but somehow she knew that she should be very afraid of him. At first his angular face set with determination, but it quickly morphed into shock and then confusion. His eyes zeroed in on Jerry, and a nearly comical look of disbelief derailed what might have been a terrible fight.

"Are you . . . are you the father of the young lady that attacked my son?" he asked in a halting voice.

Jerry nodded curtly. "My daughter, Helen," he said, gesturing back to her. "I'm Jerry Hamilton."

"Castor Delos," the big man replied. "My wife, Noel, won't be able to make it. And Helen's mother?"

Jerry shook his head. "It's just Lennie and me," he said with finality.

Castor's eyes darted to Helen and back to Jerry and he

pursed his lips as if he had set something right in his head. "Pardon me. I didn't mean to bring up personal matters. Is there any way you and I might have a word alone?"

"NO!" Helen shouted. She lunged across the cot, grabbing her father's arm and yanking him away from Castor.

"What is wrong with you?" Jerry shouted. He tried, and failed, to shake Helen off.

"Please don't go anywhere with him!" she begged, tears welling up in her eyes.

Jerry made a frustrated sound, put his arms around Helen, and held her reassuringly. "She hasn't been well," he explained to Castor, who looked on with sympathy.

"I have a daughter," Castor replied gently as if that explained everything.

Mrs. Crane and the principal, Dr. Hoover, rushed into the room as if they had been trying to catch up to Castor.

"Mr. Delos," the principal began in an irritated voice, but Castor talked over him.

"I hope your daughter feels better soon, Jerry. I've had heatstroke myself, and I was told I did all kinds of strange things. It can make you hallucinate, you know," he said to no one in particular.

Helen saw him glance quickly at her and then into the corner where the sobbing sister was still rocking back and forth. Did he see her, too, she wondered, and if he did, how the heck could two people share a hallucination?

"Well . . . okay. There's no animosity then?" Dr. Hoover said uncertainly, looking from Castor to Jerry.

"Not on my part, nor on my son's, I'm sure. I'm more

concerned about you, young lady," Castor said, turning politely to Helen. "Luke told me he had to be, well, a bit rough. Did he hurt you?" Castor inquired. On the surface, it seemed like he had extraordinarily good manners, but Helen didn't buy it. He was just trying to gauge how strong she was.

"I'm fine," she replied tartly. "Not a scratch."

His eyes widened ever so slightly. She didn't know why she was baiting a full-grown man, a very big man in the prime of his life at that, but she simply couldn't help herself. Usually, she hated arguments so much she couldn't even bear to watch those trashy daytime talk shows where everyone screamed at each other, and here she was for the second time in half an hour looking to mix it up with someone much bigger and stronger than she was. Thankfully, she wasn't as desperate to kill Castor the way she had been with his son. No one had ever enraged Helen the way that Lucas had, but she still wanted to put a few dents in Castor's fender. That urge confused her deeply.

"I'm glad you're all right," Castor said with a smile, diffusing the situation. He turned to the principal and made it clear that he and his family did not want Helen punished. As far as he was concerned Helen had been ill, and the whole incident should be forgotten. He left as abruptly as he had entered.

As soon as Castor's footsteps faded away, the sobbing sister vanished and the whispering stopped. Helen no longer felt angry. She slumped down onto the cot like a balloon with a fast leak.

"You'd best take her home now, Jerry," Mrs. Crane said with a no-nonsense voice and a comforting smile. "Lots of fluids, no direct light, and get her to take a cool bath to bring her core temperature down. All right?"

"Sure, Mrs. Crane. Thanks a lot," Jerry replied, reverting back to the teenaged boy he had been the last time he was in Mrs. Crane's office.

Helen kept her head down on their way out to the parking lot, but she could feel the other students staring at her as she passed. As she jumped up into the passenger seat of the Pig she saw the door by the principal's office open and the two Delos boys leaving with Castor. Lucas's eyes went straight to hers and held them. Castor pulled up and put his hand on the back of his son's neck, talking to him. Finally, Lucas broke his stare contest with Helen and looked at his father briefly before nodding and looking at the ground.

It started to rain. One, then two, then three big, fat drops of summer rain splashed down, and suddenly the air was full of water. Helen slammed her door shut and glanced over at her father, who was also looking back at the Delos family.

"Which one did you jump?" Jerry asked, fighting a grin.

"The bigger one," Helen answered, a half smile of her own creeping up her face.

Jerry looked at Helen, whistled once, and started the engine. "You're lucky he didn't seriously hurt you," he said, not joking around anymore.

Helen nodded meekly, but she was thinking that Lucas was the lucky one. The strangeness of her own thoughts scared her silent for the rest of the drive home.

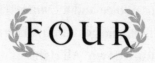

# FOUR

**H**elen sat in a bathtub of cold water, the lights in
the bathroom switched off, and listened to the
phone ring over and over. She didn't know what
to say to anyone and every time she thought about attacking Lucas Delos in front of the entire school she groaned out
loud in humiliation. She would have to leave the country, or
at least Nantucket, because there was no way she could live
down the fact that she had tried to strangle the hottest boy
on the island.

She groaned again and splashed her face, which was still
finding a way to blush even though she was submerged in
freezing-cold water. Now that she wasn't being driven half
crazy with rage she could think about Lucas objectively, and
she decided that Claire hadn't been exaggerating when she
said he was the best-looking boy she had ever seen. Helen

agreed with her. She had been trying to kill him, but she wasn't blind. Normal boys simply weren't put together the way he was.

It wasn't his height or his coloring or his muscles that made him so beautiful, she concluded. It was the way he moved. She had only seen him twice, but she could tell he thought less frequently about his looks than everyone around him did. His eyes, as pretty as they were, looked *out*, rather than back at himself.

She dunked her head underwater and screamed, just to get it all out without scaring her father. When she came back up she felt a little better, but was still disappointed in herself. One of the terrible side effects of feeling like she somehow already knew Lucas was that she was starting to idealize him, making him more perfect than was humanly possible. Which was uncomfortable because she also still wanted to kill him.

She pulled the rubber plug out with her toes and watched the water creep slowly down the sides of the bathtub until the last of it sucked down the drain. Then she sat naked in the empty tub, staring at her white, wrinkled feet until her butt hurt. Eventually, she knew, she would have to leave the dark bathroom and try to act normal.

She got dressed and went downstairs to check on her dad, finding him just walking through the front door. He had run out to buy ice cream for dinner—and not just any ice cream, but the good stuff from the gelato place that Helen had banned him from when the doctor told him to watch his diet.

"To bring down your core temperature," he said innocently, shaking the rain out of his hair.

"Is that your story?" she asked him, her hands on her hips.

"Yup. And I'm sticking to it."

She decided to let it go. There would be plenty of time to worry about his cholesterol in the morning. After so many days with so little food, rich gelato was probably not the best idea, but it did go down easily. They sat on the floor of the living room with their beloved Red Sox on television, passing the pint and spoon back and forth as they cussed out the Yankees. Neither of them answered the phone, which continued ringing periodically, and Jerry didn't push Helen to explain what had happened. Claire's mom would never have let her get off this easy. Sometimes there were advantages to being raised by a single dad.

Helen had to change her sheets before she went to bed. The stains from the night before had not disappeared as she had hoped, but tonight she had bigger things to worry about than sleepwalking. For one thing, she could hear someone or something moving around on the widow's walk. It was different from the sounds she had heard the night before. This time there were actual footsteps directly above her instead of just amorphous whispers coming from all sides. Helen didn't know what would be worse—going up there and finding a gang of intruding monsters or finding nothing at all. For a moment Helen wondered if she was starting to crack up. She decided *not* to go up to check. She'd seen enough ghosts already that day.

The next morning, Helen went to see Dr. Cunningham. After a few minutes of flashing a penlight in her eyes and thumping her on the chest, Dr. Cunningham told her father that there didn't seem to be any permanent damage done. Then he yelled at Helen and told her she was far too fair to be walking around without a hat on. She didn't know how it had happened, but after one trip to the doctor her meltdown had been brushed off as nothing more than the carelessness of not keeping her head covered. At least the checkup got her out of school for the day.

When she got home, Helen opened her computer and spent a few frustrating hours online trying to find some information on the three women who were plaguing her. Every search she did overwhelmed her with so many possibilities that her task seemed hopeless, and she couldn't narrow it down because she didn't have any real context for what it was she had seen. Were they ghosts? Demons? Or just her own personal manifestations of crazy? It was entirely possible that she had hallucinated the whole thing, and now that she didn't feel so enraged she was almost starting to think maybe she *had* had heatstroke. Almost.

Claire came over in the afternoon to deliver some bad news. "The whole school thinks you're on your way to an institution as we speak," she said as soon as they sat down in the family room. "You should've come in today."

"Why?" Helen asked with a grimace. "It doesn't matter when I come back, no one's ever going to forget this."

"True. It was pretty bad," Claire said. She paused for a moment before speaking in a rush. "You scared the crap out of me, you know."

"Sorry," Helen apologized with a weak smile. "So, was *he* in school today?" For some reason she felt like she just had to know, but she couldn't bring herself to say his name out loud.

"Yeah. He asked me about you. Well, he didn't actually talk to me, but Jason did. He's a jackass, by the way." Claire started talking with increasing heat. "Get this. So he comes up to me at lunch, right? And he starts asking me all these questions about you. Like, how long have I known you, where are you from, did I ever meet your mom before she skipped town . . ."

"My mom? That's weird," Helen interrupted.

"And I start answering him with my usual flair for clever repartee," Claire said, a bit too innocently.

"Translation: you insulted him."

"Whatever. Then that chump had the huevos to call me 'little girl'! Can you believe it?"

"Imagine. You, described as 'little,'" Helen said in a droll voice. "So what did you tell him?"

"The truth. That we've been friends since birth and neither of us really remembers your mom, and that she didn't leave any pictures or anything, but that your dad's always going on about how she was this incredible beauty and how she was so smart and talented and everything, and blah-blah-blah. It doesn't take a rocket scientist to figure out that your mom had to be hot. I mean, look at your dad and then look at *you*," Claire said with a knowing glint in her eyes.

Helen winced at the compliment. "Is that it? Lucas didn't say anything else?" Helen's hands were curled up into fists. She found it hard to so much as say his name without wanting to punch someone in the head. Obviously, she either still had heatstroke or she really was going out of her mind.

"Hasn't said a thing. But I did hear a rumor that Zach was talking trash about you and Lucas shut him down hard."

"Really?" Helen said, perking up. "Shut him down in what way?"

"He wouldn't let anyone say anything bad about you, is all. You know how Zach and Gretchen are. But Lucas wouldn't hear it. He kept saying you felt like you had a really bad fever when he . . . did that thing that he did. What would you call that, anyway? A back-assed bear hug?"

Helen groaned and buried her face in her hands.

"It's all right," Claire said, patting her back consolingly. "He's not going around telling everyone you're monkey-butt crazy, so at least you brutalized a seriously sweet guy." Helen groaned louder and tried to crawl into the sofa while Claire had a nice, long laugh at her expense.

That night, Helen had another nightmare about the dry land. When she woke she was so tired and sore that for a moment she almost believed that she had been walking for days, just like she had dreamed. She had always been good at ignoring strange things about herself, and she tried to convince herself that this was no different, but her hands shook as she bundled up her dirty sheets and took them to the laundry room.

Helen washed the grit off in the shower and tried to focus on school, though that was no comfort, either. As soon as she walked into Nantucket High, it was going to be open season on the freak, and the freak knew it.

It was still raining out, so she had to get a ride with Claire and her mother. Helen put a hand over her tummy, afraid of a cramp before she even got out of the car. She had never really understood why she got cramps; she just knew that sometimes when she did something that made people stare at her she was seized with a crippling spasm in her stomach that was so intense it made her stop whatever it was that she was doing.

"Relax," Claire said as they opened their doors to get out. "All you have to do is make it through today and then you have the whole weekend to . . ." she trailed off, thinking. "Nope. Sorry, Len, I tried to be optimistic, but this'll still suck on Monday." Claire started laughing, and the sound cheered Helen up a bit—until they got inside the school.

It was worse than she'd imagined. A group of underclassman girls literally gasped and huddled up to gossip as soon as they saw Helen come through the front doors. A senior boy with a leather fetish leered at Helen and called her "hellcat" just as he was passing by. When she turned to stare back at him in astonishment he mouthed the words "call me" before continuing on.

"I don't think I can do this," Helen whispered. Claire put a hand on her back and pushed her forward.

Every time someone's eyes landed on her and widened with recognition she got closer and closer to a panic attack. Was she going to have to suffer through the rest of junior year like this? Helen tried to melt into Claire's shadow and realized that if it was cover she was after, she was going to have to find some bigger friends.

"Quit stepping on the backs of my feet!" Claire complained. "Why don't you just go hide out with Hergie while I get your stuff out of your locker?"

Gratefully, Helen ducked into homeroom and tried to blend in with her desk. Mr. Hergeshimer asked if she was feeling better, and then ignored her completely as soon as she answered that she was feeling fine. She could have kissed him for that.

Matt just waved and sat down without a word. Helen guessed correctly that he had been threatened by Claire to act like he'd forgotten the whole thing, but he kept trying to stop himself from glancing over at her, so Helen knew he was still really worried. She caught his eye and smiled warmly, and after that he seemed a little less preoccupied. Zach turned his head and looked out the window as soon as he took his seat, making a big show of not looking at her.

She made it through the rest of the morning without incident, right up until lunch. As she walked to the cafeteria she realized too late that she was going to pass by Lucas's locker. She was about to turn and go another way, which was ridiculous because that would mean she would have to literally go around the entire school, when she was spotted.

Gretchen and Zach noticed her as she stood wavering indecisively in the middle of the hall. They were at their lockers, which just so happened to be right next to Lucas's and Jason's. Some of the fuzz fell off of Helen's memory and she recalled Gretchen's and Zach's petrified faces floating around in the background as she tried to choke Lucas. It made alphabetical sense for their lockers to be together, Brant—*B*, Clifford—*C*, Delos—*D*, but Helen blamed her terrible luck for the fact that all of the most popular people in her grade had been firsthand witnesses to her moment of utter humiliation.

She had no choice—she was just going to have to walk past them. Gretchen and Zach didn't say a word and their faces didn't show any expression at all as Helen hurried by with her shoulders practically in her ears. At least Lucas wasn't there, she thought, ducking into the cafeteria.

"Stand up straight! You're going to give yourself scoliosis," Claire scolded when Helen got to their table.

"Sorry. I just had to go by *his* locker," Helen explained quietly. Matt made a disgusted sound.

"You can calm down, Lennie," he snapped. "None of them are here today."

"Supposedly they all took the day off because the aunt and the eldest Delos kid finally got to the island this morning," Claire said.

"Oh yeah, great," Helen mused. "There's another one."

"Hector. He's a senior," Claire added helpfully, although she could have no idea that saying his name didn't help Helen at all. In fact, for some inexplicable reason, it ticked her off.

"No news on him yet. Zach will probably call me with an update this weekend," Matt said with a shrug. "He always knows where everyone is and what they're doing."

The rest of the day dragged by, although there was some relief in knowing that she wasn't going to bump into the Delos kids or the wraiths that seemed to appear whenever they did. She even started to enjoy herself during track practice as she ran through the fog and splashed in muddy puddles with Claire. Coach Tar didn't say a thing about Helen's pathetically slow run time when she came in, although Helen knew she wouldn't be able to get away with that for much longer. She had an athletic scholarship to win, and Coach Tar was not about to forget it.

Dodging her way through the day, Helen made it to work that evening with something like relief, until she realized that a lot of kids from her school were coming in to buy a single piece of candy or one can of soda.

"Why don't you go to the back and do some stocking for me?" Kate asked, giving Helen a gentle pat on the arm. "They'll stop coming in to gawk if they think you've left for the day."

"Don't they have anything else to do on a Friday night?" Helen asked hopelessly.

"What island did you grow up on?" Kate replied

sarcastically. Helen rested her forehead briefly on Kate's shoulder, stealing a second of comfort before she straightened up. "You may as well do the inventory, too. And take as long as you want," Kate added as Helen headed toward the back.

Inventory was not usually Helen's favorite job, but it was that night. She was so occupied counting every object in the store that before she knew it, they were locking the front and going through the ritual of closing down.

"So. What really happened between you and that Lucas kid?" Kate asked without looking up from the stacks of bills she was sorting.

"I wish I knew." Helen sighed as she rested on her broom handle.

"Everyone's talking about you two. And not just the kids," Kate said with a half smile. "So what's up?"

"Look, if I had an explanation, believe me, I'd be shouting it in the streets. I don't know why I attacked him," Helen said. "And the worst thing is that the attack *isn't* the worst thing."

"Oh, you're going to have to explain that," Kate said. She put aside the money. "Come on. Tell me. What's the worst thing?"

Helen shook her head and started pushing the broom around.

There had always been a voice in her head that would whisper possible explanations for her strangeness, words like *freak* or *monster* or even *witch*. No matter how deftly

Helen silenced that voice, it always came back eventually.

The absolute worst thing that Helen could think of would be to find out that she really was one of those things.

"It's nothing," Helen said, unable to look up.

"It isn't just going to go away because you don't talk about it, you know," Kate pressed. Helen knew she was right, and she also knew she could trust Kate. Besides, she needed to talk to someone about it or she'd go crazy.

"I'm having nightmares. Actually, it's the same nightmare that I keep having over and over, and it feels so real. Like I'm going someplace while I'm sleeping."

"Where do you go?" Kate asked gently. She came out from behind the counter and made Helen stop sweeping and focus.

Helen pictured the barren, hopeless world she had been forced to visit the last few nights.

"It's a dry place. Everything is bleached and colorless. I can hear running water in the distance, like there's a river somewhere, but I just can't reach it. It's like I'm trying to find something, I think."

"A dry land, huh? You know that's pretty common in dream imagery," Kate assured her. "It comes up in every dream book, in every country I've ever been to."

Helen swallowed her frustration and nodded. "Yeah, but I wake up in the morning and my feet . . ." She stopped herself, hearing how crazy she sounded. Kate studied Helen for a moment.

"Are you sleepwalking, honey? Is that it?" Kate took

Helen's shoulders, encouraging Helen to look her in the eyes. Helen threw up her hands and shook her head.

"I don't know what I'm doing. But I'm so tired, Kate," she said. A few exhausted tears slipped out. "Even if I manage to fall asleep, I wake up and I feel like I've been running and running. I think I'm going crazy." She let out a nervous laugh. Kate pulled Helen into one of her pastry-scented hugs.

"It's okay. We'll figure it out," Kate said soothingly. "Have you talked to your father yet?"

"No. And I don't want you to, either," Helen insisted, drawing back to look directly at Kate. Kate gave her a searching look, and Helen continued. "Next week, if I'm still crazy, I'll tell him, but I think we've both had enough drama for one week."

Kate nodded. "You decide when you're ready to talk about it with your dad, and I'll be there. My little *loca*," she teased smilingly. Helen smiled back, grateful that she had Kate, who could listen to her seriously when she needed it, and then stop being serious at just the right time.

"I think we can leave the rest." Kate gave Helen one final squeeze. "Ready to go?" she called over her shoulder as she went behind the counter and put the money in the safe.

Helen stowed her broom and made her way to the back door. Switching off the lights, Helen turned to lock up as Kate headed across the alley toward her car, keys in hand.

Neither of them heard a thing. There was a blur and a faint flash of blue light in the corner of Helen's eye, and a *smell*. It was a nauseating yet hauntingly familiar odor of sizzling hair mixed with stale ozone. Then Kate dropped to the ground like a puppet with her strings cut. Helen instinctively bolted forward, holding out her arms to try to break Kate's fall, but the attacker took the opportunity to put a bag over Helen's head from behind.

She was too startled to scream. As she was pulled backward against a soft chest, it suddenly registered in Helen's head that her attacker was a woman.

Helen had always known she was strong—and not just strong for a girl. Strong for a bear. She bent her knees and braced the balls of her feet against the pavement, ready to give her would-be abductor the shock of her life. She flexed her back and tried to break out of her attacker's arms, and was surprised to realize that she couldn't. The unseen woman was just as impossibly strong as Helen. But Helen had more to lose.

The soles of her sneakers shredded under the pressure of her feet as she pushed off. She took one step, and then another, walking right out of her ruined shoes as she dragged the woman along with her. Then Helen heard a thump, a gasp, and she pitched forward violently as she was released.

Struggling to get the black velvet bag off of her head, Helen heard a rapid succession of slaps, thuds, and the quick huffs of stunned breaths. There was a draft of air and the staccato sound of someone sprinting away just as she yanked the hood off and pushed her hair out of the way.

Lucas Delos stood over her, his body tense, his eyes scanning the distance for something that Helen couldn't see from her position on the ground.

"Are you injured?" he asked in a low, unsteady voice, still looking out over her head. There was blood on his lip and his shirt was torn. Helen had a bare moment to say she was fine before she heard the sobbing sisters start to whisper.

He looked down at her, and when his icy blue eyes met her warm brown ones, a thrill ran down her legs. Helen jumped up into a fighting crouch. The whispers turned to wails and Helen saw the bent heads and shivering white bodies of the three sisters blink in and out of her field of vision. She backed up and scrunched her eyes shut by force of will alone. The anger was so intense she felt as if her organs had caught fire.

"Please go away, Lucas," she begged. "You just helped me, and I'm grateful. But I still really, *really* want to kill you."

There was a short pause, and Helen heard his breath catch.

"This is hard for me, too, you know," he replied in a choked voice.

A skipping, scuffing sound from where he stood, a rush of wind, and then Helen dared to open her eyes. He was gone, and thankfully the miserable poltergeists had gone with him.

Helen crouched next to Kate, trying to see if she was bleeding anywhere. She got down on her hands and knees to inspect every visible inch, but strangely there were no cuts, bruises, or scrapes of any kind. Kate was breathing evenly but she was still unconscious. Helen risked picking her up and hoped she was doing the right thing by moving her. She gently laid Kate down in the back of the car, and then ran around to the driver's seat as she dialed her dad's cell number. She started up Kate's car as the phone rang.

"Dad! Meet me at the hospital," she blurted as soon as he answered.

"What happened? Are you—" he began in a panicked voice.

"It's not me, it's Kate. I'm on my way to the emergency room now and I can't talk and drive. Just meet me," she said, pushing END CALL and tossing the phone onto the passenger seat without waiting for a response.

Now she had to think up a really good lie, and quick, because the hospital was only a few minutes away.

She called the police as she pulled to a stop at the emergency room entrance, saying nothing more than that her friend had been attacked and that they were at the hospital. Then she dithered around in the driveway for a second, not knowing how to get Kate into the actual emergency room. Helen didn't want to leave her, but she couldn't very well pick Kate up and reveal her freakish strength in front of so many people, so she finally went inside alone.

"Help?" she mumbled timidly to the admitting nurse. That didn't work, so she raised her voice and hopped up and down. "Help! My friend is outside, and she's unconscious!" That got people running.

Once her dad got there and they both knew that Kate was going to be fine, Helen made a statement to the police. She told them that a woman she'd never had the chance to see had made Kate pass out with a blue flashy thing. When

Helen saw Kate fall, she went out into the alley and that must have scared the woman off because she ran away. Of course, Helen didn't mention anything about the near abduction, the wrestling match, or the fact that Lucas Delos had appeared out of nowhere to fight the superstrong woman off. The last thing she needed was to complicate this situation any more or tie Lucas Delos to herself in any way. What was he doing there, anyway?

"What happened to your shoes?" the police officer asked. Helen's heart started pounding. How could she have overlooked the fact that she was barefoot?

"I didn't have them on from before," she stated in a rush, and then continued haltingly. "Before, earlier, they had torn . . . while I was stocking in the back. And I had taken them off. When I saw that Kate was hurt I just dropped them, and came straight here." Worst lie ever, Helen thought. But the officer nodded.

"We found a pair of ripped sneakers in the alley," he said as if Helen had told him exactly what he expected. He went on to explain that Kate had been Tasered, and that since the assailant had used up the charge on Kate, she was forced to run off when she saw another person arrive.

"One more thing," the officer said, just before turning away. "How did you lift her into the car all by yourself?" Both the officer and her father stared at her for a moment with puzzled looks on their faces.

"Willpower?" Helen said lamely, hoping they bought it.

"She was lucky to have you there. That was very brave

of you." The officer gave her an approving smile. Helen couldn't handle being praised for lying. She looked down at her bare feet, and they reminded her of how dumb she had been not to take care of that detail from the start. She was going to have to learn to be more careful.

When the police were done questioning Kate, Helen and Jerry went in to check on her. Unlike Helen, Kate had gotten a quick look at the woman before she got zapped.

"She was older—in her late fifties at least. Short salt-and-pepper hair. She looked totally harmless, but I guess she wasn't," Kate said ruefully. "What the hell? Since when did little old ladies go around Tasering people?" She was trying to make a joke out of it, but Helen could tell she was really shaken up. Kate's face was pale and her eyes were big and shiny.

Jerry decided to stay the night with Kate and bring her to her house when she was discharged. The doctors told Kate she probably shouldn't drive for a few days, so Helen offered to take Kate's car and bring it over to her on Sunday. Kate thanked Helen for the favor, but Helen had her own reasons for wanting Kate's car. There was one more detail she had to take care of before she headed home.

She had just enough time to get scared as she drove across the island on Milestone Road to the Delos compound in Siasconset. The closer she got, the more she found herself shaking, but she had no choice. She had to make sure Lucas kept his mouth shut about the attack or she could get into serious trouble. She didn't think he would tell anyone. The

Delos family worked very hard to appear normal when Helen knew they were anything but. No one of regular human strength could have stopped Helen from strangling him if she set her mind to it. Lucas was like her.

The thought made her stomach heave. How could she be anything *like* someone she hated so desperately? First, she had to make sure he never mentioned his involvement to the police, but after that she was determined to hate him from as far a distance as she could without falling into the ocean.

Helen had to concentrate to see through the fog. In the dim predawn light, way the heck out on private property, she wasn't sure where the turn onto the long driveway started. She pulled the car over and got out, heading on foot toward the sound of the ocean. She had only seen this particular compound from the beach, and she was trying to scour her memory for any landmark she could recognize from the opposite direction. Then she heard a stumbling, thudding sound behind her. She spun on her heel and saw Lucas walking steadily toward her with long, forceful strides.

"What are you doing here?" he half barked, half whispered. Helen took a couple of steps back and then made herself stop and hold her ground. In the gray light she could see the white bodies of the three sisters dragging themselves through the sandy grass, crawling up the soft rises, shivering with sobs.

"How did you get behind me? Were you following me?" she asked in an accusing voice.

"Yeah, I was," he spat out, still coming toward her. "What the hell are you doing on my family's land?"

Too late Helen realized that by coming to his house she had crossed some line. Where there had been hatred, Helen could now see violence. It distorted his features and added menace to his stance. He was still graceful, but almost too cruel to look at. *Good,* she thought. *Let's do this.*

She lowered her shoulder and closed the distance between them, barreling into his chest and tumbling onto the ground with him under her. She reared up to drive her fist into his face, but he grabbed her arms. She was on top and should have had the upper hand, but she had never hit anything and she could tell from the way he never wasted a movement that he had been fighting his entire life. Helen felt him do something with his hips and then he was on top. Her arms were pinned above her head and her heels were left to scrape uselessly at the ground. She tried to bite his face, but he jerked his head away.

"Lie still or I will kill you," Lucas warned through gritted teeth. He was panting, not because he was winded, but because he was trying to control himself.

"Why did you come here?" he asked, almost begging.

Helen stopped struggling and looked into his infuriating face. He had his eyes closed. He was trying the trick she had used in the alley, she realized. She shut her eyes as well, and felt a tiny bit better.

"I lied to the police. I didn't tell them you were there tonight," Helen grunted, the unbelievable weight of him pressing the air out of her. "You're crushing me!"

"Good," he said, but he shifted his weight, seeming to get lighter somehow so she could fill her lungs. "Do you have your eyes closed, too?" he asked, sounding more curious than angry.

"Yeah. It helps a little," she replied quietly. "You see them, too, don't you? The three women?"

"Of course I do," he replied in a baffled voice.

"What are they?"

"The *Erinyes*. The Furies. You really don't understand. . . ." He stopped abruptly when a woman's voice called his name from what Helen assumed was his house. "Damn it. They can't find you here or you're dead. Go!" he ordered. He rolled off of her and jumped up into a run.

As soon as she was free, Helen bolted and didn't look back. She could almost feel the three sisters reaching out with their clammy white arms and bloody fingertips to touch the back of her neck. She ran in a panic for Kate's car, dove behind the wheel, and drove away as fast as she dared.

After half a mile she had to pull over and take a few deep breaths, and as she did, she noticed that she could smell Lucas on her clothes. Disgusted, she took her shirt off and drove home in her bra. No one would see her, and if they did they would just think she was out for a dawn swim. At first she left her shirt on the passenger seat, but the scent of him kept wafting up, smelling of cut grass, baking bread, and snow. In a fit of frustration she screamed at the steering wheel and tossed her shirt out the window.

She was exhausted to the point of collapse when she got home, but she couldn't lie down in her bed without taking a shower. She had to scrub Lucas off or his scent would chase her around in her dreams. She was filthy. Her elbows and back had grass stains on them and her feet were a black mess.

As she watched the dirt melt off her shins and ankles under the water she thought of the three sisters and their perpetual suffering. Lucas had called them the Furies, and no name could have suited them better. She vaguely recalled hearing Hergie saying the word at some point, but for the life of her, she couldn't remember what story they were in. For some reason Helen was picturing armor and togas, but she couldn't be sure.

She picked up a pumice stone and rubbed off every last speck of dirt before shutting off the taps. Afterward, she stayed in the steam to put on sweet-smelling lotion, letting it soak in, obliterating every last trace of Lucas. When she finally tumbled into bed, still wrapped in a damp towel, the sun was long up.

*Helen was walking through the dry lands, hearing the dead grass crackle with each step she took. Little clouds of dust puffed up around her bare feet and clung to the moisture running down her legs, as if the dirt she walked on was so desperate for water it was trying to jump up off the ground to drink her sweat. Even the air was gritty. There were no insects buzzing around in the scrub, no animals of any kind. The sky was blazingly bright with a tinny blue light, but there was no sun. There was no wind and no clouds—just a rocky, blasted landscape as far as Helen could see. Her heart told her that somewhere close there was a river, so she walked and walked and walked.*

Helen woke a few hours later with heavy limbs, a headache, and dirty feet. She flopped out of bed, rinsed off the increasingly familiar nocturnal grime, and threw on a sundress. Then she sat down at her computer to look up the Furies.

The first website she clicked on gave her chills. As soon as she opened it she saw a simple line drawing on the side of a pot. It was a perfect depiction of the three horrors that had been haunting her for days. As she read the text under the illustration it gave a nearly exact physical description of her sobbing sisters, but the rest confused her. In classical Greek mythology there were three *Erinyes*, or Furies, and they wept blood just as they did in Helen's visions. But according to her research, the Furies' job was to pursue and punish evildoers. They were the physical manifestation of the anger of the dead. Helen knew she wasn't perfect, but she had never done anything really wrong, certainly not anything that would have earned her a visit from three mythological figures of vengeance.

As she read on, she learned that the Furies first appeared in the *Oresteia*, a cycle of plays by Aeschylus. After two solid hours of untangling what had to have been the first—and bloodiest—soap opera in history, Helen finally got her head around the plot.

The gist of it was that this poor kid named Orestes was

forced to kill his mother because his mother had killed his father, Agamemnon. But the mother killed the father because the father killed their daughter, Orestes' beloved sister Iphigenia. To make it even more complicated, the father had killed the daughter because that's what the gods asked for as a sacrifice to make the winds blow so the Greeks could get to Troy to fight the Trojan War. Poor Orestes was bound by the laws of justice to kill his mother, which he did, and for *that* sin he got chased halfway across the earth by the Furies until he was nearly insane. The irony was that he never had a choice. Right from the start he was damned if he did and damned if he didn't.

After Helen got the tragedy straight, she still had no idea how it could relate to her own circumstances. The Furies wanted her to kill Lucas, that was clear, but if she did would they then chase *her* for having committed murder? It seemed to her that the Furies had no idea what justice was if they both demanded you commit murder and then punished you for doing it. It was a vicious cycle that didn't seem to have any end, and Helen didn't know how or why it had all started. The Furies had simply appeared in her life one day as if they'd moved to Nantucket with the Delos family.

She felt a shot of adrenaline rush into her bloodstream. Was it possible that the Deloses were murderers? Something in her didn't quite buy it. Lucas had had several opportunities to kill her, but he hadn't. He'd even fought someone else to save her. Helen had no doubt he *wanted* to kill her, but the fact remained that he'd never even raised his hand to her. If he'd hurt her at all, it was because he had been defending himself from her abuse.

Helen switched off her computer and went downstairs to look for her dad. When she couldn't find him she went out to the car and grabbed her cell phone off the passenger seat. Jerry had left her a text saying that he was still at Kate's. Helen looked at the time—it was 3:00 p.m. What could he possibly still be doing? A fantastic, although slightly nauseating, idea occurred to Helen.

It would make sense for the two of them to hook up, she reasoned. They made each other laugh, they worked well together, and they obviously cared about each other. Kate was a few years younger and could probably get any *guy* she wanted, but Helen didn't think she'd ever find a better *man* than her father. And Jerry definitely deserved a fresh start. He'd been treated horribly by Helen's mother and he'd never gotten over her, which ticked Helen off to no end.

She rubbed the charm on her necklace. For the hundredth time she considered taking the wretched thing off, but she knew she wouldn't. Every time she'd tried to go without wearing it she obsessed over it, unable to stop picturing it in her head. Eventually, she'd give in and put it back on in order to regain some mental peace and quiet. She realized that this probably meant she had some serious mommy issues, but compared to all the other things that were wrong with her, that was the least of her problems. An image of Lucas's face hovering over hers in the dark, his eyes scrunched tight, popped into her head. She had to think up a task to distract herself before she started throwing things, so she decided to go grocery shopping.

Helen's official term as kitchen slave—a system of alternating weeks that had started as soon as she was old enough to cook—began on Sunday morning, but there was nothing in the house for them to eat that night. She made a list, took the housekeeping cash out of the cookie-less cookie jar, and drove Kate's car to the market. In the parking lot she saw a gigantic luxury SUV and shook her head disapprovingly at it. There were a lot of disgustingly rich people on the island who drove vehicles that were too big for the old cobblestone streets, but this SUV was especially annoying for some reason. It was a hybrid, so she couldn't really get too wound up about the environment, but she felt herself getting irritated, anyway.

Helen pulled a shopping cart out of the stand and wheeled it into the store. As she waved at a few kids from school who worked at the registers, she started to hear the Furies whispering. She debated running out . . . but everyone at school already thought she was crazy. If she ran out of the grocery store now like she had seen a ghost, there would be even more gossip.

She made herself push the cart on, keeping her head down to avoid seeing the Furies—but there was nothing she could do to block out their voices. She would just have to move fast and get it over with as quickly as possible. She allowed herself a moment of self-pity for the injustice of her situation. She didn't deserve to be haunted like this. It wasn't fair.

Helen walked briskly through the store, picking only the few things she would need to get through a day or two of cooking. Her frantic thoughts were interrupted by voices, real voices, coming from the next aisle over.

"She shouldn't be here," said a young but strangely serious voice. Helen guessed it was Cassandra's.

"I know," said a male voice, possibly Jason's? "We have to find a way to get to her soon. I don't think Luke can take it much longer."

Helen froze. What did they mean, "get to her"? She stood there thinking in slow motion until she realized they were coming around the end of the aisle. Trying to back up, she plowed into someone standing right behind her. The wailing of the Furies grew so loud it was painful.

She spun around and had to tilt her head almost all the way back to find the face above the enormous male chest that confronted her. Under golden curls, bright blue eyes drilled down into Helen's. It crossed her mind that he looked like a blond version of Michelangelo's Adam on the Sistine Chapel ceiling, newly released from plaster and walking around in three gigantic dimensions. Helen had never been so afraid of anyone in her entire life.

She took an automatic step back and ran into her shopping cart. Her breath hitched painfully in the back of her throat as she stumbled to the side, her hands and feet clumsy with fear. There was a bright, momentary glimmer, and he twitched away from her, his body convulsing spasmodically.

Helen smelled the nauseating combination of singed hair

and ozone that always made her think that she had done something wrong. A brief thought of the Nantucket ferry flashed through her mind as she studied the blond monster in front of her, trying to figure out what had happened. After a stunned second, he collected himself and leaned closer to Helen with an evil grin on his angelic face. He was near enough that Helen could feel the heat coming off his body.

"Hector!" commanded a familiar voice. Helen had only a moment to register that it was Lucas before she felt him grab her arm and pull her away from the Goliath that was his cousin. Instantly furious instead of frightened, Helen rounded on Lucas and threw off his arm.

"Don't touch me," she hissed. She felt light-headed. "Why can't you just stay away from me?"

"Why can't you just stay at home?" he shot back at her. "Didn't you have enough fun last night in the alley?"

"I have errands to run! It's not like I can hide in my bedroom for the rest of my life just because some woman . . ." Helen realized she was starting to yell. She stopped herself and lowered her voice. A thought occurred to her. "Are you still following me?"

"You're lucky that's all I'm doing. Now *go home*," he growled, and grabbed her arm again.

"Careful, Luke," Hector warned, but Lucas just smiled.

"She can't control it yet," he replied.

"Can't control what?" Helen choked out furiously, her patience pushed past the limit.

"Not here. Not now," said Jason in a low, clipped voice.

Lucas nodded in agreement and started pulling Helen toward the door.

Helen ripped her arm out of Lucas's grasp again. Undeterred, he just grabbed her by the hand and held it hard. Helen had two choices. She could put up a fight in front of the entire store, or she could go quietly holding the hand of the most despicable boy in the free world. She was so frustrated she could feel a repressed scream squeezing her lungs shut, but she had no choice.

Lucas frog-marched her past a chestnut-haired beauty that Helen guessed was the other cousin, Ariadne. She tried to smile at Helen compassionately even though she was clearly just as inflamed by the Furies as everyone else was. For a second, Helen considered smiling back, but she didn't possess Ariadne's self-control. She was too angry to manage it. Fleetingly, she thought that Ariadne had to be the nicest person in the world if she could attempt to be kind in that moment.

"Don't even *look* at my sister," Lucas growled through gritted teeth, jerking brutally on Helen's hand as they walked past tiny Cassandra. Cassandra opened her mouth to say something to her brother and quickly shut it, turning away.

"I have no food in the house. What am I supposed to do for dinner?" Helen growled through her closed-off throat.

"Do I look like I care?" he replied, dragging her out of the store.

"You can't treat me like this," she said. He was leading her across the lot. "We hate each other. Fine. Why don't we just stay away from each other then?"

"And how has that worked out so far?" Lucas asked, sounding frustrated rather than sarcastic. "Do you always come to this same store at this same time every Saturday, or did you come today on a whim?"

"No, never. It's the busiest day of the week. But I needed groceries," Helen sputtered. He laughed incredulously and squeezed her arm even harder.

Helen suddenly realized how many random events and raw impulses had driven her decisions these last few days. When she thought about it, it was as if she had stopped choosing for herself days ago.

"The Furies won't allow us to avoid each other," he said in a dead voice.

"Then we can make a schedule or something . . ." Helen began, but she knew it was a lame suggestion and trailed off before he had a chance to shoot it down. An ancient, supernatural force was compelling her to kill Lucas. It probably wasn't going to be deterred by something as prosaic as a time-share.

"My family hasn't decided what we want to do about this, about you—yet. But we'll be in touch," Lucas said. They got to her car. He shoved her against the driver's door, as if he couldn't stop himself from trying to hurt her one last time. "Now go home and stay there," he ordered again, and stood over her while she fumbled with the keys.

For a moment as she backed out of her parking space she considered gunning the engine and hitting him with the car, but she didn't want to mess up Kate's paint job. Angry tears started pouring down her face as soon as she was out of the parking lot, and they didn't stop until she was at home, splashing cold water on her face in the kitchen sink.

She felt humiliated in a dozen different ways. Some of that humiliation she had brought on herself by attacking Lucas at school, but he seemed determined to belittle her. She wasn't even allowed to go grocery shopping now. How was she going to explain that to her father?

The thought of Jerry derailed any nascent plan of escape. She was hopelessly outnumbered, and unless she was willing to leave her father behind to fend for himself she had to wait until the Delos boys were done *deciding* how to handle her. She leaned against the kitchen sink and stared at the block of knives on the counter. If she had Lucas cornered the way he did her, she would have already picked out which knife to use. What she didn't know was *why*. Why did they hate each other so much? What purpose could all that anger possibly serve?

She suddenly thought about Hector, about the way he had smiled at her, and a carpet of goose bumps unrolled down her arms. If she was ever alone with him, she knew he would kill her. Not just bully her like Lucas did, but actually, joyfully, kill her.

She was still leaning up against the sink half an hour later when her dad finally made it home. He froze midstep and looked around the kitchen, giving the entire room a fast once-over.

"Did I do something wrong again?" he asked, his eyes wide.

"Why do you keep asking me that?" Helen huffed.

"Because the past few days every time I come home you look at me like I've forgotten your birthday or something equally unforgivable."

"Well, have you?"

"No! I haven't done anything! Nothing *wrong*," he said with a straight face, but the red flush rising up his neck gave him away.

"Should I ask about you and Kate or would I be too grossed out?"

"Hey. There's nothing going on there. We're just going to be friends," he said, his expression grim. Helen could tell there was a lot of backstory behind that decision, but she didn't really want to hear it at the moment.

"Your loss," Helen responded with a disinterested shrug. Jerry's head jerked up quickly, stunned by the bitterness in her voice.

"You didn't used to be so mean, Helen."

She crossed her arms and looked off to her left at absolutely nothing, too ashamed of herself to meet her father's sad gaze. She could handle the fear of being pursued by vengeful spirits from Hades, but not if turned her into a bitch. Whatever the Delos family decided, she hoped they would do it quickly. She started to mumble an apology, but was saved from having to explain herself by a knock at the door. Jerry went to answer it and after a few moments he called out to Helen to come and join him.

"What is it?" she asked, coming out of the kitchen. There was a delivery boy at the door with bags and bags of groceries.

"He says these are for you," Jerry said, holding out a note with Helen's name on it.

"I didn't order these," Helen said to the delivery boy.

"The order was made by a Mrs. Noel Delos to be delivered to a Miss Helen Hamilton. It's all paid for," he replied, anxious to be on his way.

Jerry tipped the kid and took the groceries into the kitchen while Helen read the note.

> Miss Hamilton,
>
> I am so sorry for my son's appalling behavior toward you at the market today, and I ask that you accept these few things I've sent, even if you are unable to accept an apology. I understand what it is to try to put dinner on the table with no groceries, although apparently my Lucas does not.
>
> Noel Delos

Helen stared at the page for far longer than it took to read it. She was touched by the gesture. It was a ridiculously decent thing to do. Helen got the impression that there was something different about Noel Delos, but she had no idea what it was.

"What does she mean, 'appalling behavior,' Lennie?"

Jerry asked, reading over her shoulder. Helen could see outrage beginning to build in him. "What did that Lucas kid do to you now?"

"No, Dad, it's okay. She's exaggerating," Helen said, trying to make as little of it as possible.

"Then we can't accept these. This is over a hundred dollars' worth of groceries," he argued.

"Oh, for crying out loud!" Helen moaned at the ceiling. She took a deep breath and launched into an explanation. "Okay, you win. Lucas and I had another fight today at the market, but it was a small one. In comparison, at least. Anyway, the point is that he started it and I couldn't go shopping like I needed to and one of the other Delos kids must have told his mom that I didn't do my shopping and she took it the wrong way and sent all these groceries because she's obviously a really nice woman but I don't want you to say anything to her and can we please, *please*, drop it?"

"What the hell is it with you and this Lucas kid?" Jerry said after a moment, completely flabbergasted. Then a thought occurred to him. "Are you two dating?" he asked in a terrified voice. Helen burst out laughing.

"No, we're not dating. What we're doing is trying to *not* kill each other. And that isn't working out too well," she responded, trusting that the absolute truth would be so inconceivable he would think it was a joke. She was right.

He got a pained look. "You've never had a boyfriend. Is it time for us to have that talk about what men and women do when they love each other?"

"Absolutely not," Helen replied firmly.

"Good," he said, relieved. They stood in awkward silence for a moment. "So . . . we can eat the groceries, right?"

"Heck, yeah," she said as she turned on her heel and made for the kitchen while Jerry practically ran to the living room and the dependable comfort of SportsCenter.

As she put together some bruschetta with the amazing *bufala* mozzarella, fresh tomato, basil, and crazy-good Spanish olive oil Mrs. Delos had sent, she thought about her father and how oblivious he was to the forces pulling her life apart in hunks. With all that was happening to her, she knew she might not have many more nights of dinner and baseball to look forward to, but the thought didn't bother her as much as it would have a week ago. If the Delos family wanted her, they could try and take her. She was sick of being angry all the time. Fight and kill or fight and die, she really didn't care. As long as she could keep her father out of all of this Greek tragedy nonsense, she would deal with whatever came her way.

# FIVE

The next week at school was nothing short of torture. On Monday, Helen tried to stay away from the Delos family, but every effort she made to avoid contact seemed to lead her right to them. She went to school early to try to beat them there, only to see them pull up behind her in the black Hum-Scalade she had seen at the market. She rushed to lock up her bike and get her bags together, but her rush only put her in stride with Jason and Hector. Slowing down to let them get ahead of her put her next to Lucas, who was helping his little sister get her cello out of the back. Helen took a flustered step forward, then went back toward her bike to stand and wait there as long as it took for them to go inside and get out of her way.

Later that day, she got permission to eat lunch outside, only to find Cassandra was already out on the patio practicing the fingering without using her bow on her cello. When she saw Cassandra, Helen pulled up short. As she turned to go back inside, she smacked into Ariadne. The contact made Helen's skin prickle so tight that her pores hurt, and although she tried to be gracious and smile apologetically, Ariadne's hands balled into fists around her violin case. Helen stumbled to get away from her, both of them mumbling apologies.

"Cass and I got an outdoor pass to practice. We'll be out here during lunch for the next few days," Ariadne explained quickly, avoiding eye contact as she moved away from Helen.

"Thank you," Helen managed to push out between her clenched teeth. She went back to the cafeteria to intercept Claire.

"Aren't we going to eat outside?" Claire asked, still moving toward the exit. She spotted Ariadne and Cassandra out there and then turned back to Helen with an incredulous look on her face. "Seriously? It's not like we have to sit at the same table as them."

"I know. I just don't want to be anywhere near them," Helen said defensively as she fiddled with the clasp on her lunch box. Claire rolled her eyes.

"Hey," Matt said, catching up to them. "I thought we were going out on the patio. There're still plenty of tables . . ." His voice trailed off when he saw the Delos girls. Matt had just enough willpower to stifle a whistle at Ariadne's glorious cleavage—pretty impressive since Ariadne was wearing a tank top and bending over at that particular moment. Helen knew she was ruining Matt's eye candy and Claire's sunshine, but she just couldn't eat outside.

"You guys go out. It's fine," Helen said as she abruptly left them and headed toward the cafeteria.

"Lennie! What the hell?" Claire called after her in frustration. "Could you please get your head out of your ass?"

Claire's voice carried right around the corner with Helen. The word *ass* seemed to echo in the air as she found herself facing Hector and Jason at their lockers. They were talking with Gretchen and Amy Heart, a senior girl on the cheerleading squad, both of whom were flirting their brains out. Gretchen and Amy looked at each other and then turned in unison to stare at Helen as though she was something they had just found in a hankie. The Furies started to whisper. Helen took a deep breath and tried to block them out.

"Hi, Helen," Hector said with a bright voice and eerily blank eyes. His body leaned ever so slightly forward in her direction, as if he couldn't stop himself from trying to reach out and grab her. Jason playfully smacked his brother on the chest with far more force than normal people like Amy and Gretchen could guess at.

"Rude?" Jason reminded Hector.

"Just saying hi to Helen. Hi, Helen. Helen Hamilton, hi. Get out to 'Sconset lately?" he jeered.

"No, she hasn't," Lucas said from behind her. Helen spun around and glared at him. "And I would know," he said so quietly there was no way normals could hear it. But Helen could.

All of a sudden she felt like she'd had enough intimidation

for one day. Goaded on by the Furies, she took a tiny step toward Lucas. She saw him inhale sharply, and understood in a flash that Lucas had probably spent just as much time trying to scrub away her scent after their little tumble in his front yard as she had spent trying to scrub away his. The thought made her so happy she almost laughed.

"Tell Noel the olive oil she sent was the best I've ever tasted," Helen said with a wicked little smile. She saw Lucas's eyes snap open a little wider with fear, and she knew she had guessed right. There was something different about his mother. "Anytime she wants to try my bruschetta she's more than welcome to stop by."

Lucas made a move toward Helen, but Jason was suddenly at Helen's elbow, pushing her gently to the side as he forcibly pulled Lucas to the lockers. Helen took the opportunity to be on her way, but she couldn't resist one final jab before she left.

"Tell your aunt I said hi," Helen breathed through bared teeth as she passed Hector, mimicking his menacing tone perfectly.

She didn't stop to wait for a response. As she sauntered down the hall she could feel all three Delos boys staring holes in her back, but it didn't make her the least bit nervous. She was so pleased with herself that she even forgot to slouch.

Tuesday wasn't much better, but at least Helen had stopped trying to alter her schedule to avoid the Delos kids. Instead, they were altering their schedules in order to avoid her . . . so, of course, she was running into them all day long. It seemed like every time she turned down a hallway she bumped into one of them.

To make matters worse, her friends were starting to get annoyed with her. Claire thought Helen was being a spineless wuss. Matt got all sullen and huffy every time Helen flinched because she and Lucas had made eye contact.

On Wednesday, the Delos clan changed tactics. First thing in the morning, Helen went to her locker and found Jason waiting for her there, leaning up against the wall like he'd been put there to decorate the place. Jason had the kind of body that was built to lounge, very catlike, as if he was capable of stretching out and taking a nap at any given moment. He was more gracefully built than his cousin or his brother and when he stood next to them he seemed small, but in the same way a panther is small when compared to a lion or a bull. To Helen, seeing him by himself in the relatively empty hallway, he was big. She forced herself to keep walking forward, and when he glanced over at her she noticed that he had the most outrageously long eyelashes she'd ever seen on a boy.

"Do you have a sec?" he asked in a stiff but polite manner. Helen could see him concentrating, probably trying as hard as she was to block out the Furies.

"All right," Helen answered, keeping her eyes on the floor. She could see that the kids with lockers near hers were taking their sweet time getting their stuff together. She really wished they would leave, but no one at Nantucket High would pass up an opportunity for a front row seat at another possible brawl.

"Some of us think it would be a good idea if we tried to smooth things over," he said quickly, as if he wanted to get it done with as fast as possible. Helen thought for a moment.

"Some of you? You mean there hasn't been any unanimous decision made yet? About me, I mean," Helen said pointedly.

"No, sorry," he said, understanding her meaning immediately. "But we think—well, at least a few of us think that we should at least try to be nicer to each other."

"I don't see how we're going to be able to do that, do you?" Helen replied, not meaning to sound unfriendly but unable to stop herself. She heard one of the girls loitering nearby tisk at her.

"We just want to be friends with you. Or if not friends, then at least not enemies. Think it over," he said, and then left.

It took Helen three tries to get her lock undone with everyone standing around staring at her. Using all her energy to not attack Jason as he walked away, she had none left over for patience. She wanted to scream at everyone for judging her, but that would never be possible. What would she say? *I'm not usually a bitch—I'm just super-grouchy because I'm being stalked by three blood-crying ghosts who won't let me sleep at night?*

At lunch, she was surprised to see Ariadne and Cassandra sitting at her customary table with her friends. Even from a distance Helen could see that Matt was flushed with repressed hormones. Gretchen and Zach, who never sat at their lunch table, were there, too, kissing popular ass. Helen wavered in the doorway for a moment, thinking she might still have a chance to sneak away, when Ariadne spotted her and waved her over.

During that uncomfortable lunch, Ariadne was as nice as could be to Helen, and even though there was a brittle quality to Cassandra's smiles, there were plenty of them. Despite this genuine attempt at friendship, Helen was so agitated by the insufferable presence of the Furies hovering just outside the corner of her eye that her testy behavior earned her several scandalized looks from Gretchen and a few worried ones from Claire. As they left the cafeteria, Claire pulled Helen aside.

"Would it kill you to be nice?" she asked.

"You have no idea how hard I'm trying," Helen replied though tight lips.

"Try harder. You're coming off like a total snob, and I know you're not one so don't even start." Claire continued over Helen's protestation: "I can tell there's something weird going on. Something that you're not telling me about. I'm fine with that. But you have to start *pretending* you like them or people like Gretchen and Zach are going to make sure that your life here is miserable until graduation."

Helen nodded submissively. She knew she was getting good advice, but her life was already miserable enough without cozying up to the Delos family. Still, the next day she did her best to make an effort and smiled at Ariadne and Jason as she passed them in the hall. The attempt wasn't pretty—it came off more like a toothy grimace than a grin—but it was well received by the twins.

Hector was a different story. Apparently, he didn't share in the opinion that they should all try to get along, and after another harrowing day of forcing herself not to flinch when she saw Lucas, Helen had to pass by Hector on her way to track. As if pulled by invisible wires, Hector changed direction and started following her across the field. He was calling her name under his breath, like he was singing a song to himself. Helen glanced around desperately for another person, a witness in case something happened, and sighed out loud when she saw a few girls headed in her direction. They looked at how Helen was practically running away from Hector and stared at her like she had grown horns. Most girls at school would have run toward Hector if he was smiling at them like that.

All Thursday night, Helen was kept awake by the moaning of the Furies, as though one of the Delos kids were near. On Friday, Helen had to get up at dawn to drive Kate and Jerry to the airport. They were flying to Boston to attend a small-business owners' conference for the weekend, and Helen was looking forward to a few days on her own. Between the lack of sleep and the daily harassment, Helen felt ground down to bare bone. All she had to do was make it through one more day at school and then she could crawl into bed and hide until Monday. Maybe, eventually, she would even be able to fall asleep.

Unfortunately, what she thought was the Friday Finish Line was actually a trip wire, as she found out when she got to school. At first she didn't understand why she was getting bumped into so much, and assumed it had to be some new trend that she had missed, until Claire began yelling at everyone to back off. Then Helen started to listen to what everyone was saying when they bumped into her.

People she had never even spoken to were whispering "bitch" and "slut" as they passed her in the hallway. The whole day brought one insult after another. Three separate times Helen had to run into the girls' room to hide. She managed to make it through the day without seeing any of the Delos kids, but in exchange she had become the bull's-eye on everyone else's target. By the time she was changing for track, she was such a nervous wreck she didn't know if she was going to cry or throw up. Once outside, she caught up to Claire on wobbly legs. Thankfully, the other girls gave them a wide berth as they ran the trail.

"Why do they even care?" Helen burst out in frustration. "What does it matter if I like the Delos kids or not?"

"Because that's not the whole story," Claire said gently.

"What did you hear?" Helen asked, desperate for any explanation.

"There's this rumor that Lucas and Hector are fighting over you, so of course all the girls hate you now," Claire said like she hoped the rumor was ridiculous, but wasn't entirely sure if it was.

"You're joking, right?"

Claire shook her head. "I guess Lucas and Hector got into an actual fistfight after school yesterday at football practice. That's why they weren't in school today. They got suspended."

"What happened?" Helen asked, stunned quiet.

"Lucas saw Hector following you out of the girl's locker room and he lost it. He started yelling at Hector to stay away from you. I guess Lucas sort of said . . . that you were his," Claire said timidly. Helen shook her head. Lucas had meant that Helen was his to kill, but she couldn't exactly explain that to Claire.

"All the girls hate me because Lucas is a delusional stalker? How is that fair? I loathe him," Helen said passionately. She paused. Another thought occurred to her. "But that only explains the *girls* hating me. There's more, right?"

"Oh, yeah. It gets way worse, because they didn't just get suspended," Claire continued, her brow scrunched with worry. "Zach said that Hector and Lucas went at it in this really scary way, right there in front of the whole football team, the coaches, everyone. It was bad. Like death-match bad. Jason got in between them and managed to break it up, but it was still too late. And . . . well . . . they all got kicked off the football team. That's why the whole school hates you, including the boys," she said, bringing the story to its conclusion. "All three of the Delos boys are supposed to be these amazing, legendary athletes, and everyone is saying you destroyed Nantucket High's one shot at a winning season."

"You have got to be kidding me," Helen said slowly.

"They're ruining my life." Even in the depths of her self-pity, it didn't escape her notice that she was also ruining their lives.

They had been in town for two weeks and all three boys were already singled out as disciplinary problems. If these incidents kept happening, they could get kicked out of school, and then where would they go? They would have to commute to the mainland every morning because there was only one high school on the island. And all this—the fight, the suspension, the entire school trying to trip Helen—had happened *after* they all agreed to try to get along.

A terrible truth was starting to sink in. Even if she got control over her anger and the Delos family got control over theirs, the Furies would not allow them to coexist. The fight between Lucas and Hector proved that the Delos kids would have to come after her or they would start going after each other. There was no live-and-let-live solution to this. For some reason that Helen still could not fathom, the Furies demanded blood, and they would get it no matter how it was shed.

"You're really not seeing Lucas?" Claire asked with care. Helen snapped out of her morose reverie.

"*Seeing* him? Every time I *look* at him I want to tear my eyes out," Helen replied honestly.

"There! Right there! That's what I don't get," Claire exclaimed. "You have never hated anyone before, not even Gretchen, who's been nasty to you since fifth grade. You just walked away from her like it was nothing, and you used to be just as close to her as you were to me. But this thing with you and Lucas? It's eating you up! You have been so angry since he moved here. I don't understand it at all. It's like the only explanation that makes sense is what everyone's been saying." Claire stopped herself abruptly.

"What is everyone saying?" Helen asked, pulling up short. They had been jogging at a slow pace to begin with, but Helen needed to get a straight answer. She forced Claire to stop and look at her. "What are they saying?" she repeated. Claire sighed and got it over with.

"That you and Lucas met randomly on the beach right before school started and slept together. Then he lied to you and said he was just on vacation so he wouldn't have to call you. That's why you flipped out when you saw him in the hallway, because he used you and you were in love with him."

"Wow. That's pretty dramatic," Helen said, feeling detached.

"Yeah, but is it true?" Claire said, her eyes pleading. Helen sighed and put her arm around Claire, leading her to a walk.

"First of all, Lucas and I never even met before that day in the hallway, let alone slept together. Secondly, I would have told you if I'd even kissed another boy since the disaster with Matt in the closet in seventh grade. Third, and probably most important, I was never as close to Gretchen as I am to you. You're my best friend, Gig." Helen squeezed her until Claire gave in and smiled. "I've been strange lately, I know it, and I'm really sorry. Some weird stuff is going on with me. I want to tell you everything about it, but I can't because I don't understand it yet. So please, please just stay on my side, even if I am angry and miserable all the time."

"You know I'm always on your side, but do you want me to be completely honest?" Claire stopped again and turned to face Helen. "I know I'm supposed to say that this is nothing, and that it will all work itself out, and feed you all that supportive nonsense, but I can't. I don't think this is going to get better on its own, and I'm worried about you."

After track practice, Helen went to hold down the store. She had offered to give Luis the night off so that his marathon weekend manning the store while Kate and Jerry were in Boston would start on a full night's rest.

Customers were still looking at her funny as news of her meltdown made its way to every year-rounder on the island, but she had too much to do to get bent out of shape about it. By the time she was done cleaning and setting everything up for Luis in the morning it was after midnight.

There was a moment while she was locking up and walking to the Pig when she was alert and listening for danger, but it passed by the time she was backing out and on her way home. She had been cautious, but that didn't matter. It was after she had parked in her driveway and was walking toward her house that she got jumped.

The first thing she felt was gratitude. At least the Delos clan had waited until Jerry was safely out of the way before they came to kill her. A wiry arm wrapped around her neck, simultaneously pulling back and pressing down until Helen fell to her knees. Her breath was cut off, and she was bent forward in such a way that she could see nothing of the person behind her. She wondered who had won that whole "she's mine" argument, Lucas or Hector? White and blue blobs bloomed across her field of vision from lack of oxygen. Then she pictured her dad coming home to find her dead body in the driveway, and she knew that no matter how outnumbered she might be, she had to fight back. She couldn't let him lose another person he loved. He'd never get over it.

Helen crooked her arm and rammed her elbow into her attacker's solar plexus with every bit of juice she had in her tank. She heard the person suck wind and then she felt herself get dropped. The heels of her hands scraped against the ground as she stopped her forward momentum. She took two deep breaths before she looked up, surprised that one of the others hadn't jumped in to secure her.

Lucas stared down at her, his right arm thrown out and gripping Hector by the shirt. Strangely, Hector was looking over his shoulder—away from Helen. She barely had time to register that fact before Lucas spoke. As he did the Furies began wailing behind him. Helen wondered why it had taken this long for them to show up, but she didn't have a chance to dwell on it.

"Jason! Ariadne! Bring her back alive," he commanded, stressing the word *alive* as he looked pointedly at Hector. The twins took off in the same direction Hector had been looking. Helen took that moment to jump up and run for her life.

She had never tried to run at full speed before. She'd always known that if she did she would discover every nightmare she had ever had about herself was true. *Monster, freak, animal, witch*: all of the names she had whispered to herself when she did something impossible would come gushing to the surface if she ever let herself loose. But when she heard Hector snarl her name she didn't think about what it would mean, or how it would feel, to run as fast as she could. She just did it.

Something led her out onto the moors. The dark, flat lands that stretched out under the color-bleaching light of the moon were somehow safer than the roads and the houses of her community. If she was going to die, it would be alone, with no weak normals sacrificing themselves to save poor Helen Hamilton, their lifelong neighbor and friend.

If she was going to turn and fight, she wanted to be under the broad, low sky of the uninhabited parts of her island and not hemmed in by the quaint shingle-sided whalers. She went west, across the northern side of her island, the calm waters of Nantucket Sound sighing somewhere off to her left, and Lucas and Hector calling her name from behind. They were gaining on her.

Helen crossed Polpis Road, skirting Sesachacha Pond until she saw the true Atlantic, not its calmer cousin, the Nantucket Sound, but the wild water at the end of the continent. She needed to hide, but the land was flat and open and the air was clear and bright. Helen looked out over the dark waves sparkling like inky tinfoil in the moonlight and begged for some kind of mist or haze to come and cover her. That damn ocean owed her for almost taking her life as a child, she thought hysterically, and it should pay. After a few more huge strides, Helen's plea was miraculously answered. She ran north up the coast, out onto the uninhabited sand spit on the northern tip of the island, into a damp, salty fog.

In the wet air, Helen could hear her pursuers even more clearly, and she knew they could hear her better, too. Panicked and exhausted, she blindly tossed herself into the fog and asked her body to go even faster. On the edge of collapse, she felt her body grow light and her labored breathing unexpectedly eased up. The jarring impact on her joints and spine from her gargantuan strides ended abruptly. She was still moving, but she no longer felt anything except the cold and the wind that spun her hair into whips. She burst through the edge of the fog and saw nothing but darkness and stars around her. There were stars everywhere. She looked down.

Below her were twinkling lights outlining the edges of a familiar sideways comma in the middle of the ocean. Looking around for the airplane that would normally be housing her body at this altitude, Helen saw her limbs floating in the air, buoyant and sinuous as if they were submerged in water. She looked down again and realized that the twinkling comma was her beautiful little island home. Her vision contracted into a narrowing tube of blackness. Without a sound, she fainted and fell out of the sky that had so recently claimed her.

# SIX

*I*t was nighttime in the dry lands. Helen was surprised that there was such a thing as time here. It confused her so much that she glanced around, uncertain as to where she was. After a few moments she decided that, yes, she was in the dry lands, but this time the hilly terrain was flatter and more open. The dark, empty sky seemed lower and heavier somehow. Then she looked over her shoulder. It took her a few moments to understand what she was seeing.

Miles away, there was a line across the land and sky, where the flat nightscape turned back into the more familiar, hillier dayscape. The different time zones sat next to each other like two paintings in an artist's studio—unmoving, unchanging, and both equally as real. Here, time was a place and it never moved. Somehow that made sense.

Helen walked. It was cold in the night version of the dry lands, *and her teeth chattered uselessly. In the dayscape, there was no relief from the heat, so Helen knew that in the nightscape there would be no warmth no matter how much she rubbed her arms and shivered. She saw someone up ahead. He was panicking.*

*She hurried forward until she could see that it was Lucas. He was on his hands and knees, feeling around as if he were blind— grabbing at the sharp stones, cutting his hands on their edges. He was very afraid. She called out to him, but he couldn't hear her. She knelt down next to him and took his face in her hands. He flinched away from her at first and then reached out blindly with relief. He mouthed her name, but no sound came out. In her arms, he felt very light. She made him stand up even though he was so frightened he hunched over on shaking legs. He cried silently, and Helen knew he was begging her to leave him behind. He was too frightened to move, but Helen knew she couldn't heed him or he would never leave this dark, dry land.*

*Even though he screamed, she forced him to get up and walk.*

Helen was in terrible pain. She wanted to groan but she didn't have the strength to make any noise. She could hear the ocean close by, but she couldn't move or open her eyes to see where it was. She felt her head bob gently up and down, as if she were lying, stomach down, on a lumpy raft, and her lips twitched in the faintest of grateful smiles. Something had broken her fall and was gently supporting her. She concentrated on that bit of good fortune as she divided her pain up into manageable little bits, one heartbeat at a time. After ten heartbeats she counted to twenty. At twenty she asked herself to get to forty, and so on. She heard another steady rhythm under her, and after a short time her heart was in sync with the sound coming from her life raft. They beat together, each encouraging the other. She kept very, very still.

After what seemed like hours Helen was still immobile, but she could finally open her eyes and focus them. All she could see in the sweeping, blinding flashes sent out from some distant lighthouse were walls of sand. Under her right cheek was a warm T-shirt. After a few moments she realized there was a person in it. She was lying on top of a man. The lumpiness under her head was his chest and the bobbing sensation was him breathing. She gasped. The Delos boys had caught her.

"Helen?" Lucas asked, his voice faint and breathy. "Make sound. If alive," he barely managed to say. He didn't sound like he was going to kill her so she answered.

"Alive. Can't move," she whispered back. Every syllable sent threads of pain radiating out from her diaphragm.

"Wait. Listen to waves. Calm," he said, struggling with every word as her body weight tried to press the air out of him.

Helen knew she couldn't so much as raise her arm, so she relaxed like he told her to and just watched as the world swayed up and then back down with every breath he took. They waited in the intermittent light and dark of the lighthouse signal, listening to the surf fizzing in the sand.

As the agony began to lessen into something semi-endurable, Helen was able to notice more things about her body. From what she could see, her outward shape seemed mostly normal, but her insides felt gooey and soft, as if she were a freshly microwaved chocolate chip cookie. Her bones were barely supporting the muscles and tissue they were supposed to, and there was an itchy heat in her marrow. She recognized that sensation as being similar to the one she'd experienced once when she was learning to ride a scooter and accidentally flipped the thing. Some part of her knew at the time that she had broken her arm, but by the time she got it X-rayed it was as good as new. The itch meant she was healing.

Somehow, she had fallen out of the sky and survived. She really was a monster. A freak. Maybe even a witch. She started to cry.

"Don't be scared," Lucas managed to say in one try. "Pain will pass."

"Should be dead," she whined quietly through her lique-fied jaw. "What's wrong with me?"

"No. Not wrong. You're one of us," he said with a slightly stronger voice. He was healing just as fast as Helen was.

"And what's that?"

"We call ourselves Scions," he said.

"Offspring?" Helen mumbled, remembering the definition from one of Hergie's despised Word of the Day assignments. "Offspring of what?"

Lucas answered her. Helen heard him, but she didn't. The word *demigod* was so far from what she was expecting to hear she had to think about it for a second. She had prepared herself for it to be something horrific, possibly even evil, which made her the way she was.

"Huh?" she blurted out stupidly, so confused she had stopped crying. Her view jiggled, and Helen realized that Lucas was laughing.

"Ouch. Don't make me. Laugh," he said even though his chest kept bouncing up and down.

It felt funny to have her head bobbing around like that so she started laughing, regretted it, but couldn't seem to stop. It was almost as if the pain was so awful she had to laugh it off.

"This really hurts," he said as he started to get hold of himself.

"If you stop, I'll stop," she said, her fit winding down as well.

In between recurring snickers, they went back to quietly managing their pain and waiting for their bodies to knit themselves back together. Despite the pain, the time ticked by soothingly. Out of one ear, Helen could hear the steady thump of Lucas's heart, and out of the other she could hear seagulls. Dawn was on its way, and she felt completely safe for the first time in weeks.

"Why don't I hate you anymore?" she asked when she felt like her head bones were solid enough to enunciate properly.

"I was just wondering the same thing. I think the Furies

are gone." Lucas sighed deeply, like a huge weight had just been lifted off his chest, even though Helen knew her head was probably as heavy as a bowling ball. "I was scared for a moment when we were in the air. It was very hard not to engage you."

"We? Oh, you can fly!" Helen said, realizing.

She remembered how Lucas had a habit of appearing and disappearing so suddenly, and how she had heard the thuds and scuffs of his takeoffs and landings. She had never seen him fly because she had never thought to look up.

"How did you get under me?" she asked, shifting her position ever so slightly.

"I caught you. I saw you faint and slowed your fall as best as I could, but we were already close to impact when I got an arm around you." He shifted as well, and then flinched in pain. "I can't believe we're alive."

"Neither can I. I thought you were coming to kill me tonight, but instead you caught me," she marveled, still stunned. "You saved my life."

It was as if the fall had knocked all the rage right out of her. She didn't hate Lucas at all. She felt the pressure of his arms lying across her back increase slightly, quickly, and then relax again.

"The sun's coming up," Lucas said after a while. "Hopefully, my family will be able to see us now."

"All I can see is your chest out of my right eye and mounds of sand out of my left. Where are we?"

"At the bottom of our impact crater on the last bit of beach before Great Point Light at the absolute tip of the narrowest strip of sand on the northernmost end of Nantucket Island."

"So . . . easy to find," Helen quipped.

"Practically in my backyard," Lucas joked, and then flinched painfully when he laughed. He went quiet for a moment before speaking again. "Who are you?" he finally asked.

"I'm Helen Hamilton," she replied hesitantly, not sure what he was getting at. She wished she could see his face.

"Your father's name is Hamilton, but that's not your House," he said. Helen could feel the capital *H* in the word *House* just from the inflection he used. "You would normally have taken your mother's Scion name rather than your father's mortal one. Who was she?" he asked as though he had been meaning to ask her that question all night.

"Beth Smith."

"Beth Smith. Right," he said sarcastically.

"What?"

"Well, 'Smith' is obviously an alias."

"You don't know that. You don't know anything about her. How can you say that isn't my mother's name?" Helen asked, getting defensive.

She had never even known her mother, and here was this stranger assuming he knew more than she did. It cut Helen a little to have to admit to herself that perhaps he did. For the first time in hours, she was also hyperaware of the fact that she was lying on top of him, and she didn't want to be anymore. She tried to put pressure on her forearm but a searing pain informed her that there would be none of that. After a few feeble attempts to roll off of him she gave up. She could feel him smiling, and his arms tensing to hold on to her just in case she managed to get away.

"I know your mother wasn't named Smith because you can fly, Helen, now hold still. You're hurting me," he said frankly.

"Sorry," she said, suddenly realizing that he'd taken the brunt of her weight when they hit the ground. His injuries were probably far worse than hers—and hers were awful.

As she watched the sand turn gray, then pink, then coral with the rising sun, Helen thought that this was the second dawn she had seen in as many days. Of the two, she much preferred this one. She was in far more pain, but she was also alive and completely free from anger. Helen hadn't realized how heavy the burden of hate had been until she was allowed to put it down.

She heard a voice calling for Lucas, and although she knew they were in danger lying helpless in that pit, she didn't want to be found. What if the Furies came back with the rest of the family?

"Here!" Lucas called weakly.

"Wait," Helen pleaded. "What if they still see the Furies when they look at me? I can't defend myself in this state."

"No one will hurt you," he promised, his arms tightening slightly around her.

"Hector . . ." she began.

". . . would have to get through me first," he said resolutely.

"Uh, Lucas?" she said leadingly, not wanting to insult him by pointing out the obvious.

"Yeah," he replied with a chuckle, catching her drift. "I know I'm not exactly Secret Service material right now, but trust me. I won't let any of them harm you—not even big, bad Hector. He isn't as terrible as you think, you know." He managed to tilt his head to the side enough to meet Helen's eyes.

"You're his cousin. You have to think the best of him."

"I'll leave it up to you, then. I can't hide us, but I won't call out to them if you don't want me to," he said, and let his head roll back out of her sight.

They lay there listening to his family call his name over and over, but Lucas kept his word. He didn't make a sound, although he did flinch when he heard Cassandra's exhausted voice. She sounded desperate and frightened. They all did. And Helen was to blame. After a few more moments she couldn't stand it any longer.

"Here!" Helen yelled as hard as she could. "We're over here!"

"Are you sure?" Lucas asked carefully.

"No." She chuckled nervously before calling out again, this time with Lucas's help.

There was a lot of yelling from down the beach, and the sound of feet pounding across the sand. Then Helen felt Lucas try to reposition his head to look at someone standing above them.

"Hi, Dad," he said apologetically.

Castor muttered some kind of oath that Helen didn't recognize, but the meaning was clear enough. Then he starting giving orders, and Helen felt someone thud down next to her.

"My gods," Ariadne whispered to herself. "Helen? I'm going to try to roll you off, okay? But first I'm going to have to try to speed up the healing of your bones a bit. It will feel a little hot, but don't be afraid, healing is one of my and Jason's talents. Jase, come and do her legs," she called up.

Helen felt another thud, and then she felt the twins slide their hands gently down along her arms and legs. There was a burning sensation inside Helen's bones that was nearly unbearable, and it made her wonder if she would be better off without any "healing." Right before she begged them to stop, the burning mercifully ended. The twins counted to three and gingerly flipped her onto her back like she was a runny pancake. Helen tried to be brave, but she couldn't stop a scream from slipping out. Every muscle, every inch of skin, every bone in her body was lit up with pain as though someone had filled her bloodstream with flaming-hot shards of glass.

She gritted her teeth and took deep, calming breaths before she felt like she had enough control to open her eyes. When she did, she saw Ariadne's luminous hazel eyes, fringed with the same incredibly long lashes as Jason's, looking down at her with compassion. She studied Helen's face carefully, and then gave her a tired smile. Helen thought Ariadne looked drained, as if what she had done for Helen had cost her. Her bow-shaped lips were ashy instead of their usual cherry red and her long, chestnut hair stuck to her perspiring cheeks.

"Don't worry. Your face is already going back to its right shape. You'll be your usual, exquisite self by nightfall," she said, smoothing Helen's hair comfortingly. "Keep still. I'll be right back."

Helen glanced around. For the first time she could see where she and Lucas had spent the night. It took a moment to register that they were in a hole in the ground that was at least five feet deep and three times that wide, and it took even longer to register that the hole had been made by their bodies when they fell. She felt water seep into her clothes as it leached up from the damp sand, and realized that Lucas must have been lying in a cold puddle all night. She rolled her head to the side so she could look at him.

There was a faint Helen-shaped dent running down the length of his body, and his chest was nearly caved in from the weight of her head and shoulders. His face was pinched up in a grimace. He hummed to himself a little as if to try to give his vocal cords something to do other than howl. His father hovered over him, looking Lucas directly in the eye and talking softly. She saw Lucas give a tiny nod, bite his lower lip, then take a deep breath and strain. His chest expanded into a more normal shape, and then Lucas suddenly let his breath out and panted as if he had just lifted a great weight. A tear trickled out of the corner of his eye and ran into his hair.

His father said something reassuring and then pulled

himself smoothly out of the hole and started talking strategy with Hector. After a few moments of getting his breathing right, Lucas rolled his head to the side so he could look back at Helen.

"I think the worst is over," he said, squeezing her hand. She hadn't realized that they had joined hands, but it felt right to her. She squeezed back gently and smiled. He looked horrible. Much worse than Helen could have guessed.

"Piece of cake," she said blithely, trying to distract him. "So what are you doing next Friday night?"

"What have you got in mind?"

"We could try hitting each other with cars," she suggested cheerfully.

"Did that last weekend with Jase," he said with mock regret.

"Go to the zoo and throw ourselves to the lions?" she fired back quickly, desperate to keep him focused on her rather than his caved-in chest.

"The Romans sort of wore that one out. Got anything original?"

"I'll think of something," she warned him.

"Can't wait," he breathed, and then turned his face away as he rode another shivering wave of pain.

"Hey! Little help?" Helen yelled, her voice sliding up to a shriek as she watched Lucas shake. "Lucas isn't doing so hot!"

"No, he isn't doing *so hot*," Cassandra said in a hoarse, bitter voice from somewhere around Helen's feet. Helen hadn't realized that anyone was in the hole with them while she and Lucas held hands and cracked jokes, but she had the feeling that Cassandra didn't like what she had seen.

"Lower the boards down, it's time to move them," Cassandra called up to her father, as if she was the one in charge.

Helen's eyes widened in shock that any fourteen-year-old would speak like that to her elders, let alone be obeyed, but the boards were quickly lowered down without a word of comment. Jason and Ariadne eased Helen and Lucas onto the long planks and told them to hold still. The twins ran their glowing hands an inch above Lucas's body, and Helen saw him grit his teeth as they sped up his healing. Just when she thought Lucas was about to start screaming, the twins stopped, looked at each other in silent communication, and then nodded exhaustedly. They had both lost so much color their cheeks looked gray to Helen, but they also seemed strangely happy, like nothing gave either of them more pleasure than helping someone else. Helen tried to thank them, but Ariadne told her to save her strength.

Helen and Lucas were kept level as they were raised out of the crater and loaded side by side in the back of the same giant SUV that Helen had had so many uncharitable thoughts about. Now that it was her ambulance, she made a silent promise to never rag on big trucks again.

Castor was behind the wheel and anxious to get moving. The longer they stayed on the beach, the higher the sun got, and the more opportunity there was for them to be discovered. Cassandra came with them, but Jason, Ariadne, and Hector stayed behind to fill in the crater and leave the beach looking as normal as possible.

"Can't we just put a lump of rock in the middle and pretend it was an asteroid?" Helen heard Hector ask, exhausted.

"Do you think that would work?" Jason put in, perking up at the prospect of seeing his bed an hour or so sooner.

"No," Cassandra said decisively. "This part of the island is a nature preserve. There are scientists all over the place. They would know the rock didn't come from space."

Jason and Hector gave identical groans and immediately went back to work. Again, Cassandra's opinion went unquestioned. Helen had always tacitly assumed that Lucas was the leader of the kids and that his father, Castor, was the leader of the whole family, but now she thought maybe there was another, less traditional dynamic at work in the Delos family. When Cassandra spoke, everyone listened—including Castor. And apparently, Cassandra didn't need the influence of the Furies to dislike Helen. Which reminded her . . .

"I don't see the Furies!" Helen suddenly exclaimed out loud.

"None of us do," replied Castor in a pensive voice. Helen heard a leathery squeak as he twisted around in his seat to look back at them. "We'll figure it out later. You two need your rest for now."

She couldn't argue with that; in fact, she could barely keep her eyes open. As soon as she heard the soporific purr of the engine she nodded off exactly like a fussy baby on a car trip.

She woke up in a big, white bed as the sun was going down. The room's window framed the sky, which was doing things with color that all the island painters had to be going bananas over.

She wiggled her toes. When that worked out okay she propped herself up on her arms and got into a sitting position. Swinging her legs out of bed, she realized that she was in someone else's nightgown and she wasn't wearing anything underneath it. She knew she was recovering from a near-death experience, but she was still bashful enough to blush. The nightgown was actually more what Helen would call a nightie, as gowns were generally much longer and more opaque. Testing her feet on the floor was enough to wipe her modesty away, however, and her startled cry was quickly answered with a welcome helping hand.

"Easy. Here, hold on to me," said Ariadne. "Wow, I can't believe how fast you're healing. But still, you should lie down for a bit longer."

She tried to get her to lie back, but Helen stayed perched on the edge of the bed and took a few breaths.

"I kinda can't," she replied, looking up at Ariadne sheepishly.

"Bathroom, huh? Okay," she tittered nervously. "I'll carry you. Just don't pee on me."

Helen laughed gratefully. Ariadne was making an

embarrassing situation as humorous as possible so Helen would feel more comfortable. It was something Claire would have done. Helen was still embarrassed, but with a few jokes and a little bit of tact, they both made it through.

"Is it all right if I check and see how you're healing?" Ariadne asked politely when Helen was settled back in the bed. "It would mean that I would have to lay my hands on you, and I want to make sure you're okay with that."

"You just watched me pee," Helen responded with an embarrassed laugh. "So, yeah, I'm okay with a checkup. But wait—is it going to hurt?"

"Not at all. I'm just going to take a peek, not grow cells. That's what *really* hurts you. If it's any consolation, it's no picnic for me, either. So exhausting," Ariadne said with a smile as she pushed Helen, making her lie down.

"Okay," Helen said uncertainly. She rested against the pillows and waited for the pain that she suspected was soon to follow, despite Ariadne's optimistic denial.

Ariadne put her hands on Helen's ribs and concentrated. Helen felt a faint vibrating sensation, like she was standing in front of an enormous subwoofer, but, as promised, it didn't hurt at all. After a few moments, Ariadne lifted her hands and looked at Helen.

"I couldn't ask for a better patient," she said with a beaming smile. "After seeing how much damage you and Luke sustained, I had my doubts. But you're going to be just fine."

"Thank you," Helen said earnestly. "For the healing and helping me . . ."

"And thank *you* for not peeing on me." Ariadne laughed as a beautiful pixie of a woman in her late twenties popped her head around the half-open door.

"You two are having way too much fun to be in a sickroom," she said with a mischievous look in her yellowish cat eyes. Helen had a feeling that those eyes were usually filled with some kind of worldly mischief, and she instantly liked her for it. It reminded her of Kate. She entered the room, tinkling like a shaken bag of loose change. She had short, spiky hair. Helen noticed that her wrists were buried under layer upon layer of glittering bangle bracelets, and although Helen couldn't see them, she could hear that the woman's ankles probably had a few bits of jewelry wrapped around them as well.

"Helen, this is my aunt Pandora. Dora, this is . . ." Ariadne rapped her fingertips on the bedspread like a drumroll. "The famous Helen Hamilton!"

"Ta-da," Helen replied weakly. Pandora sat down on the end of the bed.

"Gorge-ous! I can see why she's got Luke's panties in a twist," she said with a cheeky grin.

"No! That's all done with! We haven't heard the Furies since we woke up on the beach," Helen said urgently. When Pandora gave her a quizzical look, Helen felt like she had to keep going. "I don't want to kill any of you anymore. Just to be clear."

"Well, good, 'cuz I hear you've got quite the arsenal," Pandora said as if she was giving a big compliment. Helen had no idea what she was talking about so she changed the subject.

"How is Lucas?" she asked cautiously, still surprised that she could say his name without being launched into a fit of anger. Pandora and Ariadne glanced at each other.

"He'll be okay," Pandora said firmly. She shook her wrists and sent her bangles into a cascade of sparkles and jingles, almost as if she believed the cheerful sound would banish all dark thoughts.

"It was close, but he's healing," Ariadne added with an optimistic face. Helen couldn't look at either of them. The tense moment was broken by a glugging sound in Helen's stomach, which lasted for an inordinately long time.

"Well, you're hungry," Pandora said drily. "And I think you might be able to come downstairs with some help."

Helen was outfitted with a long terry-cloth bathrobe, which bore the logo of a popular Spanish soccer team, from Ariadne's closet. Then, with a few more jokes about how Helen could use a little fattening up, she was carried downstairs by her two new patronesses.

When they reached the kitchen, they were greeted with a heavenly scent blossoming off of the stove, and Helen's stomach growled again. Hector heard the noise and cocked an eyebrow as she was deposited gently in a chair at the kitchen table. He said something to the woman who was orchestrating dinner, and she spun around to look at Helen.

"I didn't think you'd be joining us," the woman said with a startled face. "I'm so glad."

"Thank you. And thank you again for the stuff you sent

my father and me," Helen said. She knew immediately that this was Noel Delos, and she could also tell that Noel was a normal woman without an ounce of demigod strength. A big, bubbling pot of guilt boiled over in Helen's chest. She had threatened this fragile human in a family of super-heroes—threatened her to her son and her nephews, no less. Noel smiled knowingly at Helen's penitent face.

"You're very welcome. Now, first things first. How do I contact your father to let him know you're okay?"

"I'd rather keep my dad out of this," Helen replied nervously.

"You've been gone all night and all day. Don't you think he'll be worried?"

"He's in Boston for the weekend. He won't be back until tomorrow night."

"All right, it's up to you, but I want you to know I think it would be better if you and your father had a long talk about all this," Noel said with piercing eyes. Then she whirled around and got busy with dinner. Helen had the feeling that she may have been granted a stay of execution, but she wasn't pardoned yet. "Are you ready to eat now?" Noel asked, buzzing around.

"I don't think I've ever been this hungry," Helen replied truthfully.

"It's the heal," Noel said, smiling at some internal thought as she laid down bread, salt, and oil in front of Helen. She poured a tall glass of milk before gesturing impatiently. "Eat. This isn't the time to be shy, Helen. You need it."

Helen ripped into the bread like a medieval glutton with low blood sugar. Noel smiled again and asked Hector to go get some hard cheese out of the fridge. He grudgingly did as he was told. As he put the cheese down he made a joke about being scared to get his fingers too close to Helen's mouth.

"You're one to talk," Pandora grumbled. "Just two weeks ago I had to count the silverware after every meal to make sure you hadn't swallowed any of it."

"You were healing two weeks ago?" Helen asked, and then remembered that Hector and Pandora had arrived later than the rest of the family.

So much had happened in just a few weeks that Helen felt like every day had telescoped out into a week in itself. As she marveled at how much her life had changed, she noticed that a silence had fallen over the kitchen. Apparently, Helen had stumbled on to a touchy subject because everyone was exchanging nervous glances over her head.

"Sorry. I don't mean to intrude," Helen amended quickly.

"No, it's fine. It's just that Hector's recent heal is part of something much bigger," Noel said. "Right now, you eat."

At first she felt the lingering reticence of a new guest, but as soon as the lentil stew was put down in front of her, Helen's whole being was lost in a flavor blur. She was vaguely aware of other people pulling up chairs or standing around by the stove while they tasted this or that, got themselves a plate, or just hung out to talk, but she was far too focused on the ever-changing dishes in front of her to pick individuals out of the crowd. Noel kept the food coming. A few times, Helen was aware of Cassandra shuttling trays up and down the stairs, but it didn't sink in that those were for Lucas until Helen was falling asleep over something sweet and nutty made out of dough.

"Ready for ice cream?" Noel asked her, absentmindedly pushing a thick swath of Helen's long hair behind her shoulder so it didn't fall into her food.

"I think I've gone blind," Helen replied, unable to chew or swallow or see straight anymore.

"Finally," Noel sighed as she sank into a chair across the table from Helen. She looked as tired as Helen felt. "Jason? Do you think you could take her up?"

"Sure," Jason replied, and scooped Helen out of her chair. She was suddenly very awake.

"I can walk! Really, you don't have to carry me," she said, squirming in his arms.

"Sure you can. Now hold still or I'll drop you," he replied with a good-natured smile. She had no choice but to relax and let him carry her.

When they got upstairs, Cassandra came through one of the many doors, holding a tray stacked to overflowing with dirty dishes, and Helen got a brief glimpse of Lucas lying in bed. She tensed and tried to crane her head around Jason's shoulders to get a better look, but Cassandra shut the door.

"Is he really going to be all right?" Helen asked Jason as he brought her into the guest room.

"Yeah," Jason said, but he didn't meet her eyes when he said it. He forced an uncomfortable laugh. "Luke's just milking it to get Cass to pamper him. He'll be fine," he said. He laid her down and turned to go.

"I'm really sorry," Helen called out as Jason reached the door. He stopped uncertainly and turned to listen as Helen unburdened herself with increasing emotion. "I was so scared and I was running away into the fog and then I felt really light and really cold. When I looked down and realized that I was flying, I fainted. I always knew I was strange, that there was something wrong with me, but I didn't know . . ." Helen trailed off. Jason came back to her bedside and touched her shoulder.

"Nobody blames you," he said, but Helen waved a dismissive hand.

"Yeah, you do. You all do. Because I started this when I attacked Lucas in the hallway at school."

"You didn't start this," Jason replied forcefully. "This war started *thousands* of years ago." Helen gave him a confused look, but he shook his head before she could ask any questions. "Get some sleep, and don't worry about Lucas. Even compared to other Sons of Apollo, he's really tough." Jason switched off the light on his way out, but left the door open a tiny crack in case she needed to call out for help in the middle of the night.

Helen snuggled into the down comforter and tried to relax, but she was jittery with exhaustion and overwhelmed with the strangeness of the room and the house. And the *flying*. She could fly—there was no denying it now. She wasn't just a gifted athlete with paranoid notions about possibly being some kind of genetic experiment. She could frigging *fly*, which is aerodynamically impossible for *Homo sapiens*, so she had to be something else. Something other than human.

The only explanation was what Lucas had said, but that didn't make much sense, either. The Greek gods were myths, anthropomorphic manifestations of powerful natural forces, not historical figures with actual descendants—or so she'd been taught in eighth grade. But now she wasn't so sure. She thought of how it felt to fly, how the air had become solid—a malleable object—and she knew that the argument was over in her heart. Somehow, she was a demigod, and she was just going to have to accept it.

In the early morning hours, Helen woke up with a start and looked around at the dark, unfamiliar room. She had been dreaming about flying, which was great, until she realized she had no idea how to land. Her first waking thought was that she would have to get Lucas to teach her. Then it occurred to her he might never be able to fly again.

Despite what his family said about him being fine, Helen knew she wouldn't be able to go back to sleep without checking for herself. She needed to see his face tanned and normal, not white and scared as it was when they were in the dry lands together.

She touched her feet to the floor and tested them, applying more pressure until she was sure she could stand, and then made her wobbly way down the hall to Lucas's room. She had never had shin splints, had never had any kind of sports injury at all, but as she crept along she imagined that what she was feeling had to be similar, if not much, much worse. Her muscles wouldn't stretch as far as usual; her joints felt swollen and hot. By the time she silently pushed Lucas's door open she was covered in a thin, sickly sweat. Lying on his back and staring at the moon in the window, Lucas spun his head to look at Helen as she appeared in the doorway. A moment passed.

"Hi," he whispered.

"Hi," she whispered back. "May I come in?"

"Yeah. But quietly." He gestured to Cassandra asleep on a couch on the other side of the room. "She was awake for two days straight."

Helen made her way into the room, crouching like an old woman and wincing at the pressure on her feet. She felt like some ridiculous fairytale hag and she started laughing silently at the thought of chasing kids off her gingerbread lawn.

"You shouldn't have come on your own. You've worn yourself out," Lucas admonished her gently.

"I was fine a second ago, but it was farther than I thought. Your house is huge," Helen whispered, aiming her creaky body at the chair next to his bed.

"You won't be able to sit up long. Here," he said as he pulled back his covers. "You'd better lie down."

Helen looked uncertainly at his bed. She had spent all of last night melded to him, but now it was different somehow. If she lay down with him, it would be a choice. She saw him smirking up at her, and realized he thought she was being silly. Which she was, because her knees were shaking with the effort to hold her up. She tried to sit down as carefully as she could so as not to disturb him, but at the last moment her legs gave out and she pretty much flopped into bed with him.

"Sorry," she whispered as she gathered the covers over them.

"It's okay. Careful of your toes—my legs are splinted," he warned her. Helen peeked under the covers and saw that his lower body was wrapped in soft casts. "See? You're completely safe with me." He grinned at her in the dark and she grinned back, until the reason for her draining trek came back to her. Her smile faded.

"How bad is it? Can you even tell right now?" she asked him seriously. She propped herself up on an elbow so she could look directly into his face and scan him for any well-intentioned lies. Even in the low moonlight dribbling through the casement she could see the intense jewel blue of his eyes.

"I'll mend," he said so softly his lips hardly moved.

"Completely? Will you still . . . you know . . . walk and run and . . . fly and all that?"

"Yeah," he whispered before she had even finished talking. "Good as new in another day."

It occurred to Helen that all she had to do was lean down and she would be kissing him. It seemed like such a natural thing to do—as if she *should* be kissing him—that she was halfway to his mouth before she stopped herself and pulled back, stunned by her lack of self-control. She saw him swallow hard.

"Lie back, Helen," he told her, which she immediately did to hide her confusion.

For a few minutes they were both breathing a lot faster than they should have been, but after a while, Lucas relaxed enough to take her hand and hold it under the covers. She watched his chest go up and down in a way that was familiar to her now, and smiled herself to sleep.

# SEVEN

"Because I didn't want to wake up Lucas!" a frustrated voice hissed.

Helen had no idea how Ariadne had made it to the tea table at the top of the Golden Gate Bridge. Ariadne couldn't fly.

"Why are you fighting me on this?" Cassandra pleaded quietly. Hmm. Helen couldn't be on top of the Golden Gate Bridge so she must be in bed, but she couldn't figure out what Cassandra was doing in bed with her. If she could only open her eyes and see.

"I don't doubt you. But what can we do?" asked Noel.

"We should leave. Now. Pack up the house and go back to Europe."

"You're overreacting," huffed Ariadne, not even bothering to whisper.

"Two nights in a row, Ari. They ate the same food. Shared a roof and a bed, and now they have witnesses!" Cassandra said just as loud.

"But they haven't done the most important thing!" Ariadne shouted back.

"Girls!"

Even though she was still so tired she felt glued to the mattress, the yelling made Helen's eyes open. She saw Ariadne, Cassandra, and Noel standing over her bed. Correction, they were standing over Lucas's bed and Helen was in it. Her eyes snapped open and her head whipped around to look at Lucas. He was frowning himself awake and starting to make some gravelly noise in the back of his throat.

"Go argue someplace else," he groaned as he rolled over onto Helen. He tucked himself up against her, awkwardly fighting the drag of the casts on his legs as he tried to bury his face in Helen's neck. She nudged him and looked up at Noel, Ariadne, and a furious Cassandra.

"I came to see how he was and then I couldn't get back to my bed," Helen tried to explain, absolutely mortified.

She gasped involuntarily as one of Lucas's hands ran up the length of her thigh and latched on to the sloping dip from her hip to her waist. Then she felt him tense, as if he'd just realized that pillows weren't shaped like hourglasses. His head jerked up and he looked around, alert for a fight.

"Oh, yeah," he said to Helen as he remembered. His eyes relaxed back into a sleepy daze. He smiled up at his family and stretched until he winced, then rubbed at his sore chest, no longer in a good mood. "Little privacy?" he asked.

His mother, sister, and cousin all either crossed their arms or put their hands on their hips. Humiliated, Helen tried to untangle herself from the sheets and roll out of bed without attracting too much attention. Cassandra spun on her heel and stomped out of the room.

"Ari, help Helen," Noel said gently as she saw Helen's difficulty. Then she turned and bellowed angrily down the hall. "Hector! Get in here and help your cousin!"

"I'm okay," Helen protested as she stood up on tender legs, only using Ariadne's helping hand to maintain her balance. She realized she was wearing that ridiculous scrap of silk Ariadne had the nerve to call a nightgown, although that detail had escaped her notice the night before when she decided to take her little stroll.

"Whoa! That's . . . interesting," said Hector as he arrived and saw Helen.

"What's interesting?" Jason asked as he passed in the hallway. He poked his head in the door and saw what his brother was looking at. "Aw, damn!"

They both stared at Helen, half naked and totally busted as she got out of Lucas's bed. Then they looked at each other, threw back their heads in unison, and laughed.

"Okay, okay. Enough," Lucas said defensively. "She was worried and came to check on me, but by the time she made it here she was practically falling over. I didn't want to wake Cassandra to carry her back to the guest room, so I had her lay down with me. *Obviously*, we just slept. Now, can everyone but Hector or Jase get out of my room, please? That includes you, Mom. I need Jason to help me out of these casts so I can take a shower."

Helen made it back to the guest room without accepting any more help than she had to. She was so embarrassed all she wanted to do was run screaming out of the house, and to do that she was going to have to prove she was healthy.

"No thanks, I got it now," she said to Ariadne when asked if she needed help bathing.

"Okay. Just shout if you need me," Ariadne replied with narrowed eyes.

Twice Helen had to sit down on the shower floor to rest, but she eventually managed to clean all the itchy sand out of her hair and towel off without calling for Ariadne. It took her ten minutes to struggle into her own freshly laundered clothes alone, but it was worth it. All she wanted do was say thank you and slip out without drawing too much attention to herself.

When she got downstairs the whole family was in the kitchen, including Lucas. His face lit up like Vegas when he saw her. She automatically went straight to him and sat down, her hopes of a quiet escape ruined by what felt like a knee-jerk reaction. She hadn't intended to stay for breakfast, but it was almost as if she needed to be near him.

"We were just about to send someone up to make sure you hadn't washed down the drain," joked Noel.

"Helen's modest. She wanted to dress herself," Ariadne

said, drizzling honey over a bowl of oatmeal and putting it down in front of Helen.

"Modest? Sure she is," Hector said sarcastically as he passed Lucas the bacon.

"That was *your sister*'s nightgown, wasn't it?" Lucas asked without skipping a beat as he served Helen and himself. Hector wisely shut his mouth.

"Yeah," Ariadne replied for him, not getting it. "So comfortable! What? What are you all laughing at?"

"Nothing, Ari. Just drop it," Jason said in a pained voice, a hand over his eyes. Everyone was cracking up, including Castor and Noel.

Helen was torn. She didn't want to laugh at the joke because it was partly on her, but she couldn't entirely stop herself. She stifled a giggle and looked down at her full plate. It was the kind of breakfast that was almost always followed by a nap, and Helen was dying to go somewhere and hide. She thought about skipping it so she could get away sooner.

"I know you're hungry," Lucas said so quietly that Helen alone could hear him. "What's the matter?"

"I feel like I should go home. I've imposed long enough. . . ." She trailed off as Lucas started shaking his head.

"That's not the reason," he said positively. "What is it?"

"I feel like a jackass! Waking up practically naked in your bed with half your family standing over us? Not okay," she said through clenched teeth as a hot blush burned her cheeks. He smiled slowly as he watched her cheeks stain red.

"If that hadn't happened, would you want to stay?" he

asked, suddenly serious, his eyes focused on hers. She looked down and nodded, still blushing. "Why?" he persisted.

"For one thing, I have questions," she said, hazarding a glance up at him. He was staring at her with an unreadable look on his face.

"Is that the only thing?" he whispered.

"Enough chat, you two. You both need to eat," Noel called across the table, making Helen jump, which in turn made Lucas chuckle. She and Lucas dug in with all the ferocity of two people who were literally rebuilding their bodies cell by cell. When Helen finally looked up after a solid hour of determined chewing, everyone else was done eating but still sitting around drinking coffee and passing around sections of the paper. It was as if they always spent half of Sunday sharing an enormous brunch, then the other half hanging out around the kitchen waiting for dinner to start. Lost in the shuffle, Helen was surprised to find herself having a good time.

Lucas was still bent over his plate, so Helen took the sports section when Hector put it down, and read up on her beloved Red Sox, who were battling their way through September. She must have been muttering to herself out loud because when she finally put down the stats sheet she had the attention of all the men at the table.

"'Pitching wins pennants,' huh?" Castor asked with a delighted smile.

"'We've got too many injuries and no closer,' do we?" Jason repeated back to Helen, then looked at Lucas. "Okay, you win," he said cryptically.

"Thank you," Lucas said through a shaky grin. He leaned back and closed his eyes, and Helen saw a sweat break out on his forehead. She touched his head to see if he had a fever, but Jason was already standing up.

"I got him, Helen," he said as he came around the table. Jason went to pick Lucas up, but Lucas wouldn't let him. Instead, he threw his arm over his cousin's shoulder and allowed Jason to prop him up.

"Just to the stairs, okay?" Lucas asked, and Jason nodded back, the bond between them so strong they didn't seem to need words to communicate. Helen saw Noel throw up her hands in frustrated helplessness.

"Let him find his own pace," Castor said gently to his wife. She nodded, like it was something they had been over a million times. Then she turned her attention back to the brunch leftovers.

"Hector! It's your turn to clear the table!"

Helen noticed Noel had a tendency to parse out her anger as judiciously as she possibly could. She needed a good yell, but she couldn't scream at Lucas because he was hurt, and she couldn't yell at Jason because he was helping Lucas, so she picked the next boy she could find. It was the same thing Noel had done when Helen was just waking up, speaking softly to Helen and then yelling for Hector. Poor Hector seemed to get the brunt of her frustration, and from the way he slunk into the kitchen shaking his head, Helen had the feeling he'd been Noel's favorite whipping boy since Lucas got hurt. For a moment she almost felt bad for him, but when she saw the way Noel stared worriedly after Lucas as he winced his way out of the kitchen, she couldn't blame her.

Lucas paused before he left the room.

"Dad?" he called back without fully turning around. "Helen has questions."

Still seated at the head of the table, Castor nodded, deep in thought for a moment, and then stood up. "I thought she might," he said, smiling kindly at Helen. "Would you like to join me in my study?"

Castor took her to a quiet end of the sprawling house and into a half-unpacked study with a spectacular view of the ocean. Leather chairs and boxes of books in a dozen different languages fought for floor space with rolled-up carpets and un-hung paintings. Two large desks stood on opposite sides of the room. The tops of each were already covered in various papers, envelopes, and parcels.

Along the back wall was a row of French doors that opened up to a patio bordering the beach. In front of the doors were two sofas and a big armchair, all three set up facing each other.

Cassandra sat in the oversized armchair reading a book, which she put aside when Helen and Castor entered. Helen expected her to leave, or at least be asked to leave, but after a few moments it was clear that Cassandra had been waiting here for Helen and Castor to come to her and have this conversation. How Cassandra knew there would be a conversation at all was beyond Helen, but Castor didn't seem surprised.

Castor offered Helen a seat on one sofa and then sat down on the other. He glanced at Cassandra, dwarfed by her giant chair, and then began.

"How much do you know about Greek mythology?" he asked.

"You mean, like the Trojan War?" she asked in return. When Castor nodded, she shrugged. "I know bits of it. A queen named Helen left her husband and ran off with a Trojan prince named Paris. Her husband came after her with a thousand ships full of Greek soldiers, and there was a long war. Something about a wooden horse . . . and that's about it." Helen grimaced sheepishly. "I never read the actual book."

"Well, that's not *exactly* how it started. But close enough for now," Cassandra said, passing Helen the book she was reading. It was an anthology containing both the *Iliad* and the *Odyssey*.

"Keep it. We've got plenty of extras," she said with a wry smile.

It was the first attempt at a joke Helen had ever seen Cassandra make, so she forced a smile in response.

"I'm pretty sure my son has already told you that we are descendants of what are known as the Greek gods," Castor began. When Helen grimaced uncomfortably, he nodded with good humor. "I imagine it's hard to grasp, but you have to understand that Homer was a historian, and the *Iliad* and the *Odyssey* were accounts of a real war that took place thousands of years ago. Most of the ancient myths and great dramas are based on real people. The gods are real, and they had children with mortals. Half human, half god. We are their descendents. Their Scions."

"Okay," Helen said, hearing how frustrated her laugh sounded. "Say I believe you, and all this did happen. Gods had babies with humans? Fine. But wouldn't all that magic, or the god-ness or whatever, been bred out of us by now? That was a *really* long time ago."

"The gifts don't dilute," Cassandra responded. "Some Scions are stronger than others, and some have a broader range of powers, but the strength of those powers isn't dependent on how strong their parents were."

Castor nodded and took over to clarify.

"For example, my wife is entirely mortal, but both of our children are stronger than I am. And I am very strong," he said without boasting. "We think it has something to do with the fact that the gods are immortal. They never fade, so neither do the talents they've given us, no matter how many generations pass. In fact—" he started, but broke off, looking at Cassandra.

"We are getting stronger, and each successive generation of Scions is being gifted with more and more talents than their parents were. But there is still some argument as to why this is so," Cassandra finished.

"Okay," Helen said mostly to herself. "I knew I had to be something not entirely human. It's actually a relief to know what I am and that I'm not something awful. But can I ask another question? What are the Furies? And why aren't they bothering us anymore?"

This question earned a long pause. Cassandra and Castor made eye contact as if they were trying to read each other's minds before Cassandra began to speak.

"We aren't completely sure why they went away. In the past, there have been rumors about pairs of Scions, usually a man and a woman, who have found a way to be together and not see the Furies, but it's never been proven. As far as we know for sure, you and Lucas are the first to manage it. I think it might have something to do with saving a life. I think somehow you managed to save each other, and this freed you from the cycle of vengeance, but I can't be certain about that," she said.

Helen had a fleeting thought about Lucas in the dry lands—blind and lost and unable to get off his knees. She pushed the horrible image aside.

"Vengeance?" Helen questioned. Castor saw her confusion.

"The Trojan War was very long with many casualties. It was the worst the world had ever seen at that point, and a lot of sins were committed. No one knows where the Furies came from; all we know is that they started plaguing our kind after the end of the war. It started in Agamemnon's family, but as the years passed it spread to all of the Four Great Houses and set them against one another. Over the years it developed into a blood feud that has left us as we are now . . . with each House set against every other House to the death."

Helen remembered the story of Orestes, and how he was forced to kill his own mother to avenge his father, Agamemnon, who had killed his sister. It still struck her as dreadfully unfair, like the Furies created a no-win situation where everyone ended up dead.

"'Houses' are what we call the four different bloodlines of Scions," Cassandra interjected when she saw Helen frowning. "They were royalty in ancient Greece."

"So, are you saying we're Greek?" Helen asked, trying to put poor Orestes out of her head and keep up with the conversation.

Castor smiled. "We don't consider ourselves either Greek or Trojan anymore, but as members of four different Houses that were started by four different gods. Who was Greek and who was Trojan doesn't matter to us. The war ended a long time ago," he said quietly. "And the Furies have been our curse ever since."

"They compel members of opposing Houses to kill each other to pay a blood debt we owe our ancestors. It's a vicious cycle. Blood for blood for more blood," Cassandra whispered, and Helen shivered at the empty gleam in her eyes.

"I know that part. Orestes had to kill his mother because she killed his father because he killed their daughter," Helen said. "But I read those plays and they had happy endings. Apollo talked the Furies into forgiving Orestes."

"That part was pure fiction," Castor said, shaking his head. "The Furies never forgive, and they never forget."

"So basically, our families have been murdering each other since the Trojan War?" Helen asked. "There can't be many of us left."

"There aren't. The House that our family belongs to is

called the House of Thebes. It was thought to be the only House left—until the Furies led us to you, of course," Castor responded.

"What House am I from?"

"We won't know that until we know who your mother was," Cassandra said.

"Her name was Beth Smith," Helen said, hoping Lucas was wrong and that his father would remember her somehow. But Castor shook his head kindly.

"Whoever she was, she obviously told you and your father a fake name to protect you. You certainly look like someone I used to know, but Scions don't always hand down physical traits the same way mortals do," Castor spoke haltingly as he shifted in his chair. "For instance, Lucas looks nothing like me—he doesn't even look like a typical Son of Apollo, like my brother or me. We Scions are half human, half archetype, and every now and again the way one of us looks has more to do with the historical figure the Fates destined that Scion to model his or her life after than who the parents were."

"So, do I look like anyone?" Helen asked.

"We don't want to jump to conclusions. Maybe you have some pictures, or some video of your mother? Then we might be able to confirm who she was," Castor said eagerly, like they were close to figuring out a huge puzzle that had been troubling them.

"I have nothing. No pictures," Helen replied in a flat voice. Cassandra exhaled sharply and nodded her head at some internal thought.

"To protect you, probably. If she severed all ties with you and made sure you grew up on a small island with a limited group of friends, it was less likely that a rival House would discover you," Cassandra observed as if she was a detective gathering together all the clues.

"Apparently, that didn't work," Helen scoffed.

"It did for a long while, but the Furies would not allow it forever," Castor said quietly.

Helen ran the charm of her necklace along its chain, and held it out for Castor and Cassandra to look at. "This is all I got from her. A piece of jewelry. Does it mean anything to you?" she asked intensely.

A part of her had always hoped that her necklace was important—that maybe someday it would answer all her questions. In her wildest daydreams she imagined it being the talisman that would someday guide her to her mother. Cassandra and Castor studied the heart charm carefully, but there was nothing special about it.

"It's very pretty," Cassandra said kindly.

"It is, isn't it? But it's from Tiffany so there are probably thousands just like it. It's just that this is all I have," Helen said, the words spilling out uncensored. "My dad says she must have been planning to leave for a long time because by the time he figured out she had left us, all the pictures were gone. Every single one. Even pictures he thought she had no idea he'd taken."

Helen stood up suddenly and started pacing around aimlessly. She walked to the far end of the library, looking at all the books that the Delos family had collected together, all of the antique furniture they probably handed down, generation to generation. It was a family legacy Helen had been denied, and she felt a sense of loss not knowing where her mother was, or where she'd come from. But she also sensed a possibility in that ignorance.

"Your family is tight, I can see that. You always know where everyone is. But my mother did something drastic, right? She ran away." Helen struggled with the right way to phrase her thought, and decided the best thing would be to ask a question. "Why were you so sure that the House of Thebes was the only House left? How could you possibly know that?"

"We keep very close watch over our numbers, Helen," Cassandra said.

"Yeah, but how can you know for sure?"

"It's barbaric," Castor said, shaking his head. When Helen gestured for him to continue he did. "When one demigod kills another from a rival House there is a traditional celebration for the champion called a Triumph. It's considered a great honor."

"But that doesn't mean *my* mother is dead. Maybe she's just missing! You don't even know who she is!" Helen said. The tears tipped over the edge of her eyelids and splashed down on her shirt.

"The fact that you exist proves that anything is possible," Cassandra said. But she wasn't able to look Helen in the eye.

"Right around the time you were born, the Houses were going through a period of intense fighting that was thought to be the final confrontation. There were a lot of deaths," Castor said, looking down at his hands as if he expected to find blood on them.

Helen turned her back on Castor and Cassandra and tried to breathe her way through the tears, but still it took a few moments before she knew she wasn't going to start sobbing. She didn't even know why she was so upset. She'd always thought she hated her mother.

"Helen, we understand that you might need some time before we continue. We still have a lot more to talk about, but we're not going anywhere and we can finish this conversation when you're ready. In the meantime, please know that we really do want to help you," Castor said gently from somewhere on the other side of the room.

Helen heard them get up to leave, but she couldn't bring herself to say good-bye. After they'd left, she opened up the French doors and went out onto the patio. The sight of the pristine beach and rolling blue water blunted the sharper edges of her emotions and before she knew it she was shuffling down the beach.

"Are you okay?" Lucas asked from behind her.

Helen just nodded, not surprised that he had appeared. They both looked down the beach, watching a big, hairy dog jump in and out of the surf with glee. After a moment Lucas moved and stood beside her.

"I'm relieved," Helen said. She turned her head to look at him. "My whole life I thought my mother hated me so much that she didn't even want me to know what she looked like."

A pained expression darkened Lucas's face, but Helen continued before he could interrupt her. "I'm not saying an ancient blood feud is a good thing, but at least it's a *reason* why she left me. I've never had one of those before."

"She could still be alive, you know," Lucas insisted. "Regardless of what Cass and my dad think."

"I don't know what to feel about that yet," Helen replied honestly. "Kate has been more of a mother to me than Beth, or whatever she was called, ever was. I guess I'll decide how I feel when I find out the truth. The whole truth."

"That works," Lucas replied, smiling out at the water for a moment before another thought occurred to him and his face fell. "For now, anyway."

He squeezed her fingers, and Helen glanced down, surprised again that they had joined hands when she wasn't paying attention. She didn't know who had initiated this new habit of theirs, but she realized that it would be nearly impossible to stop. She had never held a boy's hand before and it should have made her shy, but it didn't. It felt like the most natural thing in the world for her to touch him. That thought made her shake her head in wonder. She looked up and noticed that he was looking down at their hands as well, probably thinking the same thing.

"Do you want to sit down for a moment?" she asked, suddenly conscious of the fact that the last time she had seen him he was unable to walk without Jason's help.

"Nope. But I wouldn't mind something else to eat." He threw a distracted glance over his shoulder at the house.

"Me too. My god, I'm a pig!" Helen said, still surprised at herself.

"You went hours without eating during the heal," he said, leading her away from the water's edge. "That's crazy talk."

"You know, if it weren't for the whole 'agonizing pain' thing, I think I could get to like heals. People carry you around, and feed you nonstop. It's like being an infant, only you're old enough to appreciate it."

"Not so much fun when you have to go to the bathroom, though."

"No! Especially not when you're around strangers," Helen said, expecting a laugh or a witty response from Luke, and not getting either.

"We're not strangers," he said quietly, slowing down so he could look her in the eye.

"Well, not anymore," she agreed. She felt a hot blush stinging her cheeks and had to look down. His eyes were so honest and so blue that Helen felt if she didn't force herself to look away right from the start that she'd get stuck and never stop staring at him.

They held hands as they walked back. When they got close to the house, Helen noticed Cassandra looking down at them from one of the second-story balconies. She didn't look happy.

When they went into the kitchen, they found Noel already hard at work over half a dozen pots and pans. She set them up with a pint of ice cream, cookies, nuts, and caramel sauce and told them they were strong enough to make

146

their own darned sundaes before she went back to snarling at the ox-sized roast she was wrangling into the oven. After a decadent snack that tempted the rest of the house into the kitchen to spoil their appetites, Noel told everyone that they might as well just stay in their seats because dinner would be ready in another twenty minutes.

"I can't. I have to go home," Helen admitted in a disappointed tone as she pushed a few soggy pecans around the bottom of her bowl.

"Ridiculous. You're not going anywhere," Lucas responded.

"No, really. I have to go home, get the Jeep, and then pick Kate and my dad up at the airport."

"One of us can get them for you," Ariadne said, rising from the seat on the bench to Helen's right.

"Sit, Ari, you're still drained from healing. And don't think for a second all that blush you're wearing is fooling *me*," Pandora said with a twinkle in her eye and a snarky finger wag that set her bracelets dancing and tinkling. "I'd *love* to go and meet your dad, Helen."

"No, you can't!" Helen said a little too forcefully before she got hold of herself and continued in a steadier tone. "My dad doesn't know about any of this. Please. It's very kind of you to offer, but if you could just give me a ride back to my house, I'd really appreciate it." She couldn't look up, but she knew everyone was shooting each other meaningful looks over her head. Ariadne touched Helen's hand and opened her mouth to say something, but Lucas spoke first.

"I'll drive you home," he said as he slid out from his seat

on the bench and pulled Helen along with him by the hand. "Let's go."

"You're in no shape to travel," Noel said, shaking her head, but Lucas was already walking toward her and smiling mischievously.

"I'm driving her home, not flying her there," he said, suddenly grabbing his mom faster than she could move and kissing the top of her head with an exaggerated smooching sound. It couldn't have been too comfortable, but it was funny enough to get Noel to laugh and admit that Lucas was strong enough to drive.

Helen tried to give everyone a heartfelt thank-you but Lucas made a snoring sound, grabbed her hand, and dragged her across the room, saying, "Yeah, yeah. You'll be back tomorrow, anyway."

"What?" Helen said in a flustered daze as Lucas pulled her through the kitchen door that led to a huge garage packed with fancy cars. He bundled her in a little, classic convertible Mercedes and started the car as he hit the door opener.

"You'll be back here tomorrow afternoon," he said, finally answering her question as he pulled out and headed off the compound toward Milestone Road.

"I can't. I have track," Helen reminded him.

"I have football. I'll drive you back here after we're both done. And I can pick you up for school in the morning if you'd like."

"I thought you weren't allowed to do sports anymore."

"That's mostly cleared up," he said with a huge grin.

"Look, all I'm going to say is I've seen the football team. And believe me, they need my cousins and me."

"I should probably be offended by that, but I've seen the football team, too," Helen said, mirroring his grin. "But regardless, I can't come over after tomorrow. I have to work on Monday nights."

"Tuesday then," Lucas said.

"I can't. I have to cook dinner for my dad," she said in a rushed voice.

"He can come, too. My mom wants to meet him," Lucas said with growing uncertainty. He glanced over at Helen. "Don't you want to come?"

"It's not that," she said, feeling cornered and frustrated and not knowing why. "My dad won't allow it, okay?" Helen looked out her window at the golf course and felt Lucas take her hand and shake it a little to get her to look at him.

"No one will tell your father about you if you don't want them to," he said, glancing from her to the road and back again.

"It's not that. He doesn't let me go out on school nights," she said, looking back at him, but he was frowning deeply and staring at the road. As the minutes ticked by silently, Helen could feel Lucas's mood getting worse and worse.

"Nope. This isn't going to work," he said suddenly, pulling the car over to the side of the road, yanking on the parking brake, and turning in his seat to face Helen. When he saw Helen's startled face he took a shaky breath to control himself before he started. "I don't know if my dad explained this to you, but the different Houses are the descendants of different gods," he began.

"Yes, he said something like that," Helen responded quietly. She felt like a kid in the principal's office and she had no idea why. He tried to smile at her but gave up.

"My family's House, the House of Thebes, are the descendants of Apollo. He's primarily known as the god of Light, but he was also the god of Music, Healing, and of *Truth*. Falsefinders—Scions who can feel lies—are very rare, but I'm one of them. I always know a lie when I hear it, and if it comes from someone close to me I can't stand it. So you can't lie to me, Helen. Ever. If you don't want to tell me the truth, please, for my sake, don't say anything all," he pleaded.

"Does it hurt?" Helen asked, her curiosity piqued.

"I've tried to explain to Jase how it feels, but I've never been able to get it right. It's almost like that feeling you get when you've lost something really important and you can't find it, but it's much worse. The longer the lie hangs there, the more frantic I get to find the truth. I'll dig and dig for it . . ."

"I just need a little bit of time to adjust," Helen admitted in a rush. "I'm not ready to tell my dad about me, or about my mom, because I don't know what it would do to him. To be honest, I don't know if I'll ever tell him. But I know I need a minute to get used to all of this. A few days at least."

Lucas's face relaxed immediately and he let out a held breath.

"Why didn't you just say that to begin with?"

"Because it's, it's too . . ." she trailed off, not knowing why it was so hard.

"Too raw. Like being naked," Lucas said for her. Helen nodded her head. "Well, sorry. But with me you have to be either honest or silent." He released the brake, put the car in gear, and merged back into traffic.

As soon as he could stop shifting, he grabbed her hand and held it on his leg, and when the fading sunlight forced him to turn on the headlights, he let go of the steering wheel rather than let go of her hand.

Lucas pulled into Helen's driveway behind the Pig, then killed the lights and engine. "Stay here for a sec," he said before hopping out of the car and disappearing around the back of the house.

Helen craned her head to look for him as she waited, but she didn't hear anything—not even the sound of his footsteps. Annoyed that he would just run off like that, she got out of the car and walked up to the Pig to get a better view. She noticed her purse lying on the ground behind the front tire. Oops. She picked it up and fished out her phone. There were over a dozen missed calls.

She remembered that her purse was lying on the ground because she had been attacked, and she suddenly realized that her attacker was *not* Hector or Lucas, as she had assumed the other night.

Now that she could look back on it without the Furies there to warp her judgment, she figured out that there had been someone else here waiting for her when she came home.

Someone with wiry arms—a woman, she thought, recalling the smell of cosmetics—had grabbed her from behind, then been scared off by the arrival of the Delos family. Lucas had sent Ariadne and Jason to chase after her, but the woman must have gotten away because there was no mention of her this weekend. In the shock of the past few days, Helen had completely forgotten about the attack.

"Lucas?" she called, heading toward the shadows off to the side of her house. He had been gone too long. She heard a muffled thud behind her.

"I asked you to stay in the car. It's for your safety, Helen," Lucas said with frustration. She spun around to face him, gesturing wildly with her cell phone still in her hand.

"That woman! You're looking for that woman who jumped Kate and me," Helen said, finally understanding it all. "She's a Scion, too. She has to be!"

"Yes, of course she is. . . ." he interrupted her. "But listen to me. There are two of them—two different women are after you, and we haven't caught either of them yet."

A pair of lights flashed across the house and driveway. A car was pulling up. Lucas stood in front of Helen and looked easily through the lights that were blinding her from seeing the people in the car. "It's your father," he told her.

"Helen? There you are! Where the hell have you been?" Jerry shouted as he climbed out of the cab before the driver had even come to a full stop. He was angrier than she'd seen him in years. "I called over and over. You're never late! I thought something had happened to you!"

"Why are you here?" Helen screeched.

"We got an earlier flight. Didn't you get any of my messages?"

"I . . ." Helen trailed off, holding up her cell phone stupidly. She knew she had to make something up, but she also knew she was a terrible liar. She started to panic. Lucas grabbed her phone from her and, as he did, Helen heard an almost imperceptible crunch.

"Her phone's broken," Lucas said, passing Helen's phone to her father so he could see it. It came apart in Jerry's hand. "I came over to see why she wasn't picking up and she was out here in the driveway on her way to go get you." Helen stared at Lucas with her mouth open, wondering how someone who demanded honesty from everyone else could be so quick to lie.

"How did you do this, Len?" Jerry asked in a dismayed voice as he studied the pulverized sandwich of plastic and microchips. "This was brand-new."

"I know!" Helen said a little too emphatically. "Piece of junk, right? I'm so sorry, Dad. I had no idea you were coming early. Really."

"Oh, it's all right," Jerry said a bit sheepishly now that he wasn't so worried. He and Helen smiled at each other, all forgiven. Then Jerry turned to Lucas. "You look familiar," he said suspiciously, acknowledging Lucas's presence for the first time and distrusting it immediately.

For a moment Helen could see Lucas as her father did—a heartbreakingly beautiful young man who was too well built, too well dressed, and driving too nice of a car to ever be liked by anyone's father.

"Lucas Delos," he said, holding out his hand.

"Don't you hate this kid?" Jerry asked Helen candidly as he shook the offered hand. Lucas laughed, and it was such an open, unself-conscious sound that Jerry joined in.

"We worked it out," Helen said.

"Good," Jerry said. Then he passed Lucas's flashy convertible as he went back to the cab to pay and get his bags. "Or maybe not," he amended. Helen took that moment to roll her eyes at Lucas and point to her phone.

"What about that woman? How are you going to tell me the rest of the story now?" she whispered frantically. "If I use the phone in the kitchen, my dad will hear."

"Sorry," Lucas whispered back, his eyes laughing. "I couldn't think of anything else to do."

"Tomorrow," Helen warned. "I want the whole story."

"I'll pick you up half an hour early for school. We'll get coffee," Lucas promised.

"What's going on?" Jerry asked suspiciously, joining them again.

"Lucas has to get home for dinner," Helen said. She saw Lucas wince at the lie, but he took the hint.

"It was nice to meet you, Mr. Hamilton," Lucas said as he waved good-bye and backpedaled toward his car.

"Damn, I really wish you had acne. Or a gland problem," Jerry replied.

"Dad!" Helen huffed, embarrassed. "Good night, Lucas,"

she said apologetically.

"Good night, Helen," he replied softly, his eyes bright.

"Okay, that's enough. Get in the house, Helen," Jerry said with a nervous smile. He physically turned Helen around and gave her a little push toward the door. "I think I would prefer it if you went back to hating him."

Helen heard Lucas laughing to himself as he started his car. The warm sound made her smile.

Lucas took his time driving home from Helen's side of the island. He needed time to think and get control over himself before he faced his family. Not that it would do much good. Cassandra and Jason could always figure out how he was feeling, and they were being hypervigilant about him right now. They'd been worried about him since that day in the hallway when he'd first seen her, and now it would get worse. It was *already* worse. Jason would probably try to get him to sit down for a nice, long talk, and Lucas didn't have the patience for that. He didn't want anyone's pity; he just wanted to be left alone for once.

Lucas pulled into the garage and sat with the engine off for a few minutes, trying to put his feelings back where they belonged. The past few days he'd felt as if his emotions were spring-loaded, as though if he let the lid off them they'd all come flying out like confetti from a Christmas cracker. He knew for damn sure he couldn't handle seeing Cassandra, not right then, and he also knew she was probably waiting for him. He got out of the car, walked outside, and flew up to his bedroom window to avoid her.

But of course she knew he would do that, and she was already sitting on the couch in his room. Lucas smiled ruefully to himself before he even got his window open. He should have known better than to try and outmaneuver his little sister.

"I don't want to talk about it, Cassie," he said in what he hoped was a patient but firm voice.

"You don't get to make that choice," Cassandra responded sadly.

"No. We're Scions. We don't get to make many of our own choices, do we?" he said bitterly as he floated through the window and came in for a landing.

His body took on the burden of gravity and his feet touched down as he went from flying to walking in an instant.

"You've been gone a while," Cassandra said in an insinuating tone.

"I stayed in her area for a bit, looking around her neighborhood for any sign of those women," he said evenly, and he wasn't lying.

"I told you, you don't have to worry. She's safe for a few more days at least," Cassandra said, shaking her head. "I'm not so sure about you."

"I didn't touch her."

"But you can't stay away from her, either."

He couldn't. Even when he was still possessed by the Furies in her presence, he *couldn't* stay away from Helen. He didn't know how to describe it; it was as though it felt wrong to be separated from her. "You don't have to worry. I won't touch her."

"That's not the only thing I care about," she began in a warning tone.

He interrupted her, tired of the doublespeak. "Yeah, sure, but it's the thing you and everybody else cares about *most*, Cassie," he said. He unlatched his watch and laid it carefully on his bedside table. He wouldn't look at her, and he knew that was cruel, but he couldn't stop himself.

"That's not true. You know that, right?" she asked, suddenly no more than his sweet little sister. He looked over at her and felt his heart soften. She carried a heavier burden then he did, he knew that. Sometimes his bitterness got the better of him, but he trusted that Cassandra knew he loved her, and that she also knew he wouldn't stop loving her even if she told him he had to give up the one thing he wanted most in the world. That didn't make it any easier for either of them, though it wasn't like anyone had ever asked them what they wanted.

"What does it matter how any of us feel?" he muttered. "If I take Helen, the war starts all over again. No amount of wishing will make it different."

"I don't *know* that," Cassandra replied with more than a little self-doubt. "I'm not strong enough yet."

"But you're pretty sure it is," he said, sitting down on the end of his bed, suddenly feeling as if he had taken on two planets' worth of gravity. "And don't pretend you're not, because not even you can lie to me."

# EIGHT

Helen spent the next few hours alternately listening to the details of her father's trip and insisting that Lucas was not her boyfriend. She figured out pretty fast that the only way to get Jerry to stop asking questions about Lucas was to ask him questions about Kate instead. And besides, she genuinely wanted to know what was going on between the two of them. Jerry kept insisting that they had never been anything more than friends. Disappointed that her dad was obviously still lugging around a big bag of hurt for her mother, all Helen wanted was to escape upstairs to her room to think, but she had to wait until they finished dinner first. By the time she and her father were done eating, arguing over how much salt he was allowed to put on his dinner, and talking about the store, Helen was so exhausted she nearly fell asleep sitting on the edge of the tub as she brushed her teeth.

The next morning, Helen skipped breakfast, packed her own lunch box, and shouted good-bye to her father from the front door before he even made it downstairs. He called after her as she jumped into Lucas's car, but she pretended she didn't hear him.

"Shouldn't we wait to see what he wants?" Lucas asked her.

"Nope. Let's just go," she said a little too quickly.

Lucas shrugged and drove off as Jerry made it to the front door. Helen waved to him, but she knew she would hear about this little stunt later. In detail.

"Okay, I'm still new around here so I don't know the cafés. Where's a good place on this side of the island?" Lucas asked.

"Ah, the News Store?" Helen offered with a shrug. "I don't think we'll be able to talk there, though."

"How 'bout this," he said as he pulled into a chain restaurant that was popular with the tourists.

Helen winced but assented. There were other mom-and-pop choices, but she knew all the people who worked in those places. For this conversation she needed a little privacy.

They stood quietly together in line, waiting to sit before they started talking. Helen tried not to stare at Lucas, but it was difficult. It amazed her how comfortable he seemed wherever he went, as if the whole world was as private to him as his own bedroom.

She tried to watch him out of the corner of her eye, maybe

catch him fidgeting or shuffling his feet the way she herself did in public, but there was none of that. He really didn't care if people looked at him or not. He didn't subconsciously apologize to the world for his presence by slouching or crossing his arms or playing with his keys. It unnerved Helen to see how he could just stand there and not do anything else, but it also inspired her. Why should she slouch and feel bashful for taking up more space than most people? She stood up a little straighter while she stared at him.

"Had enough?" he asked, smiling at Helen's brazen admiration of his looks.

"Not yet," she said, a matching smile breaking across her face.

"Good."

As soon as they were seated, Lucas asked her what she wanted to know, and Helen had to think for a moment. She wasn't entirely sure.

"I guess the first thing I need to know is who hurt Kate," she said, dreading the answer.

"We have no idea," he answered, sounding earnest. Helen's heart sank. She knew from the night before that although Lucas couldn't bear to be lied to, it didn't stop him from telling a few whoppers of his own.

"That doesn't make sense, Lucas," she said carefully. "Your father told me that I was the only one of . . . our kind . . . who was not a member of your House. How can you not know two women who, by that logic, are related to you?"

Lucas nodded, like he understood why Helen doubted

him. "The House of Thebes is very large. Our immediate family—those of us who moved back here to the States—are a just a tiny splinter group, but the main part of the House of Thebes is much, much larger. They're known as the Hundred Cousins, although there are a lot more of them than that now, and they're loosely led by my uncle Tantalus," he said, looking down at his coffee, his eyes far away. "My dad knows everyone in our House on sight, but I don't, and he wasn't there when you were attacked. Helen, I've got so many cousins, there are some I've never even *heard* of, let alone seen."

"If your uncle is the leader, can't you just call and ask him which of your cousins is trying to kill me?"

"Tantalus may have been the one who sent them," he said darkly. "But we don't know that for sure yet. My uncle Pallas—Hector, Jason, and Ariadne's father—he went back to Europe after the first attack on you to see how much Tantalus knows." Helen studied his face for a moment. It was all sharp edges and glittering blue eyes.

"You mean spy on the rest of the House," Helen said, surprised. He nodded. "But why would your family go through so much for me? I'm grateful, but still. What else aren't you telling me?"

He tore at his croissant for a moment and then let out a fast breath.

"The Hundred Cousins are a kind of cult. They believe something that my family doesn't, and they believe it so fanatically that they are willing to kill for it. That's why we left Spain. Hector . . ." Lucas trailed off, and then shook his head as if to clear it before turning his focus back on Helen. "The point is that you're in a lot of danger. I've been following you since I first saw you, but I can't guard you every second. If either one of those women finds you without me there, they'll try to kill you, and you don't know how to defend yourself yet."

"Well, it's not like I've ever had to defend myself," Helen said, at a loss. "I mean, this is *Nantucket*. My dad and I forget to lock the front door more often than not!"

"You're very important to us. Much more than I can explain to you right now," Lucas said, leaning forward and taking her hands. "I know you said you needed a few days, and I didn't want to freak you out by throwing all of this at you at once, but you have to start training with us as soon as you can. My family will teach you how to fight."

"You mean like judo and stuff?"

"Sort of," Lucas said, smiling reassuringly. "Don't look so worried. With your gifts you'll be kicking ass in no time."

"What gifts?" Helen asked doubtfully.

"You really don't know, do you?" he marveled.

"Hey, Luke, what's up?" Zach asked, entering the café. He was smiling, but his smile faded as soon as he saw whom Lucas was with. Behind him stood a few guys from the football team, all of whom were staring, openmouthed, at the unlikely pairing.

"Hey, Zach. Getting some coffee. You?" Lucas answered, totally unfazed. Helen gave a watered-down smile and untucked her hair from behind her ears to hide her face. Lucas reached across the table and smoothed her hair back behind her shoulder.

"Same, yeah," Zach mumbled as he nearly tripped over himself to get away, his eyes darting between Helen and Lucas with disbelief. "See you in a few," he called out before joining the other guys in line.

Helen bit her lip and stared at her coffee cup, rubbing her stomach under the table as subtly as possible. *Please, no cramps*, she thought.

"What's the matter?" Lucas asked, watching her.

"Nothing. Can we just go?" she pleaded, desperate to change the subject, get away, maybe drop dead if at all possible.

"Sure," Lucas said, standing up. He gave her a worried look. "I know it's not nothing, Helen, and I'd rather you told me the truth, whatever it is. Ariadne gave all three of us guys a whole lecture about women's troubles years ago, you know. And by lecture, I mean beating."

"Well, I owe her one, but it's not what you think." Helen grabbed his hand and pulled him toward the door.

Lucas waved to Zach on his way out. Zach waved back, but he was still pouting.

"I think I've lowered your rank. Sorry," Helen said as they got in the little silver Mercedes.

"What are you talking about?" Lucas asked, backing out of the parking lot.

"Well, Zach and all those guys saw us together," she said,

like her meaning was obvious.

"And?"

"Zach and Gretchen aren't my biggest fans, which makes me sort of like popularity antimatter at school," Helen explained sheepishly. Lucas's face cracked into a huge smile and he grabbed her hand, but he had to let it go to shift.

"I'm going to have to start driving an automatic," he mumbled to himself before continuing. "You think you're unpopular? The first hour I was on this island I heard about the beautiful, perfect, *heavenly* Helen Hamilton. You know that's what the boys call you, right? Heaven Hamilton?" Helen dodged his seeking hand, but he eventually captured hers and held it tighter.

"Stop it, Lucas. This isn't a joke to me. And what's up with *this*?" she asked, holding up their linked hands.

"I don't know," he said with a curious tilt of his head. "But it feels right, doesn't it? Look, why don't you tell me what's really bothering you about being seen with me. Are you afraid of people talking?"

"Yes and no. You don't understand because you haven't been here long enough, but those popular people have something against me, and some of them go out of their way to be mean to me. I've never fit in with them."

"And you never will," he told her seriously. "No matter where you go you are going to be different, Helen. It's about time you got used to it."

"I am used to it! I've had my whole life to get used to it!" she exclaimed as they drove into the school parking lot.

"Good. Now stop freaking out and listen for a sec. Those guys weren't staring at us because they hate you. They were staring at us because they couldn't figure out how the hell I convinced a girl who tried to strangle me the other week to get in my car and go out for coffee."

"Oh, yeah. I forgot about that," Helen said to the ground, getting out of the car. She tossed her bag over her shoulder.

"And I'd like to go back to forgetting about it. If we never talk about trying to kill each other again, it would be fine with me," Lucas said quietly. He took her hand firmly in his and pulled her up against him so that her shoulder was touching his arm as they walked into school.

Everyone was staring. The halls were lined with blank faces and slack jaws as conversations were momentarily halted and then continued twice as loud when Helen and Lucas passed. Helen tried to pull her hand out of Lucas's, but he resisted at first. Finally, he let go when he realized that Helen was not just being modest, she was about to panic.

"Lennie?" Claire called out warily. Helen smiled briefly at Lucas and veered in Claire's direction.

"Where were you all weekend?" Claire asked, eyeing Lucas suspiciously.

"Did you try to call me?" Helen asked, grateful for an excuse to pry herself away from Lucas and hopefully away from all the stares.

"Like, five times. What happened to you?"

"My phone broke," Helen said apologetically. Then she turned to Lucas. "I have to stop at my locker before homeroom. Thanks for the ride," she told him bluntly.

"Okay. I'll see you later then," he said, accepting his dismissal as gracefully as he could. When he was no more than three steps away, Claire grabbed Helen's arm and dragged her toward her locker.

"What the holy hand grenade was that?" Claire practically shouted. Helen shushed her as she wrestled with her locker combination.

"We had a long talk," Helen said quickly. "We don't hate each other anymore."

"A talk? Yeah, right. I'm sure tongues were involved but for some reason I don't think much language was used." Claire looked angry, but Helen was suddenly angrier.

"Stop it, Claire! I mean it! I had a really rough weekend. I'm sorry I didn't think to call you last night but my father was pissed at me for leaving him stranded at the airport."

"Well, tell me about it now then!" Claire replied defensively. "Not like you have to say anything. Everyone can see that you and Lucas are suddenly a couple."

"I don't know what we are, but it's not something I can sum up with an easy label like 'couple,' okay?" Stressed, Helen shuffled through her books and realized that she hadn't done any of her homework.

"Why can't you just be honest with me? You slept with him," Claire accused her. Her eyes were hurt. Helen knew she couldn't shut her out entirely.

"Honestly? I did sleep with him. Twice. But not the way you think," she said frankly. She turned Claire around and steered them both to Hergie's. "We've never even kissed."

"Rubbish!" Claire declared, stopping dead in the middle of the hall.

"Ask him yourself. You've got classes with him all day," Helen responded, perfectly serious. The bell rang and they both had to run the last few steps to make it through the door before Hergie closed it.

Helen had a terrible morning. Several teachers considered giving her detention for not doing her homework and every single girl in school was furious with her for getting a ride with Lucas. Helen's relationships with the girls in her class had always been strained. For years she'd gone out of her way to be nice to them, but she'd finally given up when she noticed that if she kept her head down and her mouth shut she could slide under the radar.

That was all over now that she had been seen coming to school with Lucas. She had crossed some sort of imaginary line, broken the truce that she had entered into by refusing to compete, and they'd declared war on her. All day long, Helen found that if she looked anywhere but at the board or her desk she was shot nasty looks. To top everything else off, Gretchen was whispering vicious rumors about Helen to anyone who would listen, and Claire was still upset.

Helen couldn't help but smile with relief when she saw Lucas at his locker before lunch. He seemed to be the only person in the entire school who would smile back at her.

"So you like me again, huh?" he said as she made her way toward him.

"Not you too," Helen moaned. "Is there a sign on my back that says 'kick me'?"

"It's just gossip, Helen. It can't hurt us," he said, wisely deciding not to tease her anymore.

"Maybe it can't hurt you," Helen muttered. She put a hand on her belly. Lucas saw her do it and was just about to ask what was wrong when Hector and Jason joined them.

"Your mom's here," Jason told Lucas, who nodded as though he was expecting her.

"What's wrong?" Helen asked.

"Nothing. We're meeting with the principal because my mom is going to try and talk our way back on to the football team," Lucas explained.

"She's playing the 'have pity on a poor little woman raising so many gigantic boys' card and then she'll beg them to let us beat up kids from other schools instead of each other. All to the benefit of Nantucket High, of course," Jason said with a grin. "It never fails. She's like the Einstein of guilt."

"But should you three be allowed to play football?" Helen said with a disapproving frown. "I mean, you all have an unfair advantage."

"Keep talking, track star," Hector replied with a little heat.

"Helen runs because she needs a scholarship for college," Lucas said, shooting Hector a warning glance. "We play sports because it's expected of us. It's annoying, actually, because we have to pretend to be unbearably weak and slow."

"And we spend as much time making sure no one gets

hurt as we do playing," added Jason with a rueful smile. "The truth is we'd much rather be beating each *other* up than pretending to beat up mortals, but that wouldn't look normal at all."

"Well, good luck on the whole looking-normal thing," Helen said briskly, stepping aside to let Jason and Hector go past her.

"I'll find you after school," Lucas promised her as he followed his cousins. He glanced back and gave her a concerned look. Helen tried to smile for him, but her expression was so phony she wondered if Lucas could feel the lie in it.

Helen slouched into the cafeteria, hoping to duck across the room without attracting too much attention. She saw Gretchen say something to Amy Heart and then the whole table of cheerleaders started laughing mockingly at Helen. It took Helen far too long to recover, and by the time she got herself oriented, everyone in the cafeteria was staring at her. She retreated to her usual table with Matt and Claire, sure she could feel a cramp coming on.

"Would you please just stand up straight!" Claire barked at her. "There's nothing more pathetic than watching you try to dissolve feetfirst into the frigging floor, and I swear if I catch you doing it one more time I'm going to lose it."

It was the last straw. Helen spun around on her heel and fled the cafeteria. She tried to eat her lunch in the restroom, sitting on a sink, but the venue was so unappetizing that she gave up on her sandwich after a few bites.

She made it through her last three classes and practically

ran to the girls' locker room when the final bell rang, but Claire was already there waiting for her.

"Sorry I yelled at you earlier," she said bashfully. She looked so cute when she was apologizing that Helen couldn't even pick up a grudge, let alone carry one.

"Oh, forget it. I've been a flake, and I'd be angry, too, if I were you." Helen threw an arm over Claire's shoulder and led her outside after they changed.

"One thing, and then I'm going to leave you alone about it until you come to me to talk," Claire said as they walked past the football field. Helen didn't have the patience for any more questions.

"We've never even kissed, Gig," she said, cutting Claire off.

"Really?" Claire practically shouted. Helen nodded and bumped Claire playfully with her hip.

"Really, really. I almost kissed him once, but he told me to lie down and go to sleep."

"No *way!*" Claire shouted. Helen grabbed her, clamping a hand over her mouth.

"He's right over there," she said, gesturing toward him with her chin. "I told you I'd tell you if anything happened. I'm not trying to keep secrets from you."

Claire gave Helen a knowing smile.

"You've always kept secrets. But it's okay. When you're ready to tell me you will," she said patiently. Then she tackled Helen, trying to wrestle her to the ground. Helen went along with it, pretending to be overpowered by her pint-sized pal, both of them laughing hysterically. The fun only lasted a moment.

"Get a room," said a boy's amused voice.

"You wish," Claire answered back. "Wait. How'd you get over here so fast?"

Helen rolled over onto her back, blew her tangled hair out of her face, and saw Lucas and Jason standing over them.

"We saw you go down so we ran over to check it out," Lucas said, ignoring Claire's question.

"Thanks. She is pretty ferocious," Helen replied, allowing Claire to flip her over one more time before Lucas helped her up.

"Five feet and two inches of pure terror," Claire boasted as she held out her hand, expecting Jason to help her. He folded his arms across his chest deliberately.

"Is that how tall you are without those ridiculous shoes?" he said derisively. "I think I was born bigger than that."

"I bet you were. Five feet of fat head and two inches of ass," Claire muttered, standing up.

"Claire!" Helen blurted out, shocked. Lucas's shoulders were shaking with laughter. Jason pretended to take the joke okay, but Helen suspected his feelings were hurt.

Helen bit back her own laughter and gave Claire a little pinch as punishment. Claire yelped in protest, pointing out that monkey bites had been off-limits since they were ten, and was about to say something else to Jason when the Delos boys were called back to practice by their coach.

Helen watched as Lucas jogged back to the football field.

Running in the sun, he was about the most beautiful thing she'd ever seen.

"Crap. We're late," Claire said, and they picked up their pace to catch up with their teammates, having to run up to the trailhead where Coach Tar was waiting with her clipboard. She was already shouting out start times, so Helen and Claire just kept running, calling back to their coach as they crossed over the line. Coach scribbled their times down, shaking her head.

"You owe me a full minute off your last run for being late, Hamilton!" she shouted after them.

"Sure, Coach!" Helen shouted back before she lowered her voice to berate Claire privately. "Why'd you say that to him?" she asked, still feeling bad for Jason.

"Because it felt fantastic!" Claire replied unapologetically.

"I like Jason," Helen said, realizing it was true. He had always been kind to her, and he seemed to have a good head on his shoulders. "He's a really nice guy, and you were awful to him."

"Of course you like him, because Jason is nice to everyone. Everyone but me. You don't have classes with us so you haven't seen him do it, but whenever we debate, he always tries to shut me down, arguing against whatever position I take. Even when he actually agrees with me, he argues just to play devil's advocate."

"And why do you think he does that?" Helen asked with a little grin.

"I asked him, and do you know what he said?" Claire

plowed on, getting herself even more worked up. "He said everyone else in this school is afraid to stand up to me in a debate, except for him, and it's good for me to have to work a little bit for once in my life!"

"How dare he challenge you to think deeper," Helen said with mock horror.

"Believe me, it's not a favor. He's just trying to prove he's smarter than me."

"Is he?"

"Oh, I don't know. Maybe. Lucas is smarter than all of us, so there goes valedictorian. And then there's Ariadne. She's really bright, too, but I think I have her beat. We'll see what happens," Claire said, biting at her lower lip.

She was deeply worried about all the new competition, and Helen hadn't even asked her how classes were going so far. It sounded like Claire had basically given up on her life-long dream of graduating at the top of the class, and Helen hadn't noticed.

"I've been a terrible friend to you these past couple of days, haven't I?" Helen asked, suddenly disgusted with herself.

"I wouldn't say terrible," Claire said with a wry smile. "But you could do me a favor to make up for it if you like."

"Anything," Helen replied immediately.

"If you could keep Lucas awake and occupied the night before exams . . ." Claire said, already holding up her arms to defend herself from Helen's pretend slaps. "I don't know why you're fighting it, Len. One, he's frigging gorgeous. Two, he's so frigging gorgeous you need to count it twice.

Three, he saw you fall down and left practice to see if you were okay. That's, like, devotion."

Helen didn't know how to respond. She couldn't exactly explain that Lucas had only come over to make sure she was okay because several of his relatives were trying to kill her. The image of Kate lying unconscious on the dirty ground flashed into Helen's head and her stomach fluttered. Like Kate, Claire was in danger just being around her.

"I gotta pick up the pace," Helen said urgently, and Claire nodded.

"Show Lucas those legs are for more than drooling over and call me later," she said cheerfully before Helen sped off.

When Claire was out of sight, Helen sighed to herself, fighting back a fit of guilt. She didn't know what she would do if anyone ever hurt Claire. The thought distracted her from reining in her stride and she almost allowed herself to run into Coach Tar's view far too early. At the last moment she remembered to duck behind some bushes, waiting several minutes before pretending to sprint the last few yards. She still finished first, of course, and then had to spend another half hour waiting for Lucas to finish up with practice. If he was going to continue driving her to school in the morning, she decided she was going to have to come up with another plan for getting to work afterward.

As soon as Helen walked in the front door of the News Store, Kate started following her around with a stunned look on her face.

"Wow!" Kate managed to say after a few moments of

speechlessness. "He's like . . . wow! I could go to jail for even thinking what I'm thinking."

"Kate!" Helen exclaimed, throwing a balled-up napkin at her. "I thought you were a feminist!"

"What's that got to do with anything?"

"Aren't you always preaching that there can be no equality if the sexes objectify each other?"

"Yeah, but damn!" Kate said, fanning herself with her hand. "When I was your age all of the guys were trying to prove how antiestablishment they were by out-uglying each other. I so got robbed!"

"Keep on going and I'll tell my dad he's got competition," Helen teased, but the joke didn't have the effect she thought it would. The laughter went right out of Kate's eyes and the smile melted off her face.

"I don't think it would make any difference to him," she said, and then abruptly changed the subject. "But we're not talking about me. We're talking about you and Lucas and the importance of condoms."

After several rounds of denial, and a few breaks to help customers, Kate finally accepted the fact that Helen was still as pure as the driven snow.

"Is he gay?" Kate asked. "I mean, look at you, Len."

"I haven't asked, but I'm pretty sure he's straight," Helen replied, and then she sighed. "I honestly don't know what's going on."

"No reason to rush, and don't let anyone make you feel bad if you want to wait, either. It's more fun if you take your time, anyway," Kate said with a warm smile, changing the subject at the first sign of Helen's discomfort.

Although Kate seemed convinced that eventually she and Lucas would go beyond virginal hand-holding, Helen suddenly wasn't so sure. The one time she had tried to kiss Lucas he had told her to go to sleep. Despite what everyone was saying about them, the truth was that she and Lucas were no more than friends. Lucas could have anyone he wanted, and if Kate's response was any indication, that included women long out of high school.

Knowing that didn't do anything to help Helen's confidence. She could tell that Lucas liked her—she'd caught him staring at her and she'd heard his heart pound when she lay down next to him—but for some reason Lucas didn't seem to want to do anything about it. Was that the way dating always was in the beginning, or was she unintentionally doing something to push Lucas away? She'd never had a boyfriend, and she honestly didn't know what "normal" was.

After work, she went home and forced herself to do all of her school assignments before bed. By the time she switched out the light it was well past two. Helen was beyond tired, but she still couldn't fall asleep. She felt like she was missing something, or maybe misunderstanding something. Lucas obviously liked her company and felt protective of her, but neither of those things meant that he was attracted to her. Maybe she wasn't his type. Maybe he even had a girlfriend back in Spain. Helen imagined a dark siren with long black curls, olive skin, and a sexy Spanish accent waiting for Lucas to come back to Europe.

She flopped over in bed and put a pillow over her head, vowing not to be the pathetic loser who chases after a boy she can never have. She needed more information about Lucas, but since he was new in school, and no one knew his previous history with girls, Helen was going to have to see what she could get out of Ariadne and hope she didn't come off as too obvious.

# NINE

"Keep sticking your chin out like that and I'll knock it off for you," Hector yelled. He'd been doing a lot of yelling over the past hour and a half.

Helen obediently tucked in her chin and lifted her fists up to guard her face. She kept her center of gravity low and moved her feet in sweeping crescents in case there were obstacles on the ground that she would need to brush out of the way. She circled Hector, watching his hips in case he shot in to take her to the mat. She did everything he'd told her to. Then Hector smirked and punched her in the face. She fell on her butt for the tenth time and after a moment looked up at him through her ever-healing eyes.

"That was your left again, huh?" she asked mildly.

"What the hell is wrong with you?" he said in a voice that reminded Helen of Mr. Hergeshimer. "You're faster than me. Why don't you get out of my way?"

Helen shrugged and stood up, adopting a defensive stance again. Hector immediately punched her in the gut, and she fell to her knees.

"That's enough, Hector," shouted Lucas in a tight voice. Helen held up a hand, gesturing to Lucas that it was okay as she stood up. Again.

She wanted Lucas to stay out of this. For some reason, Helen's first real sparring session had turned personal for Hector, and she wanted him to go all the way to the end of whatever trip he was on so he could get it out of his system. The punishment hurt, but not nearly as badly as her cramps, so she could deal with it. As soon as she was back on her feet, Hector took them out from under her again with a leg sweep.

"Easy!" yelled Jason. "She's never fought before, you dick-head!"

Helen looked up and saw Jason place a hand on Lucas's shoulder, stopping him from jumping into the cage. "I'm fine, guys. Nothing to worry about," she said as cheerfully as she could, getting up yet again. Hector did not appreciate her tone.

"Why won't you take this seriously?" he shouted at Helen. She bent down to spit out the taste of the blood in her mouth, and Hector reeled back and punched her again in the head.

"Stop it!" screamed Cassandra from someplace beyond Helen's vision. "She isn't a natural fighter, okay? When are you going to get that through your thick skull?"

Helen felt terrible—she knew she must be a bloody mess to get someone who didn't even like her that upset.

By the time Helen had struggled back up to her knees, Cassandra was no longer in the practice room where the Scions kept their punching bags and fight cage. Helen swallowed a mouthful of spit and blood and instantly regretted it when she choked on one of her own teeth.

"May I have some water, please?" she asked Ariadne, who was standing over her with a damp cloth.

On the other side of the cage, Helen saw Jason standing between Lucas and Hector. Jason's shirt was half torn off and blood was running from a cut on his head, but still he fought to keep the two larger Delos boys from ripping each other up like wrapping paper on Christmas morning. Hector was yelling at Lucas, pleading his case.

"She can take anything. Anything! I hit her harder than I've ever hit anyone and she stood right back up! But she won't *hit back!*" Hector roared, his voice cracking with passion. He saw Helen looking at him and pointed an accusing finger at her. "You think you can just stand back and let Luke do all your fighting for you? You're stronger than all of us combined, but you're too good to fight, Princess?"

Jason wrapped both his arms around his brother and held on as Hector bucked and struggled.

"I'm *not* trying to get hit!" Helen lisped through her broken and rapidly regrowing teeth. Ariadne put her own arms around Helen and held her as she stared daggers at her big brother.

"How dare you, Hector? She wasn't raised like we were, always at each other's throats. It just isn't in her," she scolded.

Hector seemed chastened by his sister's tone and finally stopped struggling against Jason's restraint. He slumped against his brother for a moment and then abruptly pushed him away. Then, with one easy leap he jumped over the fifteen-foot-high fence surrounding the fight mat and landed with an intentionally loud slap.

"She'd better *get* it in her. Because I don't want any of the people I love to *die* defending her lazy ass," he rasped. As he walked out of the fight room, Lucas ran to Helen.

"I'm so sorry." He reached out and took Helen from Ariadne's arms. "You don't ever have to fight him again."

"Why not?" Helen asked, pushing off his chest, her speech still slurred from taking too many knocks to the head. "I may not be a natural fighter, but he's right. I need to learn this or someone else could get hurt. Someone like my father, or Claire, or Kate . . . Those women are still after me. They could hurt anyone I care about."

Lucas caught her as she fell over. He looked over her mashed-up face inch by inch as he carried her out of the cage and into a back area that served as both locker room and medical facility.

He sat her on top of a stainless-steel table and left her for just a moment to gather some gauze, a basin of water, and, strangely, a juice box and a jar of raw honey. He didn't say a word, but gestured for her to open her mouth, which she did, and then he started drizzling honey onto her tongue. As soon as her taste buds registered the oily sweet sunshine taste, she understood. Honey was the perfect health food for demigods. A feral need kicked in, and she grabbed his wrist with both her hands and held on until she was licking the jar clean.

When the honey was gone she finally caught her breath. She looked up and met Lucas's eyes, and nodded at his inquisitive look, as if to say that she was better now. Without a word, Lucas pushed a plastic straw into the juice box and gave it to Helen to hold on to as he started in on her cuts with the gauze and some hot water.

Helen was having a hard time seeing straight. Everything was out of focus, and her eyes couldn't seem to get hold of Lucas. It was strange. Her vision kept sliding off his shape, as if it was too slippery for her gaze. She tried to watch Lucas's expression as he doctored her cuts, but it was almost impossible to see him. As the minutes ticked by and Helen healed on her own, Lucas became visible again and Helen could see that the grooves of worry dug into his forehead loosened and went away. He dabbed at the leftover blood and sighed.

"Why didn't you get out of Hector's way, Helen?" he asked softly, breaking the long silence. "Why didn't you block with your hands?"

"He's faster than me," she replied, but they both knew that wasn't the whole truth, and as she took in his skeptical look she continued. "I knew if I started blocking him he'd just get angrier, and then I would eventually have no choice but to hit him so hard he wouldn't be able to hit me back."

"That's sort of the point of fighting, you know," Lucas said with a touch of a smile.

"Then I don't want any part of it," Helen said seriously. "I don't want to hurt people, Lucas. Can't you teach me something else?"

"Like what?" he asked, at a loss.

"Like what you did in the hallway at school that first time we saw each other. How you spun me around and stood between my legs so I couldn't get at you? That didn't hurt me at all, but you still had me beat. Or what you did on your lawn that night. Remember? I was on top of you and then you did that thing with your hips?" she said with building optimism. He nodded and looked away.

"It's called jujitsu. It's for hand-to-hand fighting and I'd rather you never got that close to your opponents. But I'll teach it to you if you want," he said quietly.

Looking up at Lucas, Helen realized she was still seeing spots. She had to brace herself by putting her hands on his waist. As the spots went away she could see the color rising in Lucas's cheeks, and she felt waves of heat coming off his skin. Helen could smell his scent and it made her feel quiet and still, almost drowsy.

"And flying," Helen said, suddenly breaking herself out of her languid mood. "You still have to teach me how to get airborne. Once I learn that, I can just fly away from the bad guys."

"I'll teach you how to fly," he said softly, nodding his head and looking down. Helen searched for his eyes, but he wouldn't look at her. She wiped a hand across her face and it came back streaked with blood.

"Am I really that hideous right now?" she asked as she

leaned away from him, suddenly self-conscious. To Helen's surprise he didn't reply, he just pulled her against him and held her.

"Promise me something," he said into her hair. He waited for her to nod before continuing. "Promise me that next time you fight you're not going to just stand there and let the other guy beat the crap out of you until he's too tired to lift his arms."

"If I can avoid it, believe me, I will," Helen said with a little laugh, but Lucas pulled away from her so he could look her in the eye.

"I won't watch that again. You understand me?" he said sternly.

She nodded slowly and saw his face relax a little. His eyes were so intense she had to glance around for something else to talk about.

"Your shirt," Helen said, pointing to the bloody print of her face on his chest. "Which reminds me. I've ruined these workout clothes Ariadne gave me. Should I change into another set, or are we done?"

"We're done. You can put your street clothes back on after you wash up," he said briskly as if to banish the heavy mood he had fallen into. He took her face in his hands one last time and examined her former cuts. After a few moments he released her. "You certainly do heal fast. But you'll still have some impressive bruises, so if I were you I'd avoid your father for the rest of the night."

"I'll just tell him you abuse me," Helen said with a shrug. She jumped off the examining table.

"And I'll tell him you like it," he teased back, his voice rich and slow. Helen looked up at him, feeling drowsy again. For a moment he was just a breath away from her, but then he backed away.

As he walked out of the locker room he stripped off his bloody shirt and threw it in the garbage. Helen's vision stabilized again, and she watched his bare back moving away from her. The last cobwebs clearing from her eyes, she decided that if Lucas was gay then she was going to have to get a sex change operation. He would be so worth it.

While she cleaned up she got a chance to examine her mouth. Her left front tooth was still in the process of growing back in, and Helen had to laugh at how ridiculous she looked. How Lucas had managed to keep a straight face while he looked at her when she was as gap-toothed as a six-year-old was beyond comprehension. Then she realized he must have seen it so many times that he barely noticed it. Helen thought about what Ariadne had said—that they had grown up "at each other's throats." As if summoned by Helen's thoughts, Ariadne poked her head into the locker room to check in.

"Do you need a hand healing?" she asked timidly.

"No, but come on in," Helen replied. Maybe she would get a chance to ask if Lucas still had a girlfriend somewhere. "How's Cassandra?"

"Overly sensitive, but she'll be okay. You're the one that got a Hector beat-down, and since I know what that feels like I'm going to ask you honestly—is anything still broken?" Ariadne glided into the locker room.

"Nothing broken. Well, not anymore," Helen replied. Everything about Ariadne was so feminine and round and lovely that Helen simply couldn't imagine anyone hitting her. "Do you guys do this to each other often? The fighting, I mean." Ariadne was shaking her head before Helen had even finished talking.

"No. We spar together to stay in shape, but only the boys really fight, and only when they need to get something off their chests. Lucas and Hector do most of the fighting, obviously."

"They don't get along, do they?"

"Yes and no," Ariadne began carefully. "Hector is really proud in general, but he's especially proud of our ancestry and our family. He doesn't like that we've fractured the House of Thebes. Don't get me wrong—he doesn't believe all that crap that the Hundred Cousins do, but he hates to see our House divided. And Lucas feels like it's his responsibility to keep Hector in line because, well, he's the only one who can."

"It must be really difficult being separated from the rest of your family," Helen sympathized.

"We don't have a choice," Ariadne said with a tight smile.

"Is it because of the cult?" Helen asked delicately. "Lucas never got a chance to explain . . ."

"Tantalus and the Hundred Cousins believe that if only one House exists, then they can raise Atlantis," Ariadne said. "That's why our family has always lived right on the water. Boston, Nantucket, Cádiz . . . They're all near the Atlantic Ocean. Scions are drawn to it."

"That's insane!" Helen blurted out before she realized that Ariadne was serious. "I mean, Atlantis is a myth, right?" The thought of a city existing somewhere, deep under the dark, smothering waves made Helen shudder involuntarily. She took a sip of her juice box to cover her violent reaction and waited for Ariadne to continue.

"Is Mount Olympus a myth? Or heaven? It all depends on what you believe, and most Scions believe that Atlantis is real, but the problem is that we can't get there until we accomplish a few things first. See, right after the Trojan War ended, there was a great prophecy made by Cassandra of Troy. She said that if only one Scion House remains, then we can raise Atlantis and claim it as our own land forever. The Hundred Cousins interpret that prophecy to mean that if we demigods earn our entrance into Atlantis then we will become immortal, just like the gods of Olympus."

"Wow," Helen murmured. "Why wouldn't you want that?"

"Tempting, isn't it? Except the problem is that if all four Houses unite, or if there is only one unified House left, then we would be breaking the Truce."

"What truce?"

"The Truce that ended the Trojan War."

"I thought the Greeks won. Didn't they kill all the Trojans and burn Troy to the ground?"

"They certainly did."

"Then if the Greeks won, what do you need a Truce for?"

"Right from the start, there was a third group that fought in the Trojan War." Ariadne smiled at Helen's puzzled look.

"The gods. They chose sides, either with their half-human children or with heroes who had particularly pleased them. Some of the gods even came down from Olympus to fight in the war. They fought against *each other*, and they were deeply invested in the outcome. That complicated everything. The Scions on the Greek side ended up having to make a deal with Zeus."

Ariadne explained that the Trojan War was the most destructive war the ancients had ever seen. This was the first time the separate Houses joined forces to make one giant army. It wiped out most of the Western world, nearly ending civilization as we know it, and it was just as destructive to the gods of Olympus as it was to the humans.

Apollo fought riding in Hector's chariot, Athena fought with Achilles, and Poseidon fought on both sides of the war, changing his mind as often as the tide. Even Aphrodite, the goddess of love, flew down to the battlefield on one occasion to protect Paris, and as she scooped him up to fly him away from certain death, her hand was cut by a Greek blade.

"When her father, Zeus, saw Aphrodite's injury, he forbade her to return to Troy. She disobeyed him, of course, and that enraged Zeus, but not enough to get involved. It wasn't until his daughter Athena and his son Ares nearly sent each other to Tartarus, a hellish place of no return for immortals, that Zeus knew he had to act. The human war was tearing his family apart, and it was threatening his rule over the heavens.

"Zeus's involvement was nearly too late. Ten years had passed since the war began, and all the Olympians were so invested that the only way Zeus could get the gods to stop fighting among themselves was to get the Scions to stop fighting. After ten years of the gods meddling in their affairs, ten years of the gods dragging the war out and making it worse, the only thing that both the Greeks and the Trojans wanted was to be left alone. Zeus had to bargain with the mortals, offering them something they wanted. The humans and the Scions wanted the gods to go back to Olympus and stay there, and in exchange they agreed to end the war.

"Zeus agreed as well. If the Scions ended the war, he didn't care how, he swore on the River Styx that the gods would retreat to Olympus and leave the world alone. But before he sealed his vow he wanted some assurance that such a terrible war would never threaten Olympus again. As he saw it, the Greeks' unification of the Scion Houses in order to fight the Trojans nearly tore Olympus apart. Zeus wanted to make sure that such total involvement never happened again. As he set his seal on the Truce and made his unbreakable vow that the Olympians would leave the earth, he also swore to return and wipe out the Scions if the Houses ever united again."

"It sounds like what happened at the end of World War Two when the Allies divided Germany," Helen remarked. "They broke the country up, hoping to avoid World War Three."

"It's very much like that," Ariadne agreed. "The Fates are obsessed with cycles, and they repeat the same patterns over and over all around the world—especially when it comes to the Big Three—war, love, and family." Ariadne trailed off for a moment, thinking some dark thought, before she finished the story. "Anyway, Troy was betrayed by one of their own and burned to the ground, and after a few months of confusion and tricks and payback—most of which is described in the *Odyssey*—the Olympians finally left the earth. Zeus swore that if the Houses ever united again, he would come back and the Trojan War would pretty much start all over again."

"And it left off somewhere just short of the total destruction of civilization," Helen said, trying to imagine what "the end of civilization" would mean now. "If the Trojan War was so destructive with only swords and arrows, what would happen if it was fought with today's weapons?"

"Yeah. That crossed our minds," Ariadne broke eye contact and looked at her lap. "That's why my family—my father, uncle Castor, and aunt Pandora—separated themselves from the rest of the House of Thebes. Even if Tantalus is right, even if unification is the key to immortality, we didn't think it was worth the total destruction of the earth."

"That's a lot to give up. I mean, it's the right thing to do, obviously, but immortality . . ." Helen shook her head at the thought. "And Tantalus and the Hundred Cousins just let you go?" she asked incredulously.

"What choice did they have? They can't kill us because we're all family, but lately they were starting to threaten us, trying to bully us back to the fold, and some of us—okay, Hector—were starting to fight back. He was *looking* for fights, taking the bait when they called him a coward for not wanting to fight the gods. In our tradition, to kill your own kin is the worst sin imaginable, and he came so close, Helen. My family left Spain because Hector got into a terrible fight and nearly got killed, but worse, he nearly killed someone of his own *blood*. There is no forgiveness for a kin-killer," Ariadne said in a hushed voice.

"But yours *isn't* the last House. Mine is," Helen said, the whole truth beginning to dawn on her.

"No one knew about you. About two decades ago there was this 'Final Confrontation' between the Houses. All Four Houses attacked one another, each of them trying to eliminate the others. The House of Thebes won, and it was thought that the other three, the House of Atreus, the House of Athens, and the House of Rome, were wiped out entirely. But even though everyone else was supposed to be dead, Atlantis wasn't raised and the gods did not return. My father, aunt, and uncle thought that *we* were the ones that were keeping the war at bay by refusing to join Tantalus and his cult. We thought it *had* to be us because no one else was supposed to be left." Ariadne took a deep breath and looked at Helen. "But it was you all along. Somehow your mother hid you here, preserved your House, whichever one it is, and kept the war from starting. She—*you*—also kept Tantalus from attaining Atlantis."

Helen sat in silence for a moment, realizing how many incredibly strong demigods wanted her dead. The Hundred Cousins believed that if the House of Thebes was unified and the only Scion House left on earth, they would become like gods, and Helen's life was the only thing standing in the way. Her life was also the only thing keeping the Olympians from coming back to earth and starting World War Whatever. So the Delos family had to protect her even if they all died doing it. And here she was refusing to learn how to fight. No wonder Hector hated her.

"I'm sorry," Helen finally said, so overwhelmed by her own selfishness that she had almost no emotion in her voice. "Your family is siding with me against your own kin."

"Your burden is heavier," Ariadne said, taking Helen's hand. She was going to say something else, but she was interrupted by Pandora, who burst into the locker room, looking for them.

"Hey! Am I going to have to take someone to the hospital?" she asked, only half joking. "There's a whole lot of blood out there."

"No, she's okay," Ariadne answered back with a laugh as she stood up.

Something was still bothering Helen. There was a hole in the story Ariadne had just told her.

"Who was it?" Helen asked suddenly, looking up at Ariadne's puzzled face. "The way we were taught the story, Odysseus tricked the Trojans with a giant wooden horse. Everyone knows about the Trojan horse. But you said someone *betrayed* Troy, and I don't think it was by mistake."

"I was hoping you wouldn't pick that up," Ariadne said, looking like she was mentally kicking herself. "There was no wooden horse. It's a nice fairy tale, but that's all it is. Odysseus was involved, that's true, but all he did was convince Helen to use her beauty to charm the guards into opening the gates at night. That's really all it took. It's why we Scions never name our children after her. For us, naming your daughter Helen is like a Christian naming their child Judas."

Helen ran past her dad and upstairs when she got home, claiming she wanted to turn in early. She did her homework and then made herself lie down, but she couldn't sleep. Her brain kept sifting through everything Ariadne had told her that afternoon, like how much her mother must have hated her to give her such a cursed name, but mostly she thought about the cult of the Hundred Cousins. To distract herself from reflecting on just how many people would want her dead so that they could live forever, she got out of bed and attempted to fly.

She tried to think lighter, then higher. She even tried to sneak up on it by pretending to trip, but all she succeeding in doing was jumping up and down until her father yelled up the stairs for her to stop clowning around.

Hoping a little ancient history would put her to sleep, she picked up the copy of the *Iliad* that Cassandra had given her and read as much as she could. It seemed like every page was filled with the gods meddling in the world of men. Helen could see why her ancestors had eventually decided that praying for divine intervention wasn't such a good idea. Another she noticed was how much she disliked Helen of Troy. Helen of Nantucket couldn't understand why she didn't just go back to her husband. People were *dying*. Helen promised herself she would never make the same choices her namesake did.

She was up to the part where Achilles, who struck Helen as the world's most celebrated psychopath, started sulking in his tent over a girl when she heard a definite footstep overhead. And then another. Relying on the extrasensory hearing she'd always known she had but only recently begun to let herself use, she zeroed in on her father, listening to his rib cage moving against his chair as he breathed in and out. He was watching the late news on the TV downstairs and he sounded perfectly normal to Helen. The widow's walk above her, however, was now suspiciously silent.

Helen slipped out of bed and grabbed the old baseball bat she kept in her closet. Holding her slugger at the ready she walked sideways, foot over foot, out her bedroom door and to the steps that led to the widow's walk. She paused for a moment on the landing between the stairs that led down to the first floor and the stairs that led up to the roof, listening again for her father. After a few moments of tense indecision, she heard him cluck his tongue at the antics of some camera-greedy congresswoman on TV and she relaxed. He was still okay, so she knew that whatever she had heard had not made it downstairs yet. With the intention of keeping it that way, she ascended the stairs to the widow's walk.

As soon as she stepped outside, Helen felt the cool fall air soak through the thin cotton of her nightshirt, rendering it useless against the elements. A flickering shadow in the starlight caught the corner of her eye and she swung at it, but the top of her bat was stopped before it came around in a full arc. She heard the chunky slap of wood on skin.

"Damn it, it's me!" Hector whispered harshly. Helen saw him hiding in the shadows, shaking out his right hand like it stung.

"What the hell? Hector, is that you?" Helen hissed back. He came closer so she could see him better, avoiding a dark lump on the ground. Helen looked at the lump more carefully and noticed it was her sleeping bag, the one she kept in the water-proof chest her father had given her. "What are you doing?!"

"What does it look like I'm doing?" he responded pee-vishly, still trying to shake the feeling back into his hand.

"Camping?" she said sarcastically. Then it hit her. All of those sounds she'd been hearing at night—sounds she'd thought were the Furies—had a much more mundane source. "You've been up here every night, haven't you?"

"Almost. One of us is always up here at night to watch over you," he said, and then grabbed Helen's arm as she turned away from him in embarrassment. "It's usually Lucas because he's the only one who can fly here," he continued. As if that made it better.

"And you never thought to ask if I wanted you here, eaves-dropping on my dad and me?" she asked, furious.

Hector smiled at her, smothering a laugh. "Yeah. Because I can see how you'd want to keep all those discussions about politics and baseball to yourself. So private," he said, rolling his eyes.

"Do you stay all night while I'm sleeping?" she asked,

unable to look at him. He suddenly understood why she was so upset, and his smile switched off.

"You haven't had a nightmare in a while," he started to say.

"Go home, Hector," Helen said, cutting him off and turning to leave.

"No," he responded immediately, extending his arm across the doorway to block her exit. "I don't care if you're embarrassed. I don't care if you don't want us here. There are a lot of people who'd like to see you dead, Princess, and unfortunately my family *can't* leave you unprotected until I say you can defend yourself."

"Why do *you* get to decide when I'm ready?" Helen crossed her arms and rubbed her shoulders against the cold. The wind off the water had teeth.

"Because everyone knows that I'm the only one who won't go easy on you. And just so you know, I'm not about to apologize for making sure you don't get kidnapped by one of those batty women running around the island," he warned. Helen's teeth chattered. He looked at her standing there shivering and Helen could have almost sworn that he looked guilty for a second. Then he looked off to the side and cursed to himself. "But *maybe* we should have told you that we were sleeping up here," he admitted finally.

"You think? I get it, Hector. I'm in a lot of danger. But you should have at least given me a heads-up about this."

"All right! Point taken!" he said, nearly growling with frustration. "But we're still not leaving you or your father unguarded at night."

Suddenly, Helen wasn't angry anymore. In fact, knowing

that Hector and his family extended their protection to her father made her feel ridiculously grateful. She stood there smiling at him for a second.

"Thank you," she said quietly.

He froze midbreath and stared at her, amazed that her mood had changed so quickly. "That's it? No more arguing?" he asked doubtfully.

"Why, do you *want* to—" she began, but she was interrupted by her father's voice from downstairs.

"Lennie?" Jerry called from the hallway in front of Helen's bedroom. She had been so distracted by Hector she had forgotten to listen for her dad.

"Yeah!" Helen called down, motioning desperately for Hector to get away from the door. She changed places with him and made it inside just in time.

"Are you sleeping up there again?" Jerry asked when he saw Helen shutting the door to the roof and coming down the steps. "It's way too cold out, Helen."

"Do you have any idea how late it is? Go to sleep," she scolded as she hurried past him.

"I know, I'm going to bed right now . . . Hey! *You* go to sleep," Jerry scolded back, belatedly remembering that he was the parent.

As Helen jumped into bed and burrowed into her comforter, she could have sworn she heard Hector chuckling softly to himself up on the widow's walk.

# TEN

MAJORCA, SPAIN

Creon watched the reporter for five minutes before he decided to uncloak himself from the shadows. He appeared out of the darkness behind her, barely a step away. She spun around and inhaled a startled breath so quickly it almost sounded like a sob. There was something exhilarating about seeing a woman afraid, Creon thought, especially when that woman was a pushy bitch like this one. A little fear is good; it reminded non-Scion mortals of their place, and Creon wanted this mortal in particular to remember that she might be able to force this meeting by threatening to have the police investigate his family, but she wasn't in control.

That's why he picked the docks at night. He wanted to see how committed she truly was to writing a story on his family. The fact that she met him there proved she had a spine, if not a brain, and because of that Creon decided she deserved a moment of his time. Besides, she made such a pleasant sound when she was startled. Maybe he would hear it again.

He smiled down at her innocently, as if to let her know that he was just playing a little trick. She met his eye, but she also took a step back—which meant she was brave but scared. Creon liked to see those two emotions together; it made him feel like he had won something.

"Again, I ask for the father but instead I get the son," she said in accented English.

"I speak perfect Spanish," Creon replied in her native language, still smiling at her. "And you know my father doesn't meet reporters."

"Your father doesn't meet anyone. That's why I'm here," she continued stubbornly in English. He shrugged impassively, refusing to take the bait. She crossed her arms and studied him. "Tantalus Delos hasn't let anyone see him in almost twenty years now. Strange, no?"

"He likes his privacy," Creon said through a grin that had grown tight.

"Privacy is the one luxury a billionaire aristocrat can't buy. You've heard the stories about your father, yes?"

"They're all lies," Creon said as smoothly as he could, but her eyes were so doubtful he nearly faltered. *How dare she?*

Over the years there had been many stories floating around the tabloids about his father—that he had been maimed, that he had lost his mind to an obsessive-compulsive disorder like Howard Hughes, that he was dead. Creon knew at least that his father was alive, and he had vehemently denied all of the other accusations time and time again. But the truth was, Creon hadn't seen or spoken to his father in nineteen years. *No one* had seen Tantalus except Creon's mother, Mildred Delos.

His mother insisted that Tantalus was in hiding in order to protect himself and the House of Thebes, but she never could explain to Creon why his father wouldn't call him on the phone, not even once. It seemed like such a little thing to ask.

"All lies? You know this for certain?" the reporter pressed as soon as she saw Creon fall into his own conflicted thoughts. Creon noticed that she kept speaking in English, almost as if she was taunting him. "For years now, you, your mother, your whole family, say all these things are lies, but how do you know for true? Tell me, Creon, when is the last time *you* saw your father? I know he was not at your graduation from university."

Creon gritted his teeth. "My father is a very private man. He—"

"Pssh!" she exclaimed derisively, cutting Creon off with an imperious wave of her hand. She shouldn't have done that. "This is not privacy, this is lunacy! Can any man's *privacy* mean so much that he would abandon his only son simply to stay out of the papers?"

Creon's hand shot out and he had her by the throat before

she could even raise an arm in protest. She had such a tiny throat, so slender and fragile. Creon thought it was like holding a thin kitten in his hand. Her eyes blossomed with fear. The pupils opened up and reflex tears beaded on their dark surface like dew. She was lovely in terror—a perfect, pleading mask of alabaster white skin, wide eyes, and, best of all, her mouth, an open oval of red surprise like she was waiting to be kissed. Creon wanted to hold her like that for days, but a split second of enjoyment later he heard a snap.

Like a switched-off TV, the light in her eyes contracted to pinpricks, and then went completely dark.

Creon dumped her body in the water and ran back to the citadel so quickly no normal person could see him pass, even if they were standing inches away.

Still shaking with a half-sickening thrill, he went straight up to his room, and froze when he opened the door. His mother was waiting for him. She was sitting next to his packed suitcase with her narrow, manicured hands folded neatly in her lap, holding something. Her head fell to the side as she stared at him. His mother only needed to look at him to know that the meeting that she had arranged, the meeting that was supposed to be nothing more than a polite gesture, had ended violently.

"Did you have to kill her?" she asked seriously and without reproach. Mildred was nothing if not practical.

"She provoked me," Creon said as he moved past his mother and grabbed the handle of his suitcase. "Besides, it's better this way and you know it."

Mildred dropped her eyes and nodded, accepting that her son was right. More than one reporter had "disappeared" over the years.

"Given the situation, I approve of you leaving the country for a while." She held up the plane ticket she had taken from the front pocket of his suitcase and waved it at him before he could bolt out of the room. He stopped dead, realizing that he had been caught. "What I *don't* approve of is your choice of destination. What do you think you're going to accomplish by going there? Your father forbade the Hundred to go anywhere near Nantucket."

He took a breath to calm himself down. It didn't work. "It's *their* fault we don't have what is rightfully ours, it has to be, because all the other Houses are gone! I have to know how they can live with themselves when they've sentenced the rest of their family to inevitable death. Immortality is my birthright, and regardless of what my father allows or forbids, I will *not* sit back while they deny me that!"

Creon shouldered his carry-on, wheedled the ticket out of his mother's reluctant hands, and moved past her. He hurried down the ancient stone steps at the back of the citadel, his heart still pumping with excitement.

Outside, there was a nondescript black sedan waiting. His mother's driver was behind the wheel, ready to take him to the airport. Creon realized that Mildred had known all along that he would kill that girl. She had probably known he would do it the moment she arranged for Creon to meet her.

"Son?" she called out to him from under the arched gate.

"Did you kill her just to have a reason to leave?"

He turned and faced her, forcing patience. "Did you send me there to kill her?"

His mother smiled at him, but her eyes were far away and out of focus—thinking many thoughts at once. She walked toward him slowly, making him wait for her even though she had to know that he was vibrating with adrenaline. She stepped close to him and looked up into his face. Her elegantly sculpted lips were pulled tight in a thin line of warning.

"Stay away from Hector."

Wednesday morning, Helen ran out of the house and toward Lucas's waiting car before Jerry could get it into his head to come out and "have a talk with that young man," as he had been threatening. Helen wasn't entirely sure if her dad was serious or if he was just trying to get a rise out of her, but she wasn't about to take any chances. It wouldn't be fair to put Lucas through the traditional parental screening when they weren't even officially dating.

"Ready?" she asked quickly, trying to distract Lucas.

"Should we wait?" Lucas asked when he saw Jerry standing in the front door.

"No, just drive. Quick! I don't know if he's really going to do it or not," Helen responded desperately as she waved good-bye to her father.

"Do what?" he asked. He put the car in gear and drove out.

"Try and talk to you, man-to-man," Helen said, relieved.

"Well, in that case," Lucas said. He hit the brakes and shifted into reverse.

"What are you doing?" Helen put her hand over his to stop him from shifting.

"I'm going to go inside and talk to your dad. I don't want him to feel like he can't trust me with his daughter."

"Lucas, I swear to whatever god you think is holy that I will get out of this car and walk to school if you go inside and talk to my dad."

Lucas smiled and shifted back into first, driving away from her house. "Who told you the gods were holy?" he asked with a sinister glint in his eyes. Helen punched him on the arm.

"You just did that to see me freak out, didn't you?" she asked indignantly.

"Hey, you're the one embarrassed by her own father. You're pretty cute when you panic," he said with a huge smile.

Helen tried to smile back at him, but it came out all mangled on her lips. She had no idea what to think. The use of the word *cute* could either encourage her hopes, or eulogize them.

Every person who recognized them honked and waved with a big smile on their face. Honking at passing friends was customary on the island, and it was something that Helen had grown up with, but it seemed to her as if everyone was leaning on their horns for an extra-long time this morning.

"So, listen," Lucas said, changing the tone from playful to something a little more serious. "Hector told me you found him on your roof."

"Yeah," Helen replied, trying to scrunch down in her seat so no one could see her. "About that . . ."

"I wanted to explain why we didn't tell you before. I asked to be the one to tell you, and I meant to," he said. He glanced over at her as if to check how Helen felt about what he was saying. "I just didn't figure out *how* to tell you in time. I didn't want you to think I was some shady stalker hiding out on your roof."

"I'm not going to lie—well, I can't lie to you, can I?" Helen said with a grin. "I was a little upset, but I'm fine about it now. If your family is willing to protect mine, I guess I can put up with a little shadiness."

Helen was forced to stop talking because someone was honking out "Shave and a Haircut" in the most intrusive way possible. She wanted to tell whomever it was to kiss off, but she couldn't. These were her neighbors and she had to be polite. She wasn't cramping up, but she suspected that she might start to. She stuck a fist into her stomach.

"What's going on?" Lucas asked intently. "I've seen you do that before. Are you in pain?"

"No, but I think I might be soon. Don't worry about it, there's nothing you can do. Well, I guess you could go away and never hang out with me again," Helen answered.

"That's not going to happen," he said with raised eyebrows. "But what are you talking about? Are you allergic to me or something?"

"No." Helen laughed. "I think I'm allergic to attention. And we tend to draw a lot of it when we're together."

"But it's not just me, right? You feel those pains even when I'm not around?"

"Yes. I've had this all my life. I don't know exactly what causes it, I just know that sometimes when people stare at me I get a terrible pain in my stomach."

"Allergic to attention," Lucas said to himself, absentmindedly taking Helen's hand while he thought. He had to let it go to shift as he parked at school, but as soon as they were out of the car he claimed her hand again and rolled her fingers around in his.

Helen watched Lucas as they stood at her locker together. He seemed distracted. His brow was furrowed and his gaze tuned in, but most disturbingly he seemed to be all blurry.

"What is that you're doing? It's giving me a headache," Helen said quietly while she turned the combination on her lock.

"Sorry," he said as he snapped back into focus. "I'm bending the light. It happens sometimes when I'm concentrating."

Helen remembered from her reading that Apollo was the god of Light, and at that moment Lucas was doing things with light that were impossible outside of a magic show. She realized she had seen him do this before in the locker room at his house, but she had taken so many knocks to the head at the time she thought it was just her vision that was off.

"Aren't you worried someone will notice?"

"Actually, sometimes I do this to make people stop noticing me when I want some privacy to think. People have a hard time forcing themselves to look at things that they can't see clearly, or things that shouldn't be possible."

"Because their eyes slide right off," Helen interjected, remembering how her gaze was diverted from Lucas's face in the locker room even though she had really tried to focus on him.

"Exactly. If I look far away or too hard to see, most people just block me out," he said, and then he gave her a knowing smile. "You slouch to get people to stop staring at you. I blur. It's useful in a fight, too, only it's nearly impossible to do when you're moving fast."

"Are you giving me all your fight secrets?" Helen said cheekily as she put her books in her bag and shut her locker. "Not so smart, Houdini."

"Really? Well, come and get me, *Sparky*," he said with a grin as he backed away.

*Sparky?* Helen thought, puzzled. But he was already through the double doors at the end of the hall and she had to go to class.

When the bell for first lunch rang she rushed as fast as she could, intending to get some answers, but by the time she made it to the cafeteria, Ariadne was already seated at the geek table, surrounded by admirers.

Helen shouldn't have been surprised that Ariadne would join their table, considering she was in all the AP classes. Unfortunately for Matt, Ariadne's presence usually attracted an entourage of boys—the little lambs to her Mary. Helen tried to fight her way into the circle, and nearly gave up before she was spotted by Ariadne.

"Zach? Can you make a little room for Helen, please?" Ariadne asked as she flashed a dazzling smile.

"Don't worry about it, Zach. She can have my seat," Claire said in a caustically cheerful voice, vacating the place next to Ariadne.

Claire brushed close to Helen as she passed, whispering something about the "old friends" not being cool enough to sit at the same lunch table when *someone* suddenly has a popular boyfriend. Before Helen could get into a well-deserved fight with Claire, Ariadne pulled Helen down next to her to stop one of the hormone-infested boys from getting any closer to her.

By the time the bell rang for classes, all of Helen's normal friends had been driven away from the table—a table that had been theirs since freshmen year. Matt's sad look made Helen wonder how long it had been since the two of them had been able to talk. It must have been months.

Claire wasn't waiting for her at the trail when track practice started. It was silly for her to try to avoid Helen by leaving without her, because they both knew that she could catch up with Claire no matter how far behind she was, but the intent was clear. When Helen came jogging up, Claire didn't even turn to look at her.

"Just keep running, Hamilton. I am so not into you right now," Claire said as she veered away and raised her arm in a "talk to the hand" gesture.

From many years of experience Helen knew that Claire

needed to punish her a little before she'd be ready to move forward. Then they'd talk on the phone, make up, and the next day everything would be back to normal. Just this one time, Helen wished they could skip to the end of the fight, especially since she hadn't done anything, but she knew better than to rush Claire. Instead, Helen dutifully ran past her.

After a few minutes of running alone, Helen started to get bored with the mortal pace. She looked at her watch to calculate exactly how much time she would need to kill before making her way back to the trailhead, and took off across the moors at an impossible speed. She knew Lucas could simply step up into the air and start flying, but so far that approach hadn't worked for her. Maybe she needed to be running to get airborne, kind of like an airplane. Here was a chance to test that theory.

As Helen struck out off the trail and through the marshy land surrounding Miacomet Pond, she began to sense the lightness she associated with flight. There was a fluttery feeling in her stomach, a barely contained wildness that she assumed was an expression of Scion power. She felt static energy running over her skin. It was as if she had rubbed a balloon over her entire body and then held it just far enough away so that her whole surface felt the outward tug of an electrical field.

Taking an experimental leap, Helen soared up into the air. At first she thought she had done it, that she was flying, but she soon felt herself reach the top of a very large arc and begin to descend. She had merely jumped higher than ever before—too high—and her brain was still hardwired to believe that when she hit the ground she would go splat and die.

She tried to grab at the air, and although there was a part of her that knew how to make it hold her, she was either too scared or not scared enough to do the trick in time. She hit the ground at an angle and went into a skid, her feet digging up two loamy troughs in the mud.

She was fine, of course, but still deeply shaken. Her knees were wobbly and she had to laugh to let out the crazy feeling flapping around inside her chest. After she had calmed down a bit she hauled herself up off her butt. She pulled her feet out of the mud and started to walk back toward the school, feeling like a jackass. She was covered in smelly muck up to her waist, and in her head she pictured how she must have looked as she came down from her leap, her arms pinwheeling frantically like a cartoon character falling off a cliff.

She glanced around to make sure no one had spotted her in her moment of foolishness, just out of habit, but she wasn't expecting anyone to be near. Her heart turned over when she saw a dark smudge turn into a man's shape. Then he suddenly stopped and changed direction just over the next rise. He had seen her get up and walk away laughing after falling from fifty feet high. Worse than that, Helen could see there was something wrong with the way he moved. He was going much too fast to be human.

Her entire body tensed instinctively. Without even

thinking about it she took off after the dark shape. Whoever he was, he was headed back toward the high school—back toward Claire, who was probably huffing and puffing along, slow and small and human. The image of Kate lying unconscious on the ground flashed through her head and spurred Helen to run faster. She skipped over massive swaths of landscape, bounding recklessly over hillocks and cranberry bogs, unable to think of anything but catching him.

She noticed that she was having a hard time finding him in the strange shadowy light, but as she got closer, the darkness that seemed to swath itself around him abated a little and she was able to pinpoint his location. It looked like he was sucking light out of the air. There was something creepy about the way the dark shadows radiated out from him like a sinister halo—he was definitely controlling the light. That meant he was another descendant of Apollo—one of the Hundred Cousins from the House of Thebes, and therefore a threat.

From what she could see, the shadowy man was a few years older than she was, but still barely out of his teens. When she was only a few paces behind him she could see that he had fair hair and skin. With a fresh burst of speed she reached out, trying to grab on to him, and ripped off his shirt. Finally, he allowed the last of the darkness clinging to him to be swept away by the sun glowing on his huge, bare shoulders. Up close, he looked so similar to Hector in both coloring and build that they could have been twins, except for their faces. There was a hollow look to this man, a cragginess that made him seem sickly.

A horrendous cramp crumpled up her torso like origami, and Helen tumbled to the ground with a scream. She curled up on the ground in the fetal position, unable to move or even take a breath. Through the long blades of grass that partially obscured her vision she could see the blond, shirtless Cousin trot back toward her with an inquisitive look on his face.

"Interesting," he said with a cocky smile. Something behind Helen caught his eye and he started to back away. "I'll see you sooner rather than later, *preciosa*," he promised as he ran off, a dark, ominous mist collecting to obscure his outline.

Helen tried to shout something tough and ballsy after him, but all that came out was a pathetic moan. He was gone in a second, and she was left to lie there alone until she was noticed or until she was well enough to walk away. Finally, she heard someone approach.

"Helen?" a familiar voice said as it neared. "Oh, no. It *is* you."

"Matt," Helen grunted. "Get Lucas."

He came around into Helen's field of vision and got down on his knees in front of her. "Don't you think the nurse would be a better idea? Or maybe a paramedic?"

"Please. Lucas. Quick."

He sighed once, rubbed Helen's back in an awkwardly reassuring way, and then got up and ran off. Once she got her breathing under control, Helen could see enough around her to take in the fact that she was practically in the school parking lot—much closer to the school than she had realized. Still curled up in a ball on the ground, Helen banged her forehead against her knees. She couldn't believe she had been that stupid. Her ear pressed to the ground, Helen heard approaching footsteps that were a little too heavy and a little too quick to be a normal's and smiled to herself with relief even though she was still in terrible pain.

"Thanks, Matt," she heard Lucas say from somewhere behind her. "Where are you hurt?" he asked her as he came around toward the front, Jason close behind him. Helen pointed to her stomach and spoke with her eyes. Lucas nodded and looked around, confused.

"Did you see what happened?" he asked Matt.

"I think she was running after someone. I don't know," Matt said skeptically. "I just heard from Gretchen that Helen was chasing some guy, then she screamed and fell down."

"Is that true?" Lucas asked Helen with a tense face. She nodded, and he smiled back at her, his worried eyes softening for her sake. He plucked some of her hair off her sweaty forehead and looked back over his shoulder.

"I'm on it," said Jason too quietly for an ordinary mortal to catch, and then Helen heard his rapidly retreating footsteps.

"I should go with him," began Hector's voice from someplace that Helen still couldn't see.

"No, you shouldn't," ordered Lucas sharply. "I need you to get the girls. They could have whatever sickness Helen has, and they might need you. Right?"

"Right," Hector said without bitterness, suddenly

understanding Lucas's hidden meaning. Cassandra and Ariadne were unaware, unprotected, and therefore in the most danger of being attacked by the stranger. Hector ran off so silently that Helen couldn't even hear his feet brush against the grass, and she couldn't help but be both impressed and a little frightened by his skill.

"Matt, can you help me get Helen up? If you could just grab her feet . . ." Lucas asked in an apologetic voice.

"Sure, no problem," Matt said as he slipped his hands behind her knees. "Jeez, Len, you smell awful! Did you have to fall into every cranberry bog on the island?" Helen chuckled briefly, but it hurt to laugh so she stopped.

Helen initially wondered why Lucas would ask Matt for help when he didn't need it, but as she listened to them talk and work together to carry her to Hector's SUV she realized that Lucas had to be one of the smartest people she'd ever met. Not only did asking for help make Lucas seem normal, but it also made Matt feel needed. Lucas was treating him like a partner and, more important, like a man. Helen knew that if Lucas ever asked for Matt's loyalty, this simple gesture of inclusion made it more likely that he would get it. A fresh bout of pain gripped her so tightly that a sweat broke out on her upper lip. Helen blew out her breath slowly, trying to navigate her way through the pain.

Lucas popped the back hatch of the SUV and laid Helen down, then asked if Matt didn't mind waiting with them until his sister and cousins came back.

"If Helen gets any worse, I'm not going to wait for them,

I'm just going to take her to the hospital. If that happens, I'd really appreciate it if you stayed here to tell them where I went. It shouldn't take long," Lucas explained.

"I'll stay as long as you need me," Matt offered with his usual generosity.

"Damn, Matt. Aren't you tired of watching over my sick ass yet?" Helen asked him with a half smile.

"You have no idea," he said back with a smile of his own. It faded quickly. "This makes it twice this year. You never used to get sick, Len, not even that time we all got the stomach flu after Gretchen's birthday party in fourth grade. The rest of us were puking our brains out for two days, but you were fine."

"Oh, yeah! That was so gross! Hey, at least I brought you all Gatorade and crackers, remember?" Helen said playfully. She was trying to lighten the mood, but she was still in pain. She pressed on her belly again and Matt frowned. He was worried, and so was she. Her cramps had never lasted this long before.

"Maybe you should quit track," Matt suggested suddenly.

"I think Matt's right," Lucas said, his face both surprised and pleased that Matt had suggested it. "It's obviously not good for you. You should quit."

Helen was too stunned to respond. She stared at Lucas with her mouth hanging open until Hector, Cassandra, and Ariadne arrived and ended the conversation. The girls got in the SUV with Lucas and Helen, and Hector took the keys to the Mercedes, saying he would wait for Jason. Ariadne offered

Matt a ride home in her sweetest voice, but he demurred. Then, after a brief and very quiet exchange between Lucas and Hector, Lucas got behind the wheel and drove the three girls to the Delos compound, speeding the whole way. As they drove, Cassandra climbed into the back and perched next to Helen with a calm poise that belied her age.

"Did you get a good look at him?" she asked in a level, strangely adult voice.

"Yes," Helen answered.

"If I showed you some pictures, would you be able to recognize him?"

"Like, mug shots? No problem," Helen said positively. "I'm pretty sure there aren't that many guys in the world who look exactly like a bigger, blonder version of Hector but with a scary, pockmarked face."

She sensed the mood in the SUV shift.

"Creon," whispered Cassandra.

"Are you sure?" Lucas asked, his head snapping up to look into the rearview mirror at Cassandra.

"Yes," she answered with a dreamy look on her face. "And Uncle Pallas followed him here from Europe. He's at home." Lucas apparently didn't need any more information. He fished his cell phone out of his jeans and hit speed dial.

"Jase, come in. Cassie can see him now," he said in a flat, frightened voice. He listened for just a moment and then continued, talking over Jason's questions. "When we all get back home. Your father's waiting for us there."

Helen felt like she had missed an important detail. "Who's

Creon?" she asked Cassandra as soon as she was able to sit up.

"A cousin of ours," Cassandra answered unhelpfully.

"He's the one who attacked Hector in Cádiz," Ariadne said, her voice quivering momentarily. She glanced over at Lucas, who was just about to interrupt her, and kept going. "Okay, they attacked each other. Creon is a radical fanatic, and he's looking for a fight with any of the moderates, not just us. But it's Hector he's really after. Not even you can deny that, Luke."

"That guy, huh?" Helen asked, folding her arms over her belly as she tried to make a joke. No one laughed. Her right hand felt stiff so she flexed it. A scrap of fabric fell from her balled-up fist.

"What's that?" Cassandra asked.

"Um. It's Creon's. I caught up to him, and when I tried to grab him I sort of ripped his shirt off," Helen replied apologetically.

"*You* chased *him*, caught up to him, and got close enough to rip his shirt off?" Ariadne said in disbelief. Apparently, Creon was fast, even by their standards.

"He saw me trying to fly, okay?" Helen began, sensing that she had done something very wrong. "I didn't know who he was, I just knew that he'd seen me jump about five stories into the air and I had to get to him before he got away."

"Great," Cassandra said bitterly. "He came here to check on our family and maybe pick a fight with Hector, but now that you've exposed yourself everything has changed."

"He was heading right for the school," Helen said defensively.

"And what was he going to do?" Cassandra yelled back, suddenly furious. "Attack a pathetic normal? Use your head, Helen! For some reason the two women who attacked you haven't told the rest of the Hundred Cousins that you exist, probably because they want the glory of killing you alone so they can have a Triumph. Creon might be thinking the same way, but if he isn't, he *will* tell Tantalus. That means half of the Family is going to be here in a few days—and you can't even hold a sword yet!"

"Back off, Cassie!" Lucas said heatedly. "We were raised for this, and Helen's had what? A whole week to adjust?" He looked at Cassandra through the rearview mirror, and even in reflection his eyes looked intense. Cassandra threw up her hands in surrender.

"You're right, Cassandra. I didn't use my head," Helen said, rubbing her stomach. "Maybe we could talk to him."

Ariadne made a strangled sound.

"What? Why are you all so scared of him?" Helen asked.

"He's a Shadowmaster," Ariadne said ominously from the front seat. "He can stop light. It's unnatural."

Helen thought about the darkness that wrapped itself around Creon and she knew what Ariadne meant. The sun wouldn't shine on him, and Helen had instinctively felt like there was something wrong about that.

"Shadowmasters are rare," Lucas tried to explain a bit more calmly, but Helen could still hear the fear in his voice.

"There haven't been very many of them in our House's history, but every one of them that we know about has turned out to be, well . . . evil."

A few tense minutes passed with Cassandra cupping her hands over her eyes in a posture of deep concentration. Finally, she looked up at Helen, and with a determined smile she dispelled the lingering negativity.

"Well, you're safe for now. I don't see any immediate threats," she said reassuringly, watching Helen cradle her still-tender midsection. "Any idea which human saw you chasing Creon?"

"Gretchen. Don't worry, no one will care. She's always saying stuff about me," Helen said positively. "Wait a sec. How do you know someone saw me?"

"These cramps you're having? They're the curse. Your mom cursed you to feel almost unendurable pain if you use your Scion powers in front of ordinary mortals," Cassandra said with a shrug.

"Is *that* what it is? It's been driving me crazy all week!" Lucas said from the front seat as he turned down the long Delos driveway.

"Of course you wouldn't recognize them. You're a boy," Ariadne said. "Curse Cramps are sadistic, really. I haven't even *read* about anyone doing it in centuries."

"My mother cursed me?" Helen repeated back to Cassandra, who nodded sadly.

"Way back, hundreds of years ago, it was thought to be the only way to keep women Scions in line with the society of the time. Mothers would do it to their daughters to keep them from drawing too much attention to themselves because women weren't supposed to be special or smart or talented." Cassandra wrinkled her nose, like she had said something that smelled bad as it came out of her mouth.

Helen sputtered uselessly to herself for a few seconds, unable to process what she had just learned. Cassandra took Helen's hand and smiled kindly at her. "If it's any consolation, the curse probably kept you hidden all these years."

"As much as I hate to admit anything so barbaric could be useful, I have to agree," said Ariadne as she opened her door and got out of the car. "If you hadn't been cursed, can you imagine what your mortal dad would have gone through when you were a toddler with all that strength? He tries to punish you, you throw him out a window. Bedtime would have been a bloodbath."

"Well, when you put it that way," Helen admitted as she climbed out of the back, accepting Lucas's politely offered hand. As she and Lucas walked side by side behind Ariadne and Cassandra toward the house, she started to laugh to herself.

"What is it?" he asked.

"I always knew my mother hated me, and now I find out that she literally cursed me," she replied, hearing her voice sound matter-of-fact. "I don't think I've ever heard anything that made so much sense in my whole life."

"Your mother was trying to protect you," Lucas countered judiciously.

"Oh, you are such a boy! You've never had cramps," Helen muttered. They paused on the landing.

"Maybe take your shoes off," Lucas said, looking down at Helen's feet. She was caked in black marsh mud all the way up to her waist.

"Maybe get a hose," Helen countered with a laugh.

"I can do better than a hose," he said with an easy grin, pulling on her hand to follow him to the pool. "Outdoor showers are sort of a requirement for our family."

He brought her to the outdoor shower and left her there to go to the pool house to get some towels and a change of clothes. When he was completely out of sight she self-consciously stripped down in the shower area. The beautiful teak walls of the shower curved around in a spiral that screened off the important parts of her body, but her feet and the very top of her head were still visible.

She'd taken millions of beach showers like this, but never without wearing a swimsuit. She washed as quickly as she could and was nearly finished by the time Lucas returned.

"The T-shirt's definitely mine, but I have no idea who the sweatpants belong to. Don't worry about it, though. No one will care," he said, flipping the clothes and a big beach towel over the top of the screen. Then he put a plastic shopping bag down on the ground. "That's for your uniform and sneakers."

"Thanks," Helen called out, painfully aware how little space stood between him and her naked body. It was silly, really. Everyone is naked under a few millimeters of clothes, but this felt different somehow. It felt dangerous. She watched his feet through the gap at the bottom of the screen as he began to turn away, hesitated, and then hurried off. She let out a breath she didn't realize she'd been holding.

The clothes he'd left her were gigantic, but they were soft, comfortable, and they smelled like dryer sheets. She toweled off, put the borrowed outfit on, and came out of the shower area carrying her bag of dirty clothes.

By the time she and Lucas made it into the house, Jason and Hector were sitting at the kitchen table watching Cassandra and Ariadne shower a man Helen didn't know with affection. Lucas introduced Helen before giving his uncle a big hug.

Pallas Delos was a large, blond man, still glowing with health and youth even though he was graying at the temples. He and Hector shared the same cautious smile and sharp eyes, but there was more of Jason's and Ariadne's prettiness about him than Hector's blunt masculinity. He shook Helen's hand politely, but his curious stare followed her long after the introduction was over and it began to make Helen feel uncomfortable. She wondered if he was just reacting to her taboo name or if he had heard unflattering things about her from someone in the family. His stare made Helen jumpy. She tried to hide herself behind Lucas.

"Okay, everybody out. I have to get started on dinner," Noel ordered as she entered the kitchen, waving her hands in a shooing motion. Helen found herself being pulled out the back door by Lucas.

"It's a good idea to stay out of my mom's way when she gets like that or you'll end up chopping vegetables for the next hour," he said. He led her back outside toward the grassy lawn between the tennis courts and the pool.

"I don't mind helping," Helen said, starting to head back toward the house.

"I do," Lucas said with a sly smile, tugging on her hand. "Besides, I thought you wanted to learn how to fly. Isn't that what caused all the fuss earlier this afternoon?"

Helen could tell he was upset and trying not to show it. "About that," she began, scrunching her face up guiltily.

"Yeah, that was bad. And it was all my fault. I should have taught you to fly as soon as we healed from our fall, but I didn't trust . . ." he said, stopping himself and shaking his head ruefully. "Never mind. The point is, once I learned I could fly all I wanted to do was get back in the air. I couldn't sleep, I couldn't eat. It was stupid of me to think you would wait."

"How old were you when you found out?" Helen asked.

"Ten? But it took me a while to understand it," he said as if to prepare her for something. "Scions are born with all their talents, but it takes time to discover how to use some of them. Especially if there's no one with your particular talent to act as a mentor."

"Did you have one? A mentor, I mean."

"No. I don't know any other Scions who can fly besides you. But I had books, and my family for support." He pulled up and stopped to face Helen. "You never had any of that, so this might be a little harder for you."

"I'm good at hard, it's easy I've never trusted," she responded quickly, but he gave her a look that indicated he thought she had missed his point.

"I just don't want you to get discouraged if this takes us a while. So before we start, I have to explain some things," he said, suddenly all business. "Strength, speed, agility, acute hearing and eyesight, beauty, rapid healing, and intelligence, although that last one's debatable, these are all gifts that pretty much every Scion has, and we don't have to be trained to use them. But there's another group of talents that are rare, and most of them take some work. Flying is one of the rare ones. And it's one of the hardest to get the hang of."

"I honestly don't care how hard it is to master this. I don't care if this takes me years. I'm just dying to do it again!" Helen bounced up and down on her toes impatiently.

"Okay, okay! First of all, you have to hold still. The jumping part comes later when you want speed," he said with a laugh as he put his hands on Helen's waist.

She gasped faintly at the unexpected touch, and tried to make herself stand still like he had said, but it wasn't easy. They stood for a few moments, just staring at each other.

"Close your eyes," he whispered. Helen's heart was racing and she had a feeling Lucas could hear it.

"Calm down," he said, smiling with his eyes closed. "Try and slow your pulse down if you can."

"I'm trying. Do you have to stand so close?" Helen asked, her voice thin and shaky.

"Yes. I don't want you to get away from me. That would be bad," he said in a deadpan voice, maintaining his concentration. A few seconds passed. When he next spoke he sounded very calm and far away.

"Now. Focus on your body. Take a deep breath and follow it in, like your brain is floating gently inside that air you're breathing." He waited a few moments for Helen to get to where he was.

It took her a few breaths, but eventually she was able to do it. He knew exactly when she was ready. "Good. Now you're inside of yourself," he said triumphantly. "Can you feel the weight of you, all stacked up and all tied together?"

She did feel it. She could feel the weight of her skin on top of her muscles on top of her bones, all stacked up, just like he had said. There were millions and millions of little bits of her, all marching around like soldiers with different but cohesive orders. Those were her cells, she realized at once. She giggled, thinking how strange it was to be this massive army and never feel it. She heard Lucas laugh, too, and she knew that he was right there with her, experiencing what she was experiencing.

"Now I want you to do something really hard," he said, his voice light and curious, almost childlike. "I want you to stay inside, but also look out, if you can. Don't be scared. I'm right here with you."

Helen did as he told her, but the sensation was way too intense to process.

She had lost her sunglasses once. She'd looked all over, in

the kitchen, the living room, back up in her bedroom, but she couldn't find them anywhere. It was annoying because she knew she had just had them in her hand, but she couldn't remember what she'd done with them. Then her dad told her that her sunglasses were on top of her head.

In that moment she realized that she had been using the wrong sense. She had been looking when she should have been feeling. She reached up and felt her glasses with her hand, but she also felt them with her scalp, and when she thought about it she realized that she had been feeling her glasses up there the whole time. She'd just been so busy *looking* she hadn't thought to *feel*.

This was similar. Again, she was realizing that there were many different ways to experience the world around her. Now she was still aware of all of her millions of cells, but she could also feel something new. She felt herself falling toward something truly huge, and she knew she had another sense that could stop the falling.

Scared out of her mind, she instinctively pushed with this new sense. She needed to put some distance between her little army and the big, fast monster she was falling toward—the monster she suddenly realized she had been falling toward every second of every day of her life.

A moment too late to stop herself, Helen realized that the monster was the earth, and the falling sensation was gravity—and that what she had just done was switch it off. Vertigo sucked at her, pulling her off balance. She grabbed on to Lucas, frantically burying her face against his chest.

He was the only unmovable object in the entire universe, and if Helen let him go of him she knew she would spin off into space forever and ever.

"It's okay," he whispered into her ear. His breath was warm, and his voice soothed her. "I won't let you go, Helen. I promise. Do you trust me?" The temperature dropped and great gusts of wind tossed her hair around in a tangle.

She kept her face pressed against the L-shaped hollow where Lucas's shoulder turned into his neck. She told herself that this is what difficult felt like, this was the "hard" that she had been cavalier enough to tell Lucas she preferred to "easy."

"Yes," she whispered, feeling the cold, thin air crawl into her clothes and snatch the sounds she made away from her lips as soon as she spoke.

"Then prove it," he whispered back. "Open your eyes."

They stayed in the air until the sky was almost completely dark and Helen was so cold she couldn't stop shaking. There was a lot for her to learn. Defying gravity was a big deal, but it was only half of flying. The other half was less of a mental leap, but it was also much trickier. Helen learned that to move through the air she couldn't just flap her arms or kick her feet. She had to manipulate the air around her. Lucas started to teach her how to command the air, make it denser on one side and thinner on another so that a tiny, Helen-sized current was created around her. When Lucas did it, it seemed as if he were floating underwater. The wind didn't whip at his hair or clothes but flowed around him, gently holding him or quickly pushing him, depending on how fast he wanted to go.

Lucas spent most of this first lesson just floating there in front of Helen as if he were in the ocean, his long limbs sinuously riding the currents, his fingers splayed to stave off random eddies. He kept his arms out and ready to catch her in case she shot off too fast, or slipped off a current of air pressure that she had created unevenly before she tumbled into a spin. Flying was complicated, and Helen didn't have the feel of it yet. It was a bit like learning to drive a car and aim a rifle at the same time. It required a light touch and complete concentration.

Lucas also taught her tricks for not getting spotted by the "gravity impaired," as he called the poor landlocked suckers they were looking down on. Helen was surprised to learn that early evening was actually the most dangerous time to fly. Sunset was when people looked up to admire the pretty colors, and on Nantucket it was also when half the island's residents were making their living taking photos or churning out watercolors.

Several times, Lucas had to grab Helen and fly out over the ocean so they weren't seen. Apparently, flying any time during the day was dangerous, but if Helen stayed high enough, anyone who spotted her would think she was a bird. Night was the safest time, of course, and that's when they could fly closer to the ground, which Lucas promised was a thrill. But all of it was a thrill to Helen, and when Lucas finally said that they should go in, she literally whined and asked for five more minutes. Lucas just laughed.

"Believe me, I know how you feel. But I'm freezing," he said. Helen pushed away from him with narrowed eyes and a small smile. She swooped over his shoulder and around his back, softly brushing against him as she passed.

"Tomorrow?" she asked, feeling shy and powerful at the same time. He rolled over gracefully and captured one of her arms just before she could drift away.

"Tomorrow. I promise," he said quietly as he reeled her in. "But it's nearly dark and my family will worry about us if we stay out any longer tonight."

Helen couldn't argue with that, so she let Lucas hold her shoulders and steer her down to the soft patch of grass they had taken off from. She hovered above him as he transitioned gracefully into the gravity-state.

"What do I do?" she asked, suddenly frightened again.

"It's okay. I know landing is intimidating, but I'm right here," Lucas said patiently as he stood on the ground, his arms stretched up to hold both her hands as she floated above him.

"I think I've seen a painting like this," Helen said, giddy with fear. "But the woman in the painting had wings."

"Demigods, and gods for that matter, have always been attracted to artists, and sometimes they've painted us. The wings are total bull, of course, but they are pretty," he said in a light tone. He was just giving her time to calm down, and she knew it.

"Okay. What do I do?" she asked evenly.

"I want you to pick the world back up again," he answered.

"What do you mean, pick up the world?" she sputtered.

"Concentrate. You can *feel* what I mean, I know you can, but you have to trust me."

"I trust you," Helen said for the hundredth time that day, but this time she looked him in the eyes as she said it, and he looked back at her with perfect faith. His face was glowing with it. Nothing could be impossible if Lucas had faith in her. So, she picked up the world . . . and fell, exactly like anyone else would have if they were trying to walk on six feet of air. Of course, Lucas knew what to expect, and caught her easily on her way to the ground. Snatching her out of the air, he eased her down until her feet lightly touched the grass.

Finally standing on her legs after so long without using them, Helen felt a bit unsteady. Her vision was reeling, and she rested against Lucas for a moment, her arms wrapped around his neck. When the dizzy feeling passed, she kept her arms there still, hoping to feel some kind of invitation from him. He pulled away and forced a laugh.

"See? Piece of cake. Next time, just swing your legs under you right before you change states, and you'll be good to go," he said breezily as he started walking back toward the house. "You're learning much faster than I did, you know."

"Yeah, right. I would have hit the ground like a brick if you hadn't caught me," she said, shoving Lucas away from her as she walked, laughing with him even though her heart felt a bit twisted up in her chest.

She wasn't exactly *expecting* a kiss, but she certainly had been *hoping* for one. She suddenly felt really foolish, like she was being an idiot for even *trying* to kiss someone so much smarter, so much more confident, so much more worldly than she was. She crossed her arms and sped up, but Lucas wouldn't let her pass him. Instead, he unwound her arms and took her hand. She had just enough pride to be offended that he would insist on holding her hand after refusing to kiss her.

"They can see us," he said so quietly Helen could barely hear him. She saw him jerk his chin over toward the house.

Following his gesture she saw that Pallas and Castor were sitting on the dark deck outside their shared study. They must have come outside to talk privately and been interrupted by Helen's prolonged landing. They also must have seen her angling for a little nookie, which was so horrifying to Helen that she had to banish that thought from her mind forever or instantly explode from humiliation.

"She's learning fast, isn't she, Dad?" Lucas called out.

"Much better than her first landing," Castor replied jovially, then turned to Helen. "Glad to see you've stopped trying to impersonate a comet."

"Yeah. I've also decided to do all my landings conscious from now on. Saves on food costs," Helen returned amiably, glad that it was too dark for them to see her blush. She smiled at Pallas but he didn't laugh, or even return her smile. He just watched.

"Very wise of you," Castor said. "By the way, you'd better

not be planning any side trips, Lucas," he added in warning. "Your mom's almost done with dinner and she's not in the mood to wait for anyone tonight."

"Duly noted. Thanks for the heads-up," Lucas said as he led Helen back toward the house. By the way Lucas was rushing her along it seemed as if he was purposely avoiding his father and uncle. Either that or he was keeping Helen away from them.

"Okay, what's going on?" she asked as soon as they got into the dark garage and closed the door behind them. "Your uncle is really weird around me. What did he find out in Europe?"

"No one's heard of you over there—or at least no one is talking about you. My uncle Pallas came home because he was following Creon here, but as far as we know Creon came to the States without telling his family. We think he just wants to keep an eye on us—on Hector, mostly," Lucas said with a dark look on his face.

"Did your uncle learn anything about those two women? The ones who attacked me?" Helen whispered tensely.

"No, that's still a mystery. None of Uncle Pallas's contacts know anything about them. We don't think Tantalus knows about you yet, but no one has seen Tantalus in years, so it's difficult to say for sure what he's got planned."

"No one's *seen* Tantalus?" Helen asked, stunned. "How does he lead, then?"

"Through his wife. She's the one who gives all the orders to the Hundred Cousins, and has been for almost nineteen years now."

"Why?"

"It's a long story," Lucas said, frowning and looking down. Helen could tell that meant that it was an important story.

"My favorite kind," she said, angling her head so she could catch his downcast eyes. When she did, she smiled coaxingly at him until he gave in. Lucas took her hand absentmindedly and started playing with her fingers as he spoke.

"My father had another brother. He was the youngest of the boys and everyone's favorite. Even Tantalus loved him the most," he said with a grimace, as if he had a hard time believing Tantalus loved much of anything. "His name was Ajax."

"What happened to him? Did he die?" Helen asked carefully. Lucas nodded.

"He was murdered. By someone he couldn't stay away from," he said quickly. Frustrated, he brushed a hand over his face before he continued. "Anyway. When Ajax was killed, my uncle Tantalus went into hiding to protect himself. As head of the House, he feared being overthrown. After that, all of his orders either came in writing or through his wife, Mildred. But no one has seen him in person since then."

"Mildred? That's not a Greek name."

"She's normal, of course," Lucas said with a raised eyebrow. "Scions from other Houses usually send us into a murderous rage, remember? Not exactly good for a marriage. And the only other option would be for us to marry our cousins."

"Oh, right. Forgot about the Furies for a sec. And with just one House left the only Scions around are related to you.

Gross," Helen said, rolling her eyes at herself for missing such glaringly obvious points.

"You're not related to me," he whispered, gently pulling on her hand to bring her closer to him. Then, abruptly, he turned and started leading her through the garage.

They could have walked in a straight line around the edge, but instead Lucas chose to bring her through the maze of cars. Right before they got to the door that led into the kitchen he slowed and turned back around to face her with a smile. She could hear his elevated breathing and his hand felt light in hers. For just a moment he pulled toward her, as if he were looking for a way to scuff his chest across hers and fall against her mouth, but at the last moment he turned away and brought her inside the house as if nothing was going on.

And maybe nothing was. Helen was so confused. But as soon as they entered the kitchen she had other things to worry about. Like tinnitus. In an instant, she understood why Castor and Pallas had gone outside to talk. It was really noisy in there.

Noel was working her magic over the stove, and the rest of the family seemed to be collecting around her as inevitably as water running downhill. All the chairs were taken, and the standing room up against the counter was constantly changing as Noel whirled and bullied her way around her work space. Everyone was talking and laughing and arguing at the same time, and although Helen couldn't understand a word, somehow they all seemed to be understanding each other. It was a Delos symphony, and Noel was the maestro.

As an outsider, Helen could see Noel for what she was—the center of the family, the beating heart that fed all that muscle she was tripping over while she was trying to cook. She was the personification of a warm fire and an open door, and she welcomed, even expected, strays like Helen to wander in and eat her food.

"There you are," she said without looking up from the stove. "I called your father and invited him over for dinner. I figured you'd be too worn out to do any cooking yourself." She turned the vegetables she was sautéing with a deft flick of her wrist, just like Helen had seen celebrity chefs do on TV. Helen had always wanted to learn that move, and for a moment her slightly shell-shocked brain was distracted by it. Then she registered that Noel had been talking to her.

"You invited my dad?" Helen asked shrilly.

"I sure did. Pallas is finally home, and since you're going to be spending a lot of time at our house to train I've decided it's time our families met each other. I asked Jerry to bring your Kate as well, but she's working at the store tonight, so that will have to wait. Your dad's going to be here in about fifteen minutes, so if there's anything you need to brush or wash first," she said, finally turning around to inspect the windswept girl standing in her kitchen wearing clothes that were about four sizes too big for her, "I'd do it quick," she finished with a knowing smile.

Helen looked down at her grass-stained feet. She tried to run a hand through her hair, and squeaked with pain when

235

all the short hairs on the back of her neck got yanked out. Ariadne laughed.

"You look like you've been dragged through a bush backward. But I can fix that." Ariadne stood up, pried Helen's hand away from Lucas's, and dragged her out of the kitchen.

Helen couldn't believe how many knots were in her hair, but eventually Ariadne managed to tease them out with some anti-frizz lotion and a straight comb. Then Helen washed her feet, tied her hair back in a ponytail, and threw on some flip-flops that Ariadne loaned her so fast she was halfway down the steps before she realized that they were too big on her and she could break her neck.

"What the hell are you wearing?" Jerry said as soon as he saw her. Helen burst out laughing, partly because her dad had said exactly what she was thinking, but mostly because of the dumb-ass look on his face.

"It's a loaner. My track uniform was all sweaty. Hey, they're huge, but at least they're clean," Helen said, gesturing down to the gigantic T-shirt and the rolled-up sweatpants.

"Oh. Well, you look . . . comfortable?" he said suspiciously.

"Next time I'll wear a ball gown," Helen promised. Still laughing with her dad, she turned and noticed that half the Delos family was watching them, apparently amused.

"I see what you mean," Castor said to Lucas, and the two of them shared a look that Helen didn't understand before he turned to Jerry and smiled warmly.

"It's nice to see you again, Jerry," Castor said, coming forward with his hand extended for Jerry to shake.

"And you, Castor. I intended to be the first to suggest we all sit down to a meal together, but your wife seems to be a step ahead of me," Jerry said graciously.

"Welcome to my world," Castor replied with a laconic smile, the two men already enjoying each other's company.

The introductions were as brief as possible, considering they included so many people, and Jerry handled them like a pro. He'd run a local store for almost twenty years and he was accustomed to remembering people's names and adjusting to even the most eccentric of personalities. Helen watched him respond in just the right way to make one person smile, another laugh, and yet another stop and think. She was proud of her dad, not just because he was clever and funny, but because he knew when not to be.

It also helped that Lucas's family had similar tastes, both in conversation and in food. Jerry ate up a storm and gently leaned on Noel until she confessed that she had been a chef in her pre-mom life, years ago, when she lived in France. Noel even admitted that she had made a few stealth trips to the News Store. She generously declared Kate's sea salt, rosemary, and crème fraîche croissants to be a work of crazy genius. Jerry beamed with pride, as if Kate was the buried treasure that he had been lucky enough to dig up. Helen elbowed him.

"I see you blushing," she whispered to her dad.

"Yeah, and you're not. Why is that?" he asked back.

"No reason to," she said, a traitorous glow starting to grow on her cheeks.

"Uh-huh," he said, not buying it. "Is this the part where I'm supposed to be the concerned parent and demand that you tell me exactly what's going on between you and Mr. Superfantastic over there?"

"No. This is the part where you mind your own business and eat your dinner," Helen said, sounding exactly like a mom.

"Good! Another bullet dodged," he said with a smile, and asked for seconds of Noel's potatoes au gratin.

The rest of the evening went along as well as Helen could have hoped, until the end. Helen chatted with Jason, joked around with Ariadne, and even spoke briefly with Pallas about his job as a museum curator. Up to that point, Pallas had seemed cold, even hostile toward her, but as soon as they started discussing painting, he seemed to open up a bit. Helen was no expert, but she knew enough about art to keep the conversation interesting. They were both surprised to find that they shared similar tastes, and they had a moment of mutual admiration while they discussed one of their favorite painters. Helen was beginning to think that she and Pallas could get along, but after their exchange ended she saw him turn away from her with a deep, distrusting frown.

Helen heard a merry jingling and turned when she felt a touch on her arm.

"You can't take it to heart," Pandora said consolingly. "Look, I love all my brothers, but they can be huge jackasses sometimes. Especially Pallas."

"I just wish I knew what I *did*," Helen said, frustrated.

"No, it's not you! You didn't do anything. All of this Scion crap has been going on for a lot longer than you know."

"Since the dawn of time, right?" Helen asked, trying to be humorous even though she was still hurt by Pallas's reaction.

"Yeah, right. In a literal sense that's true, but in this family there's something more specific that I'm referring to. Something that goes back to just before you were born— that's when everything started going to hell."

To Helen's surprise, Pandora took her hand and led her to a corner where they could sit down next to each other and avoid the jumble of the rest of the room. Apparently, whatever Pandora had to tell her was something she wanted to keep between them.

The Delos family was large enough to have cliques, and if Helen had to put their family into high school terms, Pandora was the artsy, mysterious girl that everyone wanted to hang out with, but only a few did on a regular basis.

"Let me start by saying that it's hardest for Pallas because he's lost more than most of us," Pandora said sadly, before she sat up straighter and smiled apologetically. "Don't get me wrong, my brother is still an ass for treating you like he did, but it might help you understand him a little better if you can flip it, and try to see that your arrival in our lives is just as big a bombshell for *us* as it is for *you*. Do you know about the way our looks are handed down?"

Helen felt her face twitch in confusion at what seemed like

a one eighty in the conversation.

"Sort of," she said. "Castor said something about archetypes, and then Cassandra said that we all look like the people who fought in the Trojan War, or something."

"So we've all got these recycled faces, right? And we don't always look like our parents, or even Scions from our own Houses, but rather like the people from history that the Fates want us to be all over again."

"Yeah, I get that. The Fates are really into repeats."

"And since Scions usually tend to fall madly in love with one person they are 'destined' to be with, and then they go and have about a billion kids really young, the older generation sometimes has the dubious honor of seeing the faces of people they once knew—and here's the real bitch—the faces of people they once *fought against*, in the younger generation. Sometimes, even in their own children or in someone who their children love."

"Oh. That doesn't sound good," Helen said, a strange dread growing in her. "Pallas hated me the first time he saw me. So who do I look like?"

Pandora sighed. The spangles on her wrist shook as she took Helen's hand.

"This totally sucks," she said apologetically. "But you look exactly like Daphne Atreus—the woman who killed our brother Ajax twenty-one years ago."

Helen noticed that Pandora stumbled over his name. For a moment, Helen thought the usually happy Pandora would cry.

"But I didn't do it! *I* didn't kill your brother," Helen said, shaken to a whisper by the depth of emotion she was seeing. Hearing Helen's urgency, Pandora snapped out of her sad thoughts and squeezed Helen's hand.

"I know that!" she exclaimed kindly. "It's insane to blame you, and most of us don't. I certainly don't. We have no way of knowing if you're even from her House."

"But Pallas does blame me," Helen said, finally getting Pallas's instant dislike of her. Pandora nodded reluctantly.

"When we lost Ajax it's like we lost the best of us," Pandora said, her eyes downcast and her lower lip momentarily catching between her teeth. "Ajax was . . . the best. You should have seen him. Actually, you *can* see him."

Pandora shook her right wrist out from under the piles of bangles. At the very bottom, clipped tightly to her skin, was a cuff. Pandora opened the oval face to reveal that the cuff was actually a wrist-locket, something Helen had never seen before. Inside was a picture of what Helen first thought was Hector, tickling the daylights out of a little girl with short dark hair.

"My brother Ajax," Pandora said wistfully. "He always had time for me, which is a big deal when you're in a family as large as ours. It's easy to get lost in the shuffle, especially when you're the littlest. I used to follow him around everywhere he went, begging him to give me jobs to do. He started calling me 'Squire' and I loved it."

Helen looked at the joyful little girl squirming under the giant hand of her big brother, and then up at Pandora's glistening eyes. "Even just looking at this picture I can tell he loved you very much."

"He did, and I loved him. I used to pretend he was a glorious knight and I was his only trusted sidekick, and he played along. He was so patient. He used to send me on dangerous quests to find his car keys or summon the elevator. I was seven when he died. I wasn't supposed to be following him that night, but I was. I was there when he was murdered."

Helen was about to speak, to say something comforting if she could, but Pandora changed abruptly, and continued. "He was like Apollo himself," she said with a bright, although slightly forced, smile. "Like Hector in a lot of ways . . . only sweet, and not a cranky wiseass. Don't get me wrong, I love my nephew, but damn! He can be a such a grouch." They both broke into a much-needed laugh at Hector's expense.

"I wish I'd met him. Your brother, I mean," Helen said, and was surprised to realize that she meant it. Ajax must have been truly special to inspire such enduring love in his younger sister.

"In a lot of ways none of us have gotten over losing him," Pandora said, shrugging as though she had run out of explanations for Helen. "But my brother Pallas is the only one who can't look at you and accept that you're a different person, even though he knows it's got nothing to do with you."

"I get it," Helen conceded. "It's not fair, and I still think he's mean, but I get why Pallas hates me."

"Don't worry, eventually he'll get over it. Deep down he knows you didn't choose your face. The Fates did," she said.

She gave Helen a cheeky smile. "And damn, girl! But you got a nice one!"

"So did you!" Helen insisted, and she meant the compliment she gave.

"Whatever," Pandora said, rolling her eyes and shaking her tinkling wrists. "I'm probably one in a hundred who gets some stupid handmaiden's face, or a vestal virgin's from Troy, considering my luck with men!"

Even while she laughed, Helen couldn't quite shake a strange doubt. Finally, she gave into it and asked, "So who from Troy do I look like?"

"Hell, no!" Pandora said, standing up. "I promised—we all did. You need to talk to Lucas about that one, Helen. Sorry, but I've already given you enough to think about for one night."

And with a considerable amount of jangling and sparkling, Pandora announced that she needed a glass of wine and disappeared in the mix of her family. Helen grimaced after her. She knew that Pandora had really opened up and entrusted her with an emotionally dense bit of information, but Helen still felt dissatisfied. She wanted to know what role the Fates intended for her to play. She was going to ask Lucas the second she got him alone.

She looked over at him. All night she had felt him watching her, and the weight of his eyes had been like an encouraging hand on the small of her back. She didn't have to slouch or pretend to be weak or less of a geek than she was. She simply fit in. She realized that this new ease with herself was partly due to the fact that for the first time in her life she was around people who were just as odd as she was . . . but it was mostly because of Lucas. He never stood next to her, but she could feel they were still tied to each other by the trust they had built during their flight. His gaze had such a positive impact on her that she felt unbalanced as soon as his eyes abandoned her. She looked around to see what had caught his attention and spotted him talking privately with Pallas.

Helen did not approve of using Scion hearing to violate another person's privacy—she and Hector had already had an argument about just that when she accused him of eavesdropping on her and Jerry from the widow's walk, but now she couldn't seem to stop herself. When she heard Pallas say her name, she had to know what they were saying about her.

"I'm not going to lie to you. Helen caught my eye," Lucas was saying in a low voice. "But nothing's going on."

"So everyone keeps telling me," Pallas replied. Helen saw him rub his lower lip in thought before continuing. "I'm not so worried about that right now, but what I am worried about is a month or two down the road when the two of you are flying off every direction together. Alone. It can't happen, Luke."

"It won't," Lucas replied coldly. "I'm teaching her to fly and I'm making sure she doesn't get killed, but there's no way I'd ever touch her. Give me some credit."

They continued talking, but Helen had stopped listening. She felt sick. Stumbling in her borrowed shoes, she went over to her dad. She stood right next to him as he talked to

Pandora, and stared at his profile until he took the hint and looked at her.

"What's the matter with you?" he asked sarcastically at first, until he took a good look at her and became concerned. "You okay, Len?"

"Can we go? I have so much stuff to do. Homework and chores. And I'm so tired," she said, making up random excuses until he responded. She was causing a bit of a scene, which she hated, but she simply couldn't stand there and suck it up for one second longer.

Jerry glanced down at his watch. "Sure, yeah. I guess it's getting kind of late. Was that supposed to be my line?" he asked with a guilty grimace.

"No, you're good. It's still early. I'm just . . . I've got stuff," Helen said before she launched immediately into the thank you, good-bye, and see-you-tomorrow crap that she wished she could just skip.

Ariadne shot Helen a worried look, but Helen didn't care about anything anymore, not anyone's feelings or whether or not they all thought she was rude or crazy or both. None of it mattered. She just needed to get out of that house before she saw Lucas again or she was going to lose her mind. It was rude and awkward, but Helen managed to drag her dad out the front door before Lucas and Pallas had even looked up from their conversation in the corner.

# ELEVEN

Helen rode her bike to school the next morning, giving her dad instructions to tell Lucas that she had a few things to do before homeroom. Jerry was a little put out that Helen refused to call Lucas to explain it herself, but she honestly couldn't make herself listen to his voice.

"Did something happen at dinner last night?" Jerry asked. She ran out the door and pedaled off before he could get a straight answer out of her.

The cool autumn wind felt good on her face, which was puffy from staying awake half the night with her eyes leaking. She hadn't really cried, and never got that explosive release that comes from a good old-fashioned weep-a-thon. Lying in bed, she'd been too shocked to sob. She felt like an idiot. She knew there had to be worse things in the world than being dissed by the boy of your dreams, but at that moment, she couldn't think of any of them.

Kate, Claire, even her dad had asked her repeatedly what was going on between her and Lucas, like it was expected that the two of them would get together eventually, but no one had ever asked Lucas what he thought about being paired off with Helen. Now Helen knew for a fact that he "would never touch her." Those words kept coming back to her, not just the words, but how passionately he had said them. The way he had spoken about her made it seem as if the very thought of kissing her was disgusting to him, and Helen was just as confused by this as she was hurt. How could he want to hold her hand all the time if he thought she was repulsive?

Helen got to school, locked up her bike, and took an alternate route to her locker. It was longer, but she knew it would be Delos-free, and therefore worth all the extra steps. She had left her house so early that even with the longer walk she beat everyone to homeroom.

When Claire arrived, she noticed immediately how awful Helen looked. Like the good friend she was, she forgot all about the argument they were supposed to be having, asking Helen a dozen questions about her red face and ratty hair before she had even put down her book bag. Helen lied as best she could, but so halfheartedly she never would have gotten away with it if Matt didn't back her up by explaining how sick Helen had been the day before. It didn't help that Zach kept making scoffing noises as Helen tried to put

Claire off. Helen ignored him, as she usually did, but she could still feel him watching her with a sneer plastered on his face.

Helen kept her head down all day and did her work. She found now that she simply didn't care anymore if she did well in class, drew attention to herself, and potentially got the cramps. As she walked to lunch she considered faking the stomach pain if it could get her farther away from Lucas. She didn't want to go into the cafeteria and face everyone, but she still had to go somewhere, and the auditorium door was right next to her. It had been left ajar, so Helen pushed it open and went in. Helen knew she wasn't allowed in there. Any room that was unsupervised by a teacher was off-limits to students, but that didn't stop her. She really didn't care if she got caught—she just needed a moment alone.

There was only a dim light onstage, and it was very quiet, exactly what Helen was looking for. She sat down on the apron of the stage and unpacked her lunch box. Chewing, Helen glanced around, taking note of all the new sets that were just beginning to be built. The drama club put on two shows a year—a winter play and a spring musical.

She wondered what play the drama club was going to put on, and saw a spare script lying in the wings. *A Midsummer Night's Dream*. Helen opened to the first page and read, SCENE I. ATHENS. THE PALACE OF THESEUS. She rolled her eyes and dropped the script, feeling set up. Maybe the Fates really did pull all the strings.

Helen zombied her way through the last three periods,

but her luck couldn't hold out all day. When the bell signaling the end of school rang, she rushed to her locker to get to track as quickly as she could, but Lucas was anticipating her.

"Hey!" he shouted from halfway down the hall. He looked big and dangerous as he walked toward her, every step sending underclassmen scurrying to get out of his way. "Where have you been all day?"

"Busy. I can't be late for track again," she replied tersely, not looking at him as she dug her stuff out of her locker.

"I'll walk you," he said. He tried to get a look at her face.

She kept her head down and her face covered with her hair and didn't reply. They walked down the hall next to each other at the same pace, but today Helen felt even more lonely with Lucas beside her than she had when she was by herself.

"Why didn't you call me this morning? I could have picked you up earlier if you needed to stop somewhere," he said when the silence became intolerable.

"Look, Lucas. The whole ride to school thing is sweet, but I think it's easier for me to just take my bike. So maybe we should just forget it."

"You don't want me to pick you up anymore?" he asked in a cold voice.

"No, I don't," she said. They neared the end of the hallway that led down to the locker rooms. She finally turned to look at him, which she shouldn't have. He looked hurt.

"Okay," he said, barely above a whisper. "Are you going to tell me what I did wrong or am I supposed to guess?"

"You didn't do anything wrong," Helen answered listlessly.

He looked at her, waiting to feel the lie, but there wasn't one. The light scattered momentarily around his face, hiding his expression.

"You'll be able to get yourself to my house after track?" he asked as he glanced around, so confused he didn't know where to look or what to say.

"About that," Helen started, trying to think up a believable excuse.

"You're coming. We still haven't found those two women and now Creon is out there. Learning to defend yourself is more important than what I did or didn't do to piss you off," he said, suddenly angry.

She nodded, knowing it was stupid of her to even suggest giving up her training. She could barely see him through the confusing images he was creating as he bent the light around him. It was as if there were three of him for a moment, whirling around like she was looking at him through a kaleidoscope. She kept her head down and her eyes behind her hair until his image stilled and she could look at him without getting dizzy.

"Do you want me to stay away from you for the rest of the day?" he asked in a carefully controlled voice.

*No*, she thought. And yes. Both answers were completely true. She *couldn't* lie to him, but the truth had suddenly become very slippery.

"I think that would be best," she mumbled.

He didn't say anything. He just turned on his heel and left her.

"Hi, Luke . . . bye, Luke," Claire said as she joined them. She looked back and forth at the two of them. "Fight?"

Helen shrugged and took Claire's hand, leading her into the locker room. "I don't really care," was all she had the energy to say.

As they ran the trail she asked about Claire's day. She let Claire in on the auditorium secret, and told her to tell Matt about it, too, in order to avoid a friendship meltdown. Claire looked at her funny, but she didn't ask any questions.

Helen felt as if the whole world had turned into some gigantic punch line that she had waited patiently for, and then when she heard it she found it insulting. If she had been in a comedy club she would have gotten up and walked out, but instead she had to go to the comedian's house after school and let his cousin beat the crap out of her.

When track was over, Helen dutifully rode her bike to the Delos compound, arriving before Lucas, Jason, and Hector did. She went down to the tennis courts, which were in the process of being converted into a proper fighting arena with a sandy bottom, and looked around. There was a sword on the ground. She picked it up and gave it a swing to see how it felt.

It felt goofy as hell. Helen supposed she wasn't a swords-woman.

"I think Hector wants you to learn the spear first. It's considered traditional," Cassandra said behind her.

"Wouldn't want to mess with tradition," Helen said sarcastically as she threw the sword down, point first, into the sand so that the hilt made a cross above the ground.

"Yes, you would. In fact, I think that's what your mother had in mind for you all along," Cassandra said in that spooky, faraway voice she had a tendency to slip into at crucial moments. "But naming you is something your mother did in the past, and I can only see the future."

"You're an oracle!" Helen said, astonished. She should have known all along.

Suddenly, she wasn't so sure she wanted to be alone with Cassandra. There was something wrong about her eyes. Helen started to circle around her, always keeping an equal distance between them, but subtly closing the gap between herself and the exit.

"Delphi, Delos. And the Oracle at Delphi was always one of Apollo's chosen priests," Helen said as evenly as she could, trying to keep Cassandra distracted.

"Close. The Oracle was always one of Apollo's Scions, and always a priest*ess*. A girl," Cassandra said bitterly. "The Oracle of Delphi is the female offspring of Apollo and the Three Fates."

"I'm pretty sure that wasn't in the book you gave me," Helen said uncertainly as Cassandra pulled the sword out of the ground, hefted it in her hand thoughtfully, and took a few steps toward her.

"It wasn't made known to any of the ancient historians, but they did know that Apollo is the son of Zeus, and not one of the original gods. He was second generation, a kind of glorified Scion, and, like us, he was going to die eventually."

Cassandra came closer to Helen, still holding the sword.

"Then why didn't he?" Helen asked cautiously, trying to stay calm so as not to provoke her. She circled back the other way, never taking her eyes off the bright bronze blade that Cassandra alternately lifted and let fall, as if she couldn't entirely bring herself to raise it.

"Apollo made a deal with the Three Fates," she said, half distracted by some darker thought. "He offered them something they couldn't have without him. A baby girl. He swore on the River Styx to give them offspring, and in return they swore never to cut his string of life. From that day on, Apollo got his immortality, and every generation one girl who is descended from him belongs to the Fates. She's their spiritual daughter, and occasionally she can see what her mothers have in store for the world."

Cassandra was stalling, Helen realized. Whatever she was planning to do unsettled her, but even though she seemed uncertain, she continued to close in. As she did, light started to dance backward into her skin, and her eyes and teeth glowed with the vaguely purple hue of black light. Helen knew that she was older, larger, and stronger than Cassandra, but she also knew she was still the one in danger. Cassandra was not the only being inside that tiny body. She was being visited and maybe even partially controlled by the Three Fates.

Helen watched as Cassandra cut off her exit. Helen could always fly away, now that she knew how to get airborne, but she wasn't sure if she could control her flight once she was aloft. She also didn't know how to land without Lucas holding her hand. But right now she was more afraid of the Oracle with the sword than she was of falling out of the sky. Helen was about to take her chances with flight when Cassandra's demeanor suddenly changed. She went from being the dark, fiery messenger of the Fates to being a very vulnerable teenager.

"I saw something, Helen," she said desperately. "Then I saw it again, and again. I've been so ashamed and frightened that I haven't told anyone else what I saw. And I am so sorry if I'm wrong—for all of our sakes. But I have to do this . . . because . . . this is what comes next."

Her eyes were filling up with tears. She looked so tormented Helen would have done anything to make her feel better. She smiled understandingly at Cassandra, who tried to control her hitching breath as she nodded in return and wrapped both hands around the hilt of her sword. She swung it over her shoulder and paused, waiting for Helen to be ready.

Helen choked back the scream that was trying to climb out of her mouth.

If Cassandra, the Oracle of Delphi, had foreseen her death, was there any sense in fighting it? Did Helen really have a choice?

Cassandra swung her sword. In that millisecond Helen knew she'd had a good life, because she suddenly loved it so much that she could have wept with gratitude. She'd had amazing friends, the best dad in the world, and a strong, healthy body. She'd even experienced the joy of flight. And once, just once, in the middle of the night, she'd *almost* kissed the only boy she'd ever wanted. . . .

Helen felt a strange, vibrating tickle, like someone had pressed a gigantic kazoo against the side of her throat and blown on it. She saw Cassandra's eyes widen as she pulled the blade back from the side of Helen's neck and looked at it.

The sword was totally mangled in the middle section, all crunched up on itself like a squeezed piece of tinfoil. Cassandra stared at Helen in shock for a moment. Relieved tears spilled down her cheeks.

"I was right." She dropped the sword and grabbed Helen in a hug. Then she started jumping up and down, making Helen jump with her. "You're not dead! This is . . . You have no idea how happy I am I didn't just kill you!" she squealed.

"Ditto," Helen said in a daze. She was alive.

"Hang on. We still have to test this," Cassandra said excitedly as she ran over to a chest of weapons in the corner of the fenced-off court. She threw open the lid and grabbed a bow and arrow. Grinning, she shot Helen.

Helen heard Ariadne scream something behind her, and someone running at demigod speed to overtake the arrow, but it was too late. The arrow struck her and bounced off her chest, making a faint twanging sound as it did so. Too late to change course, Jason plowed into her from behind and knocked her to the ground. They rolled over together until he was propped up on his elbows above her, staring at her chest with disbelief.

"I saw that arrow strike you," he said vehemently as if he were swearing in front of a grand jury.

"It did," said Cassandra from the other end of the tennis court, beaming with pleasure.

"I think Cassie's finally lost it," Hector whispered sadly, but without surprise, to Ariadne.

"No, I haven't lost it, Hector. I *saw* it," Cassandra said, still smiling from ear to ear. "Helen can't be hurt by any weapon. Try it yourself." She pulled a sword out of the box, offering it to him.

"Cass, just put the sword down," Ariadne said with a hand raised in an appeasing gesture. "We can talk about this."

"I'm not crazy!" Cassandra screamed, suddenly livid.

"She isn't crazy," Helen said with conviction. She untangled herself from Jason and stood. "Go ahead, Cass. Shoot me."

Cassandra locked another arrow in her bow and shot Helen—in the head this time. Ariadne screamed again, but the scream trailed off lamely when they all saw the arrow bounce right off. Everyone was silent for a moment.

"No frigging way!" Hector shouted, a touch of envy making him sound almost angry.

"Did that hurt?" Jason asked as he turned to Helen, a look of disbelief on his face.

"Maybe a tiny bit," Helen said, but Jason was too excited to really listen. He ran over to the box, pulled out a javelin, and chucked it at Helen. It bounced right off.

"Okay, *that* stung," Helen said, smiling and raising her

hands to signal in a friendly way that she'd had enough, but Hector had already picked up a sword and was stalking toward her.

"I'll stop as soon as you start bleeding, okay?" he said casually before he started hacking away at her. Four strokes in, and the blade was ruined.

Helen stumbled back with raised arms and fell down. She wasn't wounded, but the instinct to protect herself was still there, and Hector was absolutely terrifying when he attacked. The rain of blows ended abruptly when the sword fell apart. She tried to stand back up, but as soon as she did she was thrown down again as something fell from the sky and landed violently on top of Hector. Lucas had rammed into Hector from above, driving his cousin two feet into the dirt before he reared back on his knees to hit him.

"Lucas, stop!" Helen screamed in concert with Cassandra and Ariadne.

Jason didn't yell, but as usual, he dove on top of the other two to put himself between them. In his rage, Lucas hit Jason accidentally, and that misguided blow made him stop and look at his cousins more clearly. Hector lay at the bottom of the pile, covered in layers of dirt, his hands held up in a surrendering gesture. Jason lay across his brother's body, bleeding from the mouth and pushing on Lucas's shoulders to keep him back. Lucas blinked and looked up at Helen.

"He was trying to kill you." Lucas lowered his raised fist. He forced his eyes to focus on Hector and his voice frayed at the edges, like he was a young boy. "I saw it. You had a sword."

"I'm okay. Look at me, Lucas. No blood. I'm fine," Helen said gently as she moved to the side of the trench. She put her hands on his shoulders and tried to coax him off his frightened, panting cousins. Lucas allowed himself to be led up out of the trench, docile with regret and confusion.

Cassandra briefly explained Helen's imperviousness to her brother as Helen, Ariadne, and Jason pulled Hector up out of the collapsing ditch. He was injured—not too seriously, but badly enough that he couldn't walk on his own. Ariadne and Jason took Hector into the house, having to hold him up as he walked. Lucas watched his cousin half limp, half drag himself across the yard. He had to sit down in the sand at the sight.

Three fast-moving shapes came rushing out of the house to see what was wrong. Pallas helped his children the rest of the way into the house while Castor and Pandora briefly conferred with Ariadne and then moved toward the tennis court.

"Why didn't you warn me, Cassie?" Lucas pleaded quietly while Castor shouted questions as he and Pandora entered the tennis court. Cassandra shrugged, avoiding everyone's eyes.

"She was afraid," Helen answered defensively, cutting off Castor's questions. She took Cassandra's hand and pulled her close, a little angry that they would try to blame Cassandra for Lucas's actions. "She had a vision of herself swinging a sword at me and she thought she was going to kill me. She thought she *had* to kill me. Would you have told anyone if you were in her shoes?"

Pandora looked at Helen questioningly as if to ask if she was okay. Helen gave her an uncertain smile in response, relieved that Pandora had been sensitive enough to keep this exchange silent. Then they both turned their attention back to Lucas, who was still shell-shocked.

"If you were scared, why didn't you tell me, Cassie? You know you can always come to me," Lucas said firmly, but she shook her head.

"None of you are qualified to be my confidants anymore. I'm the only one who can decide what to reveal or keep hidden," she said gently. Cassandra stepped away from Helen's side and stood up straighter. It was as if she was throwing off her support system with one painful gesture. She took a wistful breath and turned back to Helen.

"Standing there, waiting for me to cut your head off?" said the newer, older, and slightly more melancholic Cassandra. "That was the bravest thing I've ever seen."

*That's because you couldn't see yourself,* Helen thought.

Cassandra looked down at Lucas, who was still in shock over what he'd done. She put a hand on his shoulder and shook it until he looked up at her.

"Let's go inside and check on Hector," she said as she helped her brother off his knees.

Helen still felt shaky with adrenaline. Walking back to the house next to Lucas, she wished he would take her hand like he used to, but then scolded herself for even thinking that. She sped up and walked in front of him so she wouldn't be tempted to feel sorry for herself.

All of them sat down at the kitchen table to hash out the new discovery, but no one had any answers. They asked Helen if she could ever remember a time when she had been wounded by a knife, but Helen's childhood was remarkably violence free, especially for a Scion. She couldn't remember ever getting anything bigger than a paper cut. That sparked a philosophical debate on what qualified as a weapon—if paper could cut her but a spear couldn't, could you make a spear out of paper and kill her?

"Is a fork a weapon?" Jason asked, gesturing to one sitting on the counter. Ariadne shrugged and stabbed Helen in the shoulder with it, and it squished up like a soggy ice-cream cone on contact.

"Guess so," said Ariadne. "Maybe a spoon?" She turned to find one.

"Could you stop that, please?" Lucas said with a wince. "Eventually, we're going to find something that actually *can* hurt her. Maybe even kill her. I think we should hold off on the experiments until we figure out why she's like this."

"I agree with Lucas," Castor said carefully. "And the sooner we find out how she got like this, the better."

"It can't be something she inherited or we would have seen it in another Scion before," Pallas said, staring at Helen like she was a fancy, new bug he'd found under a log. "Dipped in the River Styx?" He threw it out there, like it was the most logical explanation. "She doesn't seem like a zombie, but maybe Achilles didn't, either."

"No. I would bet anything she still has her soul," Castor said, shaking his head.

"And how would she have gotten to the River Styx? There hasn't been a Descender in millennia," Cassandra added doubtfully.

*Descender?* Helen wondered.

"What about something more basic, like a gun?" Jason asked. He was still trying to wrap his head around Helen's unbelievable talent.

"Since when were bullets ever fast enough to hit a Scion? That's why we still use swords, dummy," Ariadne said with a smirk. "We're the only things that can move fast enough to kill us."

"Yeah, but what if we had her just stand there and take a few bullets? Technically, we can be killed by them, if we're hit enough times," he said logically.

"It doesn't matter how many times she gets shot. You could drop a bomb on her and she'd be fine, that's what I'm trying to tell you," Cassandra said with tired frustration.

"There has to be a reason behind it. It isn't a talent, so she must have some form of protection we don't know about. I'll start doing some research and put together a list of possibilities," Pallas interjected, still staring at Helen.

"I'll help you, Dad," Hector said from the doorway. He limped into the kitchen, his hair damp from a shower. "I'm dying to know how Sparky here does her little impervious trick."

"I tried to get him to lie down, but he wouldn't listen," Pandora complained from the hallway behind him. Hector walked straight over to Lucas.

"How are you feeling?" Lucas asked guiltily.

Hector clasped hands with him. "It's okay, brother. I would have done the same thing if I were you," he said. Then he flashed one of his mischievous smiles. "Only I would have hit you *harder*."

They hugged each other, and just like that the whole confrontation was forgotten. Ariadne started to ask Pandora a question, but Helen couldn't hold her tongue for a second longer.

"Will someone please tell me why you all call me 'Sparky'?" she burst out in frustration. "And if I get stabbed one more time tonight I'm going to lose it!" she added, rounding on Jason, who was sneaking up behind her holding a stapler.

"You haven't told her yet?" Cassandra said to Lucas with disbelief. "You should have done it days ago."

"I was going to tell her today, but I never got the chance," he replied, looking at the floor.

Helen thought about how he had hunted her down in the hallway after school, like he had something urgent to say, and how she had told him she didn't want to see him. But that was *his* fault, she reminded herself. He was the one who was forcing himself to teach her how to fight and fly, right?

"Well, tell me now, then," she said briskly. Lucas looked up at her sharply. His eyes were angry.

"You can generate lightning. Electricity. I don't know how strong a charge you can create, but from what I've felt, and what Hector felt in the grocery store, I'm thinking it's big."

"Lightning?" Helen said with disbelief.

She remembered Hector convulsing when he first touched her in the grocery store, and then she remembered Lucas letting go of her so abruptly in the hallway the very first time she had seen him. She had been so afraid of them both, so desperate to defend herself . . . . Was it possible she had summoned a power she had never been aware of? Had she created *lightning*?

Somewhere in the back of her mind she saw a blue flash, and Kate crumple to the ground. A terrible thought occurred to her. She tried to banish it as she had done since childhood, but this time the thought wouldn't go away.

"We think that means you are descended from Zeus," Cassandra said. "But from which House is still uncertain. The Four Houses were founded by Zeus, Aphrodite, Apollo, and Poseidon. Aphrodite and Apollo were Zeus's children, so Scions from their Houses could display his traits as well. The fourth House, the House of Athens, was founded by Poseidon, so it can be ruled out. Well, maybe."

"My House?" Helen said, still so wrapped up in her own head that she was having a hard time understanding English. She was remembering a blue flash from her past, and a scary man that kept trying to touch her hair, flying away from her off the back of the Nantucket ferry. The smell of burning filled her throat. Helen rubbed her hand over her face and tried to rebury that memory. She had always believed that she *couldn't* have been the cause of that. And worse—had she hurt Kate, too?

"When we say your House, we mean your heritage, Helen," Castor said gently, noticing Helen's disquiet. "Zeus had a lot of children, so your House can't be pinpointed with any certainty yet. But don't worry, we're still trying to find out who your people were."

"Thanks," Helen muttered, still overwhelmed.

"You can't control the lightning yet, it sort of jumps out of you when you're upset," Lucas said after a long pause. He was looking at her strangely.

"Is it like a Taser?" Helen asked anxiously, suddenly snapping out of her trance.

"Yeah," Hector said as if he was recollecting both sensations and comparing them in his mind. "But stronger."

"Does it really hurt?" Helen said quietly. She felt sick to her stomach.

"I guess," Hector said with a condescending shrug. "You know, if you put in some real training, you could probably generate a lethal charge soon."

"That won't be necessary," Helen said, jumping to her feet, horrified with the suggestion. And with herself.

"Wait, Helen, it could be a good thing," Jason replied. "You could learn how to use your bolts instead of fighting."

"You don't have to use them to kill. Just to knock

people out," Lucas amended, aware now that something was disturbing Helen deeply.

He couldn't know that what he was saying to make it better only made it worse. Helen thought of Kate's unconscious body—how Kate had convulsed in that nauseating way when the blue light flashed. How her head had lolled back and her mouth fell open uncontrollably when Helen had picked her up off the ground. She couldn't get the horrifying images out of her head so she started pacing around, wringing her hands to dispel the nervous energy she felt. She knew everyone was staring at her. She looked up and locked eyes with Pandora, who was clearly attentive to her strange reaction.

"Why don't we talk about this tomorrow?" Pandora said to the room in general. "Hector needs to eat and everyone else needs a shower. No offense, but pee-ew, guys." She got a few laughs, but more important, she got the focus off Helen. Helen smiled at her gratefully.

"Are you okay?" Ariadne whispered in Helen's ear as the family meeting broke up. Helen squeezed Ariadne's hand and tried to smile, but she had no idea what to say. She started to wander toward the door.

"I'll take you home," Lucas called out over his shoulder to Helen, ending the brief conversation he was having with his father and uncle.

"I'm supposed to watch Helen tonight," Jason said apologetically.

"And I have my bike," Helen said. She couldn't bear to be with him alone.

"I don't care," Lucas replied bluntly to them both. He stared down Jason for a moment, speaking volumes with his eyes, then turned back to Hector. "I need your truck," he said with barely controlled anger. Hector nodded, glancing over at Helen and back at Lucas with something approaching sympathy.

Lucas grabbed Helen's hand and pulled her outside. He loaded her bicycle into the back of Hector's SUV, held Helen's door open for her while she got in, and drove out of the garage without a word. Once off the Delos property he pulled over into one of the many scenic park-and-gawk spots and turned in his seat to face Helen.

"What's going on?" he asked, angry and frustrated and frightened all at the same time.

Helen didn't have an answer for him.

"Will you at least tell me what I did wrong?"

"I already told you, you didn't *do* anything," Helen said to her lap.

"Then why are you treating me like this? Look at me," he pleaded, taking her hand. She stared at their linked hands like it was the first time she had ever seen anything like it.

"What the hell is this?" she asked. She pulled her hand out of his with disgust. "You know what? I take it back. You did do something to me. You led me on."

Lucas's whole face crumpled. Helen had had no reason to hope after what she had heard the night before, but for some reason there was a tiny spark still glowing in her that maybe, somehow, she had misunderstood. Or that he would change his mind. It went out completely when Lucas nodded.

"I led you on," he said, squeezing his eyes shut and clenching his fists so hard Helen thought for a moment he was going to rip the steering wheel off. His voice was harsh, almost a snarl. "You and I can't be together, so just get it out of your head and move on."

Helen unbuckled her seat belt and got out of the car.

"Wait, please," he started to say, almost as if he was in pain, but Helen slammed her door shut and cut him off.

"Wait for what? For you to tell me that I'm a really nice girl but you'd *never* touch me? Thanks, I got that part already. Now open the back so I can get my bike," she bit out. Her voice was foreign to her, so bitter and loaded with sarcasm that it sounded like someone else's.

"I promise I won't say anything the rest of the way if you don't want me to. Just let me take you home," Lucas replied calmly. She hated that he was calm.

"Open the damn door, or I'll rip it off!" Helen yelled back.

She knew she was making a fool of herself, throwing a tantrum in the middle of the road like this, but she couldn't stop. Humiliation was leaking out of every pore and she needed to get away from him fast. She didn't want to leave anything behind, either—nothing that would force her to come back to him later to ask for what was hers.

She stood at the back of his car with her head down and her arms crossed tightly over her sore heart. She knew he was looking at her in the rearview mirror, so she angled her body away. Finally, he popped the back. She got her bike out and rode off without another word.

When she got home she fell into bed without even taking her clothes off. She could hear Jason moving around on the widow's walk as he settled down for the night, but she didn't feel guilty about leaving him up there. All Helen wanted was to run as far away from the Delos family as fast as she could.

*She was on the edge of the dry lands, in a new place that she had seen from a distance, but had never thought she could reach. It was still rocky, but interspersed with the tufts of razor-sharp grass, there were tumbledown drums of mason-carved marble, a thousand Parthenons' worth of scattered columns. There had once been an empire here. No longer.*

*Far off, there was the promise of a river. Helen couldn't tell if she could hear it, or if she felt the extra part per million of moisture in the air, but she knew there was running water nearby. She felt so dry and empty inside. Where was the river?*

*As she searched, she looked down at the fallen architecture and read the names graffitied on its sides. Gracus loves Lucinda. Ethan loves Sarah. Michael loves Erin. For what seemed like days she ran her fingers over the names carved into the fragmented bones of ruined loves, stepping around the broken pillars of unkept vows and dusting the headstones in the graveyard of love with her hands. Every kind of death had a resting place in the dry lands.*

*She walked until her feet bled.*

Helen woke to a room filled with sad blue light. She tried to roll over and felt tied to her mattress, like she had been jumped by the Lilliputians in the middle of the night. Somehow in her sleep she had shucked off her shirt and shoes, but her jeans were so tangled up in her sheets that she had to push herself off the bed and fight it out on the floor to unwrap herself. It was an ugly battle, especially since she was still covered in dirt from the trench Lucas had dug with Hector's body, dried blood from her cut feet, and a gray, powdery dust from the dry lands. Her feet had healed themselves, of course, but still there were blood-encrusted foot smears all over her sheets. They were ruined, and she would have to buy new ones. Luckily, her dad was too squeamish about girl stuff to ask questions.

She shimmied out of her jeans on her way to the bathroom and climbed into the shower before the water even had a chance to heat up. Opening her mouth, she gulped down as much of the cold spray as she could catch. She was so dry inside. Her body ached from walking hundreds of miles under a dead sun—the cold water was like a blessing even though it made her shiver. Helen looked down at her skin and watched the water get forced into little rivers by the raised hairs of her goose bumps. It made her think about the river she had seen from a distance right before she woke up.

She couldn't remember it.

She knew she had felt a sigh-worthy relief, and only one thing could have made her feel that way in the dry lands. Water. But she couldn't *remember* anything about it. How could she forget a river in the dry lands? It was unthinkable, so she stopped thinking about it.

It bothered her that her brain refused to think about it. She walked, still naked and dripping wet, to the vanity in her bedroom, picked up some old viper-green eyeliner Claire had left the last time she slept over, and wrote *THE RIVER I CAN'T REMEMBER* on the mirror, just in case she forgot again. Then she got dressed.

It was getting cold out, and the air was damp with fog. Helen zipped her jacket up to her throat and regretted not bringing gloves. As she rode to school she had to keep one hand in her pocket and one on the handlebars, and then switch off when the hand she was using to steer got too numb.

When she arrived she saw Lucas waiting in the parking lot, leaning up against an Audi she'd seen in the Deloses' garage but had never seen him drive before. It reminded her how stupid she'd been to think he was going to kiss her that night in his garage. She dropped her head and hurried toward the school without waving to him. He took a step after her and opened his mouth to say something, but stopped himself and let her go.

When Helen got to the door, she heard Claire call out from behind. She paused and waited for her to catch up.

"Are you two fighting?" she asked, glancing back at Lucas's stooped form. When she got a good look at how terrible Helen looked she burst out, "Holy crap! What the hell happened to you?"

"I didn't sleep well last night," Helen mumbled.

"Your eyes look black and blue, Len. Like you haven't slept in weeks," Claire responded, sounding seriously worried. "Were you crying a lot?"

"No. Not at all," Helen said. It was true, too. She was sad, but she never felt like crying when she was depressed. She felt like sleeping.

"Can you tell me what the fight was about?" Claire asked cautiously.

"There was no fight, really. Lucas just doesn't want to be with me," Helen said. She rammed her fists into her pockets. She found that if she tensed her muscles she could keep herself from giving up on moving.

"I don't believe that," Claire said doubtfully. "He punched Hector in the face for just talking to you and pretty much announced to the whole school that you were his girlfriend."

"Well, I guess he must have changed his mind since then," Helen said, shrugging. She didn't have the strength to argue. She barely had the energy to turn the combination on her locker. She was so tired from walking for weeks, but that had been a dream, hadn't it? How could she be physically worn out from something that had only happened in her mind?

"You're serious, aren't you?" Claire asked, studying Helen's hunched-up body.

"Uh-huh. He doesn't want me, Gig. He told me so himself. Can we drop it now? I'm just too tired."

"Yeah. No problem," Claire said, rubbing Helen's back.

For a second, Helen let herself lean against Claire in a sideways hug.

"Shit. I'll kill him," Claire offered. Helen tried to laugh at that, but what came out of her sounded more like a hacking cough.

"Thanks, but no. I don't want him dead," Helen said. She shuffled after Claire to homeroom.

Mr. Hergeshimer asked about her health as soon as he had a chance to process how wretched she looked. Helen assured him she was fine, and after studying her face skeptically for a moment he gave up and went back to harassing Zach about his choice for the Word of the Day. Matt asked Helen in a whisper if her stomach felt better, and then restated his opinion that she should quit track.

"You're wearing yourself too thin," he said, sounding an awful lot like her father.

The rest of the morning went similarly. Every teacher asked if she needed to go to the nurse, and all of her acquaintances worried that she wasn't better yet from her "fit" during track the other day. Except for Zach.

"I had no idea you were so fast, Hamilton," he said as he ran to catch up to her in the hall.

"Yeah, I'm pretty fast," she countered, trying to sound disinterested.

"Right before you collapsed I saw you chasing that shirtless guy and I realized that I've had it backward all these years. See, I always thought you were the one who liked to be chased, you being such a tease and all," he said with a faint sneer. "But it's hard to believe any guy could outrun you. I don't think I've ever seen anyone run that fast."

"Wait, *you* told *Gretchen*?" Helen asked, a sinking feeling in her stomach. "I thought it was the other way around."

"I gotta admit," he said, taunting her, "when you want to, you can move so fast it's, like, inhuman. The only other time I've ever seen anyone move that fast was when one of those Delos kids was playing the hero during football practice and this freshman went down on the other end of the line—" Zach was cut off by Helen's history teacher, who gestured for Helen to hurry up and get in the room.

For the moment, Helen was saved, but from the way Zach was looking at her, she had the feeling that this wasn't the end of the problem. She tried to put it out of her head by telling herself that he could spread as many rumors as he liked, but everyone would think he was exaggerating. Zach liked to gossip and even though people generally listened to him, Scion speed was something that a person had to see to believe.

On her way to the auditorium to meet Claire and Matt, Helen got intercepted by Cassandra and Ariadne. They asked where she was going, and she didn't feel like lying to them, so she invited them along.

When the coast was clear, they sneaked in the unlocked fire door and came into the auditorium from the backstage entrance. Matt and Claire were already sitting on the apron of the stage, their lunches laid out on napkins like a picnic.

"Good. You invited them," Matt said with a satisfied nod when he saw that Helen wasn't alone. "But don't bring anyone else along or we're going to get caught."

"We'll probably get caught, anyway," Claire said with a

smirk. "But it's totally worth it. Where else could we get such atmosphere?" She gestured to the beautiful, glittery set that was growing, piece by piece.

Cassandra and Ariadne looked around appreciatively, especially at the parts of the set that were to be Theseus's palace. They shared a conspiratorial grin with Helen, who managed to lift up half her face in something sort of like a smile. The fairyland parts of the *Midsummer* set appealed to Helen, but the Greek bits disturbed her. The faux Doric columns were half painted and lying sideways on the ground as if they'd been toppled, and they made Helen think of the arduous journey she'd taken the night before.

She never wanted to go back to the dry land, but if she could find that river . . . *Wait, what river?* she thought. She turned her back on the half-built columns and sat down next to Claire to eat her lunch.

Helen tried her best to get into the conversation, but she barely had the initiative to chew, let alone laugh and joke. She could tell that her friends were being clever and fun by the way Cassandra and Ariadne were reacting, but she could barely stay awake, let alone participate in the conversation.

She kept thinking about flying. Well, really she kept catching herself thinking about Lucas, but as soon as her thoughts slid down that hot knife, she shuffled her imagination over to the side and thought about flying instead. Maybe she would try it again on her own later, she decided, but this time she would do it inside her house so she wouldn't be in danger of floating away. Although the prospect of blowing away on the breeze didn't seem like such a bad idea right about now.

"Lennie! The bell's ringing," Claire said, her bag already over her shoulder. Helen jumped up and got her things together while her friends shot each other looks behind her back.

Claire tried to talk to Helen during track, but eventually gave up when Helen kept turning the conversation around to ask how Claire was instead. Helen didn't want pity, and she didn't want to talk about herself. She just wanted to switch her brain off and float.

Eventually, Claire got the hint and started talking about the bonfire party on the beach that night. She was having trouble deciding if she was going to get a ride with Ariadne or not.

"On the one hand I want to get to know her better, but it would mean I would have to go with her and Jason, and he always finds a way to start an argument with me. Are you sure you can't take the night off from work? We could get a ride with Matt together," Claire said optimistically.

"You know I can't."

"If you asked Kate, I'm sure she'd let you," Claire coaxed

"Gig? I really don't want to spend the night sitting on cold sand watching everyone make out," Helen said with finality. "But you should go and have fun. And who knows? Maybe you and Jason will get along tonight, for once."

Claire launched into a tirade about how annoying Jason

was for always disagreeing with her. Only half listening, Helen finessed the air currents around her, practicing flying with the gravity on. She couldn't wait to get home after work that night and give it a try.

Hidden behind a sand dune, Creon counted the minutes that passed while his cousins Hector and Jason stayed submerged. He hadn't known about this talent, and he was happy that circumstance had led him there to witness it. He had lost track of Lucas earlier, which happened often considering his little cousin could fly, and he had to settle for following Jason and Hector to this ridiculous beach party. As he watched his cousins breach the waves and stroll out of the thundering surf, he seethed with resentment. All that talent wasted on cowards who were too frightened of the gods to challenge them, and too interested in their own pleasure to consider the implications that flirting with human girls could have for their entire House.

Jason spent most of the evening talking to a tiny Japanese girl. He seemed to be able to control himself around women, but Hector was a different story. It wasn't even midnight yet, and Creon had seen him rolling around in the sand with *two* different girls already. Didn't Hector know how easy it was for Scions to impregnate women? Did his idiot cousin really want his firstborn to be from some foolish child with no character? Obviously, Hector didn't care about their House, or he wouldn't waste his time with such silly girls. It rankled so much, Creon had to look away and grit his teeth. There was only one girl on this island who was equal to any of them in status. Only one girl worthy of his attention.

Helen. But Lucas wouldn't leave her for a moment, and it forced Creon to keep his distance from her. He couldn't confront his cousins directly or his undercover mission would be spoiled, but there had been a few times when Creon had considered it. Helen's face had stayed with him. He thought back again to their confrontation out on the moors. The fear and anger in her eyes while she chased him had been pure, so passionate it was almost too much to resist. She was powerful, and yet so unaware of her potential she was nearly helpless. His hands shook at the thought of conquering her, but he had to be patient.

His mother had begged him to wait until she could quietly ask around and find out if there was a possibility someone in the family had left a bastard in Massachusetts. Creon had reluctantly agreed to wait a week on her reply, but he knew what the answer would be. Even though he hadn't seen the Furies when he first encountered her, he knew Helen wasn't his cousin.

There were rumors that a few Scions in the past had found a way around the Furies, and Creon believed Helen was one of them. His mother said it was impossible—that all the other Houses had been destroyed—but Creon had more to go on than a gut feeling. The traitors were guarding her like she was the last enemy Scion, and she was so untrained, so ignorant of who and what she was, it seemed obvious to Creon that she had been purposely hidden away from all the Houses, even her own. But above any of these other reasons, it was Creon's body that told him she was not related

277

to him. He had met dozens of his female cousins, all beautiful as the daughters of Apollo should be, but not one of them kept him up at night the way Helen did. He *knew* she was from another House.

He was obligated by family duty to watch and wait for a few more days in order to remain true to the promise he had made his mother, but very soon he would prove himself. He was up to this challenge, and although there was an alternative for unification of the Houses other than combat, Creon forced himself not to think about it, no matter how tempting it was. This was his one chance at the glory he deserved, the last chance at this type of glory for any Scion. There was another Triumph waiting to be captured, and in his heart he knew that this Triumph would be the one to open the gates of Atlantis.

Creon was destined to be the Scion to make his family immortal, and for that his father would honor him above all others.

# TWELVE

Helen heard something up on the roof. She ran up the stairs to the widow's walk and threw the door open as fast as she could, but the widow's walk was empty. She sighed, relieved. She didn't want any of the Delos kids sleeping on her roof anymore. She especially didn't want Lucas listening to her while she had nightmares, and she had just woken up from another horrible one. She looked around at the empty widow's walk, feeling desolate and lonely, but she wasn't sure if that was because of a dream or because of her waking life.

She went back down to her bedroom and forced herself to notice the writing on the mirror. Then she wrote *I SAW IT AGAIN* in Claire's green eyeliner and made herself stare at the words. That was two nights in a row she'd seen the river she couldn't remember. She was racking her brain trying to picture it, but her mind's eye kept looking away. Suddenly, she spotted her own reflection in the mirror and gasped.

Her cheeks were sunken in, her nightshirt was pulled out of shape, and her arms and legs were covered in icky black muck. River muck.

She had seen a river with black banks and gray water. She could remember thirst and not being able to drink. But why was it such a struggle to remember anything else that had happened? She focused her thoughts to try and bring the memory back.

*Her thirst was tormenting her so she had gone down to the water. She leaned over the foul banks of black mud and saw pale, crippled fish bumping around clumsily, as if they had forgotten how to swim. She backed away from the river, refusing to drink that water even if she died of thirst with the sound of its current rushing in her ears. . . .*

Helen ran to the bathroom and threw herself into the shower, rubbing at the black mud and rinsing her mouth out with gulp after gulp of water. She felt polluted. She scrubbed until her skin turned red and her eyes were stinging from being open in the spray.

When she got out of the shower, she dragged her sheets and nightshirt over to the washing machine. There was no blood this time, but Helen doubted she'd be able to get out that river mud. She put a half a cup of bleach into the washing machine and made sure the water was hot, hoping that she would be able to salvage something. Then she went back upstairs to clean all the dirty footprints she'd tracked through the house.

It was early Saturday morning, and usually her father would be home during the day and working at night, but he had opted to work a double to give Kate the day off. Helen had a feeling that the two of them were avoiding each other. She had tried to talk to Kate about it the night before, after Claire left to go to the bonfire, but she just didn't have the energy to push Kate to open up. Everything felt duller to Helen. Muffled, like her feelings were in storage, buried under mounds of packaging peanuts.

Helen went to her room and switched gravity off and on, alternately floating up and thumping down until she figured out how to swing her legs under her and land on the balls of her feet instead of all over the damn place. She worked a bit with the air currents, but she couldn't do anything more than finesse her position as she floated or she risked blowing her room to pieces. After a few hours, the constantly ringing phone drove her out of doors. The Delos family wanted to know why she wasn't at their house yet for practice, and they wouldn't stop calling until she answered.

Helen had been thinking. She just couldn't see the point of learning how to swing a sword if she couldn't be wounded by weapons, and she didn't need to fight if she could simply fly away. She knew that eventually Hector or Jason would come looking for her at home, so she wandered outside with no clear destination, hoping that a little speed would help clear her head. She was in jeans and a sweater, not exactly running gear, but it didn't matter. As soon as she was out of the town center she went off Polpis Road, heading east. She didn't care where she ended up, as long as it was away from people. As she ran she realized that she had come this way once before, and although she didn't want to think about her first flight and everything that came after it, she knew it was the perfect place to find the solitude she was after.

The sun was going down and she was grateful to be numb enough to experience something beautiful without her depressing thoughts barging in and ruining it. Looking around, she saw a familiar lighthouse. She glanced down at the sand under her feet and wondered if it was the same sand that had cradled her and Lucas when they were in so much pain. When they had *died* for a moment, she realized.

As soon as the thought occurred to her, she knew it was true. They had done more than just suffer terrible injury that night, they had started to cross over. Or at least Lucas had. And she had followed him down to stop him. And there was a river . . . *Wait, what river?*

"Hey! What the hell do you think you're doing?" Hector shouted.

He was furious. He stalked up the beach, his legs eating up far more distance than a human's could as he came toward her.

"How did you find me?" Helen sputtered.

"Your moves aren't so hard to anticipate," he sneered. "Now get your ass to my house."

"I don't want to practice anymore. It's pointless," Helen called over her shoulder as she turned on her heel to walk away. "I just want to be left alone."

"You want to be left alone, huh, Princess? Sorry, it doesn't work that way," he said as he grabbed her shoulders and spun her around. That did it for her. She gave one hysterical laugh—it was either that or start crying—and shoved Hector away from her. Hard.

"What are you going to do? What? Are you going to beat me to death? You can't! You're not strong enough," Helen said as she hit him repeatedly on the shoulders, trying to instigate a fight. "So go get a sword. Go ahead. Oh, wait, I forgot. That doesn't hurt me, either. So what are you going to do, you big bully? What do you have to teach me?"

"Humility," he said quietly. He moved fast, but he was also bending the light funny the way Lucas did. While she was still trying to focus her eyes, pissed that she hadn't even considered that Hector could have this talent as well, Hector grabbed her, threw her over his shoulder, and started walking toward the water.

Enraged, Helen used her full strength against him for the first time. She didn't care how much she hurt him. She pushed until she unlocked herself from Hector's grip. She heard his arm break as she physically separated herself from him. Then she changed states to fly away. As she summoned a wind to take her away, he grabbed her with his other hand. His more dominant hand. Helen realized, a bit too late, that Hector had allowed her to break his left arm so that she would chose weightlessness—weightlessness and momentary weakness. Before she could digest what he was doing and shift back to the gravity-state to get enough purchase to push him off, he dragged her easily into the water where her weight mattered not at all.

Hector walked right into the water and trudged down, down, down until they were both completely submerged under what seemed to Helen like fathoms of dark water. She struggled uselessly. This was Hector's element and he had complete control. He could even speak and be heard underwater.

"You aren't the only one with talents, Princess," he said.

There were no bubbles streaming out of his mouth, just clear speech. He could breathe, he could talk, he could walk on the seabed as if he was walking on firm ground. Helen finally understood why Hector terrified her so much. He was an ocean creature, and she was deathly afraid of the ocean.

Ever since she'd almost drowned as a child, Helen had suspected that the ocean had it in for her, but she'd never told anyone that because she was pretty sure they would think she was crazy. Now, almost a decade later, as she looked into Hector's blank blue eyes, she knew she had been right. Helen bucked and squirmed under Hector's relentless grip. Great gouts of bubbles flew from her mouth as she screamed in soundless panic. She scratched at his face and kicked her feet, but there was nothing she could do to make him let her go. She was going to drown.

Acid fizzed in her veins and the edges of her vision

smudged as she started to black out. As her eyes closed, she felt him tug on her legs as he towed her back to shore. He hauled her out of the water by an ankle and swung her over his head and down onto the sand like a mallet, hard enough to dislodge the liquid from her lungs. She puked burning salt water and coughed until her inner ears stung and she could hear the blood thumping in her head.

"If you had been training with me today, you would have known that you can use your bolts underwater," he said, yanking on his broken arm to straighten out the bones with a sickening crack. He screamed and fell to his knees, panting for a moment before continuing through gritted teeth. "But you didn't show up for practice."

They sat next to each other on the sand for a while, both of them too injured to move. As they healed, the setting sun seemed to give up on the day and jump headlong into the water. The sky grew dark.

"I thought you were descended from Apollo," Helen rasped.

Her vocal cords were still damaged, but she didn't need to say anything more, anyway. Hector didn't come off like the smartest member of the Delos clan, but Helen was starting to suspect that even if he didn't spend as much time reading books as Cassandra did, he was every bit as clever as the rest of his family.

"A minor sea goddess called a Nereid mixed with our House somewhere along the way. There are a lot of minor gods and spirits of the water or the woods still running around here and there, and things happen over thousands of years. None of the House lines are purely descended from one god or another anymore, and all the younger generation of Scions have more talents than their parents," he answered.

"Why is that?"

"Cassandra thinks it has something to do with the Fates wanting the Scions to acquire more talents and become more powerful so they can rule Atlantis, but personally I just think it's because we're all mutts. My great-great-grandfather sleeps with a nymph, and I get to walk underwater. You don't need the Fates to explain that one."

"Is that how you knew I can drown? Because you have power over water?"

"That was common sense. And I don't have power over water, I'm just at home in it," he said. He turned to look her in the eye. When he continued speaking it was in a tone that was excruciatingly similar to the voice Lucas used when he'd taught her to fly, and it tugged at Helen. "You don't think like a fighter yet. You have all these amazing talents—talents most Scions would trade half the years of their lives for—but you can't use them because you don't think tactically. Just stop and use your head for a second. The ocean isn't a weapon, but it can kill. The air isn't a weapon, but if I were to deprive you of it, you would die. The earth isn't a weapon . . ." he began.

"But if I were to slam into it hard enough . . . I get it," she finished for him, swallowing hard and staring out at the unforgiving waves.

"Water is your Achilles' heel. It's the one element you fear because you have no control over it."

Helen didn't know how he had figured that out, but she knew he was right. Somehow, even when she had been ignorant of her abilities, she had known deep down on an unconscious level that she had less to fear from three of the four elements. She could command the air and summon winds, she could manipulate the gravity of the earth, and she could easily tolerate the heat of fire because in order for her to create lightning she had to be able to withstand temperatures that were hotter than any flame. But water was the one element that rendered her completely helpless. Finally, she understood her own fear, even if she wasn't any closer to conquering it.

"How could you have known that about me?" Helen asked, slightly awed.

"Because I've been trained to think tactically and find my opponent's weaknesses since the day I was born. You haven't. There are so many ways to kill a person, Helen. You think you're safe because you passed Cassandra's test with the sword, but you're not," Hector said, his voice thick with frustration and worry. "I know you're still in shock, but I don't have time to wait for you to get comfortable with what you are. People are coming for you. You have to grow up, and you have to do it now or a lot of people are going to die. So go home. Eat something and get some rest. You look sick and I don't want Luke blaming that on me. But tomorrow you come to train. No more excuses."

Without waiting for a response, Hector stood up and left her alone on the dark beach. She fiddled with her heart necklace, running the charm along her lower lip as she sat there feeling ashamed of how she had acted. Her clothes were heavy with water, but she didn't wring them out. She felt like she deserved to be waterlogged and uncomfortable a little longer.

Obviously, she had to keep training with Hector, but that meant she had to go to the Delos house. That meant she had to see Lucas, and she absolutely could not do that. No matter how she turned it over in her mind she felt like she was choking whenever she thought about having to see him every day, knowing that he was forcing himself to be nice to her, that he probably pitied her. She still couldn't figure out how she could have been so wrong about Lucas in the first place, and it stuck inside her like a splinter that can't be found and dug out. She didn't expect him to fall at her feet or anything, but to go from holding her hand everywhere they went to saying he would never touch her? How could that be?

Unable to sit still with these thoughts in her head, Helen jumped up into the air with a little cry and let an easterly wind take her out over the water. For a few heartbeats she hung in a calm envelope of air as the stars switched on, desperately sucking up the beauty of that experience like it was emotional Novocain.

When she was calmer, she circled higher and hitched a ride on a steady westerly gust that brought her back over the island. She was not a graceful flyer yet—in fact she was barely competent—but if she didn't think about it too much she knew what to do to move herself along. She had no clear idea where to go, but suddenly she was freezing cold and in need of comfort. Without making a conscious choice, she found herself circling over Claire's house.

Helen alit in Claire's front yard, and then realized that in her condition she couldn't just go up and ring the bell. She was soaking wet and shaking with cold. Mr. and Mrs. Aoki would call her father immediately if they laid eyes on her like this.

Circling the house on foot, Helen peeked inside the windows, trying to figure out where Claire was. She fished her cell phone out of her jeans to call Claire and get her to come outside, and then smacked herself on the forehead when she saw that her two-day-old phone had been ruined by the salt water. She heard Claire yelling at her mother in Japanese as she stomped upstairs to her room. Claire's bedroom light switched on, and she slammed her door shut behind her.

It was a terrible way to come out to Claire, and Helen was vaguely aware of that fact as she floated toward the window and saw her best friend sitting on her bed with her mouth hanging open. Helen waited for her to scream, but when Claire didn't, she motioned to the locked window.

"Let me in," she said urgently through her chattering teeth.

"Oh, damn it. You *are* a vampire," Claire said. She had a disappointed but completely unsurprised expression on her face.

"What the hell? No! Just open the window, Gig, I'm freezing!" Helen said in a loud whisper. Claire dragged herself off her bed and walked to the window with her shoulders slumping dejectedly.

"I know it's popular and all that, but I really don't want you to suck my blood. It's just so unsanitary!" Claire whined pitifully as she opened the window.

She put a protective hand over her bare throat, but she still let Helen inside despite the danger, and that fact was not lost on Helen.

"Oh, for the love of Pete, I'm not a frigging vampire, Gig! See? No fangs! No crazy eyes." Helen lifted up her upper lip to expose entirely normal incisors, and then opened her eyes extra wide to show a complete lack of bloodlust.

"All right! But it was a valid question, considering the circumstances!" Claire replied defensively as Helen wafted through the window and then transitioned into the gravity-state in front of her.

"All right! I agree, it's a valid concern," Helen conceded, but something was wrong. "I just flew in your window. Why aren't you more surprised?"

"I've known you could fly since we were kids. I even pushed you off your roof once to make sure. Sorry about that, by the way," she said sheepishly.

"You *did* push me!" Helen breathed, suddenly remembering the whole incident in a flash.

They had been maybe seven years old and goofing off on Helen's widow's walk. Helen fell, but she never hit the ground. She'd sort of settled to earth like a leaf falling from a tree. Claire swore up and down that Helen had slipped, but Helen never remembered losing her balance, and because of the way Claire looked at her for weeks afterward, Helen had suspected something fishy before putting it out of her mind. Now it all made sense. Helen stared at Claire, speechless.

"What? I didn't think you'd die or anything! Long story short—I saw you *not* fall down my stairs the day before when you actually *did* slip, so I needed to test my theory," Claire said as if it all made perfect sense.

"By pushing me off the roof?"

"You have no idea how angry I've been with you since then for keeping it from me! You can *fly*, Lennie, and you never told me!" Claire yelled, completely shifting the argument away from herself, but Helen decided that she should allow it, considering Claire's obvious hurt.

"I didn't know until a few weeks ago!" Helen insisted.

"You are such a liar!" Claire said, jabbing a fist against her hip.

"It's true! My mom put a curse on me when I was a baby so I wouldn't be able to use my . . . Aw, crap! It would be so much easier if I *was* a vampire. Then you'd just understand!" Helen huffed, frustrated and feeling misunderstood. She paced around for a bit, raking her fingers through her tangled hair, before she was able to put her thoughts in order.

"Hergie made you read the *Iliad*, right? You remember how all the heroes had superhuman strength and they could do all kinds of things that normal people can't?" she asked.

"Yeah. That's because they were demigods. But that wasn't real," Claire said like it was obvious. Then she got it. "Oh, my . . ."

"I'm one of those heroes' descendents. We're called Scions, and I have a whole bunch of powers—stuff you wouldn't believe. But I had no idea what I was or what I could do until just days ago. I wish I could tell you everything, but I don't know what I can or can't say. Please, Gig. I know it sounds insane, but I've never lied to you. You just have to believe me."

"Okay," Claire said, nodding her head once and looking Helen directly in the eye, as if she finally felt like she was getting the respect she deserved. "I've had this mostly figured out for a while now, you know. You found out that you were a demigod—how cool is that by the way?—when the Delos family moved here. Because they're like you. I knew that as soon as I saw them. I just didn't know *what* you all were."

"See?" Helen said with a flustered smile. "That's why I had to tell you, I need to be able to talk to you about all this so you can help me figure it out. But you can't tell the Delos family I told you until I find out if that's okay or not."

"It doesn't matter. I can bluff, or pretend I guessed on my own. I sort of did, anyway," Claire said with a satisfied smile. Then something occurred to her and made her switch to a more serious attitude. "Where have you been, by the way? And why are you such a damn mess?"

Helen was about to explain what happened between her and Hector when Claire's phone buzzed. Claire checked the text and then started typing in a response.

"It's Jason. I have to tell him you're here, he's been looking for you all day," Claire told Helen. The phone buzzed again.

"It's him." She read the screen. "He wants me to keep you here. He's on his way over."

"No! I'm not ready to talk to any of them yet!" Helen exclaimed, backing away.

"Len, he's really worried about you, they all are."

"I gotta get out of here," Helen stammered. She ran a hand over her face and turned for the window.

"Where are you going?" Claire asked, trying to block Helen's path with an outstretched arm. "I'll tell him to go away if you want, but you have to let me know that you'll be okay."

"I'm just going home. Promise you won't let him follow me, okay?"

Claire promised and gave Helen a hug. Then Helen jumped out the window, transitioning states in midair. She heard Claire gasp as she flew away. A minute later Helen was landing in her front yard and heading right for the stairs to take a shower and warm up.

He was waiting for her behind the front door. He swept her feet out from under her before he even bothered to slam the front door shut. Everything went completely dark, darker than any night, any blindfold, or any closed room that Helen had ever experienced. She was enveloped in a disorienting blackness that made her feel so dizzy and cut off from the rest of the world that she couldn't even remember the layout of her own house anymore. Where were the stairs? The furniture? She didn't know. It was as if she had fallen into a black hole.

Helen was so shocked she didn't have time to roll over before she felt a very large man cover her from behind. He took her head between his hands and wrenched it to the side, trying to break her neck. She grabbed on to his wrists and pulled them outward, trying to get him to release his grip, but he had leverage on his side. Her neck muscles strained dangerously, and she felt herself start to panic for the second time in an hour. But it was that recent brush with death that informed her as she kicked and struggled. The thought of using her lightning made her stomach turn, but she knew she had no choice.

Helen felt the current start in her belly. It was naturally trying to arc out of her toward the ground, and all she had to do was release it. Untrained as she was, she let the bolt go, and it shot down her legs uselessly, causing her to convulse. In her desperation, she got the last few volts to run up to her hands and jump across her skin into the man's wrists.

For a brief moment the blue spark lit up the room with a flash, and she saw his eyes widen in surprise. Then she felt him shake with the current, and heard him scream as he was electrocuted.

Helen smelled burnt hair and ozone like a calling card from her darkest childhood nightmare. She felt what must have been half her body's energy empty out of her, leaving her as weak as a kitten. The burden of the large man on top of her grew intolerably heavy, and she knew she had to get out from under him before he recovered or she would be no better off than she was when he'd had her by the head. While her attacker was still shaking, she managed to kick some of his weight off of her, and as the barest amount of light was allowed to creep back into the room, she finally got a look at him.

The gleaming blond curls and the thick body were Hector's, and for a moment she feared she had killed him while he might have been trying to teach her a lesson. She leaned right over him to see if he was still breathing. Hanging inches away from his face in the regular darkness of night, she saw it was Creon, but it was too late. The moment she recognized him he opened his eyes and grabbed her to his chest in a deadly bear hug.

Helen screamed and struggled. She reached down into her belly looking for the current, but all that was left was weak static. She had already discharged all the voltage stored up in her muscles. The release of all that energy had left her weak and vulnerable. Her arms and legs had no strength, and she crumpled under Creon's renewed attack like a paper bag. He fell on top of her, pinning her to the ground as he pulled a bronze knife out of his belt.

"Such a shame, *preciosa*. You're the most beautiful girl I've ever seen. Almost too perfect to cut," he grunted into her ear. "But Atlantis . . ."

She squirmed her neck away from his lips, shivers of disgust running across her skin. Then he pushed off of her, raising his knife up high over his head. He paused, and for a brief moment Helen thought he wouldn't do it, but she saw his eyes harden. He brought it down directly over her heart.

Creon's knife made a dozen pinging noises as it shattered and scattered off of her skin. He had just a moment to register what had happened before a foot connected with his head and sent him flying off of Helen.

Lucas jumped on Creon with a vicious snarl, and the two of them began to fight so fast Helen could barely see their hands move. They punched and grabbed and gouged at each other, both of them changing from claw-handed boxing to some kind of strange wrestling in which they tried to bend each other's joints in the wrong direction. Helen barely had time to roll onto her knees before it was over. Cornered and still weak from having been electrocuted, Creon cloaked himself inside an eerie shadow and ran at top speed out of the house as soon as he could put even one inch in between himself and Lucas, who chased him halfway across Helen's lawn before turning around and coming back inside.

"Are you okay?" Lucas practically shouted.

"Yeah, I just can't . . ." Helen said as she tried to stand and then fell back down on the ground with a woozy thump.

"What did he do to you?" Lucas asked, his voice high-pitched with worry. He picked Helen up and tried to balance her so she could stand on her own. "Are your legs broken?" He suddenly reclaimed her weight as he frantically assessed the damage.

"No, I just . . . Hector said to use my bolts to fight, and I did, but they went the wrong way, I think," she mumbled. She was confused and seeing spots.

"Why can't you stand?" Lucas asked as he tried to get her to her feet again. Her heart hurt from seeing Lucas's beautiful face and smelling his body and feeling his hands on her. She had a vague sense where the ground was, but the whole world was falling over, and she was too tired for this crap. She just couldn't do this anymore. She needed a nap.

The next thing she knew, Helen could taste something sweet on her tongue. Honey. She opened her eyes all the way and saw that she was sitting on the counter in her kitchen with Lucas standing between her knees, holding her head up and tilted back as he drizzled honey into her mouth from a plastic bear.

"There you are," he breathed through a small smile when she looked at him. He looked back at her with so much tenderness Helen had to remind herself that Lucas wasn't really interested. For the thousandth time she wondered what had happened to make him push her away the way he had.

"Hi," she said, her voice cracking like she'd just woken from a full night's sleep. "How'd you get here?"

"Cassie got a glimpse of Creon's attack, but she didn't know where it was going to take place because all she could see was darkness. I took a guess," he said, brushing her hair back from her face and placing a long lock behind her shoulder. "Sorry I was late."

"Don't sweat it," she said, her voice still shaking with fear.

She took a deep breath to steady herself and pulled herself together.

"You messed him up pretty good. I've never seen Creon bolt from a fight like that before," Lucas said with admiration.

"I just softened him up for you." She couldn't resist smiling at him, even though she knew she'd spend hours rethinking and regretting it. "Did I miss anything while I was out?"

"Just a trip from there to here," he said, pointing over his shoulder then to the counter. "And a quick call to Jason for backup."

"Lennie!" Claire shrieked frantically as she barged through the front door. She gasped at the knocked-over furniture in the foyer.

"In here. Don't freak out, I'm all right," Helen called out to Claire. Then she saw Lucas's questioning look. "It's okay, she knows some of it," she told him. She pushed him back so she could jump down off the counter. Claire came in first, followed by Jason, who looked like he was ready to strangle her.

"Sorry, Luke. I was at her place looking for Helen when you called. I tried to come alone but Five-Two latched on to my arm and wouldn't let me go without her," Jason growled, nearly tearing his hair out in frustration.

"Um, excuse me? But she's my best friend and I could tell something was up," Claire snapped at Jason. "How could this have happened? You just flew out my window, like, two seconds ago." Claire grabbed Helen in a hug.

"You know about . . . stuff?" Jason asked, surprised, not

sure how much he should say.

"I told her," Helen admitted as she pulled out of Claire's enthusiastic hug and rubbed her sore neck.

"But I've always sort of known. I just thought she was undead or something," Claire said with a dismissive wave of her hand. "Believe me, I'm much happier you're all part Greek god instead of part something disgusting like bat or wolf or mosquito."

Jason and Lucas shared a look over Claire's head. Helen explained what had happened as quickly as she could while Lucas took Jason outside to look at the tracks, but it was too late to try to follow Creon. They came back inside with grim looks on their faces to find Helen and Claire had switched the lights on to assess the damage in the entryway.

"Are those pieces of a knife?" Claire asked.

"Yeah. He kinda stabbed me in the heart," Helen said tentatively, not knowing how Claire would react.

"You can still do that? Stop blades?" Claire asked, unsurprised. "What about the lightning thing? Can you still do that, too?"

"How do you know all this about me?" Helen sputtered. Claire sighed.

"After I pushed you off the roof . . ." she began.

"After you *what*?" Lucas yelled.

"It was when we were seven! And she wasn't hurt!" Claire yelled back. "Anyway. I knew about the knife thing because, well, I tried to stab you once, too," she continued bashfully. "But I already knew you'd be fine because of what happened with Gretchen and the scissors in second grade. Remember?"

Helen grimaced. "Oh, yeah! Gretchen and the scissors! She really *was* trying to kill me, wasn't she?"

"Yeah, she was. She was crazy jealous of you. But I *never* wanted to hurt you, I just had to be sure I wasn't losing my mind. It was scary, you know?" she asked apologetically.

Helen smiled, forgiving her instantly.

"I guess I can't blame you. But how'd you know about the lightning-bolt thing?"

"Remember when we were nine, we were going off island on the ferry to see the Boston Aquarium, and that creepy guy with that huge gut kept trying to talk to us? Remember how he kept 'accidentally' bumping up against you and stroking your hair?"

Helen did remember, even though she had spent a lot of time trying to forget. There had been that horrible smell of burnt hair, and the empty look in his eyes. Helen nodded, shivering at the thought, and dreading where Claire was going.

"Remember how he just disappeared suddenly before we docked? Well, he didn't just disappear. He tried to grab you, Len, and I saw an electric spark jump from you to him. It blew him right off the deck of the ferry. It looked like lightning, except it came *out of you*."

"I think I killed him," Helen whispered, needing finally to admit what she had done.

"Good! He was a child molester! You should probably get a medal," Claire insisted. Helen looked at Claire's earnest face. The man probably *did* mean to do something terrible, but did that justify frying him?

"First, you don't *know* that you killed him. Second, it was a reflex. Whether he deserved to die or not isn't the point. You shouldn't feel guilty about something that was done in self-defense," Lucas insisted. He touched Helen's shoulder. She moved away from him uncertainly, not knowing how to feel. Luckily, Jason changed the subject.

"So you've always known she wasn't entirely human," Jason said to Claire with a wry smile. "Didn't that ever bother you?"

"I was a little worried she might try to drag me off to hell and drain my essence at some point, but I figured that was still better than having Gretchen for a best friend," Claire said with just enough honesty to get a laugh. "Plus, I don't know if you've noticed or not, but this island is full of white people. Not exactly easy growing up Japanese here. But with Lennie around I always knew no matter how strange I was, she would always be way stranger. So that was nice."

"And you never told anyone else over all of these years? You never mentioned it to someone when you were little, even by accident?" Lucas asked skeptically.

"Come on Lucas, I'm not stupid! I saw *E.T.*, you know, and I know what the men in the white coats did to him and Elliot," she replied with a disgusted look on her face. "I'd never tell on Lennie. Or you, for that matter."

"Thanks," Lucas replied, a little confused by the alien metaphor.

He and Jason shared another look, and this time there was obvious admiration in their eyes.

"You know what I don't get?" Helen asked, changing the subject. "Why can she be around when I do Scion stuff but it doesn't affect me? All of these times she saw me use my powers over the years, but I don't remember ever feeling pain in my stomach."

Helen explained her mother's curse to Claire, but no one had an answer to her question. They turned their attention to cleaning up as best they could before Jerry got home. Claire offered to stay with Helen for the night, in case she was too freaked out to sleep alone, but Jason nixed that idea right away.

"And what are you going to do if Creon shows up again? Throw your pocketbook at him and give him a piece of your mind?" he said shaking his head. "Uh-uh. I know you two are like sisters, but you're not staying here."

"I'll stay. You take Claire home," Lucas said, quietly assuming control before Claire could start another argument with Jason. "Let me know if you see anything around her house."

"Right," Jason said with a nod as he guided Claire toward the door.

He didn't seem surprised that there might be something dangerous lurking around Claire's house, but Helen and Claire were. Helen lifted her arm to stop them from leaving, suddenly terrified again. It was night and any shadow could have Creon inside it. Sensing Helen's fear, Lucas intercepted her hand and held it tightly.

"Jase can handle it," he told her confidently.

"Wait, what do you mean, my house? My parents are home," Claire said, her anxiety resurfacing as well. "You don't think the guy who did this . . ."

"Don't worry," Jason said with a sensitivity he usually reserved for everyone in the world *except* Claire. "I'm not going to let anything happen to you or your parents."

"Thank you," she said slowly, looking a bit surprised that she had any reason to say those words to him.

She turned and waved at Helen, who thought to herself that the impossible had just happened. Claire had finally run out of nasty things to say to Jason. Helen shut the door behind them and took a deep breath. Then she glanced over at Lucas, and prayed to a pantheon of gods that looking at him would get easier someday.

"You look tired," she said, realizing it was true as she said it.

"So do you. I hear you've been having a lot of nightmares," he said back, completely unashamed to admit he was asking his cousins about her.

"Why do you care? Please, Lucas, just go away," she begged, rubbing her face with her hands.

"I can't. I won't," he said, moving forward and pulling her into his arms.

She felt too fragile to fight him off. She melted into his chest and rested there for a few moments.

"Why do you smell like the ocean?" he said suddenly, pulling away from her to get a better look. He studied her bedraggled clothes speckled with sand, and asked suspiciously, "What happened to you today *besides* Creon?"

"How is that fair?" she demanded. She pushed him from her with a bitter laugh. "If I lie to you you'll know, and if I stay silent you'll assume something worse than the truth."

"Then just tell me as much or as little as you want," he said quietly, stepping away from her to allow her some personal space. "But tell me *something*. What happened?"

"I was dodging practice because I couldn't bear to see you. Hector found me hiding on the beach, I got in his face, and he nearly drowned me to teach me a lesson in humility," she blurted, tears of exhaustion brimming in her eyes. "Then I went to Claire's to cry on her shoulder and tell her I was a Scion. Then I flew home, where Creon attacked me, tried to break my neck, and stabbed me in the heart. You pretty much know the rest. Now I just want to take a hot shower and lie down because I'm freezing cold and itchy and I don't think I can handle anything else happening today."

"Okay. You go shower," Lucas said, nodding tightly as he stepped out of her path. "I'll wait for you in your room."

Helen staggered up the stairs and ran into the bathroom. She got into the shower and began to cry. Sitting down in the tub with the spray fanning out all around her she couldn't stop the tears any longer. She tried to be as quiet as she could, and hoped that the droning rush of water would mask the sound of her crying.

When she finally got it all out she dried off and put on a sweet-smelling tank top and pair of sweatpants fresh from the laundry. As she flossed and brushed her teeth in the foggy bathroom, she heard her dad come home and turn on the TV in the living room. She went to the top of the stairs and shouted a good night down to him. He grunted a good night back, but he was too engrossed in the Red Sox race to October to start a conversation. Helen went into her bedroom.

Lucas was waiting for her in there. When Helen saw him, lying on top of her covers fully dressed with his shoes kicked off, she stopped and stared at him from the doorway. He was too long for her little-girl bed, but even so he looked just right lying in it. He stared back at her for a moment before he swallowed painfully, lifted up the covers, and motioned for her to get in. When she paused, caught between arguing that her father could walk in at any second and asking him to take his clothes off, he spoke.

"I only have so much willpower, Helen," he whispered. "And since you apparently sleep in the most ridiculously transparent tank top I've ever seen, I'm going to have to ask you to get under the covers before I do something stupid."

The blood rushed to Helen's face, and she immediately crossed her arms to cover her chest. She ran and jumped under the covers. Lucas just laughed and folded the comforter up over her as if it were some uncrossable line that would magically keep the two of them from doing "something stupid." As she snuggled down, he wrapped an arm around her and rubbed his face into the back of her neck.

"No need to be embarrassed. After seeing you in my cousin's nightgown, you've got nothing to hide. But why were you crying in the shower?" he murmured into her hair. She could feel his lips moving against her scalp, and feel the press of his hips through the covers, but his arms were an unyielding cage. She tried to turn over to face him, to welcome him under the covers with her, but he wouldn't let her.

"I was crying because I'm frustrated! Why are you doing this?" she whispered into her pillow.

"We can't, Helen," was all he said.

He kissed her neck and said he was sorry over and over, but try as she might, he wouldn't let her face him. She began to feel like she was being used.

"Please be patient," he begged as he stopped her hand from reaching back to touch him.

She tried to sit up, to push him out of her bed, anything but suffer lying next to someone who would play with her so terribly. They wrestled a bit, but he was much better at it than she was and felt even heavier than he looked. He easily blocked every attempt she made to wrap her arms or legs or lips around him.

"Do you want me at all, or do you just think it's fun to tease me like this?" she asked, feeling rejected and humiliated. "Won't you even kiss me?" She finally struggled onto her back where she could at least see his face.

"If I kiss you, I won't stop," he said in a desperate whisper as he propped himself up on his elbows to look her in the eye.

She looked back at him, really seeing him for the first time that night. His expression was vulnerable and uncertain. His mouth was swollen with want. His body was shaking, and there was a fine layer of anxious sweat wilting his clothes. Helen relaxed back into the bed with a sigh. For some reason that obviously had nothing to do with desire, he wouldn't allow himself to be with her.

"You're not laughing at me, are you?" she asked warily, just as a precaution.

"No. There's nothing funny about this," he answered. He shifted himself off her and lay back down alongside her, still breathing hard.

"But for some reason, you and I will never happen," she said, feeling calm.

"Never say never," he said urgently, rolling back on top of her and using all of his unusually heavy mass to press her deep into the cocoon of her little-girl bed. "The gods love to toy with people who use absolutes."

Lucas ran his lips across her throat and let her put her arms around him, but that was all. He kept her pinned under the blankets, mummified in miserable chastity, allowing her to hold, but not fully embrace him.

"Do you care for me? More than just in a life or death 'we need to stop the Hundred Cousins from starting a war with the gods' type of way?" she asked flippantly.

She knew that on some level she was being petty and insecure, but she needed to know how he felt about her. He propped himself up on his elbows so he could see her more clearly and so that she could see him back.

"Of course I care for you," he said intently. "The only thing

I wouldn't do to be with you is cause innocent people to die. And that's pretty much it." He moved on to his back again, jabbing a hand in his hair. "But apparently that's enough."

Helen knew there was a lot more behind what he was saying than he was letting on, but she couldn't bear to ask any questions that might have awful answers. She'd had enough awful for one day. She rolled on top of him and tucked herself into that spot on his chest that she was convinced still held a Helen-shaped dent in it.

"Just so you know? Just so we're clear. I care about you, too. And if this hug is all I can have, I'd prefer it over anything else from anyone else."

"That's because you've never been with a man," Lucas said as he kissed the bit of skin on her forehead that was just about to be hair. "Now go to sleep," he ordered.

Helen would have argued, but she was too damn tired from fighting for her life twice in one day to do more than blink contrarily. Lucas's arms wove a safe basket around her mending heart and she relaxed completely into him. She listened to the particular resonance of his breathing, a sound that she already knew so well, and fell into a deep, nightmare-free sleep.

# THIRTEEN

Swathed in black shadows, Creon crouched outside Helen's house, his eyes glued to her bedroom window. He could hear Hector four doors down, slipping through the neighbor's yard, searching for him. But Creon knew Hector didn't have a prayer. No one could find Creon at night if he didn't want to be found.

His little cousin Lucas was up there, in Helen's bed, holding her while she slept. Creon shook from head to toe, resisting the nearly all-consuming urge to leap through the glass and fight his cousin for her life. Or maybe just for her. Creon wasn't sure what he would do anymore, and he didn't like this newfound uncertainty. He gritted his teeth and forced himself to get control. If he challenged his cousin, it would be a fight to the death. Creon had no doubt he would win, but in winning he would lose everything. He would become an Outcast, and Atlantis would remain lost.

The choice was clear: immortality or Helen. So why was he sweating with the effort to resist? He heard Helen sighing in her sleep and Lucas shifting his body under hers, pulling her even closer. Creon's legs straightened as if of their own accord. He took two steps toward the window, his head swimming in the red-lit haze of bloodlust.

His phone vibrated in his pocket.

Alerted to the danger, Hector broke into a sprint and headed straight for that slight sound. Creon had no choice but to run. He couldn't take both his cousins *and* Helen. He would have to come back some other time.

It took him ten minutes to lose Hector in the center of the island. His cousin was persistent, but eventually the suffocating darkness of Creon's shadows disoriented Hector enough so that Creon could slip away.

Trotting up the eastern side of the beach, Creon finally checked the ID on the call that had saved him from a terrible mistake. It didn't surprise him that it was from his mother. She might not be a Scion, but she had uncanny timing. He called her back and told her what he had discovered when he tried to stab Helen.

At first she didn't believe him, though in her careful choice of words, Creon sensed that her incredulity came not from a belief that what he had described was impossible, but rather that she doubted Helen herself was responsible for the phenomenon he had witnessed. Somehow, his mother had seen or heard of a Scion being able to break blades with his or her skin before, and Creon pressed her to tell him who it was. Instead of answering, she asked yet again for Creon to describe Helen. He did.

"Well, it must have been that your blade was defective. From how you describe Helen, it can't be *her* or her daughter," Mildred said quickly.

Creon continued to press his mother and she grew increasingly frustrated, raising her voice and even swearing a bit. Creon was shocked by her crass behavior. A lady never cheapened herself by using foul language, and he hadn't even considered his mother capable of it until that moment. He asked her politely how she could be so sure his blade was defective.

"Because if this girl truly was impervious to weapons, then you would have also said she has the most beautiful face you've ever seen. You wouldn't be able to ignore that fact—it's in your blood," she replied petulantly.

"And if she does have the most beautiful face I've ever seen? What then?" Creon asked calmly, although a wonderful rush of adrenaline was sending a chill across his skin. The line went silent for a full five seconds.

"You need to come home *now*. We need to tell your father. This is much bigger than you know," Mildred finally choked out before she abruptly ended the call.

The next morning Helen jerked herself awake, her entire body snapping from sleep to high alert in a blink. Her hand flew to that spot on her chest where Creon's blade had broken, and she had to press her fingers into her breastbone to convince herself that there was no gaping hole there.

She heard faint whispers coming from across the room. Sitting up, she saw Lucas standing in the window, talking to someone outside in such a low voice that no human could hear. The clock by her bed read 5:25, and the sky was barely gray with the dawn.

"She's safe, that's all that matters," Lucas said out the window.

"Not *all* that matters," came the whispered reply.

Helen got out of bed and joined Lucas at the window. She looked down and saw Hector standing on the edge of her lawn. He looked up at them, glancing back and forth from Helen to Lucas, an indignant look on his face.

"You okay?" Hector asked Helen gruffly.

"Yeah. But *you* don't look so hot," she said. Even from one flight up she could see that Hector's eyes were bloodshot with fatigue and worry. He grimaced sarcastically at her compassionate look, and turned to Lucas with a warning.

"Stay high until we're sure. She's safer in the air."

Hector ran off so fast that Helen could only make out his blur. Lucas shut the window and leaned against it. His eyes were wide and unblinking.

"What was that about?" Helen asked in a nearly inaudible voice. She could hear her dad's deep breathing from his bedroom. Thankfully, he was still asleep.

"My family went looking for Creon last night," Lucas answered with downturned eyes. "We think he caught a charter flight off the island, but we aren't sure yet."

"He's gone?" Helen asked, a little too hopefully.

"Maybe. But if he *did* leave, it won't be forever." Lucas stared at Helen so intensely she had to reach out and touch him somehow just to break the tension. She stepped forward and placed her hand on his chest. He was shaking.

Straightening suddenly, Lucas crossed to the door. "Put on something warm."

"Why? Where are we going?" she whispered.

"Up."

As soon as they were airborne, Lucas seemed to relax a little, but not much. She asked for a flying lesson, partly because she wanted to learn, but mostly just to distract him. They worked on Helen's air-pressure control for over an hour before they got a call from his family. Castor had called from the airport, finally confirming that Creon had left the island by private charter like they had suspected, and it was safe for Lucas to bring Helen in.

Hector took the phone and *insisted* they come in right away—he wanted her to resume her combat training that morning. The cousins got into a heated exchange. Finally, Lucas agreed to land, but he seemed put out by the request.

"What's wrong?" Helen asked, confused that he wasn't happier to learn that Creon was gone.

"Hector has the wrong idea about us being up here alone. I'm not *keeping* you aloft so we can . . . damn it, you need to learn this!" he snapped, raking a hand through his hair. "I want you to be able to fly away from trouble, rather than try to stand and fight."

"Me too," she replied enthusiastically, grabbing on to Lucas's shoulders so she didn't waft away. "Call your cousins back and tell them we're not done. I'd rather spend the day flying with you than getting sweated on by Hector any time."

Lucas gave Helen a sinking look, like he was thinking a painful thought. "We'd better go in," he finally decided, his face darkening. "You need to learn both."

Helen knew Lucas was worried, but after spending the morning soaring weightless, she couldn't feel anything but elated. She took both his hands and swung him around her so they spun in a spiral and tumbled in the air like they were on a roller coaster. The swooping sensation in her stomach made Helen shriek, but it worked. Lucas grinned and took the bait.

He seized on her arms and brought her into a dive that had her screaming bloody murder. At the last moment he pulled up, holding Helen cradled in his arms before allowing her to float to his side. They hovered over the Delos lawn like that for a moment, holding hands and laughing hysterically. They failed to notice the worried stares they were getting from the rest of the Delos family inside the house.

"Now, before you land I'm going to teach you another skill," Lucas said as he looped over her shoulder and put an arm around her from behind. "I'm going to teach you how to transition into the massive-state—turn up the gravity pulling on you. The best way to get the hang of it is to do it while you're landing."

"Is that what you did when you landed on Hector the other day in the tennis courts?" Helen guessed. "And last night?" She was thinking of how heavy he'd made his body when they were wrestling in her bed. She pinched her lips together to keep herself from smiling.

"Exactly," he said against her ear, letting his lower lip brush against her skin. "It's the third state of gravity for fliers, and it could save your life in a fight."

With his arm around her waist and the two of them floating ten feet above the ground, he taught her how to warp the way the world pulled on her. Lucas guided her to reverse the impulse that made her weightless and imagine her body becoming heavier. She was able to pick up the basics right away and when Lucas told her to touch down she thudded into the lawn with a jarring blow, kicking up two great divots of grass with her heels. She was impressed with herself and looked up at Lucas for approval, but apparently, there was still a lot left for her to learn.

"You'll get better at it," he said encouragingly as he pounded into the lawn next to her, skidding two deep trenches with his feet.

"You are such a show-off!" she said, grinning at him.

"Hey, I've got to impress you as much as I can, while I can. Soon you'll be flying circles around me," he said. He took her hand and pulled her tight up against his side as he led her toward the house.

"I doubt that," Helen said, shaking her head. Lucas was so graceful in the air. There was no way she'd ever fly the way he did.

"You're stronger than me," he said without any envy or

judgment, just as a fact. "When you realize that, you're going to be able to do things that I never dreamed of."

"If I'm so strong, then why do I always need you to come and save my sorry ass?" she asked sarcastically.

"Because fighting is about much more than strength," he said seriously. "Which is good, or Hector would still be able to beat the crap out of me in a fight."

"I can still beat the crap out of you in a fight," Hector shouted from inside the house. Lucas smirked at Helen and shook his head as they walked into the kitchen. They didn't get far.

"Not on my clean floors!" Noel shouted, pointing to Lucas's and Helen's muddy shoes. Then she realized why they were so muddy. "What did you savages do to my new lawn?" she groaned.

"I had to, Mom. Helen needs to learn." Lucas dutifully backed out of the house and took off his shoes, and Helen did the same.

"Helen, dear. You look hungry. Make sure you eat something before you leave," Noel said kindly, before shifting right back into scolding mode. "About that lawn, you know the rules, Luke."

"'Fix what you break,' yeah, yeah. And you know I always do," he said with a mischievous smile as he came into the house and started chasing his poor, hassled mother out of the kitchen with the threat of a tickle. She tried to beat him off with a dish towel, but she didn't stand a chance.

As Lucas ran upstairs to change his clothes, Helen could

see he was happy. And so was she. She knew she was still in danger and should be terrified, but watching Lucas bound up the stairs three at a time, all she could feel was giddy, bubbly happiness. She still had no idea what the heck was going on between them, but she was *happy*.

Apparently, Helen wasn't the only one. Pandora came into the kitchen with a yoga glow, humming to herself. She didn't have on her bracelets. Instead, it was her anklets and a spangled belly chain that were jingling away cheerily with every step and sway of her hips.

"Oh my gods, I love that!" she exclaimed, reaching out and touching the charm Helen always wore around her neck. "I always say, if it isn't plastered with diamonds it isn't *really* jewelry."

"What?" Helen asked, puzzled, looking down. Pandora was chugging from a bottle she took from the fridge and didn't hear.

"The workout room is all yours," she tossed back over her shoulder at Hector. Helen fingered her heart necklace and wondered why Pandora had mentioned diamonds. There were no diamonds on her charm.

"You ready for a beating, Princess?" Hector asked once his aunt had danced out of the room.

"Do you have to call me that?" Helen huffed, wondering if being a dick was part of his strategy or if it was just his personality baseline.

"Well, *now* I do," he smirked, pleased with himself for hitting a nerve.

"Let's go before I wreck Noel's kitchen with your big, stupid face."

"That's the spirit," he said encouragingly. Helen had to laugh. He really could be quite charming when he wasn't trying to kill her.

Hector and Lucas started Helen out on the heavy bag, thinking that it was the most basic place to begin. She didn't get it. She tried to follow through with her hips like they told her, but she kept positioning herself strangely at the last moment and taking all of the momentum out of her swing. She just didn't like to punch things. It didn't come naturally to her. Hector couldn't even watch.

"You've got the killer instincts of a houseplant," he groaned, covering his face.

"Maybe we should move on to grappling. It'd probably be more useful for her, anyway, considering all of her attacks have been close-quarter struggles," Lucas suggested.

Helen readily agreed. She was a terrible fighter, but not even Hector could deny that she was *trying*. The boys gave her a brief rundown of dojo etiquette, and then she entered the ring with a bow, as she had been taught. She was expecting Lucas to be her teacher, but he stood back and let Hector go into the dojo with her instead.

"I thought this was your specialty," Helen said uncertainly to Lucas.

"It is. He's way better on the ground than I am," Hector replied for him with a grin. "Now get down on your hands and knees. You know, like you're a dog."

Despite the fact that Hector was deliberately trying to get Helen's back up, she stayed calm and focused on the instructions she was given. Jujitsu was part physical, which was fun, but the main part of it, the real challenge, was mental. She felt like she was trying to solve a puzzle, trying to unwind out of the human pretzel that Hector had made out of her. A few times she pissed him off by giggling and shying away from the sexually suggestive shapes he was trying to bend her into, but he gutted it out and kept working with her rather than let Lucas take over the lesson.

"Nah-uh!" Hector said when Lucas tried to enter the ring. "You. Out."

"You're not breaking it down step-by-step for her, Hector!" Lucas called from outside the cage. He wouldn't come in the ring and break the rules of the dojo, but he could still yell from the sidelines. "She doesn't know the first thing about pulling guard!"

"Well, tough," Hector replied as he raised himself up from between her knees. "There's no way I'm letting you in here, brother, so just forget it." He gestured meaningfully at her prone body and open legs, and raised his eyebrows. Helen started laughing hysterically.

"You have nothing to worry about, Hector!" she managed to choke out. "Trust me!"

That got Lucas blushing. Helen heard a familiar laugh from outside the ring. "Giggles? Is that you?" She propped herself up and shoved Hector off of her.

"Yeah, it's me. I gotta say, Len, I would have thought it

would be harder to get between your legs, but Hector doesn't seem to be having any trouble at all," Claire teased.

"What are you doing here?" Helen said, surprised.

"I tried to stop her, but she just barged in and . . ." Jason began, his voice fraying with frustration.

"I *really* wanted to see you do demigod stuff!" Claire said, cutting him off. "I've never gotten to see you do all your tricks on purpose before."

"Tricks? We're not show ponies, Claire!" Jason yelled at her.

Helen looked at Hector and shrugged while Claire and Jason continued to bicker. "You know what? I think they enjoy fighting," she commented.

"She's your friend," Hector said to her.

"He's your brother," Helen said back.

Then she heard the door slam. Lucas had left the room. Helen stood up and called after him, but she couldn't leave the ring until Hector, her dojo master for the day, dismissed her. She turned to him and pleaded with her eyes.

"You may be safe for today, but you're still in a lot of danger, you know. I know you don't like this, but you need to train. And anyway, it would be better if you just let him start hating you now, Helen," he said heavily.

"What are you talking about?" she asked, surprised that Hector could be so unfeeling.

"Then chase after him if you have to," he said, looking away. Helen bowed to him and ran out of the practice ring. "But it will only get harder," he warned as she turned to close the door. She slammed it behind her to make her point . . . though she didn't exactly know what that point was.

She ran outside and heard a deep *thunking* noise coming from the tennis courts. She started to run and then realized that, duh, she could fly. Leaping into the air, she looked down to see Lucas in the tennis-courts-turned-arena, chucking spears at a target. He saw her and took flight, meeting her in the air.

"Come on," he said, taking her hand and looking down at a couple of people on the nearly empty beach below them. "Someone could still see us."

They flew high, going north to Great Point, where they could be alone. They touched down on the soft sand around the lighthouse and transitioned into two normal people walking on the chilly beach, holding hands. Lucas was still silent after a few moments so Helen decided to go first.

"You know we were all joking around, right? I wasn't trying to hurt your feelings. I'm sorry if I did," Helen told him.

"You didn't hurt my feelings," he said, shaking his head and clenching his fists. "It's much simpler than that. Much more basic. I hate seeing Hector on top of you. I'm jealous, Helen."

"Then *you* train me," she said hopefully, and he stopped walking and turned away from her with a groan. "Wait, why not?" she persisted.

"I'm a demigod, not a saint," he said with a self-deprecating laugh. "There's only so much I can take."

"Exactly. So, what *can't* you take? Decide which of the

two options is harder, and do the other. That way, no matter how hard your choice turns out to be, at least you can find comfort in knowing you're avoiding something even worse," Helen said logically. Lucas looked at her sidelong and smiled.

"You give good advice, you know that?"

"Maybe, maybe not. I've got my own agenda," she said through a playful smirk.

"You're betting I'm going to choose to train you, aren't you?" he asked, a laugh bubbling up in his chest.

"Flat-out banking on it."

They walked along for a bit, smiling at their own thoughts. She could feel him struggling to make his decision, and she let him be. Then, finally, she felt him give in to something and take a deep breath.

"The twins will still be teaching you archery and spears, and Hector will still be in charge of boxing and sword fighting, but I'm taking over for all the grappling disciplines. Just a warning, this could still be vetoed by my father and uncle, no matter what I say."

"Don't I have any say?" Helen asked, slightly annoyed. "Castor and Pallas can't tell me what to do. If I want you to train me, then why shouldn't I get what I want?"

"Um . . . maybe leave my family to me," Lucas said good-naturedly, and Helen decided to let the subject drop. "Come on, we need to go back. I don't like having you out in the open like this."

"Everything is so close," Helen said as they hovered over the Delos lawn, still in awe over how fast and simple it was for her to get from one end of the island to the other. "Don't you ever get sick of being stuck over Nantucket?"

"I would if I was stuck," he said wryly as they touched down in the backyard, "but I just went to New York the other day."

"You did! For what?"

"Bagels. There's this place out in Brooklyn that I love. It only takes me ten minutes at subsonic to get there."

Helen stopped dead when she realized what that meant.

"You mean, any day at school, you and I can just fly to Boston and eat our lunches in Harvard Square and then be back in time for fifth period?"

"Sure," he said with a shrug. "I want you to get a few more weeks of experience before we go off island, but soon you'll be strong enough to go everywhere with me."

"I want to see the statues on Easter Island! And Machu Picchu! And the Great Wall of China!" Helen exclaimed, practically hysterical with excitement.

She started bouncing up and down on the balls of her feet as they walked toward the house. Lucas grabbed her hands.

"We'll need to wait a bit before we go overseas. You can barely stay in the air as it is and it's harder to navigate with no point of reference, plus oceanic air currents can be a nightmare."

"But I'll be with you, and you know all that stuff already!" She stopped dead and gripped his hand tightly to her chest. "I'm strong enough now, I swear! Please? I've always dreamed of traveling! Lucas, you have no idea! My whole life I've wanted off this island."

"I know, and we will—soon! We'll tape a map to a dartboard and wherever we hit, we'll go. Fiji, Finland, Florence, whatever!" he said indulgently, pulling her against him to stop her from jumping into the air and leaving without him. "We can go eat sushi in Tokyo every night until it gets boring. We can do whatever you want, Helen. When you're a better flier."

"We really can, can't we?" she asked breathlessly, noticing the fact that they had both used the word "we." Then a less-pleasing thought occurred to her. "You've been doing this for a while now, haven't you? Running off to other continents when you have a few hours to kill."

"Yes, I have."

"But always alone?"

"We can carry people short distances when we fly if we have to, but it's unbelievably exhausting to tamper with other people's gravity. You'd be better off just walking there."

He was attempting to sound lighthearted about it, but his face was turned down. Helen looked at him sideways, trying to figure out what it must be like to know that you could go to the Louvre and see the *Mona Lisa* instead of just looking at a picture of it in a book, but you'd have to go there by yourself. It must have been so lonely for him. He'd been the only Scion who could fly for his entire life, and that meant that he'd been isolated in a lot of ways—until he met her.

"There's plenty of time for us to see the world, but for now, I think you'd better stay local. And since I can't ask you to do something that I wouldn't be willing to do myself, I promise I won't go off island without you," he said.

"Yeah, right," Helen said, laughing and trying to pull her hand out of his, but he held on to her.

"I'm serious," he said, tugging on her hand and pulling her toward him until she was practically stepping on his feet. "There's another reason I want you stay over the island, especially when I'm not with you. My family can't protect you if they can't find you. Don't forget, those women are still out there. And Creon *will* be back for you. . . ."

At the mention of Creon's name, it came flooding back to her. He had tried to kill her, and he very nearly succeeded. The dizzying *darkness* had been bad enough, but he had forced her to use her lightning and relive another terrible memory as well.

"Helen?" Lucas said, touching the side of her face and turning her eyes to his. "I'm sorry to bring him up, but you know I had to."

"I know, Lucas, it's not that," she began and stopped, needed a second to regroup. "Do you think my lightning is dangerous?"

"Very," he said seriously. "But only if you don't learn to use it."

"I don't want to use it! I want to go back to forgetting about it!"

"Helen, you don't need to run away from yourself anymore," he said, scowling down at the ground. "Look, this is partly my fault. I should have told you about your lightning sooner, but I could tell you were avoiding it, maybe even repressing it, for some reason. What I really wanted was for you to discover it yourself and *want* to learn about it, like you did with flying."

"Lucas, I . . ." Helen broke off, shaking her head. "I think I killed someone with it, and even if he was trying to hurt me, it still terrifies me."

"You can't be afraid of your power anymore, Helen," Lucas said gently. "You are the strongest of us all, but all that strength is for nothing until you *own* it."

"But I've spent my entire life scared to death of using any of my powers," Helen said in a strangled voice, thinking about her cramps.

"I know I'm asking you to forget about years and years of conditioning, and it probably won't happen overnight, but it still has to happen, and you have to be the one to decide to *make* it happen. You are the most amazingly talented Scion I've ever seen." Lucas raked a hand through his hair and shook his head, at a loss. "Really, Helen, you can't see yourself the way I do, but if you could, you'd be speechless. It's time for you to stop fearing what you can do, and it's definitely time for you to start using all your talents when you train, especially your lightning."

"How am I supposed to do that without frying everyone? I don't suppose you have a garage full of lightning rods?" she tried to joke, flustered that Lucas thought she was powerful, but more important, that he seemed to love that about her.

"I haven't worked out the details yet," he said with a grin. "But I'll think of something."

When they went into the house it was dinnertime. Helen was happy to see that Claire was still there, sitting at the table, waiting to be fed like the rest of the family, chatting away with the twins about a paper due the next morning for one of their brainiac classes, and stopped only to wave excitedly at Helen when she and Lucas came through the back door.

As usual, the kitchen was packed. Pallas and Castor were hovering hungrily over the stove, burning themselves every time they dipped a finger into a pot to taste what Noel was cooking, but not caring enough to stop. Pandora and Hector were joking around with each other by the sink, laughing identical laughs as they tried to see who was better at spitting a grape into the air and then catching it again in their mouths. Poor Noel couldn't turn one way or the other without tripping over one of her offspring, a guest, a husband, an in-law, a nephew, or a niece—and, yet again, no one seemed to be lending her a hand.

"You know I can cook, right? Should I offer to help your mom?" Helen asked Lucas sheepishly.

"Are you kidding? My mom loves this. Sometimes I think she's just waiting for all of us to get married and move out so she can open her own restaurant." He saw Helen's dubious look. "I'm serious! She was telling my dad the other day she wants to have a dinner party and invite half the island. She's insane."

"There you are, Helen, dear," Noel said when she looked up, as if she had been truly anxious about Helen's whereabouts. Then she turned back to her stove top and started talking to herself. "She'll need extras. So damned thin all of a sudden . . . Father still doesn't know the first thing about her so he isn't feeding her properly and Kate is so worried! Now where is Cassie?"

Noel was mumbling to herself, but loud enough so Helen could hear. She couldn't tell if Noel was out of her mind with stress, used to being talked over in such a loud room, or if she was intentionally letting Helen in on her thoughts. Noel took a lungful of air and hollered Cassandra's name.

There was a startled thump from upstairs, and Cassandra's distant voice yelling back, "Start without me, I'm busy!"

Helen and Claire shared a wide-eyed stare, which melted into identical warm smiles. They had both been only children, both growing up not being allowed to raise their voices indoors. Together, they'd dreamed of having big families and full houses with a thousand things happening at once, and now they saw in the other the remembrance of that girlish wish. The yelling jangled the nerves a bit, but there was no denying that it made the Delos house feel like a home.

"Hec-Jace-Castor-Lucas!" Noel sputtered while she stared at her son's face and repeatedly forgot what she had named him. "Go drag your little sister down here. We have guests tonight."

Lucas did as his mother asked, returning with a very grouchy Cassandra thrown over his shoulder.

"But I see them every day!" Cassandra whined as Lucas bent forward and put her down on her own feet next to Helen.

"Mom said," Lucas replied with an apologetic shrug. Apparently, there was no arguing with that because Cassandra rolled her eyes and sat down at the table without another word.

"Hi," Cassandra said in a slightly miffed way to Helen. "Do you eat a lot of garlic?"

"No. Why? Does my breath stink?" Helen replied uncertainly, already working up a blush at the thought of having gassed Lucas all day with dragon breath.

"Not at all. Just trying to figure out why you're impervious to weapons," she said. She held up a book she had clutched in her hand and waved it at Noel's uncaring back. "I'm trying to solve a problem here," she said loudly, obviously intending for her mother to hear, but Noel kept right on cooking.

"I've been looking stuff up, too," Hector added, hands behind his head, exactly like someone who hadn't.

"You just worry about teaching her to defend herself, and I'll take care of the research," Cassandra said in a frazzled way as she opened her book and started leafing through it. Hector smiled, obviously glad he was off the hook.

Castor, Pallas, and Cassandra asked Helen about different habits—foods she ate, daily routines, even prayers her mother might have taught her to say before bed. Nothing yielded an answer, and they gave up when dinner was served.

It was good. Really, really good. Helen ate like she hadn't been fed in weeks. She drank glass after glass of water. She was so dehydrated she could feel the cool water fanning out in her system and thickening her tissues like a dry rag fattening up as it absorbs a puddle. She felt guilty at one point for hogging all the food and forced herself to put her knife and fork down, but Noel looked at her sharply and asked her if she didn't like the meal. Helen murmured an apology and gladly resumed chowing down.

After dinner, Lucas drove her back to her house, which by now was a waste of both time and fuel, but something they had to do to keep Jerry from getting suspicious about how Helen was traveling around the island.

"I don't like leaving you alone," Lucas said, glancing nervously at every shadow in the yard.

"I'll be okay," Helen lied. Actually, now that it was dark out she didn't want Lucas to get farther than a few inches away from her, but with her dad home there was no option but for them to separate.

"I'll be back in an hour or so," Lucas told her as she got out of the car. Helen shut the door but kept hold of it, looking at him uncertainly through the open window. "What is it?" he asked.

"I feel horrible, Lucas! It's autumn, and you and your cousins are sleeping outside at night. That just isn't acceptable."

"We don't have much of a choice. We can't leave you by yourself until you can fight."

"I won't allow it anymore," she said, tucking her hair behind her ear and crossing her arms stubbornly. "You're just going to have to stay in my room."

"Because that's relaxing," he replied with gentle sarcasm. "I barely shut my eyes last night. Trust me, I'll get more sleep on your roof."

"No," she said, sticking to her guns, even though she was getting warm and jittery at the thought of him in her room again. "You either come inside or you don't spend the night here at all."

Lucas looked up at her. "We'll figure something out when I get back. Okay?"

Helen reluctantly agreed and went into the house to see her dad. Through a wide yawn, he tried to ask her how her weekend had gone but after working double shifts for two days straight he could barely keep his eyes open. Helen sent him to bed, promising to fix breakfast in the morning. Jerry was snoring away before she'd even brushed her teeth. She finished up in the bathroom and put on a pair of boxer shorts and a baggy V-neck tee, thinking that Lucas would appreciate her attempt to cover up, and then went to the linen closet to find an air mattress she was pretty sure her dad had gotten for his birthday a few years ago.

At the bottom of the closet she found the unused kit

herding dust bunnies around its corners and brought it back into her bedroom. She sat down on the floor, opened the box, and took out the different components. As she tried to find any part of the instructions that was written in English, she heard a tap. She smiled involuntarily, and waved for Lucas to come through her unlatched window, marveling at how lovely he looked as he soared in her window, quite certain that she looked nothing like that when she flew.

"Is that spine cracker for me?" he whispered with a smile as he pointed at the air mattress.

"Hey, if you don't like it, I'm all for you sleeping in my bed," Helen whispered back, making a show of closing up the kit.

"No, it's perfect," he said, stopping her by grabbing her hands and pulling her into his arms. He held on to her like he hadn't seen her in forty days, instead of forty minutes, and then he grinned and rubbed his face against her cheek.

"You need a shave!" she said, squirming away from his scratchy chin. He chuckled sadistically and turned his attention to the air mattress.

"I was going to sleep on the couch downstairs," he said uncertainly, still deciding if that would be better.

"My dad . . ."

"Wouldn't be able to get down the stairs fast enough to catch me."

"And what if you didn't hear him and didn't get out in time? I'd never be able to explain it," Helen countered.

"Better that than the alternative," he said, gathering up

the mattress. "Look, I'm fine on the roof, Helen. I'm really not comfortable sleeping in here with you. I think it would be a mistake."

No matter how guilty it made her feel to make Lucas sleep on the roof, she could tell that she wasn't going to win this one. They dragged the air mattress up to the widow's walk and eventually figured out how it was supposed to inflate, but Lucas had to read the instructions in Spanish because the English ones were nearly incomprehensible. Hilariously so.

"Insert mouth to the purpose inflation," Helen whispered, quoting one of the stranger lines of the English instructions as she fixed up the newly filled mattress with sheets.

"Expel lung into inflator tube," Lucas whispered back. He stuffed a pillow into a fresh case. "That sounds like it would hurt."

Trying to silence their giggle fit only made it harder to stop. They both crumpled up on top of the mattress, stifling their laughs. Every now and again they would get control over themselves—only to snort and stuff their hands back over their faces as soon as they made eye contact. It went on way past the time when their throats started stinging with the tension of holding in the sound. Finally, they got it all out and just lay there on their backs, breathing heavily with the exhaustion of a damn good laugh. Helen felt Lucas take her hand and shake his head at the night sky.

"What am I doing?" he whispered to himself, digging his other hand into his hair.

"What? We're not allowed to laugh together now?" she whispered, the ghost of a smile still haunting her lips.

"It's not that," he said, turning his face to her tenderly. "But it's not exactly healthy for me to enjoy your company so much that something as stupid as blowing up a mattress is this much fun. As soon as I think I'm in control, you make me laugh or you say something so smart, and I feel like I lose a little bit of myself. I thought I was prepared, but this is much harder than I imagined."

"And what exactly is 'this,' Lucas? Why are you sleeping on my roof and not in my bed?" Helen asked. She rolled over onto her side to face him and reached out to run her fingers over the U-shaped hollow under his Adam's apple.

"Go downstairs," he ordered desperately, brushing her hand away before she made contact. "Please, Helen. Go to your own bed."

There was a part of Helen that knew exactly how to seduce Lucas whether he wanted to be seduced or not, and that freaked her out enough to make her get up and walk on shaky legs to her own bed. It rattled her that she could be so aggressive, so unconcerned with what he wanted that she would consider forcing herself on him.

As she settled down under the covers she heard Lucas tossing and turning above her. She heard him stand up with a sharp exhale and go to the door on the widow's walk.

Her heart started joyfully hammering away when she heard him put his hand on the knob and turn it. Helen sat up, listening to him listening to her.

Both of them could hear the other's breath, the other's blood rushing around under the skin, and, for just a second, Helen could have sworn that she was so aware of him that she could feel his body heat from so far away. Finally, he seemed to win some kind of fight, and forced himself to go lie back down on his air mattress.

Helen lay back as well. After getting control over her thumping heart, she fell into the dreamless sleep that she was usually blessed with when Lucas was watching over her.

# FOURTEEN

Just before dawn, Lucas touched her face to wake her up. When she opened her eyes, he kissed her forehead and told her he'd be back in a bit to take her to school. Then he jumped out her window and flew away. Helen decided there was no way she was going to be able to fall back asleep, so she got up and made a big elaborate breakfast for her dad.

"You okay?" Jerry asked between mouthfuls of pancake, syrup, and bacon.

"Considering? I'm great," she answered honestly as she sipped her coffee.

"How are things with you and Lucas?" he asked cautiously.

"Weirder 'n hell," she replied with a smile. Then she shrugged and laughed. "But what can you do?"

"What can you do?" her father repeated. His chewing

slowed down as an all-consuming thought hijacked his motor skills.

Helen knew he must be thinking about Kate, but an instinct told her to let him be. He still needed more time, and when he was ready he would come to her to talk about it.

Lucas picked her up as planned; they sparked and blushed at the sight of each other. Just sitting in the same car with him put Helen in such a good mood that when one of her favorite songs came on the radio she danced in her seat and somehow convinced Lucas to sing along with her as they drove to school. He would deny it later, but he got really into it, and Helen stopped to listen to him with her mouth hanging open.

"What?" he said, stunned when he noticed he was belting out the refrain all by himself.

"You have a beautiful voice! Is there anything you're *not* good at?" she asked with exasperation as she hit his arm playfully.

"Apollo also happens to be the god of music. Now quit complaining and sing along with me," he said, turning up the volume until the bass was rattling the car windows.

Helen's voice was not nearly as pretty as his, but she made up for her lack of skill with sheer enthusiasm. They finished the song together, and even stayed in the car after they had parked to play the instrumental ending. Lucas was on steering-wheel drums, and Helen was lead air guitar.

"God, we sound amazing! My guitar solo was just inspired!" Helen enthused as she hopped out of the car.

"We should tour," Lucas agreed as he took her hand and led her into school.

They were getting stares, but Helen didn't care. She didn't feel stomach pains anymore. She could relax now that she knew the Curse Cramps would only come as a result of her using her powers in front of normals and not from any other kind of attention. She began to wonder how many of her past episodes had been real, and how many had been brought on by the *fear* of them. It was a relief to know that she had some control over the curse, and for the first time in her life, Helen felt like it might actually be okay to be a little bit different.

"Aren't we old news yet?" she asked him with a sly glint in her eye.

"I don't know. Let me check CNN," Lucas said, pulling out his phone and pretending to open a browser. Helen gasped and clapped a hand to her mouth.

"Oh no, my phone! I forgot to tell my dad it's broken again!" She stopped dead in the hall as she remembered how Hector had made her take a little swim with it.

"Hector will buy you another phone. A better one," was all he'd say as he kissed her forehead. "I'll make sure of it."

"That sounds *really* bad," Helen groaned, but the bell rang and she had to run or suffer Hergie's wrath.

The rest of the day was as near to perfect as a day spent in high school can get. Helen felt hugely energetic, Claire was a ninety-pound ray of sunshine, and Ariadne, too, seemed in fantastic spirits as Matt helped her with her golf swing in the auditorium at lunch. Matt was the captain of the golf team, and Ariadne was thinking about joining, although first she had to learn how to play.

"No, you're still gripping the club too tight," Matt directed her gently. "Think of it as a rapier, not an ax," he said, unwittingly hitting the metaphoric nail on the head for her. Her swing instantly improved.

"Cassie, why don't you put that book down and come learn how to golf?" Ariadne called to her cousin.

In response, Cassandra opened another book.

"What are you looking for, anyway?" Matt called.

"Charms or spells in ancient Greek myth that protect against wounds," she said as she wiped a hand over her face. The gesture reminded Helen of Lucas. If Matt found Cassandra's response strange, he let it go easily enough and focused on Ariadne and her "stance" instead.

"How much longer do you think we have before we get caught in here?" Claire asked.

"Who cares? This is one of the best ideas Lennie's ever had. We should enjoy it while we have it and not ruin the moment worrying about losing it," Matt answered serenely.

Claire looked at Helen and they both nodded, surprised by Matt's wise answer.

"To Matt Millis. Friend. Philosopher. Golf Pro," Helen called back, saluting him with her thermos.

"Here, here," called Claire. She raised her soy milk in a lazy toast. Matt took a dignified bow and blushed when Ariadne smiled at him.

"Hey, Len? Did you get a new necklace?" Claire asked, reaching out to touch the charm that Helen always wore.

"No, it's the same old same old. Are you going crazy again, Gig?" Helen responded, trying to eye her heart charm.

"It looks like a strawberry, not a heart. Or maybe it's just shinier. Probably I'm crazy."

The next few days were blissful, and Helen felt a peace she hadn't experienced since the Deloses had arrived on the island. It was as if someone had put a combination of Spanish fly and Prozac in the water. Helen kept up her training in the afternoons, but as the days passed with no sign that Creon had returned to the island, Helen found herself forgetting about the danger. The only person who seemed immune to the good cheer in the air was Zach. He kept trying to talk to Helen alone but she was avoiding him, which was easy enough when she was being guarded by a family of demigods. Still, each time she dodged him she could tell that he got more and more resentful.

She was hoping that if she put the whole situation off for long enough no one would even remember how she had collapsed as she chased some shirtless stranger. Hoping that if she stalled him long enough, Zach would let it go. But instead his attitude was becoming more and more urgent. The last thing Helen wanted was to tell Lucas and make an issue out of it. After the whole "Hector tried to drown me and ruined my phone in the process" incident, Lucas had happily beat the stuffing out of his cousin in the newly finished arena, and an hour later a toothless Hector had given Helen a new phone that she was pretty sure had enough computing power to put a satellite into orbit.

But Zach was making it impossible for Helen to protect him. The more he kept trying to corner her, the more suspicious Lucas became, until the inevitable happened. After school on Wednesday as Lucas walked with Helen to track practice, he saw Zach wandering around nearby. When Zach saw Lucas he changed direction and went to the boys' locker room, but not before his suspicious behavior was noticed.

"Is Zach after you?" Lucas asked with wide eyes.

"Oh, not really. He wants to talk to me about something, I think," Helen said as if it wasn't important. She shut her mouth before she could say too much.

"Yeah, I'll bet," Lucas said with a sneer, his blue eyes turning nearly black as he sensed her untruth. "Is there any reason for Zach to think that you might be single?"

"No! Wait, what?" Helen stammered, not understanding Lucas's anger.

"Did you tell him that you and I weren't really a couple because I won't . . ." he trailed off, and ripped a hand through his hair as he paced around in a circle. "What are you telling people about us?" The outline of his body began to smear as he scattered the light around him in agitation.

"I haven't told anyone anything!" Helen said, her voice pitching up to an unnaturally high register.

"Are you *trying* to make me jealous or are you just so frustrated that you're already looking for someone else?

Someone who'll give in to you?" He was so angry Helen could barely see him as he began to blur himself out, but she was angry, too.

"I am NOT looking for anyone else!" she howled at him.

Lucas took an involuntary step back as he stared at the halo of pale blue light crackling around Helen's head and hands. Her lightning didn't seem to respond to Lucas's light control, and as the distortions he created were thrown back by Helen's metallic glow he was forced to shade his eyes.

"Oh, boy," she tittered nervously. She felt like she was going over the top peak on a roller coaster—and she was just about to drop down.

She threw an arm out to the side to steady herself. Lucas took a step forward to grab on to her, but wisely stopped himself before he touched her and got electrocuted. Then the blue light went out like a switch had been turned off and Helen plopped onto the floor like a half-baked soufflé.

"I feel awful," she told him, a bewildered look on her face.

"Are you . . . grounded yet?" he asked her, practically vibrating with worry.

Helen looked at the floor and giggled insanely as the electricity running around her body tickled her brain.

"Nope. Linoleum," she said, slapping the palm of her hand against the nonconductive floor. Her vision swam in static. "You were r.r.right. I should have learned to u.u.use this." She had to get rid of the energy, stat.

"Luk.k.k. Run.n.n," she said, her jaw jittering uncontrollably with energy as her bolt demanded to be released. She had held it too long.

Lucas wouldn't leave her, and Helen knew she could kill him if she didn't do this right. She racked her lightning-filled brain and luckily remembered fourth-grade science class. Desperate to rid herself of the monster she had summoned, she slid on her knees to the exit door at the end of the hall and rammed her shoulder against it.

As soon as she came in contact with the metal release bar that ran across the middle of the door it glowed orange with heat and started melting. She barely moved fast enough to open it before the whole door turned into a solid block of smoldering metal. Tumbling down the short flight of steps and crawling outside on her knees, she threw herself forward onto her hands. With a welcome sigh she discharged her bolt into the one place that it would be safely dismantled—the ground.

After a few seconds she felt herself get pulled up from the forgiving earth and carried away.

"Are you injured?" Lucas asked anxiously.

"Just wicked tired," she sighed, a little surprised at herself for using the word *wicked*. She was too weary to care. "Really, put me down," she demanded when he didn't respond. He stopped and balanced her on her feet. She rubbed her tongue across her teeth and then sucked at the roof of her mouth.

"Wow, I'm thirsty! And I think I know why! It's like lightning, right? So that means I'm generating the electic—I mean, erlecic—I mean, the bolt—by ripping apart the water in my body! That makes total sense," she said, hearing herself sound like a cheerleader who had suddenly figured out how her pom-poms were made.

"Helen? You're scaring me. Here, sit, please. Do you need something?" Lucas asked, making her look him in the eye. She still seemed to be throwing off sparks.

"I do need something," she said, struggling to control her diction and her fuzzy brain as best she could. "I need to tell you what's going on, so that you and I don't accidentally kill each other over a dumb misunderstanding, and I need you to promise me that if I tell you, you're not going to beat anyone up."

"I don't think I like this deal," he said dubiously.

"Tough."

He nodded his agreement. She looked around for a moment and then decided to sit down on the top step of the outside stairs before she fell down.

"Zach was the one who saw me chasing Creon. He dropped some pretty threatening hints in class the other day, about me and about you and how abnormally fast and strong we all are. Now he keeps trying to talk to me alone and I think he might be trying to blackmail me or something. I've been dodging him for as long as I can because . . ."

"The longer you wait, the more likely it is that the whole thing turns into a big fish story and no one believes him, anyway," Lucas finished for her with a knowing nod.

"Right. You are *so* smart," Helen marveled.

"And your brain is fried," Lucas said, smiling at her indulgently. The smile fell away. "Because of me. I'm such an idiot," he mumbled, looking down at his twisting hands.

"Correction, you're a *jealous* idiot, and that has to change right now," Helen replied seriously, still feeling light-headed, but fighting her way through it. "You have no reason to be jealous. I told you that I don't want anyone but you. I never have."

"You've lived your whole life on this island, you don't know what 'anyone' means yet," he sighed. "And you have no idea how . . . *Attractive* isn't the right word. It doesn't fully describe the effect you have on men. On me. Look, I'm not a jealous person, Helen, really. All the other girls I've dated . . ." Lucas broke off, took a breath, and regrouped his thoughts before starting again.

"You know, I never believed in 'The Face That Launched a Thousand Ships' thing. I used to hate that part in the *Iliad*. I even laughed at it," he said. Then he paused and shook his head ruefully as he raised his eyes to the sky for a moment, mentally kicking himself. "It's ridiculous, when you think about it. A ten-year war because some selfish coward ran off with an unfaithful woman? It made me angry, and I hated Paris and Helen for being so weak. Then I did something very, very stupid. I swore I would never have made the same choices they did—that I would have been stronger. Then, two weeks later, I saw your face for the first time."

"Wait," Helen said. She blinked with thirst, fatigue, and shock. "I'm not some spoiled queen who left her husband,

345

ran off with another guy, and destroyed an entire city. I don't care what my rotten mother named me, I'm *nothing* like Helen of Troy."

"It doesn't matter what either of our mothers named us," he said with an ironic laugh. "Trust me."

"Hamilton!" yelled Coach Tar, clutching her clipboard and marching toward them with her eyes wide. "Are you *on fire*?!"

Helen looked at where Coach was pointing and realized that the ground all around her was seared and black. The exit door looked like something out of a Dali painting.

Luckily, Lucas was a fantastic liar. As a bevy of teachers came rushing to their aid, he explained that there had been some kind of electrical sparking from above the door, suggesting that perhaps the exit sign had shorted. He and Helen had run outside to stomp out the sparks that had drifted onto the grass. As he wove his story, Helen could hear how honest he sounded, how convincing. She nodded every time he looked at her, knowing that she needed to keep her mouth shut or she'd ruin the whole thing. Since the fire was obviously electrical and the only possible source was the exit sign, the story was believed.

Helen and Lucas insisted they were uninjured, but as a precaution they were told to go to the nurse's office for a quick checkup. Just before Lucas led her away, Helen spotted Zach staring at them from the crowd, his eyes frightened and resentful. He knew they'd caused the fire. Helen touched Lucas's shoulder and pointed Zach out, and Lucas nodded, understanding her meaning perfectly.

"So much for letting it blow over," she murmured ruefully.

"We'll discuss it tonight with my family. Cassie will know what to do," he whispered, taking her sooty hand in one of his and texting his cousins with the other as they walked down the hall to the nurse.

Mrs. Crane checked them over, shook her head in wonder, and declared them both perfectly well enough to go home, or even back to practice if they wanted, though she gave both of them a nonsensical lecture about hanging around under electrical death traps.

Then she looked at Helen's necklace and smiled sweetly. "I've always loved butterflies," she murmured, lightly touching Helen's charm, before shooing them both out of her office in her stern but kindly way.

Helen and Lucas beat everyone else back to the Delos compound, deciding once they arrived that they were entitled to a few moments of relaxation before they began what Helen had started thinking of as her superhero lessons. They stopped in the kitchen to get Helen another bottle of water and then went for a little fly.

"Jase and Hector will call when they're home from practice. We've still got about another hour or so," Lucas said confidently when they touched down in the dunes. They walked down to the half-damp sand that was flat and firm and perfect for a stroll.

"We're supposed to have our first track meet next weekend," Helen said suddenly, biting her lip with worry. "I don't know if Coach'll let me run after missing so many practices."

"Yeah, about that," Lucas said, sighing heavily and making her stop and face him. "You need to quit track."

Helen stared at him for a moment. "Quit track? Are you nuts? How else am I going to get a scholarship?"

"That doesn't matter anymore," Lucas said, shaking his head.

"Doesn't matter? Lucas, this is my *life* you're talking about."

"Exactly. You've been attacked, how many times now? We still don't know who those women are. And I don't think you realize just how big a threat Creon is even with me standing right next to you, let alone when you go running off by yourself across the island. This is your *life* we're talking about, not just an athletic scholarship," he said evenly, calmly. "I want you to quit. For now, anyway."

"You have got to be kidding me," she replied, completely deadpan.

"I'm not. Quit track. Until we figure out how to deal with Creon, it's too dangerous."

"What if I just walked up to you and told you to quit football?" she asked sarcastically.

"Done," he said, holding his hands out in a placating gesture. "I told you once, and I meant it, that I'd never ask you to do something that I wouldn't do myself. We're in this together."

"You're . . . That's . . . I can't believe you're putting this on me!" she yelled, pointing a finger at him childishly. She stomped around in a circle, kicking at the sand and trying to figure out why she was so upset.

"I'm not putting it on you! It's on both of us! That's what I've been trying to tell you," he urged, raising his voice in frustration.

"I've always felt stuck on this island, and I always thought track would be my one way to get off of it. Now you're telling me to give up on all of my plans like it's the easiest thing in the world!"

"It's easier than dying!" he shouted at her, but there was a humorous lilt creeping into his voice and a smile tugging at his lips. "And I don't know if you've noticed this or not, but you can *fly*. You're not going to be *stuck* anywhere again!"

Helen didn't want to laugh. In fact, she was working very hard to give him a penetrating glare, but no matter how hard she tried, she couldn't keep a straight face. She made a horrible noise, a huge piggy-sounding snort, and that made Lucas double up and laugh so hard he had to put his hands on his knees to brace himself. As Helen covered her face and really let herself laugh, she felt Lucas put his arms around her.

They held on to each other, each of them propping the other up. That's when Helen started to understand how things really worked between her and Lucas. They had to do this together, had to share fifty-fifty the huge burdens that had been placed on them, or they would be crushed.

Lucas turned his lips toward her cheek as he ran his hand up her spine and began to stroke the back of her neck. She felt the muscles across his shoulders tense and he suddenly pushed a knee between her thighs. Helen gasped and tried to decide if she should pull him down on top of her like *she* wanted, or push him away like *he* wanted, but she didn't get the chance to do either. As quickly as he had changed, he switched back. He pulled away from her with a sad smile, and then jumped into the air.

"You know, you don't need to run track to get into a good school. You're going to kill it on your SATs," he said breezily, but with the faintest bit of a quiver still lingering in his voice.

"That's what Hergie thinks, too," Helen said. She still felt a bit dazed and shaky. She joined him in the sky and continued her thought when she finally had one. "I just didn't want to be that girl, you know? The girl who does whatever her boyfriend tells her to do because she wants someone else to make all the tough decisions for her."

"I hate that girl," Lucas said with a wrinkled nose as they flew back, hand in hand, to his house.

"Everyone hates that girl. That's why I can't automatically do whatever you say, even if you are right. I've got my pride," Helen said jokingly as they landed in his yard, but he didn't laugh. She squeezed his hand. "What is it?"

"Pride is a really dangerous thing for Scions. We're prone to it, and it's usually our downfall. I know you were kidding, but be careful, okay?" he said gently.

"Oh, yeah. Hubris. Ancient Greece's big no-no." Helen nodded sagely. Lucas gave her a surprised look. "What? I've been doing my mythology homework. Actually, I guess it's my history homework, isn't it?"

"It is. Family history," he said, and pulled her close to him.

They walked down to the fight cage with their arms around each other before separating. They changed into workout clothes and met back on the practice mat.

Helen was expecting there to be a little lingering tension between her and Lucas after his "slip" at Great Point, but if anything, that momentary loss of self-control only served to make him more focused on training. Usually, there was a moment or two when one or the other of them would become conscious of the intimate positions they pressed each other into as Helen tried to grasp the basics of jujitsu, but not that afternoon. Lucas was all business.

"I just realized, we've been fighting all day," Helen said as she tried and failed to break out of his armbar for the tenth time. "And I don't think I've won *once*."

"How long has it been?" he asked, suddenly curious about something she didn't understand right away. He craned his head and looked at the clock on the wall, then back at Helen. "Do you have your bolts back yet?"

Helen connected to that strange sense at the bottom of her belly and felt a spark there. She nodded at Lucas, a bit surprised, and he grabbed her hand, pulling her to her feet.

"Then let's go try it out," he said with a grin as he led her out of the gym.

"Wait," Helen said uncertainly, stopping him with an outstretched hand. "My lightning almost killed you today."

"Because you don't know how to control it yet." Lucas turned and cupped her shoulders in his hands. "You have to accept this. I know it freaks you out, but as harsh as it sounds, you've just got to get over it. This is who you are, Helen, and I'm not afraid of you, or your lightning. So you shouldn't be, either."

Helen looked up at Lucas. His eyes were so sure, so accepting.

"You know what?" she said, standing up straighter. "I *want* to learn how to control my lightning."

"Yeah, you do!" he nearly shouted. When they got outside, they saw Hector's truck pull up and the rest of the Delos siblings pile out.

"We're going to test her bolts!" Lucas yelled toward them. Jason and Hector glanced at each other briefly with wide eyes. They both broke into a run.

"How long has it been?" Hector shouted, sprinting toward them, giddy as a schoolgirl.

"About an hour and forty-five minutes," Lucas said. "She drank two gallons of water."

"And I still feel a little thirsty," Helen admitted.

"Well, get her some more water, Lucas!" Cassandra ordered as she and Ariadne caught up. "How is she supposed to make lightning bolts without hydrogen?"

"Right," Lucas said distractedly. Jumping into the air, he flew to the house and back in about twenty seconds. "Why didn't you tell me you were thirsty?" he asked Helen, handing her a large bottle still cold from the fridge.

352

"I didn't know. I guess I should start paying better attention to that," Helen mumbled to herself sheepishly.

"You have to pay attention to everything that makes you more powerful. And your bolts make you very powerful," Hector said, a feline grin spreading across his face. Helen tipped the bottle back and drank deeply.

"That door was insane!" Jason exclaimed. Recalling it, he rubbed a hand across his face in that Delos gesture that Helen always noticed. "It was like you had taken an industrial-strength welder to it."

"How many volts do you think you have stored right now?" Cassandra asked. They all entered the arena.

"No idea." Helen shrugged. She felt for the charge and tried to gauge it, but she couldn't describe it. "It's a feeling, not a digital readout, Cass."

"Oh, then wait!" Cassandra said, holding up her hands. "Maybe I can devise a way to measure it."

"Cassie, geek out later! We're all dying to see this right now," Hector whined.

"All right, fine! Sorry, Helen. Whenever you're ready," she reluctantly allowed.

The Delos family moved behind Helen, giving her plenty of room to aim her bolt out across the nonconductive sand of the arena. She held up her right hand. That was the hand she wrote with, but it didn't feel like the best fit, so she switched to her left. Then she summoned her bolt—deliberately for the first time.

Lightning shot out of her hand. Not static, not some

pathetic splinter of a spark, but actual lightning. It arced forward in a bright, branching blur, and it made a huge cracking sound, like an orchestra of leather bullwhips snapping simultaneously. One second the air was full of blinding icy blue light, and the next second half of the arena was coated in a thick sheet of smoking amber-colored glass.

No one said anything for a second.

"Unbefrickinglievable," Hector cussed quietly into the silence.

Helen smacked her tongue against the roof of her mouth and stumbled toward the water bottle that Lucas automatically held out for her. She finished an entire liter in five gulps.

"Maybe that was a bit much," she said as she leaned against Lucas.

"You could have fried about fifty people," Ariadne murmured distractedly, looking from Helen to the irregular sheet of glass.

"I don't want to fry fifty people. Fifty French fries, sure. Who wouldn't want fifty French fries? Delicious," Helen said. She felt herself give a goofy grin.

"The electricity makes her a little confused," Lucas explained to his siblings in an embarrassed tone. "I hope it isn't bad for her."

"It's not the voltage, Lucas. It's severe dehydration!" Cassandra chastised. "Her body is built to handle electricity. It's the drain of the fluids out of her tissues that makes her seem like an airhead. And that isn't permanent or damaging, so stop worrying."

In the kitchen, Helen put her lips under the faucet. Everyone waited patiently for Helen to drink her fill while they stared at one another behind her back. She could feel their fear. It was exactly why she had suppressed her power to begin with. That power was so intense, so destructive, it was impossible for anyone to trust it.

Helen shut off the tap and turned to face them. "Did I just freak everyone out?" she asked.

"Yeah," Lucas said, his face a mask. Helen's throat closed and her whole body went still. She kept her eyes on Lucas, but she was waiting for any one of them to condemn her for going too far. Lucas looked at Helen and smiled at her. He smiled like he was *proud* of her.

"But that's our problem, not yours," he said firmly. "There's nothing wrong with what you can do. There's nothing wrong *with you*."

"Plus, I bet you're real good at making s'mores," Ariadne added.

"But the real question is, can she do it without liquefying the chocolate?" Jason asked, like he was some kind of s'mores guru. Helen looked from face to face, her heart aching a bit with gratitude to find nothing but acceptance and compassion wherever her eyes landed.

After all the talk of French fries and s'mores, everyone had junk food on the brain, so they headed to a local mom-and-pop burger shack by the beach. When Helen and Lucas got up to the counter, the cashier reached out to touch Helen's necklace.

"It's a sea horse! I love sea horses," the woman enthused, raising her hand to touch it, and dropping it again in embarrassment. Helen thanked her—because she would have felt rude if she didn't—put in her order with Lucas and then they sat down in one of the booths, where they looked at each other, confused.

"Your necklace isn't a sea horse, it's a heart," Lucas disagreed vehemently.

"What are you talking about, Luke?" Hector said, sounding disparaging. "Helen's necklace is a cockleshell. Always has been, although I just noticed it today. Weird," he said, twisting up his face in confusion.

"Nuh-uh," Jason said with a disagreeing grimace. "It's a strawberry. I was *just* looking at it this morning."

"Heart," Lucas insisted.

"Has everyone lost their minds? She's wearing a golden key with pavé rubies on the top," Ariadne said, reaching out to touch it. "Which, by the way, I think is so lovely."

Helen, still a little punch-drunk with dehydration, got up and went over to a pair of complete strangers at another booth. She smiled at the two shocked tourists, pointed to her necklace, and asked the man closest to her what he thought it looked like.

"A rose. Of course," he said with a hopeful smile. His friend leaned in and took a look, as if he were drawn to it.

"That's a locket," he said with a faraway look in his eye. "Just like my mom used to wear."

"Thanks," Helen said to them, then turned and went back to her table with a shrug. "You're all wrong, except for Lucas. My mom gave me this charm when I was a baby. It's a heart, and I've never worn anything but this heart since, like, forever."

"That's what I see!" Cassandra said like she had just solved a mystery. "I've been wondering what everyone was talking about!"

Helen sat back down next to Lucas. "Personally, I think you all see what you want to see."

Cassandra's mouth dropped open. "Oh my gods! She's projecting! That's why everyone is so cheerful and suddenly started jumping on top of each other like it's mating season at the zoo." she said. Her eyes were wide. She looked at Hector. "I need to go home right now."

"But . . . our burgers," he said, slightly forlorn but also aware of the fact that he was going to end up doing whatever Cassandra told him to do.

"We'll need all this to go," Cassandra said to the food runner. She turned to Helen. "I think I've figured this out, but I still need to test it."

They raced back to the Delos compound, the rowdy group storming into the library and upsetting Castor and Pallas. Cassandra dragged one of the ladders over to a high shelf of her choosing and then had Lucas hold the bottom for her while she climbed. As she did so she told her father and uncle to look at Helen's necklace and describe what they saw.

"It looks like . . . That's impossible," Pallas said, his eyes hardening with anger as he took an involuntary step back.

"What do you see?" Castor cautiously asked his brother.

"I gave that to Aileen," Pallas said, pointing to Helen's necklace like he was accusing Helen of stealing it.

"Cass?" Lucas called up to his sister, worried.

"Her necklace looks like whatever would attract the person who *looks at it*. That ability is only related to one goddess and one relic," Cassandra called down, still searching for something. "Aphrodite's cestus."

"That can't be," Pallas said, shaking his head. "We might as well say she has the aegis of Zeus. Or the Loch Ness monster, for that matter. It's folklore, it doesn't exist."

"What's a cestus?" Helen asked quietly, in case it was such a stupid question everyone needed to be able to pretend like they didn't hear her.

"The cestus is Aphrodite's girdle," Lucas responded automatically, his eyes darting from Cassandra to Castor before they landed back on Helen. "It's a mythical object that makes the wearer impervious to any weapon."

"And impossible to resist," Castor added. He cast a worried look at his son.

"And I'm supposed to have this thing on me? Well, I hate to break it to you, but I'm fresh out of mythical girdles," Helen said with a sarcastic laugh, but no one laughed with her.

"Let me see that necklace your mother gave you," Cassandra replied, coming down the ladder with a book tucked under an arm. Reaching the bottom, she stretched out her hand.

"How long are you going to want it for?" Helen asked as she fingered her necklace uneasily. She really hated to take it off for any reason, even if that reason was as important as Cassandra was making it seem.

"I'll give it right back. I promise," Cassandra said, keeping her eyes locked on Helen.

"Yes, of course," Helen replied, feeling silly for balking. She obediently muscled through the naked, panicky feeling that came along with the thought of removing her necklace. Taking it off, she handed it over. As soon as she placed it in Cassandra's outstretched hand she felt a burning sensation across her forearm.

"Cass, are you crazy?" Lucas yelled. He snatched a small blade out of his sister's grip.

Helen felt someone step against her back and put a hand on her shoulder, and, from his size, Helen knew it was Hector, supporting and protecting her.

"I'm sorry, Helen. But it was the only way to prove it," Cassandra said, biting her lower lip and looking up with defensive eyes.

"It's okay," Helen mumbled, not understanding what had happened yet. Everyone was staring at her arm. She looked down and saw a thin red cut dripping blood onto the carpet.

"But it's just a necklace," Helen repeated as she ran the charm along the chain and looked at her arm. The cut had already healed.

"It becomes whatever you need it to be, that's part of its

359

magic," Cassandra said, grasping for words with frustration. "It's like the way it looks different to everyone. That's because there's no such thing as the most beautiful ornament, or the most beautiful *anything* for that matter. How can I explain this?"

"What I think is beautiful is very different from what even my twin would think is beautiful because we're all turned on by different things," Ariadne explained bluntly for her.

"That's right," Cassandra said.

"But why a girdle?" Helen persisted.

"You have to remember, a few thousand years ago girdles were considered very attractive, but they were also a form of protection for the wearer. Some even had bone or bronze plates in them, like lightweight armor," Castor explained. He looked remote, though, not his good-natured self. "But there were two parts to the cestus. The girdle itself, and its adornments. It was the adornments that made the goddess irresistible to whomever she wanted to seduce, and they had the power to change to suit the tastes of whoever was looking at them. Time passed and girdles fell out of fashion, but the transformative magic of the cestus is still the same. It can become whatever you need it to be to make yourself more attractive, Helen. And all these years you've only needed it to be a simple necklace."

"I've always loved it," Lucas admitted softly. "The way it falls into that place." He touched the dent at the bottom of her throat for the briefest of moments. "I think it's perfect."

Helen could see a hot flush wash across his cheekbones,

but he kept his eyes down, conscious of the fact that everyone was staring at them with worried frowns. Castor especially looked so stricken he could have been at a funeral.

"What I don't understand is why are we all noticing it now? It's like it just got charged with love mojo in the past few days or something," Jason mused to no one in particular. Then a thought occurred to him and he looked from Helen to Lucas, then away.

"Like it just switched on," Ariadne said. She looked over at Helen and Lucas, sharing the same idea as her twin.

"What if I wanted it to be something else?" Helen asked, ignoring the strange stares she was suddenly getting from everyone. Cassandra shrugged.

"I don't know. Maybe try changing it?" she asked with an excited look. "But I'd take it off first! You never know," she added quickly.

Helen unlatched her necklace and tried to think about sexy things, but she couldn't come up with anything. After a moment she realized that it didn't matter what she thought was sexy, but what other people thought that would be important. She needed a guinea pig. She looked at Hector, focusing on him alone, and she felt her necklace change shape in her hand.

"Helen!" Hector exclaimed.

Helen looked down and saw that she was holding a tiny scrap of lace that more closely resembled diamond-encrusted dental floss than underpants. Everyone burst out laughing, pointing at Hector and making fun of his trashy taste. She looked at Lucas, concentrated, and it turned back into her necklace. He grinned.

"I told you. I love that necklace," he said openly.

His gaze was so warm Helen felt she had to do something to divert all the stares they were getting. She looked around the room, pointedly seeking out a new victim. Everyone wisely decided to scatter.

"Don't even think about it!" Ariadne shrieked, running out of the room so Helen couldn't focus on her.

"Come on! That's not fair!" Jason said. He backed away from her, alternately covering his eyes so he couldn't see her and covering his face so she couldn't see him.

"All right, nobody panic!" Helen put her necklace back on and laughed, but no one was left in the library to witness her mercy but Lucas and Cassandra. "I like it best like this, myself."

"Good," Lucas said, averting his eyes and trying to pretend he wasn't embarrassed.

"Why aren't you running?" Helen asked Cassandra playfully, but when she saw the dark look on her face she knew she had said something terribly wrong.

"That will never work on me," Cassandra said in a flat, distant voice. She brushed past Helen.

"I'm sorry," Helen said to Lucas, as Cassandra stalked out of the room. She put her hand on Lucas's arm and made him look at her. "I don't understand, Lucas. What did I say?"

"Aphrodite's power only works on adults—on sexually mature individuals," he answered with a raspy voice, like his throat had gone dry.

"Oh. I didn't know, but that's nothing for her to be ashamed of. She's only fourteen. So she's a late bloomer—"

Lucas cut her off. "My sister will never bloom. She was taken by the Fates."

"What does that mean?"

"It means that even if she wants to, even if she feels what other woman feel, she'll never fall in love or have children. She won't even be able to have the kind of careless physical relationships that Hector has pretty much once a week," Lucas said. "She is sacrosanct to the Three Fates, and they will not share their daughter."

"But if she feels like a woman, why can't she act like one? Who cares what three dusty old spinsters say?" Helen asked persuasively, but that made Lucas even more upset.

"You're not understanding this, Helen. We're talking about the Fates, not a couple of overprotective parents with virginity issues. The *Moirai* can't be avoided or tricked. Cassandra won't be able to sneak out of her bedroom window and have sex with some hot guy she met at a party," he said, pacing around. "Even if he was a man she truly respected, a man she could grow to *love*, the Fates would separate them. Fate herself would make sure Cassandra never laid eyes on that man again."

"How cruel," Helen said, horrified.

"And someday the Fates will separate her from us, her own family. You can barely tell now, but she and I used to be so close. She used to take my hand anytime we walked next

363

to each other, but not anymore," he said, his voice breaking with emotion. "She was the sweetest little sister ever, I
swear. Such a big, warm heart and such a big, clever mind—
all packed into the tiniest girl you've ever seen. Now she's
becoming more like *them*. Cold, meticulous, unrelenting."

Helen put her hands on his waist and waited silently until
he was ready to pull her into his arms and relax against her,
which he finally did in a wave. She had held him for only a
few minutes when Ariadne came into the library and told
Helen she needed to come out to the kitchen.

"What is it?" Lucas asked.

"Your mom found out about the whole cestus of
Aphrodite thing and she's sort of throwing a fit, Luke,"
Ariadne admitted with a heavy heart, her gentle eyes darting between the two of them with sympathy. "Aunt Noel
has asked for a meeting with Helen."

All the air seemed to leave the room, most of it sucked
into Lucas's lungs. Ariadne spun on her heel and Lucas took
Helen's hand.

"Is this bad?" Helen asked Lucas breathlessly as they followed Ariadne through the house.

"Yes," he whispered. "Listen, will you promise me something?"

"What?"

"Promise me that no matter what my mother says, that
this isn't the last time you talk to me." Lucas made her stop
and face him. He held her by her stiff shoulders and placed
his lips against her forehead as he spoke. "Promise that you

will speak to me again. Even if it's just once."

"I promise," she stammered, not sure if this was really happening to her or if she'd wandered into some bizarre dream.

She and Lucas went into the kitchen holding hands tightly, as though for the last time.

Noel looked over at Castor and gestured to them as if they were "Exhibit A" in her prosecution.

"Luke, go upstairs," Castor said without being able to look him in the eye.

"I think I'm entitled to hear this," he replied calmly. Helen clutched his hand and glanced around at everyone's solemn faces.

Something was very wrong. Helen started to breathe so fast she felt like for the first time in her life she might actually hyperventilate.

"I want you all out. It's my hearth, and my sacred right by Hestia," Noel said firmly, as if she were invoking some old ritual. "This is between Helen and me now."

After a few moments of silence, Jason was the first to move. Seeing the look in Noel's eyes, he went to Lucas and physically separated his hand from Helen's. If it had been anyone else, Helen was convinced Lucas would have put up a fight, but he allowed Jason to lead him upstairs. Everyone else filed out of the kitchen, looking sad. Everyone except for Pallas, that is. Helen noticed that he looked satisfied. Even a little smug.

"Sit," Noel said, pulling out a chair for herself, facing Helen. "You don't understand what's happening, do you?"

Helen shook her head and swallowed. Noel asked another question. "Ariadne explained the Truce to you, right?"

"She said the Houses have to stay separate or the gods will come back and start the Trojan War all over again," Helen croaked through a tight throat.

"Right. Now what does that mean? What would be the simplest way for the Houses to be unified?" Noel asked sharply. Helen shook her head again, scared dumb, and Noel continued. "There are two obvious ways. One House can destroy the others, or the Houses can intermarry. Usually this is impossible for Scions because the Furies keep everyone hating everyone else, but that isn't an issue for you and Lucas."

Helen let out a giant breath of relief.

"Is that it?" she asked. "Nobody's marrying anybody! Lucas and I are way too young! We're not that stupid."

Noel shook her head, as if Helen had missed the point.

"Do you know how marriage was defined in ancient Greece?" Noel said in a calmer tone. "It's really simple. A virgin goes to a man's house with the family gathered as witnesses. The virgin and the man share a fire, a meal, and a bed. If the girl wasn't a virgin in the morning, then the couple was considered married. That's it. That's all it took. You're still a virgin, right?"

Helen blushed furiously, her jaw dropping. "Yes. But that's no one's business but my own!"

"It certainly is our business. Because you and Lucas have shared almost everything else on the list, all that's left is the consummation of the marriage. If that happens, then as far as the gods are concerned you will be his wife. If you're his wife, then that unites the final two Houses. And you know what *that* means."

"War," Helen said, completely stunned. Her brain scrambled to find the flaw in Noel's argument—the one thing that would make it untrue—but she didn't come up with anything. "It's impossible."

"No, it's ironic. The first Trojan War started because two teenagers fell in love and ran off together, and here are you and Lucas, poised to make exactly the same mistake," Noel said, her pity beginning to show through her anger.

"And Lucas knew all this? Right from the start?" Helen asked. She felt strangely numb.

"From the first moment he saw you," Noel replied.

"That explains a lot," Helen whispered, still putting the pieces together in her head. "I thought he was just old-fashioned or something."

"Lucas? No." Noel laughed, shaking her head at the thought. "But he is honorable, so I trusted him with you. I allowed this to go on because I believed that he would be able to control himself and not do anything that the world would regret. But the cestus changes things."

"Why?" Helen asked, suddenly perking up. "I've always worn it, and he's always been able to control himself. And I didn't exactly make it easy on him, either," she added with regret. "But from now on I won't pressure him, and that way we can still be together, right?"

"And then what?" Noel pleaded gently. All the anger had

gone from her once she saw how invested Helen was, how much Helen cared. "You could both stay true to your word and never touch each other, but what do you think that will do to your relationship over time? What do you think it will do to Lucas?" Noel paused and looked at her hands in her lap.

"It'll be hard, but we know what's at stake. . . ." Helen began, trying to bargain.

"I've already been told that I'm going to lose my daughter to madness. I can't lose my son as well," Noel interrupted, her eyes wide with fear. "Please, Helen. I'm begging you. Stay away from Lucas. If you get a little distance from each other, maybe he'll be able to let you go before it's too late."

"You're talking like I'm going to drive him crazy or something," Helen said, frustrated. Noel gave her a piercing look that warned Helen not to belittle the situation.

"The cestus isn't some silly love potion you can buy at the county fair. This is a relic from the goddess of love herself, and if you don't think it's possible for someone to be driven mad by love, it's only because you haven't truly felt it yet."

"Then I'll take it off. . . ."

"You will not," Noel ordered. "The cestus has probably saved you more times than you can know. Do I need to remind you *again* how important your life is?"

They sat staring at each other for a few moments while Helen struggled with her thoughts. She'd read the *Iliad*, and she'd hated Paris and Helen as much as Lucas had. She saw them as selfish. So selfish that they were willing to watch a city burn to the ground rather than part. But was Helen Hamilton any better than Helen of Troy if she wouldn't give up the man she wanted when it was required?

"Why didn't anyone tell me this before?" Helen burst out.

"Lucas forbade it. He said he wanted a little time and a little privacy, and no one blamed him for that. Relationships are private things."

"But we're not allowed to have a relationship, are we?" Tears tried to make hot puddles out of her eyes. "This isn't fair."

"I know it isn't," Noel said, brushing a lock of Helen's hair behind her shoulder so she could see her face.

"Are none of us are allowed to choose?" Helen said, thinking of Cassandra and what she had to suffer. Her whole body was clammy with nervous sweat and starting to shake. How could she stay away from Lucas? She didn't think she could make herself do that any sooner than she could make one of her hands shrivel up and fall off.

"Castor and I tried to choose differently," Noel said sadly. "We tried to run away just before Lucas was born. We wanted a fresh start so badly that we didn't even give him a traditional name."

"So what happened?" Helen asked, desperate to keep Noel talking and maybe learn something that might give her a reason to hope.

"What always happens," Noel said with a knowing smile. "Family."

Helen sat still for a moment, unwilling to stand up for

fear that it would end the interview and therefore end her welcome in this house. She knew from witnessing everyone else's obedient reaction that what Noel said in her kitchen was law for the entire family. Helen had always thought that Noel was the weak one, the one who needed protecting, but she was beginning to realize that Noel had a power all her own. When it came down to the matter of who was to be accepted into the family and who was denied hospitality, Noel had the final say for everyone who lived under her roof. Not even Lucas would be able to break away from that without being forced to leave his entire family behind. Helen had been denied Noel's blessing, and that was the end of it.

Helen managed to stand up and make her way to the door but when she got there she paused. "May I ask you one more question?" Helen said, following an impulse. She waited politely for Noel to nod before continuing. "What *would* you have named Lucas?"

"Tradition would have led us to name him after Castor's father, who died just before Lucas was born." Noel's face was closed.

"And what was that?" Helen asked, already half knowing what Lucas's name would have been, what it should have been if his mother and father had followed the rules.

"Paris," Noel replied, unable to look Helen in the eye.

# FIFTEEN

*T*he meadow went on and on and on—endlessly. There was only one type of flower that grew here—a small blossom so pale it was nearly transparent. No bees buzzed around these flowers and none of them altered from their precise alignment unless Helen brushed against them. They were infertile things that had no scent, sustained no life with their nectar. They were never going to bear fruit.

The terrain she plodded through was no longer hilly nor toilsome, the temperature was neither hot nor cold, and no sharp stones or thorny bushes cut her feet, but still, the place was intolerable. Helen may as well have stood in one spot for weeks, staring at the same uninspiring flower and breathing the same stale air, as walk. The land she had entered was unchanging, repetitive, pointless, and the longer she stayed there the more numb she became.

It was a meadow of misery.

Helen woke up and couldn't remember what day it was. Did it matter? she wondered, but then she remembered that if it was Saturday she wouldn't have to go to school. That meant she wouldn't have to put up with any more of the random awkward questions she kept getting from eager girls trying to determine whether she and Lucas were still dating. The vultures were circling, painting their lips or flexing their muscles, all of them hoping to be the first to land on one or the other of the carcasses.

If it was Saturday, Helen wouldn't run the risk of seeing Lucas from afar as he went from class to class. She wouldn't have to recognize the graceful curve of his shoulder or the curious tilt of his head rising over the throngs of nondescript shapes that made up the rest of the population. If it was Saturday, she could go to the Delos house knowing that he wouldn't be there while she trained. But if it was Saturday, that only left her with a different pile of crap to shovel for the next sixteen or seventeen hours—all day she'd have to be where he wasn't.

Helen rolled over on the air mattress, looked at the clock, and saw that it was indeed Saturday. Nine and a half days had passed since Noel had banned her from Lucas's presence, and Helen was still waiting to feel something—but all she felt was numb. She heard Ariadne stir and then scoot over to the edge of the bed to look down at her where she lay on the air mattress.

"Morning," Ariadne said with a wan smile. "How'd you sleep?"

Helen answered by throwing the covers off to reveal the untouched jingle bells still wrapped around her ankles. They were exactly as they'd been when the two girls went to bed, but under the bells, Helen's feet were dirty, swollen, and red from what looked like weeks of walking.

"Again?" Ariadne asked, dismayed. "You *have* to be floating out of the window, because I swear I didn't hear a thing, and I barely shut my eyes last night!"

"It's not your fault," Helen said, shaking her head and unstrapping the useless bells. For a moment, Helen considered telling Ariadne about her vivid nightmares. They all knew she had them, but Helen hadn't shared what her dreams were *about* with anyone since she'd told them to Kate. Helen took a breath, intending to confide in Ariadne, and then stopped herself. Would Ari think she was going crazy like Cassandra? Helen decided she should keep her mouth shut. "You know, I really don't see the point in you spending every night here if I'm wafting out the window as soon as you nod off."

"Don't even start with that, because it isn't going to happen," Ariadne said peevishly. She threw her covers off and stood. "Lucas is probably gonna kill me dead enough as it is," she mumbled nonsensically as she headed to the bathroom.

"Oh, hey! Sorry!" Jerry said with surprise as he ran into a scantily clad Ariadne in the hallway.

"Hi," Ariadne growled at Jerry as she slammed the bathroom door.

Helen tossed the silly bells under the bed and looked up at her dad, who was peeking timidly around her door.

"I didn't know Ariadne was here. Again," he said.

"Yup," Helen replied, like it was obvious.

"Okay," he said wavering in and out of the doorway. "And you'll be at her house all day, I suppose? Working on that project for school still?"

"Yup."

"Okay," he said, confusion scrunching his brow. "Uh . . . Happy birthday?"

"Thanks," Helen replied with a nod. Then she stared at him until he went away.

"Did I hear your dad say it was your birthday?" Ariadne asked with wide eyes as she came back into the room.

"Uh-huh," Helen said. "Not a word to anyone. I just want to practice and then come home and go to back to bed."

"No! We should do something!" Ariadne protested. "We should take the day off and go shopping, then maybe go out for dinner!"

"I'm sorry, Ari, but I can't. I just woke up and I'm already exhausted," Helen replied, hearing her voice sound low. "Practice, then back to bed. That's all I want for my birthday."

Ariadne shook her head sadly and stared at Helen while she made up the inflatable bed she insisted on sleeping in every night. Helen could see that Ariadne wanted to argue, wanted to insist that Helen at least try to enjoy herself on her birthday, but thankfully, she gave in.

Helen could barely keep her eyes open, and she was starving. She wondered again if she actually *had* walked for days, like she did in her dream, or if there was something wrong with her mentally. Noel's words about love being able to drive a person mad came back to haunt Helen. Were her all-too-vivid nightmares what Noel had meant? And then she had to consider if, at that point, it might not be a comfort to go stark, raving mad.

Creon stepped onto the dock from the private yacht his father had supplied for him and his team. The trip across the Atlantic from Spain to Nantucket had been long and tedious, but necessary. They required tools that would never make it through customs, even on a privately owned plane, and what was more, they could never fly their quarry back, anyway. That would be foolish. She needed to be properly secured no matter how much the preparation inconvenienced Creon and his team.

His father had explained it all to him—how years ago he'd had the chance to kill her, but that he had fallen under the spell of her face—*the* Face. Creon was surprised that his father had been weaker than him, but that, too, was a sign of the coming of Atlantis. The Scion generations were fated to get stronger and stronger, to be born with more and more talents until finally, a generation was to come that could defeat the gods. His father's moment of weakness, as unfortunate as it was, had its benefits. In that moment, Tantalus had learned of her phobia for the water. Creon's quarry feared and hated the ocean, and that was an advantage for the Hundred Cousins. By using a boat to transport her, she would be virtually imprisoned by an element she could not control, and considering how powerful she was, they needed to give her prison as many layers of walls as they could find.

As he disembarked, Creon turned to tell his crew to stay on the yacht and wait for his return. He wanted to make it clear to them that he was in charge by keeping them as far away from the action as possible. Any one of his dear cousins might be tempted to take whatever opportunity they could to insert themselves into the annals of Scion history by stealing his Triumph. Creon couldn't allow that to happen, not even by accident. After all of the risks he'd taken, after all of his patience, he would finally be the one to bring his House the glory that it deserved. He was destined to be equal to the heroes of old, like Hercules or Perseus. Maybe even better, because Creon would do more than kill a hydra or a gorgon. Much more. He would be the giver of immortality to his family, and to his father.

Only one life stood in his way, and that life would be delivered to Tantalus, Head of the House of Thebes and future ruler of Atlantis, by Creon, his son and Heir, who would receive the honor for the capture. And maybe he would also be given the hauntingly beautiful prize that he deserved— his quarry's daughter.

Ariadne and Helen drove to the compound in total silence. When they stopped behind Matt at a light in town Ariadne waved. They could both see his eyes and forehead pinched up with worry as he stared at Helen in his rearview mirror.

"I know you're sad, but you shouldn't ignore Matt like that," Ariadne said with a little heat. "He's one of the best people I've ever met, and you're hurting him."

"You're right. I'm being selfish," Helen said. She felt blank inside. Empty. "I know it, and I hate it, but I just can't seem to *stop*."

"That's not what I meant," Ariadne stammered apologetically, her eyes on the road. "I know what you're sacrificing, and I know why. But you know what? I think you need to cry, even just once. Maybe then you could let it out and feel a little better."

Helen had tried to cry, but no tears came. Instead, all that she felt was this creeping *nothing* inside her. She knew she should care about how Matt felt, but she didn't even care how *she* felt, not even when she was fighting for her life against Hector on the mat. Their workouts had become brief and brutal. Now that Helen no longer had an emotional block against using her bolts she was learning how to control them and let them out bit by bit. Only someone who didn't mind getting fried could fight her hand to hand. Now, coupled with the power of the cestus, which made her impervious to any weapon, Helen had become nearly undefeatable.

Toward the end of their session that day Hector tried to put her in a Kimura and she electrocuted him for the third time. He dropped unconscious to the mat. After a moment, she approached him and nudged him with her toe.

"Are we done here?" she asked him with raised eyebrows when he came around.

"You still don't know how to fight," he mumbled as he wiped blood off of his lips.

"You bit through your tongue," Helen said flatly. "You should probably take a break."

Helen went to her corner to drink some water. She saw Claire, Jason, Cassandra, and Ariadne all staring at her from outside the fight cage. Jason was the first to move. He took two long strides, jumped fluidly over the metal fence, and landed next to his shaking brother.

"I think that's enough, Hector," Jason said. "She doesn't need any more training."

"She can't even throw a punch!" Hector protested, slurring his words.

"She doesn't need to," Cassandra said with finality. "She doesn't need to learn to punch or hold a sword or shoot an arrow to defend herself. She's already ten times more lethal than you are, Hector, and if you keep trying to find a way to beat her you're going to end up brain-dead. These sessions are over."

Cassandra stood up and walked out of the dojo.

"She's still vulnerable!" Hector shouted after Cassandra's retreating figure. "There are a million ways to subdue her once you find a way to get around her bolts!"

"Enough, Hector," Jason said gently. "Cassandra's right. Figure out her vulnerabilities and train her to deal with them, but the dojo work is done. Hand-to-hand combat is not something she ever has to fear."

"So no more chaperone?" Helen asked, raising her eyes from her empty water bottle. The Delos kids looked at each other, shrugging.

"I guess not," Hector finally concluded. "At least not until Cassandra foresees a threat. Then, I don't care how lethal you are, one of us will be with you at all times again."

"May I go until then?" Helen asked, looking at Hector and waiting politely for permission. He nodded. She bowed to him and then jumped into the air.

"Wait, Lennie!" Claire shouted up at her. "We were going to throw you a party. Kate made you a cake!"

Helen saw Claire, saw how worried she was, but she couldn't do what Claire wanted. She *couldn't* pretend to be cheerful. Not for a few hours while everyone threw her a party, not for half an hour to let them at least sing "Happy Birthday" and scarf down some cake, and not even for the five minutes it would take to explain to Claire why she couldn't do any of those things.

"Love you," she called out to her best friend before she flew away. She thought she heard Jason say something like "Lucas is the same" while she pulled open the door and soared out, but she might have imagined it.

She didn't have a destination or a time limit—she only

379

knew that she wasn't allowed off island. She'd given Lucas her word, and she wasn't about to break it now. Helen needed so desperately for their promises to be true, she wasn't willing to break any of them—not even the one that might bring her some comfort. She might never get to go to Patagonia with Lucas, but the least she could do to keep faith between them was to not fly over the ocean until he told her it was okay.

She could, however, go right to the edge. She'd avoided Great Point for the past week—not because she was worried she'd break down and cry if she went there, but because she was worried she wouldn't. She was starting to get frightened that she would never going to feel anything again. That she would become as sterile and lifeless as one of those pale flowers she saw in her nighttime wandering. She had enough sense to ask herself why she was reacting the way she was, but not enough clarity to discover the answer. Until she saw Lucas sitting on top of the lighthouse.

He was perched right on the edge of the catwalk that wrapped around the glass dome at the top of the lighthouse, watching the last bit of the day drag itself down behind the horizon. A storm was gathering over the water, and the fruit-punch colors of the sunset seemed to be trying to claw their way out of the rain clouds. His skin was painted with that dying light and he was, as always, beautiful.

Then Helen understood why she was pent up like a dam instead of bawling like a waterfall. She wasn't sad. She was furious.

As she flew toward him, he saw her and stood. Helen didn't land on the catwalk. Instead, she floated in front of him, claiming the air for herself. For a moment, they just stared at each other, both of them too overwhelmed to break the silence with speech.

"What are you doing here?" Lucas said at last, his sunken eyes wide and hungry for the sight of her. Helen ignored his stupid question and said the first thing that came to mind.

"Why didn't you tell me?" she demanded, angry and hurt and not sure what she wanted to hear from him. "Right from the start. Why couldn't you at least *explain* to me why we couldn't be together?"

"If you wanted to know, why didn't you just *answer the phone* one of the thousand times I've called you this past week?" he demanded in return, just as angry and hurt as she was.

"Stop it! Stop asking me questions when you're the one with all the answers!" she bellowed at him, finally feeling the hitch and sting of tears in her throat.

The dam was about to burst, and she knew that what was going to come out would be ugly, red-faced sobbing. She had to get as far away from Lucas as possible. She summoned one of the turbulent storm winds to yank her body away and take her wherever it chose, but Lucas felt her recklessness. He dove into the air and caught her before she could be chewed up by the storm she was so drastically underestimating. As soon as he had her safe again in his arms he broke down and kissed her.

Helen was so stunned she stopped crying before she had a chance to start and nearly fell out of the sky. Still the better flyer, Lucas caught her and supported her as they tumbled on the wind, holding and kissing each other as he guided them safely back down to the catwalk. As their feet touched down, the light inside the lighthouse switched on and projected the shadows of their embracing figures out onto the choppy waves of the ocean.

"I can't lose you," Lucas said, pulling his mouth away from hers. "That's why I didn't tell you the whole truth. I thought if you knew how bad it was you'd send me away. I didn't want you to give up hope. I can't do this if you give up on us."

"I don't want to give up," Helen cried. "But there can never be an *us*, Lucas. You should have told me that."

"Don't say never," he said. He brushed his face against her neck, no longer kissing her, but unable to let her go completely. "Nothing is forever, and there are no absolutes. We'll find a way."

"Lucas," Helen said, frowning and pushing against his chest until he let her go. She sat down on the catwalk and pulled him down next to her so they could talk. "We would hate ourselves. And eventually, we'd hate each other."

"I know that!" he said, his voice rising desperately. "I'm not talking about running off and doing whatever we want!"

"Then, what?" Helen asked softly, calming him down. "What are we supposed to do?"

"I don't know yet," he admitted. He leaned back against

the glass wall of the lighthouse and pulled Helen against his chest. "But I will not go through another week like this last one."

"Me neither," she said. She rested against him, fully relaxing for the first time in days. "I don't care how hard being together is, nothing is worse than being apart."

"What was it you told me? Decide what you *can't* do and then do the opposite?" he asked with an amused smile, pressing his lips against her forehead. "At least now we know we can't be apart."

"It was like being dead," she said fearfully, as if even mentioning the numbness she had felt would allow it to creep back into her body.

"For me too," he said in a strange, strangled voice.

"What about your mother? She won't allow us to be together."

"We'll have to talk with her. We'll have to talk to my whole family."

"And if they still want to separate us?"

"Then we run," Lucas said, his voice low and even.

Neither of them said anything for a while. They just watched the beacon light flash across the foaming waves of the storm-churned ocean. Helen could hear his heart pounding, but his grip on her only tightened as if he was already bracing himself for the battle he would have to fight to keep her close to him.

"They'll chase us," she whispered. "They'll think we've started the war."

"I know," Lucas said. "But we won't. We'll keep the Truce, even if they don't believe that we can."

"We don't have to make the same mistakes that *they* did," Helen said defiantly. "It makes me so angry that everyone assumes that even though we know what would happen, we'll still go out and do the same stupid thing."

Lucas laughed, but there was no joy in the sound.

"It's almost as if we don't need to live our lives or feel our feelings at all, because someone already told us what the ending was going to be," he said bitterly. She could feel him tensing with indignation, until a new and serious thought stilled him. "Are you really willing to do this? You know that it would mean you'd have to leave your father behind?"

"I know," she said, knowing full well she'd be hurting her father far worse than her mother ever did, but also knowing that she would do it for Lucas—for both of them.

"I understand if you can't do this—" he began, but Helen cut him off.

"If they won't let us stay together, we have no choice. We have to run away."

"It won't be forever," he said, trying to console her as well as himself. "Just until we can figure out a way around this. And we *will* figure it out. There has to be a way."

"I've thought of something," Helen said, her whole body going still. She felt Lucas tense.

"I think I know where you're going with this, and I don't think I want to hear you say it," he said uncertainly.

"What if I wasn't a virgin?" Helen said quickly, just to get it over with.

"I'm not sharing you, Helen," he replied immediately. "Besides, it won't work."

"I'm serious, we have to consider it," she insisted, struggling in his arms until he loosened his grip enough for her to lean back and look at him. "Tell me the truth. Would you stop wanting me if I was with someone else first?"

"Of course not," he said, smiling tenderly at her. "And I don't just *want* you, Helen. I *love* you. Big difference."

"Okay, look. I hate to even think about this, but I'll do it," Helen pleaded as Lucas started to shake his head vehemently. "I love you, too, and I'll do whatever I have to do if it will let us be together. What? Why are you shaking your head? You're not the only one making this decision, you know."

"Tricks like that won't work, not unless you just want something physical. Is that all you want from me? Sex?" he teased.

"Of course not, you know that!" Helen said in frustration, shoving him away from her. "I just told you I loved you!"

"That's why it won't work," he said. He took her hands and pulled her closer to him. "If you and I were to be together the way we want, or at least the way I want—" he began uncertainly.

"And what do you want, exactly?" Helen interrupted urgently.

"I want it all. Everything we talked about. I want us to go

to school, learn a dozen languages, live all over the world. Most of all, I want us to be together."

"I do, too!" Helen said excitedly as if she had found a way out. "And we can do all that without ever getting married!"

"We'd share everything," he said, shaking his head like Helen wasn't understanding him. "And because of that, we'd be considered a married couple in the eyes of the gods, regardless of who took your virginity. I want a whole life with you, and because I want that, you would be my wife. I can't even pretend I would settle for less."

"You're saying that it's our commitment to each other that will define us to the gods, not a white dress or a ring?" Helen asked, already knowing the answer.

"Exactly," he said. Then he suddenly laughed at a thought. "Also, it'd be kinda hard to be together if I was in prison."

"What are you talking about?" Helen asked, suddenly alarmed. "Why would you go to prison?"

"For killing the guy that took your virginity," he replied. "You I would forgive. But the guy? Dead man."

Helen smirked at Lucas like she didn't believe him, but she wisely decided not to question his sincerity.

"Then what's the plan?" She sighed, resting back against him. "We can't be together and we definitely can't be apart."

"We stick together and play by the rules until we can rewrite them. We're going to find a way to make this work. I promise."

"Isn't that hubris?" she asked, raising her eyes to his. "Thinking we can beat the Fates?"

"I don't care what it is anymore. I need to hope," he responded before he allowed himself to kiss her.

Helen fell against him, and this time she was able to enjoy his mouth without the shock that came along with the unexpectedness of their first kiss. This time she could pay attention to him, feel him responding to her. Far sooner than Helen wanted, Lucas pulled back, pinched his eyes together like it hurt, and gently pushed her hands off of him.

"You have to stop," he said, forcing himself to laugh, even if it was a shaky, watered-down laugh.

"Sorry. I don't know what I'm doing yet," Helen said through her tingling lips.

"Could have fooled me," he mumbled as he took both of her hands and stood up, pulling her to her feet with him. "I think a little cold air will do us good."

"Where to? Venice?" Helen asked with a cheeky grin.

"Sure. Because that's exactly what you and I need—a more romantic setting," he replied sarcastically. "Sorry, Sparky, but I'm taking you home to your father before I start a war."

He leapt into the air and spun back to face her, holding out a hand like they were in an old movie and he was asking her to dance. She groaned at how gorgeous he was, then joined him with a smile, taking his hand and rolling her body over the playful eddies he carved into the wind for her.

Moments later, they were landing in Helen's yard and strolling toward the door, hand in hand. Just as Helen was about to go inside the house, Lucas stopped her.

"You actually thought I didn't know, didn't you?" he asked

her incredulously. "Happy birthday."

"I totally forgot!" Helen exclaimed with a bemused smile.

"I didn't," he said, kissing her. He looked up at the brightly lit house, and they both listened briefly to an emergency weather report blaring away on the TV. "Your dad's waiting for you. You'd better go in."

"Yeah. Kate made me a cake," Helen said. She grimaced, guilty over how she'd treated her family this past week.

"Tomorrow, first thing, I'll be back to get you," Lucas promised as he brushed his mouth lightly against hers. "Then we'll go to my house and tell my family. Together."

"Right. We still have to plead our case," Helen said. Wrapped around each other, they kissed for a few more moments, stalling for time that the storm wouldn't give them. Finally, Lucas pulled away. Glancing around at every shadow suspiciously, he told her to hurry into the house. It was dark out and he was unwilling to leave her unguarded for even a moment. Helen ran inside and closed the front door behind her, peering out the window in time to see Lucas fly away. She called out for her father as she walked into the family room.

"Jerry isn't here, Helen," said a woman's voice behind her. Helen spun around, already calling up a bolt, but the woman grabbed her tightly by the wrists and shook her head.

"That won't work on me," she said. Electricity danced across her flawless face, making her long, blonde hair crackle and fluff, and circling the pupils of her warm brown eyes.

"Oh my god," Helen said, looking at the heart-shaped

charm that fell neatly into the groove at the base of her attacker's throat.

The woman ripped off Helen's identical necklace with one hand and jabbed a needle into her neck with the other. Helen felt her muscles go limp and refuse to follow her commands. The world faded into a pale gray haze, and even though she kept trying to see, her eyes could only chase the bright squiggles that tracked across the backs of her eyelids. She was losing consciousness so fast, Helen knew that she had to have been given a powerful drug, maybe even a lethal one. The last thing Helen felt was her attacker tenderly supporting her body as it swooned to the floor. Helen couldn't see, couldn't move, but for just one moment longer she could still hear.

"My sweet little girl," the woman whispered, and then Helen experienced nothing, not even nightmares.

Lucas was only halfway home when the wind tried to throw him down to the ground and the sky started to flash with the first bolts of lightning. He landed immediately, and had to go the rest of the way on foot rather than get electrocuted or crushed. He wondered if Helen could fly through the lightning and if she would be able to control it so that he could fly with her in a storm if the situation ever arose. That would be beautiful, he thought as he walked through the garage and into the kitchen, flying through lightning-bright clouds.

As soon as he opened the door, he stopped, sensing something wrong.

"Didn't you bring Helen with you?" Cassandra asked nervously as he stood in the doorway. "I could have sworn I saw you together today."

Lucas looked around the room and saw Jerry and Kate, the promised cake bristling with unlit candles, and Claire sitting wide-eyed next to Jason.

"I just left her at home to be with you two," he said gesturing to Jerry and Kate. Panic washed down his legs, nearly making his knees buckle.

Lucas ran out the kitchen door, past the cars in the garage, and ripped the outside door off its hinges as he leapt up into the apoplectic sky. Jumping up twenty feet, Jason tackled him out of the air and dragged him back down, pinning Lucas's weightless body to the ground.

"Sorry, brother, but the storm is too big. We drive tonight," Jason said.

"There was someone waiting for her inside her house!" Lucas yelled, taking on mass and throwing Jason off of him.

"We know, you idiot! This afternoon, while you had your phone shut off, Cassie saw that Creon came back to the island," Jason said, latching on to Lucas to make sure he didn't change states again and fly off. "But Creon isn't the one at her house!"

"Then who is it?" Lucas asked, visibly calming down. He and Jason stood up and waited for Hector to pull his truck out.

"Cassandra was getting little images all day long, but she didn't understand them. One of the things she saw was a woman tailing Creon as he came back to the island. She had this habit of tucking her hair behind her ear with her pinkie finger," Jason began. The truck pulled out and Lucas and Jason jumped onto it. They eased themselves inside as the truck sped off into the punishing wind and rain.

"Then Cass said she kept seeing flashes of several different women, over and over," Jason continued. "She didn't know why she was having visions about women that she didn't recognize and that didn't seem to have anything to do with each other. It took a while, but Cass finally noticed that they all had exactly the same way of putting their hair behind their ear, like a nervous tic. Because of that, Cass realized that they were *all the same person,* and the most persistent vision she kept having was of one of these women waiting for Helen at her house like she *lived* there."

"The woman let herself into Helen's house with her own key and turned on the TV like she'd done it a million times, so at first Cass didn't think there was any danger. Probably a relative Helen never mentioned, right?" Hector interjected. "It wasn't until just a few seconds before you walked in the door that she put it all together and knew that she had been seeing Helen's attacker all day long. We tried to call you. . . ."

"But I had my phone shut off," Lucas finished for him, adding a foul curse on the end. "What did the woman waiting at Helen's house look like?" Lucas asked urgently, trying to get a mental image of the threat. "Is she that brunette? Or the old woman who attacked Kate?"

"Neither. Cassandra said she was unbelievably beautiful. Like Helen," Jason replied.

"Not just beautiful *like* Helen—you're telling it wrong, dumb-ass," Hector interrupted. He wove through traffic like a madman, blowing through red lights and passing cars illegally. "Cassie said this woman looked almost *exactly* like her. But whoever she is, Cass is certain this woman is not on Creon's side. He doesn't even know he's being followed, which may or may not be good for us."

"Why the hell wasn't someone guarding the house?" Lucas shouted in frustration, too upset to think about what Cassandra's vision meant yet.

"It's my fault," Hector said, and then continued before his little brother could argue. "Shut up, Jase, I'm the one who allowed her to go off on her own after practice. It was my call, and I made it, even though I knew in my gut it was wrong."

Lucas wanted to rip Hector's face off for taking the blame when he knew whose fault it really was. He should have checked his phone, he should have checked the house, he should have paid more attention to Helen's safety and less attention to her soft hands and warm skin. He scrubbed his hands over his face and made himself take a series of deep breaths. He needed to trust Hector to get them there, and then he needed to focus and be ready for whatever they encountered. If he was going to be at all useful, he was going to have to shut up and calm down.

When they got to Helen's house, the TV and the lights

were off and the front door was locked. Lucas flew up to Helen's bedroom window, which he knew she always forgot to latch. He let himself in and then went downstairs to open the front door for the others. Nothing was taken and nothing was disturbed in the entire house. It was as if Helen hadn't even put up a fight.

"She must have known the woman and gone with her willingly," Hector said, tossing up his hands. "It's the only reason this place isn't melting."

"Unless whoever kidnapped her is just *that* good," Jason added.

"What are you talking about?" Hector said derisively. "Helen's a full-on monster now with her lightning. I don't care who this evil twin is, no one is *that* good."

"Twin," Lucas repeated, thinking. "It could be that simple. She'd have the same lightning, the same strength, and a lot more experience."

The brothers looked at him as he got down on his hands and knees and examined the floor. He reached under an end table and came up with a drained hypodermic needle.

"That rules out Helen going willingly. Whoever she was, she came prepared. And she must have known about the cestus and how it works, or she never would have been able to penetrate Helen's skin," Lucas said, his breath catching only slightly when he said her name.

He handed the needle to Jason and dropped back down to examine the floor one last time, in case he missed something. When he was satisfied, he stood up and looked through his cousins instead of at them, still thinking. Then he went to the windows by the door and looked out at the raging storm. Lucas watched mini mudslides slosh down Helen's driveway and out into the street and knew that any path Helen might have left would be long gone.

"Was there anything else in Cassandra's vision?" Lucas asked hopefully.

"The last thing she said was that she thought Helen would still be safe tomorrow morning," Jason replied, shaking his head doubtfully. "Cass had a brief flash of Helen standing in a window that looked like some kind of hotel on Nantucket, but she couldn't be sure."

"Maybe Cass has seen something else," Hector said as optimistically as he could. He opened his phone and tried to dial, but a NO SIGNAL sign was flashing on his screen. "Check your phones," he said to his brother and cousin. Neither of them could connect a call, either.

Lucas went into Helen's kitchen and checked her landline for a dial tone, but it was dead. As he joined his cousins back in the entryway, the power in the house went out. Jason went over to the window and looked at the other houses in the area.

"The whole block is out," he said. "And massive lightning bolts are headed this way. I guess we're stuck here for a while."

"You two stay here in case Helen gets free and makes her way back," Lucas said as he turned for the door.

"Where the hell do you think you're going?" Hector

demanded, grabbing Lucas by the shoulder and trying to turn him around.

"Don't," Lucas warned quietly. They stared at each other until Hector finally backed down and removed his hand from Lucas's shoulder.

"Just stay out of the sky," he cautioned. "You're no good to her dead."

Lucas strode off into the dark storm without responding. He was frustrated with not being able to fly and trying to think of where to start. If he could get airborne he could see around, get his bearings and look for anything suspicious, but the storm had him completely grounded. It suddenly occurred to him that if he had just drugged a girl who was known on sight by most of the locals of a tiny island, he would want to get off that island as soon as possible, and if Lucas was grounded, all air travel was almost certainly canceled as well. The only way to get Helen off island would be by boat, and even that was a long shot. Going out on the water would be suicide.

He ran to the dock, where he learned that the last ferry had left over an hour earlier and that the coast guard had officially suspended all travel in and out of the marina and airport while the storm lasted. New England was going to get pummeled with a good old-fashioned nor'easter that night, and the impassable weather would probably last into the next day. Lucas relaxed a little when he heard that. He'd left Helen less than an hour earlier, after the last ferry had already departed, so the chances were high that she was still on island. Hopefully, she was in a hotel, and relatively safe.

He wasted a few more hours wandering in and out of every motel and bed-and-breakfast near the ferry, asking if two women had checked in that evening. Unfortunately, although there were a lot of people stranded on the island and filling up the hotels due to the storm, there were none that fit Helen's description. Lucas knew it was futile. No Scion would be stupid enough to walk into a hotel with an unconscious girl slung over her shoulder and ask for a room. Whoever had taken Helen may have broken in someplace, or even bribed someone at the desk, but either way, Lucas knew they weren't going to announce themselves. He was chasing his own tail, but still, he couldn't give up. He checked back at home, found out what Cassandra had seen in her next vision while he'd been gone, and then ran back into the storm before his father could even start to argue.

The wind was so strong it was tearing down trees and taking apart the stoic Nantucket architecture. Even Lucas, as strong as he was, had to switch over into his supermassive state to stay anchored to the ground as bits and pieces of people's houses tumbled down the streets around him. His bare face was getting lashed by the swirling debris in the air, and the sideways rain was clawing at his eyes. All night he wandered around outside every hotel, inn, and bed-and-breakfast he could think of, looking in the windows with eyes that could see in even the dimmest of light, hoping for a glimpse of Helen.

He knew he wouldn't get it. Cassandra had told him that

Helen would be standing in a hotel window the next morning, but he still couldn't make himself stop. He wouldn't stop, because if by some miracle he did find her, take her out of that hotel, and bring her back to her family, he could prove Cassandra wrong. All he needed was to beat Fate once and he would know that he was the master of himself—not just a prewritten story that gets reread every now and again to amuse the cosmos—but a truly blank slate that he would be allowed to fill with whatever future he decided to write for himself. If he could just find Helen that night and bring her home, then he knew that someday they would beat Fate, and that they could be together.

He walked all night.

Helen's head was pounding and there was a sour, chalky taste in the back of her mouth, like she had chewed an aspirin and didn't rinse afterward. Her eyes felt swollen and puffy, and the skin on her face felt clammy and hot, but she didn't feel as dehydrated as she usually did when she visited the dry lands. This was different. She'd been drugged, she suddenly remembered, by a woman. A woman that looked just like her, but older.

"Take a sip," said a voice as Helen felt a straw being pressed to her lips. Her eyes flipped open and she saw the woman again, leaning over her and holding a glass of water.

"Who are you?" Helen asked, her voice crackling. She jerked her mouth away from the suspicious glass of liquid and felt her arms strain against bonds. She was tied to a bed. Still unbearably weak from whatever drug she had been given, Helen knew it would be a while before she was strong enough to break free. She looked around frantically. She was in a hotel room that was lit by candles. It was still night, and she could hear wind and rain battering the window behind the closed curtain.

"Look at me, Helen! Who do you think I am?" the woman asked so forcefully it momentarily stopped Helen from panicking. "Here, I know you'll need proof. I would."

The woman took out an envelope full of pictures. They were pictures of herself, when she was in her late teens. In one picture she was holding a tiny baby. In another she was sitting and talking to a young Mrs. Aoki while two baby girls, one blonde, one black-haired, played together on the floor. In yet another she was kissing Jerry over her swollen, pregnant belly.

"Beth," Helen whispered, her eyes darting over the pictures that she had spent a hefty portion of her childhood searching for.

"My real name is Daphne. Daphne Atreus. I guess it would be too much to ask for you to call me 'Mom,' huh?" Daphne said with a wry smile.

Helen gestured to her bound wrists. "You guessed right," she replied, starting to get angry. "You want to tell me why you knocked me out and tied me up?"

"Because we are out of time, and if I were you I would hate me so much I wouldn't even give me a second to explain," Daphne replied with a loving look on her face. "Unless I had been knocked out and tied down first."

Helen glared at her, furious and still groggy from the drug. "What do you want from me?"

Daphne's face and body began to shift, not just changed in mood, but in shape. One moment Helen was looking at an older version of herself, and the next moment she was looking at a woman in her sixties with salt-and-pepper hair. Before Helen could even gasp, the dowdy woman disappeared and was replaced by a brunette in her late thirties. Then that woman disappeared and Helen was looking at her mother again. She held up Helen's heart-shaped necklace in one hand and touched her own identical necklace with the other.

"There are a lot of things I need to tell you about who you are and where you come from. Things that are going to hurt you," Daphne said in a direct, almost brutal way. "But I don't have any choice. Creon is on this island right now, and he is coming for you."

# SIXTEEN

At around six o'clock in the morning, Lucas finally accepted the fact that he had run out of time. The sun was up. It was the next day, and Helen was probably already standing in a hotel window somewhere, in fulfillment of Cassandra's prophecy. He knew his best bet would be to give up, go home, and wait for his little sister to see something else, even if it half killed him to admit that. He hadn't beaten Fate. Again.

Lucas saw the Pig still parked out in front of his house, and had to sneak in. It looked like Jerry, Kate, and Claire had all been forced to spend the night to wait out the storm, and that meant Jerry and Kate still didn't know that Helen was missing. As far as they knew, Helen was safe at home and stranded there with all three Delos boys on the other side of the island. Lucas knew that lie wouldn't hold up much longer, but he decided someone else was going to have to think up a new cover story to tell Jerry. He couldn't control his emotions about Helen long enough to convince anyone she was still safe, let alone her father.

Lucas flew in through his window and paced around his room for another hour. He was vaguely aware of the fact that he should eat or rest or dry off, but the only thought he could keep in his head was the thought of Helen. Cass would know it if she was injured, wouldn't she?

The houseguests woke and went downstairs. Lucas heard Claire's phone buzzing with text alerts, and knew that the phones were back on. He listened from his room while Jerry and Kate tried to call Helen. When she didn't answer either her cell or the phone at the Hamilton household, they got worried and decided to go back home to see if she was there. The roads were a mess, but even though that would slow them down, Lucas knew he only had a few more hours tops to find Helen before her dad realized she was missing and called the police. As soon as Jerry and Kate departed, Lucas met Hector and Jason on the stairs as all three of them came out from hiding in their rooms at the same time.

"Bro, put a clean shirt on, at least!" Hector admonished as soon as he saw Lucas.

"Leave it," Lucas mumbled, shaking his head and trying to pass his cousins, but Jason stepped in front of him.

"Don't you think your mom is worried enough as it is? Go clean up before you come downstairs," Jason said quietly.

It was a guilt trip, pure and simple, but Jason was still

right. Lucas nodded and pulled his shirt off over his head on his way to the bathroom. He washed, dressed, and met the rest of his family down in the kitchen. Even so, everyone stared at him when he walked in the room, and his mother looked like she had seen a ghost. Lucas checked his edges and realized that he was blurring himself. His mom always got upset when he did that because she knew that meant that *he* was upset. He made a conscious effort to let the light do what it wanted, and sat down in a corner, his eyes on Cassandra. Then the sound of bickering made him realize that Claire was there.

"What are you still doing here?" Jason was saying in a dismayed voice. "Why didn't you go back with them?"

"I'm not going anywhere until we find Lennie," Claire huffed back at him.

"We?" Jason sputtered, but Claire held up an imperious hand and fished her vibrating phone out of her back pocket.

"Guys?" Claire said, looking at the incoming number. "It's Helen."

"Let me talk to her," Lucas demanded as he jumped up out of his chair and held out his hand to take the phone.

"She called me, not you," Claire said gently.

She answered her phone, immediately asking Helen several questions at once. Then Claire was quiet for a moment. She put the call on speakerphone.

"Okay, Len, we can all hear you. What is it?" Claire asked, looking around at the rest of his family but avoiding eye contact with Lucas.

"I'm with my mother, Daphne, and my mother only. We are not being coerced by any other individual, family, or House," Helen announced to the room as smoothly as if she were playing a recording. "My mother and I are preparing to leave the island together, and we ask that you allow us to leave it in peace. I am not in any physical danger. You know all of this is true, because your Falsefinders can hear it in my voice. Good-bye. I will miss you all."

The line went silent. Lucas stared at the phone as Claire switched out of speaker mode, put her phone to her ear, and repeated Helen's name a few times.

"That wasn't her," Lucas insisted, shaking his head repeatedly. He felt something was off, like there was a lie lurking somewhere. Helen wasn't supposed to leave him. Ever. "She'd never call me a 'Falsefinder' like that."

"Lucas, it was her," Claire insisted, finally meeting Lucas's eyes and giving him a sad look as she did so. "I know she sounded really weird, but it was Helen. You know that."

"Was she lying?" Castor asked Lucas.

"No," Lucas answered hoarsely, as though his voice couldn't entirely commit to something that the rest of him knew was so *wrong*. "She told no lies."

"So Daphne is alive," Pallas breathed, his eyes wide and blank with shock.

"We still don't know if 'Daphne' is Daphne Atreus," Castor said, blocking his brother from leaving the room.

"Enough, Castor. Just stop it," Pallas said, a note of weariness weighing his voice down. "I thought Helen *was* that

Atreus whore when I first saw her!"

"And Hector is a dead ringer for Ajax, and Lucas looks like one of *Poseidon's* children from the House of Athens!" Castor shouted, losing his patience. "More often than not the way we look is about fate, not our Houses. You know that as well as anyone! Helen's mother could be any one of the five different Daphnes we heard were killed in the slaughter eighteen-plus years ago."

"You'd do anything to keep the peace, wouldn't you? Even let that woman get away," Pallas said, pushing past Castor and throwing Hector's restraining hand off his shoulder.

Lucas took an automatic step forward to get his cousin's back. Hector could easily overpower his father if he had to, but Lucas didn't want them to fight at all. A fight would delay him from finding Helen, and he *had* to see her. They weren't supposed to be separated, and Lucas couldn't shake the overwhelming sensation that something very wrong was happening.

"Where are you going, Dad?" Hector asked wearily, backing off from a physical fight.

"To find the woman who murdered my brother," Pallas said through gritted teeth as he strode toward the door.

"You will not go," Cassandra said.

Everyone in the room froze at the sound of her voice. There was a chiming tone to it, as if more than one person was speaking at the same time. The voices coming out of her were old and young and everything in between, all speaking in harmony. Lucas saw Claire take an instinctive step back toward Jason in terror. Cassandra's mouth was glowing, and her hair was writhing around her head like snakes.

"Lucas, son of the sun, is the only one who can see the face he seeks," she continued to prophesy. "He will find the daughters of Zeus, they who are beloved by Aphrodite, and give them shelter in the Royal House of Thebes. Oh! Caution! Betrayal . . ." She broke off uncertainly. The light left her, and she began to shake. She looked frightened, but not even Lucas wanted to go near her.

"Are you okay?" Lucas asked her quietly from across the room, breaking the unnatural silence. She nodded and rubbed her hands over her shoulders and upper arms, suddenly looking much smaller than she was.

"You're going to need to take Hector and the twins with you," she warned. "I think there's going to be a fight."

"I'll go, too," Castor said, but Cassandra shook her head.

"If Daphne sees you or Pallas, she'll run," she said with an apologetic shrug.

"So our children are to go face her alone? No. Daphne is too dangerous. We can't let them anywhere *near* her," Pallas objected as his anger gave way to fear. "She seduced Ajax and murdered him!"

"We don't know that!" Castor yelled out in frustration.

For a moment it looked like Castor was going to hit his brother, but Hector insinuated himself in between them. Lucas nearly screamed with frustration, wondering how Scions had ever survived this long. They were always at each other's throats, and none of this infighting got him any closer to Helen.

"Everyone calm down! Uncle. Father," Hector said, turning from one to the other, and assuring both of them. "We can handle this."

There was a gasping laugh, a bitter sound that caught everyone's attention. When Lucas looked over, Pandora had a hand over her mouth and her eyes were filling up with tears. She looked tenderly at Hector, and spoke to him from behind her hand.

"You sound just like him, you know," she said with an odd smile. "Like Ajax. It's as if another cycle is starting."

"There's no cycle waiting for me, Aunt Dora. I'll be fine," Hector said with a cocky smile. "We'll all be back in a couple of hours with Helen and Daphne, safe and sound."

"Where is she?" Lucas asked Cassandra, relieved to finally be doing something.

"Helen and her mother are somewhere close to the ferry, but they are moving around so I can't see exactly where," she replied.

Lucas felt his cousins fall in behind him as he turned and headed for the door.

"Wait! I'm going with you," Claire insisted as she scurried to catch up with the fast-moving Scions. "Lennie needs me."

"You really are insane, you know that?" Jason said scornfully, but Lucas could hear admiration behind his false anger. "You're staying here."

"But *I* can talk to her! She'll listen to me," Claire reasoned, holding up her hands and pressing against Jason's chest to keep him from walking past her. She looked at Lucas, begging him to agree with her, but he couldn't do that.

"You're not going, Five-Two," Hector said, ending the argument. "If there's a fight you'd be a target, and I don't want anyone getting hurt trying to protect you." He glanced at his brother meaningfully.

"Don't worry, I'll bring her back," Lucas assured Claire. He followed his cousins and jumped into the truck. "Just *please* stay here, and stay safe."

"Of course," Claire replied in her most deferential tone. Lucas didn't need to be a Falsefinder to know she was lying.

He hoped she wouldn't do anything too stupid, but he couldn't stop to find out what she was scheming. Helen was about to leave the island. Lucas didn't know if he had a touch of his little sister's talent or not, but he just *knew* that if Helen left him then, he might lose her forever.

# SEVENTEEN

Creon stood along the side of the compound, entirely cloaked in shadows, and waited until his cousins sped off in their black SUV before he ran after them. He could easily keep pace with the moving car, and as long as he stayed inside a cloud of darkness, he could depend on the dreary weather to keep him perfectly hidden. No other Scion for hundreds of years had Creon's control over light, and on a cloudy day not even another Son of Apollo could see him.

Creon had followed Hector and Jason back to the compound from Helen's place that morning. Having nothing else to go on, he decided the best thing to do would be to eavesdrop on his estranged family. His father had told him about the shape-shifting qualities of the cestus, and he knew that he had no other choice but to wait for his quarry to reveal herself. He guessed that eventually she would make contact with the traitors, and he had been right. Now all he had to do was follow them and trust that eventually his cousins would lead him right to her.

Helen looked out the window of the hotel, searching the nearly empty street below, but she didn't see Lucas anywhere. She'd hoped to see him one last time before she left, even if he didn't see her. It was little enough to hope for, but apparently, little was still too much. Lucas was gone, the storm was ending, and soon she and her mother would be on the first ferry off island.

"Helen," Daphne called from behind her. "You're wearing your own face. You have to be consistent or we'll be discovered."

Helen turned around and concentrated on projecting the image of the cute brunette she and her mother had decided Helen would become when they ran away.

"Much better," Daphne said with a pleased nod. "I still can't believe you never stumbled on to this power by yourself."

Helen didn't have an answer for that. She was too disturbed by her newfound power and her newfound mother to decide whether she was being complimented or insulted. She walked over to the vanity in the bedroom to look at the stranger in the mirror. The cestus could make her look like any woman in the world, but she'd only had a few hours to practice with it. Her mother had promised to teach her how to become any age, any race, any gender in the future, but although she'd kept her disguise simple for now, she was still unrecognizable, as long as she remembered to keep up the illusion.

"You don't have to keep your half of the cestus as the heart necklace, you know," her mother told her, standing behind Helen and looking at her in the glass.

"Yeah, I know. I figured out how to do that much on my own, at least," Helen answered in the stranger's voice.

Helen's necklace was the actual girdle of Aphrodite, the protective half that made her impervious to weapons. Daphne's half was the adornments of Aphrodite, and although she couldn't stop a blade or a bomb with her skin like Helen could, what she could do was potentially more frightening. Daphne was irresistible to whomever she decided to charm.

"Well, I'm glad. I've always worn my half as the heart, and I always hoped you did, too," Daphne said shyly. "I guess you probably think I've got no right to be nostalgic about you. But I am."

Daphne fingered her heart-shaped charm and opened her mouth to say something else, but she stopped herself and went into the other room to sort through her luggage for the tenth time. A part of Helen wanted to run after her mother and say she had always hoped her necklace was a tie between them, too. But another part of her wanted to rip the thing off her neck and throw it in her mother's borrowed face.

Helen wasn't certain how far Daphne's power of persuasion went just yet. It came from the cestus, so it might be that Daphne was irresistible only in a sexual way, but Helen was painfully aware of how quickly she had agreed to leave her home and the people she loved. She was following a woman she couldn't remember to a place she had never seen, and she had made the decision to do so in less than an hour. Helen thought through everything she had learned, looking for some clue that she was being controlled, but as she added up all the evidence, she knew that she didn't need to be brainwashed to want to run away.

After what Daphne had told her, Helen was so disgusted with herself she would have run away, regardless.

"Are you hungry?" Daphne asked. Helen jumped away from the window at the sound and dropped the curtain guiltily. Without even realizing it, she had been looking for Lucas again.

"No," she replied, unable to look up from the rug.

"Well, you're still going to have to eat, and we should try out your new face before we get on the ferry," Daphne said with a grimace. "We're going out for breakfast before we have to travel over that blasted ocean."

Helen tried to argue—to point out how silly it would be to test her ability to hold her new shape with so little practice—but Daphne only shrugged and said that it would be easier to test it on land before they ventured out on the water. It seemed that Helen's fear of the ocean was inherited. Daphne loathed it, and remembering what Hector had told her about how her own dislike of the ocean came from not being able to control it, Helen assumed that her mother must be a huge control freak to hate the ocean so passionately. After a quick check to make sure that neither of them was wearing clothes that might get them recognized, Daphne dragged Helen out onto the street with a promise that it would be "fun."

The storm had mashed the fallen autumn leaves into a kind of red-brown paste that coated the cobblestone streets and clogged the overwhelmed gutters. The rain was petering out and the wind was dying down, but the bottoms of the clouds were still a smudged-mascara color, and water ran in impromptu rivers down the sidewalks on their way out to sea. Fallen branches lay here and there, the bushy ends denuded of leaves, and the trunk ends, newly ripped from the trees, ended in fresh white splinters that stuck out in all directions like dropped boxes of toothpicks. Helen could smell the tree sap in the air as the few trees that the island had to offer bled out after losing their battle with the wind. With the disturbing image of dead wooden soldiers and giant wooden horses in her mind, the last thing that she wanted to do was eat.

"Nothing's going to be open," Helen protested, but she knew she it wasn't true.

"I used to live here, too, you know. And if there's one thing I learned . . ." Daphne stomped confidently past the boarded-up windows of the nervous art dealers and down the block, where a line was forming outside the Overeasy Café. "It's that Whalers love nothing more than a really *good* storm," she finished with relish.

It was true. Helen's fellow Nantucketers were proud of their ability to live through whatever Mother Nature threw at them. It was a macho thing, but also a chance to bond. They shared a good laugh over the howling wind, ice, snow, or rain while they all looked for their hysterical cats and retrieved their lawn decorations from each other's living rooms.

The block didn't have electricity, and folks were still sweeping up glass from the broken windows. In spite of all this, Helen wasn't at all surprised that the café was seating people. In fact, she knew that at that moment her father and Kate were six blocks away at the News Store, checking out the damage. She also knew that if people started hanging around out front looking hungry, Jerry and Kate would open the doors and feed them. With the refrigerators out, the perishables would have to be eaten or thrown out, anyway, and Kate would much rather give food to her neighbors than watch it spoil.

Helen thought for a moment of how she should be there with them, but then she caught a glimpse of her new reflection in the one window outside the Overeasy Café that wasn't broken. She wasn't Helen. She was a cute brunette from the mainland, and she and her tacky, horse-faced mother were on vacation in Nantucket. These two tourists owed nothing to anyone.

Helen sat, put her napkin in her lap, and ordered whatever the café could make on a gas stove—eggs, bacon, and

French-pressed coffee. As she pushed her food around, Matt walked into the diner. Helen's eyes widened when Matt looked right at her and, out of habit, she pulled in a breath to call out to him, but his eyes skipped right past her.

It was obvious that Matt had come into the café looking for her. Helen groaned to herself and rubbed her tired eyes—Claire must have told him that Helen was missing. Helen wondered how much else he knew about her. Knowing Matt and how clever he was, Helen was sure he had figured out some of her secret on his own, like Claire had.

For a moment she wanted him to find her, but he was scanning the room for Helen's bright blonde hair. When his eyes didn't immediately spot her, he gave up. She wanted to throw her napkin at Matt and yell that she was sitting ten feet away from him, but she realized that it was silly of her to blame him for not recognizing her. Still, it hurt not to be recognized by a guy she'd known since she was in diapers. As she watched Matt walk out of the café, she couldn't help but feel like she was faceless, alone, and about as substantial as a ghost.

"It's better for him," Daphne said consolingly as she reached across the table to take Helen's hand. "The humans who love us never last long. Scions are tragedy magnets. It's safer for them if we leave before the trouble starts. That's why I didn't give Jerry more time . . ."

"You never loved my father, I mean Jerry," Helen interrupted bitterly. She snatched her hand out from underneath her mother's.

"No, I didn't. I'm not going to lie to you to make myself more sympathetic," Daphne replied, moving her rejected hand to reach for the check. "But I would never wish harm on that man. Remember, he's the only person I trusted with my daughter. You hate me for not loving Jerry? Fine. But the least you can do is respect me for understanding how special he was and giving you the gift of thinking he was your father."

"Jerry *is* my father in every way that counts," Helen said, wrenching herself out from the sinking seat of the booth.

She waited with her back turned while Daphne threw down some bills. On their way to the hotel to get their things, Helen spotted Hector. He looked right at her and then right past her, just as Matt had done. The twins were with him, wandering around by the ferry. Helen heard Ariadne call out to Matt, sounding surprised to see him, but Daphne pulled her into the hotel before she could find out what they said to each other. Helen heard Claire's name mentioned right before the door shut behind her making it impossible even to tell what they were saying about her, even with Scion hearing.

Lucas was in the lobby. Helen didn't see his face, but then she didn't need to. If she had only caught a glimpse of him as he disappeared around a corner half a mile away she would still have been able to recognize him. She turned her face away, knowing she couldn't look at him or she would lose concentration and allow her mask to slip away. As she hurried up the stairs behind her mother, she both hoped and feared that he would yell her name, but of course, he didn't.

Back in their room, Helen grabbed what few things she had and brought them to the entryway by the door, hiding her streaming eyes and her red nose from her mother as best she could. She tried to let the stranger's dark hair fall across her face, but unfortunately this girl had bangs. As her mother checked over the room one last time before they left for the dock, Helen let out an incongruous laugh, suddenly remembering the last time she had taken the ferry. It was when Claire first told her about the new family that had moved into the big compound out in 'Sconset. Claire had been sure that there would be a dream boy to fall in love with each of them, and Helen had been sure that Claire was being ridiculous. So sure that she'd changed the subject, and wondered aloud whether she should cut her hair.

"Well, Claire was absolutely right," Helen said to herself, laughing through her tears. "I *do* hate having bangs."

Her breath still catching on the half-crazy laugh, Helen yanked open the door of the hotel room to leave, and ran right into Lucas. In a split second he registered Helen's tears and the shocked face of the strange woman next to her. Lucas grabbed Helen's arm and pulled her away from the woman, putting himself between them.

"What did you do to her?" he said, threatening Daphne.

"And just who are you?" Daphne said with a southern drawl. Lucas gave the woman a confused look and then looked back at Helen.

"Helen, who is this woman?" he asked.

"Come inside," Daphne said, dropping the fake accent. "Come on, Helen. We've been discovered. He can see your true face."

"How?" Helen asked, looking down at the hands that weren't hers, at a body that wasn't hers, as she followed Lucas back into the room.

"Because he loves you." Daphne shut the door behind them. "The cestus can't hide the face of a beloved, it can only reveal it. You'll never be anyone but yourself to him because he loves you exactly as you are."

Daphne rubbed her temples in frustration at this new and annoying development. She turned to Lucas and dropped her disguise. He gasped.

"You *are* all of the women," Lucas said, remembering what Cassandra had seen. "Helen, this is the woman that's been attacking you, this isn't her real face . . ."

"I know. I even know that she was the one who hurt Kate in the alley," Helen said, swallowing painfully. "I thought it was me—that I had shocked Kate by accident."

"Helen, you aren't to blame," Daphne said, sounding almost annoyed at the idea.

"She was trying to kidnap me to get me away from your family before you found out who I really was," Helen continued, ignoring Daphne. "She knew I wouldn't trust her, and that she would literally have to tie me down to get me to listen to her. So that's what she did. But this is my true mother, and this is her true face, Lucas. It's our face."

"It's not possible," Lucas said, looking from Helen to

417

Daphne and back again. "No Scion resembles another *this* closely."

"The bearers of the cestus always look like the first Scion to ever possess it," Daphne said.

"Helen of Troy," Lucas said quietly.

Helen nodded, then clarified while looking at her mother. "Aphrodite and Helen were half sisters, and they loved each other very much. When the siege of Troy began, Aphrodite gave Helen the cestus to protect her. Since then, it's been passed from mother to daughter, along with the Face."

"The Face?" Lucas asked.

"That Launched a Thousand Ships," Daphne said, repeating the title automatically. "It's our curse."

"Helen of Troy was in the House of Atreus," Lucas said as he slumped down into a straight-backed chair that decorated the entryway. "So Pallas was right. You are Daphne Atreus."

"I suppose Pallas had to be right about something eventually," Daphne snapped before she stopped herself and softened her tone. "I know he's your uncle, but we have a complicated history. Your father was different. He was very kind to me, or at least he tried to be. The Furies make kindness a very relative term."

"The Furies," Lucas said as an idea struck him. "Why don't I see the Furies when I'm around you?"

"For the same reason your family doesn't see them around Helen anymore. You two risked your lives to save each other, and that released you from your blood debt. A long time ago

I went through something similar with another member of the House of Thebes. But I don't have time to explain the whole story to you," Daphne said not unkindly. "Helen and I have to get off this island, and we have to do it now."

"No," Lucas said, looking at Helen. "Come back with me, both of you. My family . . ."

"Your family wants me dead," Daphne replied coldly. "And Creon is here to hunt Helen down. I have to get her off this island, and if you love her the way I know you do, you'll help me do it."

"I can protect Helen from Creon," Lucas said defiantly, still waiting for Helen to look at him, but she wouldn't.

"How? Are you ready to become a kin-killer? An Outcast?" Daphne asked harshly.

Lucas snapped his head around to look at Daphne, responding to a phrase that he had been raised to abhor. For a moment he hated her, but only because she was right.

"You can't defend Helen against your own family—not to the death. I'm the only one who can protect her now," Daphne continued, her tone suggesting that she was genuinely sorry for him. "And the best way for me to do that is to get her away from Creon."

"I won't let him near her. I don't care what I have to become," Lucas said, preoccupied with Helen and troubled by the way she seemed to be avoiding him. He took her hands.

"Lucas. Let me go," Helen said quietly, pulling her hands out of his. He went silent, sensing something very wrong was about to happen. Again. "If you love me, you'll let me go. Do you love me?" Her voice was so thin and papery it crackled.

"You know I do," he replied, confused. "If you're frightened, run away with *me*, like we planned. You know we're *meant* to be together, I know you can feel that, just like I do."

"I want you to let me go," she said simply as she finally met his eyes and held them.

Instead of thinking about the way Lucas's face fell under the weight of his surprise and sadness, Helen imagined her heart as a giant tub full of water. Everything she had ever felt in her life, all the good and all bad, were just ribbons of food coloring in that water, and the whole beautiful mess was swirling down the drain. The only thing she needed to do was wait a few more seconds and the basin would be empty.

"You can hear the truth in what I say, can't you?" she continued mercilessly. "I want you to let me go."

Lucas caught his breath and held it for a long moment as he registered that Helen wasn't lying to him. Then he nodded and breathed again, his face impassive.

"I believe that you want to get away from me right now, but I also know what is *going to happen*, regardless of what anyone wants," he said.

"The Oracle!" Daphne exclaimed to herself, understanding Lucas's meaning. "She survived her first prophecy? Is she still sane?" she asked breathlessly.

He gave a curt nod in response to her insensitive questions.

Daphne began to pace distractedly, as if a thousand thoughts had started elbowing around in her head. Suddenly, she stopped moving and stared at Lucas.

"What did she say about us?" she asked.

"That the beloved of Aphrodite were to find shelter in the House of Thebes," Lucas replied, emotionless. "So you see, you *will* come back with me."

"Obviously," Daphne said turning her palms up in acquiescence. "Helen, get your things."

Helen's jaw dropped and she stared at her mother in disbelief. After everything Daphne had told her to get her away from the House of Thebes, this change didn't make any sense.

"But, we'll miss the ferry. . . ." Helen stammered, still uncertain.

"The Oracle has spoken," Daphne said, shouldering her bag with a greedy look in her eyes. Helen had no idea what her mother was up to, but lacking any reason to object, she had no choice but to obey.

Helen and Daphne assumed their disguises and the three of them went down to the lobby. Lucas asked them to wait a moment when they got to the front door. He pulled out his phone and called Hector, telling him to bring the car around to the entrance of the hotel.

"Stay here," he said, firmly. "Let me check the street before you go out there. Hector said that Creon was headed our way."

"That's not necessary, Lucas. As long as you keep your distance from us, we're well hidden," Daphne said confidently as she stepped out onto the sidewalk, rolling her fancy leather suitcase behind her.

As Helen watched her mother walk out the door, she happened to glance across the street. Creon was standing on the other side, staring up at the hotel windows with his reflection-defying vision. His eyes dropped down when he saw Daphne.

As soon as she saw Creon, Helen's senses rewound to her last encounter with him. She could still feel his humid breath on her neck as he whispered *preciosa* in her ear right before he stabbed her. Most of all, she remembered the suffocating darkness that had left her feeling like she was lost in space and utterly helpless. The terror-echo she felt made her forget for a moment that both she and her mother were protected by their borrowed shapes.

"Mom! Stop!" she screamed instinctively, reaching out to pull Daphne back into the hotel.

Creon made eye contact with Helen as she shouted. Then he saw his cousin Lucas stride up and grab the strange girl frantically. Creon looked from the cute brunette to Lucas, noticing how they held each other so protectively. Then he looked back at the tacky woman with the expensive luggage and smiled. He ran across the street, his head lowered and his shoulders rounded like a bull.

"Daphne! He knows!" Lucas shouted, throwing Helen behind him and moving impossibly fast to intercept Creon.

The cousins collided in the middle of the street, both of them using their momentum to put power into their first punches. But Lucas could do something Creon wasn't expecting. At the last moment he made gravity pull harder on him, and in his massive-state he pushed his stunned opponent back into the asphalt with so much force he fractured the surface of the street.

A split second later Lucas glanced up and saw Matt's terrified face through the windshield of his car as he slammed on his brakes. Matt tried to stop, but it was too late. He hit the two figures that had appeared out of thin air in the middle of the street and his car crumpled in on itself as if it had run into a brick wall.

"Lucas!" Helen screamed as she tried to run past her mother.

Daphne grabbed Helen and restrained her just as Hector's big SUV screeched to a halt in front of them, blocking Helen's way to the accident. Ariadne jumped out of the passenger side before Hector had even come to a full stop and sprinted to the wreck.

"Get in the truck!" Hector bellowed at Daphne as he came around from the driver's side and stomped to the smoking front end of Matt's car.

Helen struggled, unable to see what was going on. She was still calling Lucas's name as Jason and Daphne bundled her into the back of the SUV.

"Luke's fine!" Jason said to her through gritted teeth as he wrestled with her. "Helen, please! We're attracting enough attention as it is."

Reminded of where she was, Helen forced herself to calm

down and get into the backseat. She slid over to one of the tinted windows, and sighed with relief when she saw Lucas standing up in front of Matt's destroyed car. He was uninjured and holding on to Hector to keep him from running off somewhere. Creon was gone, so Helen assumed that Hector was trying to follow him. For a moment, it looked like Lucas was going to hit Hector, but then he whispered something that seemed to convince his stubborn cousin, and all at once Hector calmed down and nodded.

"He looks just like Ajax," Daphne whispered behind her, her eyes glued to Hector.

Helen glanced briefly at her mother, then turned her attention back to the wreck. Ariadne was helping Matt out of his car, holding him up. He was reeling and bleeding from the head, ash-white and owl-eyed with astonishment, but he didn't seem to be badly hurt.

"We should get you to a hospital," Ariadne insisted as she studied Matt's uneven pupils.

"No," Matt said vehemently. "There's no way to explain this. Normal people don't get up and walk away after you run them over with a car."

They all knew he was right. Even concussed, Matt was a quick thinker.

"You hit your head," Jason warned as the Scions shot each other uncertain looks.

"And I *still* know what I saw. Look, don't worry about me, I'd never rat out a friend, but we have to go now," Matt insisted. "Before the police come."

"Ari?" Jason asked as he met his twin's eyes in an honest exchange. "Is it life threatening?"

Ariadne ran her hands just over Matt's skull, a faint glow coming out of her palms. "He'll be just fine," she said after a brief moment. She started to lead Matt toward Hector's truck, but Matt giggled and stopped dead.

"Wow. What did you do to me?" He gave her a goofy smile.

"I healed you. That's my gift," she answered as she smiled back at him, suddenly looking exhausted.

"Thanks," Matt said. He allowed himself to be moved toward Hector's truck. "Wait. Where's Claire?"

Helen was out of the truck and barreling down on Matt before her mother could even hold out an arm to stop her.

"What do you mean 'where's Claire'?" Helen demanded, balling her fists so hard her arms started shaking. "Where did you last see her?"

"The front seat," Matt replied weakly as he gestured toward his car.

Jason's whole body went rigid. Moving so fast he was little more than a blur, Jason tore the door of the car off with one hand and tenderly scooped Claire out from underneath the dashboard with the other. She was unconscious, bleeding, and as limp as a wet cotton doll.

"No," Jason whispered to her. "You were supposed to stay away from me." He placed his lips a hair's width away from hers and held statue still.

"How is she?" Ariadne asked urgently.

"She's breathing," he said after a moment, his voice breaking. He lifted his head up and met his twin's eyes.

"Well, can you heal her or not?" she asked him calmly, as though she and her twin had prepared themselves for this.

He clenched his jaw and nodded but didn't speak, carrying Claire into the back of the truck and holding her carefully on his lap while everyone else organized.

"I'll take care of Matt's car and meet you back at home," Lucas said to Hector, already obscuring the particulars of the wreck by bending the light around it.

"Wait," Daphne commanded. She raised a hand like she was hailing a cab and closed her eyes. "This will draw less attention," she said. Thick wreaths of pearl gray fog rolled off the water and down the street, the long, ropy tendrils racing toward her delicately tilted fingers. Helen had the feeling that the recent storm was no accident, and wondered if her mother had conjured it.

"Great Zeus, Cloud-Gatherer," Hector said under his breath, thinking along the same lines as Helen. The scene of the accident disappeared in the fog, and then he turned to Lucas. "Where are you going to hide the car?"

"In the ocean. We can clean it up after dark," Lucas answered as he plunged into the thick mist to push Matt's lump of twisted metal and leaking toxins off the dock.

Everyone else squeezed into Hector's truck. The whole incident, from Creon's attack to their getaway, had only taken a few minutes and they were a full four blocks from the scene before they heard the first siren sounding through the fog.

They drove in complete silence, at a completely lawful speed, out to Siasconset, each of them stuck inside their own thought box of shock and worry. As they cruised along, Helen couldn't take her eyes off of Jason and Claire. Jason had started moving his hands an inch above her body, his palms glowing like his sister's had when she healed Matt. He whispered in her ear. He blew soft, sparkling breaths against her closed eyes as if he was exhaling energy directly into her unconscious dreams.

Whatever he was doing was helping Claire, but it was also causing him excruciating pain. A thick, slick sweat beaded up on his graying skin as Claire seemed to settle with more comfort in his arms and gather more color in her cheeks. By the time they parked at the Delos compound, Jason was so spent Helen didn't even ask, she just picked Claire up off his lap and carried her into the house for him.

"My room. Quickly," Jason croaked as Helen carried Claire into the crowded kitchen.

She ducked past the startled faces of the Delos family, cradling Claire close to her chest to shield her from prying eyes as she and Jason made their way to the stairs. Halfway up the staircase she felt Jason put his hand on her shoulder and lean into her for support. He was so weak he could barely put one foot in front of the other. Eventually, he made it the rest of the way.

"How can I help you?" Helen asked Jason, easing Claire down into his bed.

"You can't," he replied as he stretched his big frame out

alongside Claire. "I made my choice, and we're tied to each other until she recovers. It's sort of like a Healer's last stand. At this point we'll either make it through that desert together or we won't."

"Oh, good," Helen sighed, finally feeling hopeful. "Claire would never allow someone she cared about to just go and die, especially not to save her own life."

She saw Jason smile and nod humorously as he remembered that no matter how dire the situation seemed, at least he had tied his life force to a genuinely legendary fighter.

"I did everything I could to keep her out of this, to protect her from our kind," he whispered, meeting Helen's eyes.

"Yeah, I know. All that arguing you two did, even though you're obviously perfect for each other," Helen said, feeling guilty. Jason had tried to push Claire away to keep her safe, but Helen hadn't. "I get it now."

"You have other things to deal with," he said, his eyes already starting to close. "Go. I'll guide her through."

"If you lose your way, I'll follow you down," Helen told him, already feeling the baked air of the dry lands leaching all the moisture out of the atmosphere.

Suddenly, Helen knew what the dry lands were and why she had always been too frightened to recognize the truth when it was staring her in the face. The desert that she wandered into while she slept, the land Jason now had to traverse to save Claire, was the land of the dead. For the briefest of moments she could see Claire's fetch, confused, scared, and soundlessly calling out Jason's name. Helen banished that disturbing image and spoke directly into Jason's ear. "I know the way through the rubble, and I promise, if you can't make it on your own, I'll come down and carry you both out."

Jason's eyes snapped back open in shock, but his spirit was already following Claire's, and although he tried to fight it, his eyes closed again as he slipped into a deep comalike slumber. Helen left the room, trusting him completely with Claire's heal. Mentally, she was already joining the battle that awaited her in the living room.

Helen picked her way down the stairs, hearing her mother's raised voice as she neared. It was already hauntingly familiar even though she had known the woman only a few short hours. Daphne's voice was Helen's own, coming from outside her head like a recording played back on a crappy answering machine. Helen hated it—not the sound, but feeling like she was stuck in someone else's mistake, doomed to adopt the worst qualities of the people she was supposed to love the most.

Helen paused for a moment to steel herself before she went into the living room. In the few short minutes Helen had been upstairs, a fight had begun.

"I'm to blame?" Daphne shrieked at Pallas, reacting to something he'd just said. "If you all had just stayed in Cádiz, away from Helen, none of this would have happened!"

"That was my fault," Hector admitted, trying to get everyone to calm down. "My family had to leave because I nearly killed one of my own kin."

"You wouldn't be the first," Daphne said out of the side of her mouth.

"What's that supposed to mean?" Pallas asked indignantly.

"Are you finally ready to talk about the elephant in the room?" Daphne said bitterly. "I didn't kill Ajax. Tantalus did."

"You're a liar!" Pallas said, taking a menacing step toward her.

"Then how come I'm alive? Tantalus told all of you that he killed me himself, didn't he?"

Pallas stared at her furiously.

"Just answer this one question. If I killed your brother Ajax, then why don't you see the Furies right now?" Daphne asked, throwing her arms out as if to show she wasn't hiding them anywhere.

Everyone looked around at one another, as if they were expecting someone else to have an explanation, but no one did.

"Pallas, do you remember how Ajax and I hated each other, more than just the rage of the Furies could account for, but at the same time we wouldn't allow ourselves be parted? Do you remember how we used to seek each other out, like we couldn't bear to be separated for even a moment?" Daphne asked in a softer tone.

"You were his obsession," Pallas said darkly, his eyes shooting briefly over to Lucas.

"And he was mine. Eventually, we fought, but at the last moment, instead of killing each other, there was a terrible accident. We ended up saving each other's lives. When we did that, I paid my debt to the House of Thebes. And he paid his debt to the House of Atreus. After that, Ajax could be with my family without inciting the Furies, and I could be with his. How could I stand in front of you if this weren't the truth?" Daphne motioned to Helen and Lucas. "You've seen it happen again, right in front of your eyes, and you all already know what the outcome is. Once the Furies were gone, Ajax and I fell in love."

"Liar!" Pandora hissed.

"No," Lucas said, shaking his head with a stricken, almost fearful look in his eyes. "She's telling the truth."

"I touched his body with my own hand," Pandora screamed, tears tangling her pretty pixie face into a snarl. "He was dead!"

"I think we were both dead for a few seconds," Daphne said compassionately. She was trying to get Pandora to listen to her, but in vain. Pandora shook her head at everything Daphne tried to tell her. "Ajax and I never really understood exactly what happened, but I swear to you, I didn't kill him."

Pandora whirled away from Daphne, turning her back and still shaking her head in denial. Ariadne went and stood next to her and took her hand, but Pandora would accept no comfort. She dropped Ariadne's hand and crossed her arms tightly across her chest, like her insides hurt, her left hand cupping the cuff-locket on her right wrist.

"Oh, how typical! The House of Thebes thinks it knows *everything* because it's the House of the Oracle," Daphne said to Pandora's back, almost pleading with her. "And the irony is that it's *because* you think you know it all that the other Houses have been able to hide so much from you—our relics, like the cestus—even our very existence. You thought the House of Atreus was extinct, but *here I am*. Open your eyes! Whether you want to believe it or not, Pandora, Ajax and I saved each other's lives that night, and then we fell deeply in love."

"Then the two of you ran away together?" Castor asked, shocking everyone with his sympathetic tone.

"We had no choice. Even though I had paid my debt to the House of Thebes, and I could be near any of you without inciting the Furies, you all still wanted me dead," Daphne replied with a shrug. "Ajax said that if we could explain what had happened to Tantalus, he would take our side. He really believed your brother would help us. We were so young, only seventeen." A powerful emotion overwhelmed her and she suddenly clenched her fists and her jaw, as if she was refusing to cry.

"Finish your story," Lucas said evenly.

"'Jax and I were living on a sailboat, hiding at sea. Tantalus rowed out to meet us because we were too frightened of an ambush to come ashore. As soon as Tantalus saw my face he went mad. They fought over me in the rowboat. I can't swim—I swear, I *couldn't* get to them. Ajax lost," Daphne said. She stared directly into Lucas's eyes. "Tantalus claimed that he killed me that day, but obviously that's a lie. He has been chasing me ever since, maybe because he wants me for himself, or maybe because he intends to kill me and he doesn't want anyone else coming after me for the sake of a Triumph. I'm not entirely sure what he wants anymore."

"I don't believe it, no matter what you say, Lucas," Pallas said, shaking his head in denial. "Tantalus loved Ajax."

"Yes, he did. He loved his brother, and then he killed him," Daphne said, frustrated to the point of cruelty. "Now, as a kin-killer, he's an Outcast, and he can't have contact with anyone from the House of Thebes without the Furies revealing his sin to you."

"Pallas," Castor said gently. "Didn't it ever bother you that our brother stayed hidden even when there were no other Houses left to fight?"

"But there were other Houses, and there still are!" Pallas shouted, pointing to Helen and her mother. "He must have known she was still alive, and that she can seduce anyone, even us, to help her get to him."

"I haven't used the cestus on you, Pallas. Not even to get you to believe me," Daphne said tiredly. "I want you to know in your own heart who killed Ajax. I need you to believe that I wasn't the one who killed *my husband*."

"Everything she's saying is true," Lucas said, locking eyes with Helen. "She hasn't used the cestus. And she and Ajax were married."

Helen looked away, although she could feel him studying her face.

"The Fates have done this many times," Cassandra intoned, a hint of the Oracle's glow in her eyes and voice as she momentarily peeked through the Veil. "The Star-Crossed Lovers are in the warp and weft of the pattern, and my mothers are compelled to repeat it again and again. Symmetry must be maintained or the fabric of the universe will be ruined. All Four Houses have been preserved this way."

"All four?" Lucas repeated as his eyes sought out Helen's. A glimmer of hope flared up in him, but instead of seeing his own elation echoed in Helen, her face was pale and empty. She looked away.

"Four Houses in Three Heirs," the many voices continued to chant. "The Star-Crossed Lovers have preserved the bloodlines. And the Three shall raise Atlantis."

A strange hush overtook the room, like the pause between a blinding flash of lightning and the deafening roar of thunder that inevitably follows.

"Sibyl!" Daphne said suddenly, addressing Cassandra by the most ancient title of her office. "I beg you to answer me! How can the Scions rid themselves of the Furies?"

"She can't control them yet!" Castor gasped at Daphne, whose face had grown greedy and desperate. Helen's mind flashed back to Daphne's sudden decision to come back to the House of Thebes with Lucas, and she knew that this was what her mother had wanted all along.

Castor grabbed Daphne's arm, pulling her away from his daughter, but it was too late. The Three Fates had been officially summoned into the body of the Oracle to answer a direct question, and they would not be stopped. Cassandra's mouth glowed, her hair writhed, and her head snapped back. Her eyes grew rheumy with cataracts and her skin wrinkled. An old woman forcibly pushed her way through a young girl's shell like she was tearing through a piece of paper. Convulsing, the old woman turned into another woman, and then a third, as the many voices chimed out of her.

"The Descender must go down to those who cannot forgive and cannot forget. The Descender and her Shield will free the Three from their suffering as she will free the Houses from the cycle of blood for blood," they said, and then went silent.

Cassandra's head righted itself. The wrinkles smoothed and her eyes cleared, but the eerie extra presences were still in her. Daphne pulled herself away from Castor and approached the Oracle with her arms crossed and her palms pressed flat against her chest in reverence.

"The House of Atreus owes you a debt, Sibyl," Daphne said with a deep bow, completing her part of the ritual.

"And the House of Atreus will pay it when asked," the Oracle said before the glow died completely and Cassandra returned fully to herself with a series of blinks and an exhalation. Everyone stared at Daphne with shock and anger.

"I'm sorry, but I had to," she said barely above a whisper.

"You could have killed her," Lucas said, clenching his fists. "She's still too young."

"If the vengeance cycle isn't broken, she has no future, anyway. None of us do," Daphne mumbled, unable to look at him. Several people raised their voices to argue.

"She's right," Cassandra said, cutting everyone off. "Things will change, Prophecy has been made, and like it or not, I am the Oracle. I can't hide anymore."

"Maybe not," Castor said somberly. "But next time, we decide together what questions to ask and when to ask them." He turned and pointed a finger at Daphne. "Another trick like that and I'll make sure you don't live long enough to hear Sibyl's answer."

Daphne nodded once with a passive face that placated Castor, but not Lucas. He'd seen Helen make that face before, and he knew it was bogus. Lucas glanced at Helen, who had noticed the same thing he did, and they shared an anxious look.

Cassandra said that she was tired, and Pandora took her upstairs to lie down for a while. Ariadne went into the kitchen to check on Matt, who was still icing a few bumps and bruises while Noel gave him a crash course in demigods.

Lucas gestured with his head for Helen to meet him in the next room. She tried to shake her head no, but he had already turned away and started moving toward the door. She had to follow.

He led her to an unfamiliar part of the house, the wing directly opposite his father's office, one that Helen had never entered. As they moved through the empty hallways and past the unused rooms, she could see Lucas tilt his head ever so slightly over his shoulder, aware of her presence.

As she followed him, never more than a few paces behind,

she could see his shoulders tense and his breathing quicken. She watched the warm skin of his back moving under his shirt with every breath, and she had to rub her tight fists against each other to keep herself from reaching out to touch him. Finally, he entered the empty solarium on the easternmost end of the compound and turned around. She had one second to open her mouth in protest before he was kissing it. The second after that she felt him gently pushing her down to the floor. The second after that Helen very nearly gave in to him.

A wave of nausea swept up from her stomach and she clamped her mouth shut as she turned her head away from him. Lucas pulled back carefully, thinking he had hurt her in some way. She braced her elbows against the marble floor and shoved against his chest.

"Stop," she begged.

He shifted off of her immediately, holding his hands up in a placating gesture. As they both sat up and faced each other, his eyes looked so confused, so wounded, that Helen's eyes started leaking tears, even though she had promised herself the night before that she would never cry again.

"What is it?" he asked, bewildered and in pain.

"We can't do this," she said, shaking her head in a rapid motion.

"What are you talking about?" He tried to get her to look at him as he reached for her hands. "Helen, we're free. There are two other Houses left to preserve the Truce. We can be together."

"We can't do this," she repeated, balling her hands into fists so he couldn't take them.

"Why?" he asked in a strangled voice, sensing that Helen was being honest with him, but still not understanding why. "Have your feelings for me changed so much in one night? Did you stop wanting me?"

"That's not it," she said, agonized. "I wish I didn't want you."

"How can you say that?" Lucas asked, relieved to know that at least Helen still felt the same about him. "I know you've been through a lot today, and maybe you're not ready right this second. That's fine, we'll wait as long as you want. . . ." He tried to pull her into his arms, just to hold her, but she pushed hard against his chest and turned her face away from his.

"We're first cousins!" she cried out hopelessly, her shoulders beginning to jump up and down with uncontrollable sobs. "Jerry wasn't my father, Lucas. Ajax was."

Lucas's whole body went still with fear. In the silence that followed, all Helen could hear was the sound of the rain on the glass roof.

"That's not possible," he whispered, even though he could hear that she wasn't lying. He shook his head. "No. We saw the Furies when we met. We can't be related."

"Yes, we can," Helen said, wiping one cheek, then the other, then back again to the first in what seemed like an endless procession of tears that needed to be wiped away. "The children of mixed lineage can only be claimed by one

House, and I was claimed by the House of Atreus. It's been happening like this from the start."

"From the start?" Lucas asked, recalling Cassandra's earlier statement. "Star-Crossed Lovers are repeated in the pattern. How *many* other Scions of mixed lineage are out there in hiding?"

Helen sniffed and stared at him with a tiny smile. He was so sensitive, so quick to pick up on every detail she couldn't stop herself from adoring him. There were an infinite number of ways for her to admire this one person, and because of that, there were an infinite number of ways for her to fall in love with him over and over again. She realized that she wasn't going to have to give up Lucas just this once and be done with it; she was going to have to give up all the different ways she could have learned to love him every day from that day forward. The weight of all of those future heartbreaks pressed down on Helen until she had to drop her head, unable to look at him as she answered his question.

"Daphne calls us Rogues, and yes, there are quite a few of us," she said quietly. "No one knows how many, but there are at least twenty that my mother can locate."

"So if these kids can only belong to one House, but their parents are from enemy Houses, one side of the family . . ."

"Is sent into a Fury rage and hunts that baby down. Daphne said the urge to kill the newborn is almost irresistible, the same as it it for a newly made Outcast. One of the parents has to fight their family for their child, and it usually means that parent either dies at the hands of their own parents or siblings or they end up having to kill them."

"That's disgusting," Lucas breathed. Helen nodded.

"It is disgusting. Babies shouldn't be part of the blood feud. It's just wrong. Daphne swore to get rid of the Furies so that Rogue babies like me can be with both of their families, and so that no one ever has to go through the horror of choosing between protecting their child and fighting their own brother or sister—or parent. In fact, she's made it her mission in life to free the Scions from the curse of the Furies forever."

Lucas nodded, finally understanding. He started pacing, as if he couldn't remain in one posture for more than a millisecond with so many thoughts pushing and pulling on him at the same time.

"What do we do? We can't stay away from each other," he said as he stopped pacing and stared at Helen, who was still sitting slumped on the floor.

"I know, but I can't be near you, either," she said, standing up with an exhausted sigh.

Lucas groaned and covered his face. Neither could bear to look at the other, but they reached out blindly and embraced in a tight hug. They rocked back and forth, both of them needing comfort.

"My mother and I planned to leave today," Helen whispered.

"Don't leave me," Lucas whispered back, tightening his arms around her.

"What are we going to do?" Helen murmured desperately, knowing he didn't have an answer.

They stood clinging to each other in the unused room with the intermittent rain patting the glass walls until they heard worried voices shouting their names down the empty halls.

"I don't think I can do this," Helen said. She pulled away from him and wiped her hair off her feverish forehead. "I can't explain it again."

"I'll do it," Lucas said, instinctively reaching out for her hand, then stopping himself and withdrawing his hand.

Hector reached the door just as Lucas opened it. His face was a mask of anxiety and his chest was swelling with fast breaths. He looked back and forth between their devastated faces several times before it sank in that they were okay.

"You two are . . . alive. That's good," he said with relief.

"We should get back," Lucas said with a blank look before he started walking stiffly down the hallway, leaving Hector with Helen.

"Daphne told us," Hector said directly. "I'm sorry, cousin."

Helen nodded a few times, not trusting herself to say anything, and started down the hallway. To her surprise, Hector caught up to her and put an arm over her shoulder as they walked. He squeezed her tight for a second and kissed the top of her head. As they neared the occupied part of the house, Helen realized just how much she was leaning on him.

# EIGHTEEN

Waiting in the shadows outside the Hamilton house was a long shot, but Creon had no other choice. He couldn't get within a thousand yards of the Delos compound now that he had shown his hand and put them on the defensive. He had been so close, *so close*, but underestimating his cousin had cost him. Lucas was stronger than he had thought. He would never make that mistake again, but it was possible that once was all it would take to change Creon from a savior to an embarrassment.

Now that his target was being protected by his own family, he had few options but to wait and see if she was stupid enough to go out on her own. He was hoping that if she went anywhere it would be to the place she had once called home.

It wasn't much of a chance, but it was all he had at this point. He couldn't go back to the yacht and face his other cousins empty-handed. He had to come up with something else—a lead, an opportunity, something—before he involved any of the Hundred. No matter how this turned out, his father could never know about his failure outside the hotel. It was too humiliating to even think about.

Tantalus had finally entrusted Creon with the truth, and for the first time in over nineteen years, Creon had been allowed to hear his father's actual voice. He hadn't been allowed in the same room, or seen his father's face, because that woman had deformed it so monstrously it would be death to look upon him, but for the first time in such a long time Creon had actually *spoken* to his father and learned about the burden he carried.

His father praised him for being so strong and faithful over the years. Then he told his son what had really happened in that rowboat, how his thoughts and his will had been so grievously twisted that he had had been led into a type of sin that had marked him forever—marked like Medusa. Tantalus admitted his wrongs, repented for them, and told his son that he had been trying to right them ever since. He had sworn to remove the feminine evil of the cestus from the world so that all men, Scions and normals alike, could finally control their lust. Then he had entrusted Creon with the same sacred mission.

And Creon had failed.

Creon felt his phone vibrate in his pocket for the fifth time.

He had been ignoring it for a while and he didn't even want to know who was trying to contact him, but this time he caved and pulled it out to look at the screen. It was his mother. He debated answering for a moment, then finally relented.

"Where are you?" Mildred asked in a low voice.

"Hunting," Creon replied vaguely, sensing his mother was being watched, maybe even listened to. It had happened before.

"One of the traitors just called me," she said in an urgent whisper. "She told me about your failure in front of the hotel, and she wants to change sides. She wants her men freed of the cestus. . . ."

Creon heard the crackling sound of his mother's phone as it brushed up against fabric, as if it had been shoved into a pocket or under a sweater. A few seconds passed during which all Creon could hear was the rhythmic brushing of clothes against the mouthpiece as his mother walked somewhere else.

"Are you still there?" she finally asked when she got to relative safety.

"Yes. Mother, what's going on?"

"Sssh. Just listen. The Hundred are starting to doubt you. I can't let them know we're in contact," she whispered urgently. "Where are you? She wants to meet right now, to make a plan."

Helen spent fifteen minutes on the phone with her dad, trying to get him to calm down. He had been just about ready to go down to the police station, and he demanded to know where she had been all night. She didn't have an answer for him. Jerry was as angry as he had ever been with her. He demanded that she come home immediately. He even yelled at her, which he hadn't done since she was a kid. Helen wasn't used to disobeying her father, but she found herself telling him that she was safe and that she wasn't coming home just yet. She hung up on him while he was still sputtering.

She knew she was being unfair to him, but she didn't know what else to do. She hadn't decided if she was going to tell her father about Daphne's return and then tell him that she was leaving to live with her, or if it was kinder to just disappear. Daphne insisted that a clean break would be better for everyone, including Jerry, but Helen couldn't quite bring herself to accept that. He might be physically safer, but emotionally he would be destroyed. Helen went through both scenarios in her head, and neither of them felt right. Either way her father, the person who deserved to suffer the least, was the one who would be hurt the most. Eventually, her brooding was interrupted by Noel, who let Helen know that Claire and Jason were awake.

Helen went upstairs to Jason's room and pushed the door open a crack. Daphne was sitting on the edge of the bed next to Claire, holding her hand and looking down at her with a fretful tenderness. Daphne had loved Claire when she was a baby, she had explained to Helen the night before, and she had always worried for Claire's safety growing up alongside a Scion. In the hotel during the storm, Daphne had removed

Helen's curse, and she had also explained that she had left Claire excluded from being able to trigger the cramps, even though it could have exposed Helen, just in case Helen ever needed to protect Claire. Helen had thanked her for that, although there was little else her mother told her that night to make her grateful.

"Did you sort things out with Lucas?" Daphne asked as Helen entered the room. Helen flinched when she heard his name, nodded hastily, and put the attention back on Claire.

"Hey, Gig. You really freaked me out," she said. She came over to stand next to the bed.

"Freaked myself out," Claire said, gesturing for her to sit down. Then she noticed Helen's puffy face. "Are you okay?"

"Not important," Helen said as she perched next to her mother. "How are you two?"

"It was easier than I thought it would be," Jason replied. "We never went into the rubble, all we did was climb the dry hills."

"Good," Helen said, smiling with relief. "That's far away from the river."

"I know," Jason said, smiling back at Helen before he looked back down at Claire. "She really is strong."

"What river? What rubble?" Daphne interjected, glancing from Jason to Helen, but she was overruled by Claire's urgency.

"That was real?" she blurted out, her eyes dark and wide with fear.

"Yes and no," Jason said softy, briefly brushing his lips

446

against Claire's forehead as he sat up painfully and gently pulled her up with him. "It's a real place, but we only went there in spirit."

"But I was so hungry. So thirsty," Claire whispered, suddenly terrified.

She trustingly turned her face into Jason's neck and he held her close to him. The bond they had forged in the dry lands still tied them to each other, and Helen had a feeling that Jason was reluctant to let it dissolve.

"Don't be afraid, we only walked along the edge of it, we never crossed the river and went in. Not even the best Healers can go all the way in and make it out alive," Jason said reassuringly. He met Helen's eyes as if to ask her to help him explain.

"The place you went is just beyond the place you go when you're sleeping. It's not something you should be afraid of," Helen said, putting her hand on Claire's back and trying to comfort her. "Just think of it as an intense dream if that makes it easier, because that's what it feels like."

"Nightmare is more like it," Claire said as she pulled her face away from Jason and got ahold of herself.

"Well, you almost died," Helen said with a shrug. "That shouldn't be fun."

"Helen?" Daphne asked, comprehension dawning on her face. "How many times have you been to this place you're talking about?"

"I've lost count," Helen said softly, shaking her head.

Daphne stared at her daughter with a hard look on her

face. There was a knock on the door. Matt poked his head in sheepishly.

"Sorry to interrupt," Matt said with a slight grimace. "Hey, Claire. You okay?"

"Come in," Claire responded as she tried to sit up a little straighter. She reached out to Helen, who helped brace her. "I'm glad you're in one piece," she said gratefully.

"Yeah, so am I," Matt said with relief. "But there's still a big problem that we need to fix. I noticed some people staring at us when we . . . uh . . ."

"Hit Luke with your car?" Jason finished for him with a humorous glint in his eye.

"Right. So I need to go take care of that. Before it gets out of control," Matt said uncomfortably. "The longer I stay here, the more everyone will talk. If I start denying it, showing everyone that I couldn't have been in an accident because I'm not injured . . ."

"Then the whole thing goes away before it gets started," Daphne finished for him. "Are you really willing to lie to your own kind for us?" she asked coldly.

"I don't see it as your kind or my kind. All I see are my friends and they need my help," Matt said with narrowed eyes. He glanced over at Helen uncertainly, as if to ask if she was sure about this new mother she had acquired.

"I'll take you wherever you need to go," Helen said as she stood. "I've got to go talk to my dad, anyway. I'll drop you off on the way."

"You're not going anywhere," Daphne said, surprised that

Helen would even suggest it. "It's far too dangerous."

"I can't just leave him," Helen said. "That's what you did, and I've spent my whole life cleaning up the mess you left behind. If I've learned one thing, it's that I don't want to repeat your mistakes. Not now, not ever."

"Well, I can't tie you down every time we disagree, but I can tell you to be careful, Helen, especially when you use words like 'never,'" Daphne replied, her eyes soft with understanding. "The gods know what it is to be eternal, and they love to toy with mortals who use absolutes."

Helen turned and half stumbled for the door, so shaken to hear an echo of Lucas in her mother that she lost all sensation for a moment.

"I got you," Matt whispered into her ear as he took Helen's elbow and steered her through the door so she didn't clip her shoulder on the frame.

"Your mom's a real trip," he said with a touch of fear when they were outside and the door was shut safely behind them.

"I haven't decided if she's right about everything that ever mattered to me, or if she's just evil," Helen said honestly.

"That's what everyone wonders about their mother," Matt said with a smile as he rolled his eyes. "The thing is, nobody's mom is entirely one or the other."

Helen smiled at Matt, hoping he was right, and led him downstairs. They went into the kitchen, looking for someone to lend them a car, but the only person they saw was Pandora, who was just coming back into the house from the garage.

"Helen," Pandora said, surprised. "You're not leaving, are you?"

"Matt needs to go home and I need to . . ." Helen started to say, but Pandora shook her head.

"I can't let you leave this house. You know that," she said forcefully.

"Then maybe you can take him?" Helen asked.

"I'm sorry, I can't right now," Pandora said, looking down at her unadorned hands. "Why don't you ask Ariadne? She's in the library." She smiled briefly at Helen and Matt, and silently hurried off toward the fight cage. It took Helen a moment to realize what was missing. For the first time Helen could remember, Pandora wasn't wearing any jewelry.

Helen led Matt to the library, where Castor, Pallas, Hector, Ariadne, Cassandra, and Lucas were all talking in a tight circle around Cassandra's chair. The conversation ended as soon as they saw Helen.

"Matt needs a ride home," Helen announced nervously. She tried to keep her gaze away from Lucas, but her eyes kept jumping back to him.

"I'll take him," Ariadne offered, immediately coming forward and motioning for Helen and Matt to leave the room.

"What's going on?" Helen mouthed to Ariadne, who took her hand and led her away. When they were a few paces from the library, Ariadne answered.

"We're trying to figure out what Creon's up to," she said.

"Why was I excluded?" Helen asked, offended.

"Come on, Helen," Ariadne replied with a chiding look on her face. "Lucas can't bear to be in the same room with you right now, and no offense, but he's a much better soldier than you are. We need him at the table and we need him focused."

Matt shot her a confused look, but thankfully, he didn't ask any questions about her and Lucas. It wouldn't matter in a few hours, anyway. Helen would be gone and she would never see him or any of them again. Later, she'd crawl into some strange bed in some strange state and then she didn't care if she ever got out of it or not. But she couldn't let herself think about that yet. First, she needed to make sure that the people she loved were taken care of.

When they reached the kitchen, Ariadne grabbed her bag off the back of one of the chairs and fished her keys out, looking around like she had misplaced something. She looked out in the garage, counted the cars, and then glanced back into the house, whispering, "She's back?" to herself. Before Helen could ask what was wrong, Ariadne said goodbye and hurried Matt out to her car.

Helen waited a few moments for Ariadne's little car to disappear down the drive before she crept out onto the lawn. It wasn't dark out yet, but Helen still felt like even the shadows under the bushes were reaching out to grab at her. As soon as she was clear of the house she jumped up into the air, frantic to get into the sky, the one place she knew Creon couldn't catch her. Calmer once she was safely airborne, Helen flew home, circling high for a few moments to watch for random neighbors before coming in steep and fast to avoid being seen. Touching down in her backyard, Helen listened for the usual sounds of her father and heard that he wasn't alone. Kate was with him.

They were talking softly, and here and there they would laugh or lapse into silence as one or the other gathered their thoughts to make sure the words came out right. Helen looked in the window and saw them sitting on the couch together, TV off, having what looked like an important conversation. If she concentrated she could probably make out what they were saying, but Helen didn't want to intrude on such a private moment between two people who were obviously falling in love.

She touched her heart-shaped necklace and wished them perfect happiness together. She wasn't sure if the cestus worked like that, but all that mattered was that Jerry would have someone to care for him when she was gone. Helen realized that if she left now, without confronting him, he would never have to know about Daphne returning to the island, and if that wound was left unopened, then this fragile understanding between him and Kate might stand a chance.

She stood at the window for a moment, deciding which course to take, until finally the sharp drop in temperature and the tangerine color staining the clouds told her she had run out of time. She flew up to her window, sat down at her desk, and wrote a note to her father. She told him that she loved him, that she was safe, and that she was never coming back, making the note brief so she wouldn't have to fill it up with lies. He had been a good father, and if she couldn't be completely honest with him, the least she could do was lie as little as possible.

She flew out of her window and back to the Delos compound as soon as she was done writing. It was a comfort to Helen to know that while she was sneaking away later that night her father would still be oblivious. Hopefully, for all of their sakes, Kate would be there for Jerry in the morning when he found the note. Thinking of that, she flew east across the darkening island with a feeling that approached peace.

Before she even touched down, Castor was running out of the house to meet her on the lawn, waving his arms over his head as if to signal her to hurry. He was shouting something about her mother.

Daphne had to wait until the little strategy session broke up before she could sneak into the library and look around. All she needed was the return address on the last few bits of mail from Tantalus to the Nantucket faction of the House of Thebes. Then, after so many years, she might finally be able to figure out Tantalus's pattern of motion.

She was only missing a few bits of information—a city name and she would know where to go from there. Then she would find Tantalus and kill him exactly the same way he had killed her sweet Ajax. Daphne had imagined it a million times. As soon as he came to the door she was going to chop off his head while his wife watched. If she avenged him, then maybe when Atropos cut her string, Ajax would be waiting for her on the other side of the river. She still had a ways to go and a lot of work to do before she could allow that to happen. First, she needed a city.

Daphne started reading the postmarks on the topmost letters on Castor's desk, but a quick glance told her that what she was looking for wasn't there. She knew Tantalus's handwriting like she knew her own, and she didn't see it anywhere. Then she realized that although Castor was the smartest and the bravest of the Delos clan, he would be the last person Tantalus would contact. She went over to the other side of the library and began another search in another desk.

She saw a safe under the other desk, put her hand on the spin dial and hoped that it wasn't designed by a Scion. After a few moments on her knees listening for the click inside the tumbler, her search was abruptly ended. She felt the hot, thick jab of a needle invading the vein in her neck. She gasped, recognizing the drug cocktail she used on other Scions. She dimly remembered that when she had subdued Helen, she had left a spare syringe in her bag, loaded and ready, just in case. In seconds, her field of vision shrank to nothing.

When she woke, Daphne could feel that her hands had been shackled with something metallic. As she blearily tried to focus her eyes she saw that she was on a dark beach. She heard the jingling of chains as she moved her hands closer to her face, and saw that her wrists had been cuffed. There were deep vertical slashes on both her forearms that were still leaking fast-pumping blood even as they healed. She was thirsty from the blood loss, but she ignored that and summoned a bolt.

The cuffs heated up until they glowed so bright Daphne had to turn her closed eyes away or be blinded by the light. The brightness was nearly unendurable, but the cuffs didn't melt, not even as she drained the last of her volts. There were few substances that could withstand so much heat at normal atmospheric pressure without turning into a liquid or a gas.

"Tungsten," she whispered through her dry, cracked lips, angry with herself for acting without thinking first.

The white-hot links of nearly unmeltable metal led to a lightning rod that was jammed into the ground like a stake. Not only was she immobile, but any attempt she made to throw a bolt at an enemy would only end up dissipating in the sand.

"I wouldn't have thought you had any bolts left," a woman's voice called from down by the waterline. The crouching shape rose and walked over to Daphne. "I took a lot of your blood to dehydrate you, or at least I thought I did."

"Why are you doing this?" Daphne asked softly. "You're not a killer, Pandora."

"I know I'm not," Pandora admitted with a humiliated nod. "I tried to kill you while you were unconscious, but I couldn't do it."

"Then let me go," Daphne said with a sad smile. "I know why you're doing this. Denial is a powerful thing, and grief can make a good person evil." Daphne hauled herself up onto her knees. "But why don't you believe me? Or if not me, why not Lucas, your own nephew? He's a *Falsefinder*."

"Lucas has every reason in the world to want your version of the story to be true," Pandora hissed, kicking at the sand as she began to pace. "He is blinded by his love for Helen, and he would do anything to keep her. Maybe even lie to his own family."

"First of all, Lucas can only have half of Helen," Daphne said darkly. "And second, you know there are easier ways to see if I'm telling the truth about who killed Ajax than kidnapping me. Have you ever asked Tantalus why he's still in hiding?"

"Probably because he knows you can look or sound like anyone!" Pandora shouted back, furious. "The only thing you can't do is fake someone's handwriting. That's why he's only communicated through letters—to protect himself because he knows you want him dead!"

"And why would I want him dead?" Daphne's own temper rose. "If it's a Triumph I wanted, why wouldn't I have killed any one of you Theban rats as soon as I saw you? Why would I want Tantalus, and Tantalus alone, unless he stole something precious from me?" she asked, her voice breaking at last.

Pandora watched Daphne as she settled back into the sand, turning her back on the ocean she dreaded, to stare slack-jawed at her own feet. Pandora moved away from her and crossed her arms, tilting her face into the wind. She was breathing hard and her eyes darted from left to right as if she was reading the dark horizon. Suddenly, she snapped back to attention.

"You snake," she said, turning to stare at Daphne with awed rage. "Creon said you were cunning, but this is something else entirely. You actually believe what you're saying! That's why Lucas couldn't find anything false in what you said. All those years of hiding behind other people's faces and now all you are is one big lie. This is why I have to keep you away from Castor and Pallas—from everyone I love. I know in my heart that you used the cestus to trick my brother. You never loved him, and he could never have loved you." Her words were harsh, but doubt was beginning to creep into her tone. "Ajax was too good, he was too pure. . . ."

"And too noble, and tender, and generous, and brave," Daphne said, raising her voice to talk over Pandora. She was blinking repeatedly as her eyes squeezed at dry tear ducts and came up with nothing. Her body was crying, but the moisture was missing, and somehow that made it hurt more than it usually did. "Since Ajax left the world nineteen years ago, there has been no good in it for me," Daphne whispered.

"What about Helen? She's good. And she's at least a part of Ajax. . ." Pandora trailed off when Daphne's eyes began to drill into hers.

"Helen's birthday was yesterday—her *seventeenth* birthday," Pandora whispered in shock. "But why? Why would you want to make her think that Lucas is her cousin. . ."

Pandora looked away, shaking her head with grief. She couldn't understand how Daphne, how any mother, could hurt her own daughter like that. But they had run out of time. Creon was coming up the beach, behind Pandora's back. Daphne had tried to win her over, had honestly hoped to spare her, but there had never been a real chance for that. Daphne could only pray that Ajax would forgive her in the Underworld.

"That's right, Pandora, Helen isn't his child. I have *nothing* of Ajax, and so I have nothing in this world that's of any value to me. Even you, the baby sister he loved so much, the one he made me promise to protect, even you have been polluted beyond hope. You know, it would kill Ajax to see you like this."

"Don't you dare tell me what my brother would feel!" Pandora screeched as something snapped inside of her, just as Daphne knew it would. She dove for Daphne, her fingers hooked into claws, trying to scratch her eyes out. Daphne rolled under Pandora, protecting herself as well as she could while shackled. She knew she only needed to defend herself for a moment.

"Don't touch her, she could have more bolts!" Creon yelled as he caught Pandora from behind and hauled her off of Daphne.

Daphne turned away from Creon and Pandora as they

struggled. Covering her face with her arms, she adopted short, dark hair and pretended to cower.

"He would never have fallen in love with her!" Pandora screamed, lost in her grief as she struggled with Creon. "He would have despised her just like I do, I know it!"

Pandora strained against Creon's strong arms, but Creon followed every motion of her desperate attempt to break free. Daphne couldn't have asked for a better distraction.

"Don't let her confuse you, cousin! She is one of Aphrodite's chosen, and you don't have to be a man to feel her influence. She can twist anyone's heart with a look," he said as he finally managed to drag Pandora away.

He led her down the beach and away from the valuable capture, talking to her the entire time. They moved just far enough away that Daphne could be sure they didn't see her make the full transformation, as she adopted Pandora's shape. Then she hit herself in the eye and the mouth and started groaning.

"Creon!" Daphne-as-Pandora yelled out hoarsely. "What are you doing? Get away from her. That's Daphne! She tricked us! Don't listen to her!"

Daphne screamed and howled until she saw Creon waver and then grab Pandora harshly by the arm and haul her back to where Daphne was staked to the ground.

"When we were rolling around on the ground!" Daphne sobbed, pointing a finger at Pandora and using the influence of the cestus. "She got out of the shackles and put me in them. She's so strong—I had no idea!"

459

"She's lying," Pandora stammered. She tried to pull her wrist out of Creon's grasp, but he didn't let go. She glanced from Creon to Daphne, so shocked she didn't know what to do.

"Don't believe a word she says!" Daphne said, her eyes locking with Creon's as she folded up his will like a piece of tissue paper and tucked it into one of the back pockets of his mind. "She *wants* to be taken to your father, but she wants to be taken to him *as Pandora* so she can get close enough to kill him! She's been planning this from the start and I played right into her hands! I'm so sorry, cousin. I had no idea how cunning she was!"

Creon stared at Pandora with perfect hate. He wrenched her arm in its socket and she fell to her knees, screaming. With blank eyes he drew a small bronze blade from his belt and slit Pandora's neck so deeply he nearly cut off her head. She was dead before her blood had a chance to soak into the sand.

Helen flew about fifty feet over Hector as he ran out the front door of the Delos compound and began a circuit around the edge of the island. It was dark, unbelievably dark, especially since most of the island didn't have power back yet. It was also cold. Everyone on the island would be inside, huddling around fires, or turning on their emergency generators. The rest of the Delos family was certain that Creon would take advantage of the fact that the streets were deserted to move her mother off island. Cassandra was exhausted and drawing a blank, so they were forced to guess as to how that would be done. After a long discussion, the family was convinced that Creon would leave by helicopter or private plane. Lucas was to fly over Castor and Pallas while they covered the airport on the west side of the island, and Ariadne was to watch the ferry landing in the northwest, just in case Creon tried to sneak Daphne off by boat. Hector did something unexpected. He *chose* to run around the dark, deserted east-northeast shoreline, apparently on a fool's errand.

Of course, Helen immediately volunteered to fly over him. If there was one thing she had learned in her few short weeks of training, it was that Hector could get inside his opponent's head and figure out exactly what he or she would do next. No matter how logical the Delos family's strategy was, Helen would bank on Hector's gut instincts about Creon over *any* carefully laid plan. There had been a heated argument about whether or not Helen should be allowed outside the compound at all, but in the end, no one from the House of Thebes could deny the Heir the right to look for her mother, the Head of the House of Atreus. It also helped that everyone thought Helen would just end up flying around in the pitch-black over Hector, safe and useless and on the wrong side of the island.

Below her, Helen watched Hector plow into the waves a few times. She stared at him, perplexed. Each time he would pause, fan his hands out as he ran them through the water, and then bound out again, looking thwarted. She knew he had a Scion talent that had to do with the water, and from

461

the way he seemed to be testing the waves, almost communicating with them, Helen guessed that he was looking for something out in the dark ocean. She suddenly realized why Hector had chosen this gods-forsaken route—he *was* looking for something in the water, probably a boat offshore. Why bother with airport records or ferry manifests when you were on an island? In the dark of night all you needed was a rowboat and a small ship of some kind anchored in deeper waters and you could move on and off the continent without having to declare anything to the authorities. You could even move a kidnapped woman.

Helen's heart turned over and she started to scan the black water frantically for any hint of a boat. She couldn't stop picturing the animal look Creon had in his eyes as he brought his dagger down over her heart. Helen didn't love her mother—she barely knew her—but she wouldn't wish the terror that she had felt in that moment on anyone. There was an evil inside Creon, and Helen suspected she had only seen a tiny fraction of what he was capable of in their one brief struggle.

Hector's shape suddenly darted forward, urged on by a huge burst of speed. Helen's eyes weren't as keen in low light as Hector's and she had to squint to see what he had seen, but when she did, she faltered and nearly fell out of the sky.

There were dark shapes on the beach. There was no fire, no flashlights to illuminate the scene so it was hard to tell how many people were there. Helen sped up, overtaking Hector from the air, and watched helplessly as a woman was brought to her knees by a big man. Helen heard the woman scream, and suddenly the scream was silenced with a gurgle. Flying faster than ever before, Helen swooped down and got close enough to see Pandora fall lifeless onto the sand at Creon's feet, and another Pandora, chained and staked to the ground behind them, shimmer and shift into Daphne's form.

A second later, a bestial roar erupted out of Hector as he saw the body lying in the sand. His whole frame shook with unnatural rage and pain, and Helen knew the Furies had possessed him. Still far away, Hector bounded across the wet sand, his eyes locked on Creon, as Creon turned and stared at Daphne. Creon clutched the bloody knife he held in his hand and advanced with murderous purpose toward Daphne.

"Get back!" Helen yelled at Creon as she thumped down into the sand next to her chained mother.

Helen's hands glowed icy blue with the light of a gathering bolt. Knowing he was outnumbered and outgunned, Creon immediately turned and ran inland. Just seconds away from reaching his target, Hector snarled and changed direction, chasing after Creon.

"Hector, wait! Don't go after him alone!" Helen called after him, unable to leave her bound and wounded mother behind. But Hector didn't listen to her. Helen saw the two of them sprint away, so similar in physique, from the back they could be twins. For all the world, it looked to her like Hector was chasing a shadowy version of himself.

Helen turned back to Daphne and ripped the chains off the shackles with her bare hands.

"What did you do, Mother?" she asked through gritted teeth.

"Not this!" Daphne said breathlessly as she gestured to Pandora's body.

"I saw you in Pandora's shape from the air!" Helen yelled, raking her hands through her hair and starting to pace with frustration.

"I did that to confuse Creon—I had no idea he would kill her!"

"And you didn't use the cestus to influence him?" Helen asked skeptically.

"I never influenced him to kill!" Daphne asserted vehemently as she got up off her knees and faced Helen. "I was just trying to buy some time, stall for as long as I could. I never thought he'd do this!"

"Okay. Whatever," Helen said, suddenly done with the conversation. She took her jacket off and put it over the gruesome corpse—*Pandora's corpse*—Helen thought in grief before she turned back to her mother. "Are you badly injured?" she asked.

"I'll be fine. You need to go stop Hector," Daphne said as she changed gears seamlessly. "Go. I'll take Pandora back to her family. Then I'll find you."

Helen nodded at her mother, knowing there was more to the story, but that would have to wait. She jumped into the air and headed west, staying low to the ground so she didn't miss Hector and Creon as they ran through the unbelievably dark interior of the island. Her eyes couldn't manipulate light the way the eyes of the Children of Apollo could; out here she was the one at a disadvantage. She wished Lucas was with her. He would be able to see perfectly even in the dark of the moors. He would also know where to look because he was a better strategist. Most of all, she just wished he was with her so that she wouldn't have to face Hector and Creon alone.

Putting that thought aside, she flew from one end of the island to the other, but she didn't see them anywhere. She backtracked, knowing that her adversary wasn't stupid enough to keep running until he fell into the ocean. Creon was trapped on the island, unless he was trying to get to someplace where he could get off of it. Helen took a sharp turn and flew north toward the ferry.

It was late, too late to catch the last ferry, but maybe Creon didn't know that. In a second, Helen was approaching the more populated area by the town center, and she had to either fly up high to avoid being seen or touch down and run the rest of the way. She decided to land while she still knew she could do so without being spotted. She started to trot toward the ferry, looking and listening as she went. As she passed India Street, she heard the slaps and thuds of what sounded like a massive hand-to-hand fight. Her feet pounded against the pavement as she ran up the middle of the road toward the sounds, already knowing where she was going, where the Fates would have arranged this. The Nantucket Atheneum.

Helen rounded a corner and saw that a dark pall erased the entire end of the street. Even in a dark room it's possible to sense other things around you, but Creon's shadows were so complete they robbed Helen of more than just her vision; they uprooted her, tilting all of her other senses off balance as well. Looking at the *thing* he created, Helen understood why Creon was called a Shadowmaster. He did more than simply take away the light; he made that same thing that lurks under the basement stairs or at the back of the closet— that full darkness that your brain believes is stuffed with serial killers and monsters. Helen had to swallow down a scream just looking at it.

Somewhere inside that terrifying black hole, she could hear Creon and Hector hammering away at each other in a blind rage. Helen was at a loss. She was so scared of the disorienting nothingness that Creon had created she couldn't force her feet to run into it. She screamed Hector's name and scrunched her fists up in frustration, and as she did so her hands began to glow with the stark blue-white glow of electricity. Then something occurred to her.

When she was fighting for her life against Creon in her foyer, her spark had thrown back the gloom so she could see him. Even though he could control other kinds of light, her lightning had to be different somehow. Acting immediately, Helen held out her hands and summoned a bright spark to dance between her palms. She lit up the whole scene in front of her.

Hector was on his back and Creon was over him, beating

his head repeatedly into the marble steps of the library. The blue glow snapped and hummed with increasing intensity around Helen's hands, and Hector turned his swollen eyes toward her bright light. He smiled. Freed from Creon's disorienting shadows, Hector was able to struggle out from under his cousin's grip and he stood to face him.

They came at each other before Helen could take another step. Clashing together, Creon and Hector ground each other's faces into the marble steps. They threw each other into the Doric columns, and yanked at each other's skin and bones, each trying to pull the other apart. Helen began running, yelling at them to stop, but she was too late. While she was still half a block away, Hector managed to get behind Creon. With one cracking yank, he broke Creon's neck.

Helen stopped running and froze in the middle of the street, her mouth hanging open as Creon's lifeless body tumbled down the steps. Hector looked down at the body, and then up at Helen, momentarily free of the Furies and in complete possession of his own passion. For a split second, Helen knew that Hector understood what he had done, and that what he had done was unthinkable. He had killed his own cousin.

A dark comet fell out of the sky and plowed into Hector's distracted body, knocking him through three columns and cracking the very foundation of the faux temple.

"Lucas, stop!" Helen screamed, her voice breaking painfully as she cried out with all of her strength.

Lucas couldn't hear her. The Furies had him. All he could

hear were their commands to kill the kin-killer. Lucas hit Hector over and over, trying to beat him to death.

Helen half flew the last few strides to the battling pair. She threw herself up into the air and then came crashing back down on top of them with as much gravity as she could muster. Pushing the two boys back into the cracked rubble of the library steps, Helen threw her arms up in a V over her head and summoned matching bolts for each hand. Before either of them could block her, she brought her bolts down onto the heads of the warring cousins and shocked them both into unconsciousness. As they fell still under her hands, Helen could hear rapid footsteps behind her. The rest of the Delos family was coming.

"Get back," she screamed with her ruined voice as she spun around to face Ariadne and Pallas, who were both running toward her from opposing streets.

Hector was unconscious, but he could still incite the Furies in his family. His sin was so recent that the impulse to kill him would be urgent and blinding, even to those who loved him the most. Helen had made peace with the House of Thebes, but she had not become a part of it, so she was mercifully free of the urge to kill Hector, who had now become their greatest enemy—an Outcast. She got in touch with the sensation that connected her to her lightning and felt a disappointingly small spark. She had been running around for hours now without a sip to drink.

She looked back at Hector and Lucas, made sure that they were both breathing, and then stood up and walked out into the street, putting herself in between Hector's unconscious form and his infuriated family.

"Don't come any closer," Helen said, forcing what voltage she had left to spark out of her fingertips in a false show of power.

Helen held out her icy blue hands as she came down what was left of the steps and looked from Ariadne's sly eyes to Pallas's bared teeth. They were not themselves anymore, but blunt instruments for the Furies. She stepped into the street and raised her glowing hands to warn them off. At the sight of Helen's lightning, they backed off a step or two, but just as they were about to back off completely, Castor rounded a corner, following the whispers of the Furies.

Helen was ridiculously outnumbered. She had no idea how far she would have to go to protect Hector from his own family. She couldn't kill any of them any more than she could let them kill him. If they didn't buy her bluff, she was out of options. She had never felt so alone in her entire life.

"Helen, I've got Hector! Stay between us while I take him away," Daphne called out behind her. "Whatever you do, don't let them lay eyes on him or we will lose this fight!"

Helen sighed at the sound of her mother's voice, so relieved that she had someone on her side that she found the strength she needed to make the only choice that she could.

She didn't care if she drained every last drop of water out of her body. The only thing that concerned her was stopping the vengeance cycle before it devoured a family that she loved. She flung her arms out wide and with a last gasping push made her lightning dance in a great, blinding circle around her body. Ariadne, Pallas, and Castor threw up their arms to protect their eyes from the one kind of light they had no control over.

Helen's halo of ball lightning was hotter than the surface of the sun. It melted the pavement under her feet into lava and heated up the air around her until it literally hummed. The Delos family jumped away from the intolerable light and heat, but more important, they jumped away from Daphne as she ran into the darkness with Hector's unconscious body slung over her shoulder.

The pain was unbearable. Helen couldn't hold the ball of electricity for more than a few seconds. As soon as she heard Daphne's footsteps move away, she switched off like a fried lightbulb and stumbled desperately out of the white-hot liquid asphalt that was pooling below her, burning her and choking her with noxious gases. She crawled on hands and knees toward Ariadne, Castor, and Pallas, their faces matching masks of agony as they all suddenly became aware of what they had nearly done. But Helen couldn't let them fall apart just yet.

"Lucas needs help!" she rasped, gesturing back to the shattered steps of the Atheneum.

"Ariadne," Castor said in a brittle voice. "Go get Lucas. Helen, can you walk?"

"No," she admitted, shaking her head.

"People will be coming," Castor said as he picked Helen up and started to carry her off, but he stopped when he noticed his brother wasn't following. "Pallas! We need to go!"

"My son," Pallas whispered, unable to move.

"Dad, come on! You have to take Creon's body!" Ariadne hissed from the stairs of the Atheneum. She had Lucas draped over her shoulders and she was glancing around frantically to see if there were any witnesses.

The sound of his daughter's voice managed to distract Pallas enough to get him to pick up Creon and follow Castor out of the town center and out into the moors.

# NINETEEN

Helen stared at the glass of water in front of her as it sweated condensed moisture onto the kitchen table. She'd already drunk what seemed like a bathtub full of water and she wasn't thirsty anymore, but she held on to this last glass to give herself something else to look at besides the bereft faces around her.

"His whole life is this family. This House," Ariadne said. Her eyes were wide, red, and staring, like someone who had been stuck in too many different airports in too many different time zones for too long. They all looked like that— like they'd woken up to find themselves on the wrong side of the planet. "How can *Hector* be Outcast from the House of Thebes?"

"I could have stopped him," Jason said with grim certainty.

"You can barely sit up straight in your chair right now,

Jase," Ariadne said, shaking her head. Jason had yet to recover from healing Claire, and his twin wouldn't let him take responsibility for something that he hadn't even seen. "I was there. I should have stopped it."

"You weren't on India Street when Hector killed Creon, Ari," Helen said, still staring at her water glass. "I was."

"Stop it, Helen," Lucas said. "You and your mother saved this family, or at least, you saved what's left of it."

Lucas's words brought fresh tears for Pandora. After several minutes of quiet crying, the family lapsed back into silence. Everyone was thinking the same thought, that if each of them had done one thing differently that day they could have staved off the pain that they were all suffering. Cassandra had told everyone they couldn't have known what was going to happen, but in saying that she seemed to take the burden of guilt onto herself. She seemed locked in her own head, unable to let go of the fact that she, of all people, should have been able to protect her family.

"Call your mother," Noel said suddenly to Helen, breaking everyone out of their tortured thoughts. "I'm the only one who can bear to be near Hector now, and I want to see my nephew. He'll need me."

Helen nodded and pulled out her cell phone. It was the same phone Hector had given her with bloody knuckles and a toothless grin after Lucas had beat the stuffing out of him, but she buried that memory and dialed her mother's number. As her phone connected, she stood up to leave the

473

kitchen and wandered toward the front of the house, which was usually quieter.

She heard two rings at the same time, one in her ear and one somewhere inside the house. Helen looked around and found her mother's bag hanging on a hook in the front entryway. She chided herself for not being more aware. Daphne had been kidnapped; of course she had left her things behind. Helen hit END and heard the phone in the bag cease ringing. She stared at her mother's purse, and was overcome with an irresistible urge. Just as Helen reached for it, there was a knock at the front door a few feet away from her.

Helen hastily opened her mother's bag and took out the cell phone. She quickly scrolled down the list of latest calls as footsteps approached from the kitchen. Concentrating on the glowing screen, Helen saw a few incoming unlisted numbers and a single outgoing call to someone named Daedalus before she had to shove the phone back in the bag.

Ariadne appeared in the entryway to answer the door, and a moment later Castor and Pallas appeared behind her. They were tense and probably expecting either the police or a member of the Hundred Cousins. After the briefest of pauses they nodded to Ariadne, signaling that it was okay for her to open the door. When she did, Daphne was standing on the doorstep.

"I call for a meeting between the House of Atreus and the House of Thebes," Daphne announced as she crossed her arms in an X over her breast and tilted her upper body forward, giving the suggestion of a bow.

Castor and Pallas looked at each other. Whatever hatred they carried toward Daphne needed to be put down now, and they both knew it. Pallas swallowed hard and finally nodded.

"You are welcome in this House and you have our hospitality," Castor offered formally as he bowed, stepped aside, and let Daphne over the threshold as his sacred guest.

The official meeting between the Houses took place in the library, with everyone arranged around Cassandra's chair. Helen took her place next to her mother on the couch, and tried not to look at Lucas even though he was sitting directly opposite her.

"First of all, I would like to make amends for the violation of your safety while you were a guest in my House," Castor began humbly, but Daphne cut him off before he finished his thought.

"Pandora was distraught. She and Ajax had a special bond, and because of that I could never hold a grudge against her for trying to avenge him, especially not now that she's lost to us," she said, waving a hand through the air as if to banish the thought. "As far as I'm concerned the laws of hospitality were not violated."

As she said those last words, Helen noticed Lucas's eyes snap over to Daphne, and she knew that he had sensed a lie, but decided to overlook it for the greater good.

"I called this meeting to address two very important matters that concern both our Houses," Daphne continued in a smooth voice. "The first is Hector and his future, and the second is my daughter and her part in the prophecy." Helen's head spun around to face her mother.

"My what?" she asked, completely at a loss.

Helen wasn't the only one in the room who didn't understand. Castor and Pallas looked around, confused, and even Cassandra shrugged as if to admit she had no idea what Daphne meant.

Jason stood up and took a stiff step forward.

"Helen is the Descender that the Oracle mentioned in their prophecy—the prophecy that says that the Descender will free the Houses from the cycle of revenge," he said from his place behind his father's seat. "I only realized it this afternoon, when Helen described the dry lands so perfectly that I knew she'd seen them. That puzzled me at first because I know she isn't a Healer. Then she told me that she would *come down* and drag both Claire and me out if I wasn't strong enough to make the journey on my own. From her confidence, I knew she meant what she said, and I also suspected that she had physically been there more than once."

"The dust on your feet!" Ariadne exclaimed as she recalled Helen's dirty feet and the mystery of the unrung jingle bells.

"What about it?" Helen asked, looking around at everyone's immobile faces.

"The Descender doesn't just dream about the Underworld, the Descender literally goes down into it in his or her body," Ariadne answered with a shocked face. "You physically went into hell every night?"

"Your nightmares," Lucas said, looking at Helen as he began to understand.

"You were with me in one of them," Helen said back to him in a confused voice. "The night we fell, before we woke up on the beach, I went down to get you, remember? You were lost and blind and I made you to stand up and walk. I made you follow me out. . . ."

Here, Helen had to stop. Forcing Lucas to walk through the Underworld had been like doing surgery on an animal without painkillers. He didn't understand that what she was doing was for his own good, he only knew that she was hurting him.

"That was real?" Lucas whispered.

Helen nodded and reached out to take his hand, needing to touch him to reassure herself that he wasn't afraid of her now, but Daphne stopped her hand in midair and pulled it back, shaking her head in disapproval.

"You knew," Lucas said, turning to Daphne.

"Like Jason, I discovered Helen's talent this afternoon," Daphne replied. "That's one of the reasons I asked for this meeting."

"And what are the rest of your reasons?" Cassandra asked coldly as flashes of the Oracle aura began to brighten the outline of her face. Daphne bowed her head reverently to the multiple presences that had begun to grace Cassandra.

"Like Aeneas, my daughter will need Sibyl's help in the Underworld," Daphne said in a formal tone. "I ask that the House of Thebes care for their cousin, Helen, Heir to

477

the House of Atreus, while she fulfills her destiny in the Underworld. In exchange, I, Daphne, Head of the House of Atreus, will grant refuge and protection to Hector Delos, Outcast of the House of Thebes."

Everyone shot each other looks, stunned by both the request and the offer that Daphne had made. The room hung in silence as expectations recalibrated.

"Why would you do this for my son?" Pallas asked as he partially rose from his seat, torn between thanks and indignation.

"Because he is one of the strongest Scions I've ever seen, but he's also one of the proudest. The loss of his place in this House is going to change him, and without guidance he could become a danger to us all. I've seen it before," Daphne said evenly. Then she turned to Lucas and looked him in the eye to ensure that what she said was proved true by him. "We are all family, and it's time we started acting like it."

"She isn't lying," Lucas said, looking over at Pallas, who nodded with relief. Lucas, however, looked devastated. He had heard the truth from Daphne herself—Helen was a member of his family.

Castor and Pallas looked at each other, already in agreement, then glanced over at Cassandra for final approval. She nodded her head once, and then stood up and left the room without another word.

"One last thing," Daphne continued, tactfully ignoring Cassandra's rude exit. "Hector wants to know what's to happen to Creon's body."

"We'll be contacting Mildred to come and retrieve her son," Castor said, looking down at his hands. "She'll want to bring him back to his father for the funeral."

"Of course," Daphne said sadly. "Will you let me know when she'll be here? Hector mentioned something about facing her to ask for forgiveness . . . " she trailed off uncertainly, as if she wasn't sure Hector should do that.

"I'll call you," Pallas promised stiffly, and then hurried out of the room.

Daphne stayed for a bit longer and reassured the rest of the family that physically Hector was going to be fine; but she was blunt about the fact that he wasn't doing well emotionally. After letting them all know that she would convey their love to him, she departed hastily, saying that she had left Hector alone for as long as she dared. Helen walked her to the door.

"Did Hector see you in Pandora's shape on the beach tonight?" she asked her mother quietly when they got to the front door.

"No. And he can never know," Daphne said, staring at Helen intensely. "You and I are the only family he has now and he needs to trust me. You both do."

Helen knew her mother had risked her life to help Hector, but the way Helen saw it, trust was something that was earned, not something that another person could demand from her. Even if that person was her own mother.

"I'll be in touch with you over the next few days to let you know what the plan is," Daphne promised as she took her bag down off the hook and opened the door.

"One last thing?" Helen asked as she held the door open. "I'll stay quiet about what I saw on the beach if you agree to release Jerry from the influence of the cestus. You never loved him, but Kate does, and I think it's about time you let someone in your life be happy, don't you?"

Daphne stared at Helen, shocked that her obedient daughter had finally expressed a mind of her own, then looked off to the side distractedly, like she was listening to a faraway sound.

"It's done," she said in a brisk voice, snapping out of her momentary trance. "I can't make any promises about his relationship with Kate working out, but Jerry's heart is his own to give or to keep as he sees fit."

"It's about time," Helen said coldly.

"All of this pain I've caused, I did it to protect you. And it worked. So I'm not sorry for any of it," Daphne said, giving Helen a sad smile before turning and walking away.

Helen shut the door and wandered back to the rest of the family, forehead furrowed in thought. As soon as she stepped into the living room, Lucas's head snapped around to look at her. He gestured for her to come to him. Although she knew it was the last thing that she should do, it was the only thing she wanted to do.

"I have to go home," she told him as soon as she got to him, trying not to shake too much. "I left a good-bye note for my father on my desk when I thought . . ." She broke off and had to take a breath. "Anyway, I have to get rid of it before he wakes up and finds it. He's been through too much already."

Lucas balled his right hand into a fist and shoved it into his pocket. Helen had never seen him make that gesture before, and she realized he was doing it to stop himself from taking her hand.

"Let's go, then," Lucas said, turning his face away from hers.

"But I thought you and I were staying away from each other?" She broke off awkwardly.

Lucas shook his head decisively. "Creon had Pandora drag Daphne to that beach because he was going to take her off this island by boat. Which means he was supposed to rendezvous with someone out there on the water," Lucas said, his expression steely. "When they realize that Creon is missing, they're going to come looking for him, and when they don't find him they're going to come looking for Daphne— and then you. You're in more danger now than you ever were and I don't care how hard it is on either of us. I'm not letting you out of my sight for a second."

"Well, what are we supposed to do then?" she nearly cried out, throwing her hands up in surrender. She had reached the end of her emotional and physical tether.

"Come on," Lucas said grabbing her hand and pulling her out of the room. Everyone turned and looked at them, but they were too overwhelmed by the losses they had suffered to pay much attention to Helen's outburst.

"I'm taking her home and staying there to watch over

her," Lucas barked at Ariadne, who was weeping quietly in a chair. As soon as they were outside they leapt in unison into the night sky.

The cold air was like a slap in the face. It knocked Helen out of her confused state and she realized that no matter what she had been through that day, Lucas had been through far worse. It was time to stop feeling sorry for herself and pay attention to him.

Moments later, they landed on Helen's widow's walk, and Lucas turned to her with an empty face, letting go of her hand.

"Go in. I'll be fine up here," he whispered. Helen took a step closer to him, but he just shook his head.

"I can't come in," he whispered, his voice breaking hopelessly. "I've lost too much today. I'm not strong enough."

"I know," she said. "I'm so sorry, Lucas."

Helen wrapped her arms around his shoulders, wanting nothing but to console him. She held on to him, propping him up until Lucas was strong enough to stand on his own again. He eased himself away from Helen and gave her a small smile to let her know that he was better.

"Wait here a sec. I have to let my dad know I'm home."

"I'm not going anywhere," Lucas promised.

Helen flew down to the front yard and noticed that Kate's car was still parked in the driveway. She landed and went in the front door, not at all sure what she was going to say or do. She found her dad sleeping on the couch in the living room, sat down next to him, and shook him gently until he woke. Jerry looked relieved for about two seconds, then sat up and sighed at Helen in disappointment.

"You know what you put me through, right?" he asked, heartbroken. Helen felt so guilty she couldn't meet his eyes. She just nodded her head. "You'd better start explaining."

Helen thought about how so many people in her life already knew what she was, and for just a moment she considered telling her father everything. But if she opened that can of worms she'd also have to tell him Daphne was back, and she couldn't bring herself to do that. Not after she had finally released him from his unnatural attachment to her. For the first time in almost two decades, Jerry had the chance to have a real life with a woman who actually loved him in return. Helen wouldn't allow anything to endanger that.

"I can't, Dad. At least I can't right now. I guess I could make up an excuse, but it would be a lie," Helen said hopelessly as she rubbed her hands over her tired face and aching skull. "And I don't ever want to lie to you."

"Is this how things are going to be between us now? No trust, no communication, no respect?"

"No, Dad. Don't even say that," Helen said shaking her head tiredly and meeting her father's eyes.

"I've been through this before, you know," Jerry said quietly. "I've spent a lot of nights waiting right here on this couch for someone to come home. And she never did. I won't do it anymore, Helen."

"Good," Helen said, seeing a spark in her father that she had never seen before. "I don't want you to waste one more second of your life waiting for anyone. Not even me. My life is crazy right now and I can't promise that I'll never disappear again, but I can promise that I will always come back to you. I'm not going to leave you, Dad. Ever."

"I know you won't," he said as if he was just realizing that it was true. He took a deep breath and sat quietly for a moment, thinking. "Well, I always knew you were different, and I also knew that someday you were going to realize it. That's all the explanation I'm going to get out of you right now, isn't it?"

"For now." Helen said smiling warmly at what had to be the best father ever.

"Would it do any good to ground you?" he asked with a humorous glint in his eyes as he stood up and stretched.

"Probably not," Helen laughed.

She stood up and gave her father a hug. He hugged her back with more than forgiveness. He hugged her to let her know he accepted her exactly as she was—sleepless nights and all. As they walked to the stairs together a happy thought occurred to Helen.

"You're going to bed?" she asked, glancing over at him with a sly look in her eyes. He nodded. "I saw Kate's car outside. Is she in your room?"

"She is," he said with narrowed eyes and pursed lips. "That's why I was on the couch."

"You're not on the couch anymore," Helen observed innocently. Jerry paused at his bedroom door and turned to face her.

"Are you going to be okay with this?" he asked seriously.

Helen knew that if she said it bothered her he would turn right around and spend the rest of the night alone.

"Dad. I've never been more okay with anything in my life," Helen said honestly. She went into her room and closed the door firmly behind her to let him know that she was going to give him some privacy.

Helen heard her dad wake Kate up and let her know that everything was okay, and then turned to tear up the note she had left on her desk. She flew out her window to meet Lucas on the widow's walk.

"Did you hear all that?" she asked when she saw the sympathetic look on his face.

"Does it bother you?" He took the sleeping bag from the chest and spread it out for both of them to sit on.

"No," she said, shaking her head. "I would have told you, anyway. Somehow, it's like whatever I'm going through hasn't happened to me until you know about it."

"I know what you mean," he whispered.

They sat down next to each other on the edge of the widow's walk, their thighs threaded between the bars of the railing and their feet dangling off the side of the house.

"It's Monday. We've got school in a few hours," Helen said. "I suppose if we all stayed home it would look suspicious, huh?"

"Very suspicious," Lucas replied. "Besides, you're safer in a public place. The Hundred won't attack you in front of human witnesses."

"And what about you?" Helen asked, looking at her hands. "Are the Hundred going to come after you and your family now?"

"I don't know," Lucas replied with a tired shake of his head. "But whatever they do, they know that if they kill one of their own kin they'll become Outcasts, and the more Outcasts there are, the farther they are from attaining Atlantis. I think they'll focus their energy on Daphne and Hector. And you."

Helen nodded, and debated whether or not she should keep asking questions.

"And tomorrow—what should I say about Hector if anyone asks? Or Pandora?" Helen asked gently, knowing that every time she said their names it hurt Lucas a little more.

"Pandora went back to Europe to study art in Paris," Lucas said in a hushed tone. "And Hector is home with a nasty case of the flu for the next few days until we can coordinate a plan with your mother."

"I don't trust my mother," Helen said as she stared out at the rising sun.

"Neither does Cassandra," Lucas replied without looking over at her. "She thinks Daphne is hiding something."

"Do you think my mother is dangerous?" Helen asked. She turned to Lucas with worried eyes.

"I think she's entirely committed to freeing the Rogues and the Outcasts," he answered, choosing his words carefully. "As long as we remember that, I don't think there's any reason not to trust her. She hasn't lied."

Helen nodded, accepting Lucas's interpretation. "I've got too much baggage to think rationally about my mother."

"That's the funny thing about being a Scion," Lucas said, smiling in the petal-colored air of the chilly dawn. "Our fights tear the whole world apart, but for us, they're really just family feuds. And no one ever acts rationally when it comes to their family."

Helen smiled back at him, struck yet again by how perceptive he was. Then she caught herself, and remembered how important it was to keep her distance from him. She turned her face away and forced herself to stand.

"Are you going to be okay?" she asked him. He didn't answer, but just smiled up her and nodded before turning his face back to the horizon.

"Good morning, Lucas," she said, her voice soft and sad as she walked away.

"Good morning, Helen," he replied, not allowing himself to turn and look at her as she left him.

Helen, beloved of the goddess of love, went downstairs to crawl into her empty bed as Lucas, the son of the sun, leaned back on his elbows and watched his father-god brighten the bare wooden planks of her widow's walk.

### ACKNOWLEDGMENTS

I would like to thank Robyn Shwer, my dear friend and guardian angel, for giving me over a decade of her big hugs and unswerving faith. A million thanks to my manager, Rachel Miller, who probably deserves some kind of medal for champion handholding, as does her partner, Jesse Hara. I'd also like to thank my fantastic agent, Mollie Glick, as well as Hannah Gordon and the rest of the Foundry gang for their guidance; Tara "the Dope Show" Kole; my editor Laura Arnold; and every one at HarperTeen for helping me make my story better and better with every rewrite. Special thanks go to Dr. Rey "Cookie" Perez, Stephanie Aoki, and Liz York for all their support. A special shout-out to the termites in my desk—bon appétit, bitches! Finally, all my love and gratitude go to my husband, Juan Alberto, and my big, crazy, beautiful family.

# JOSEPHINE ANGELINI

is a Massachusetts native and the youngest of eight siblings. A real-live farmer's daughter, Josie graduated from New York University's Tisch School of the Arts in theater, with a focus on the classics. She now lives in Los Angeles with her screenwriter husband . . . and she can still drive a tractor.